the WARLOCK'S CURSE

M.K. Hobson

The Warlock's Curse is a work of fiction. Names, characters, places, and incidents are either the product of the author's imagination or are used fictitiously. Any resemblance to actual persons, living or dead, events, or locales is entirely coincidental.

Printed in the United States of America
First Printing: October 2012

ISBN: 978-1-938860-00-3

www.demimonde.com

Translation of "Alcestis" by Rainer Maria Rilke
used by permission of A. S. Kline

Library of Congress Control Number: 2012943773

The *Veneficas Americana* Series
By M.K. Hobson

— 1876 —
The Native Star
The Hidden Goddess

— 1910 —
The Warlock's Curse
The Unsteady Earth

Once more he still saw
the girl's face, that turned towards him
with a smile, bright as hope,
that was almost a promise: fulfilled,
to come back up from the depths of Death
to him, the Living —

At that, indeed, he threw
his hands over his face, as he knelt there,
so as to see nothing more than that smile.

"Alcestis," Rainer Maria Rilke

Prologue

Special Magistrate Anson Kendall sat on the ladderback chair his son had fetched him and watched blood drip from the tips of Aebedel Cowdray's fingers. Three days ago, the warlock's hands had been fine and white as a woman's, framed by pristine silk cuffs edged with Flemish lace. Now the cuffs were soiled and torn, the lace stiff and brown, and the slim fingers swollen and purple.

Peine forte et dure. Punishment, strong and hard. The practice of pressing a warlock beneath heavy stones was commonly reserved for cases in which the accused refused to make a plea—but in Cowdray's case, no plea was necessary. He was an unabashed practitioner of Satan's arts; two score and five had he lived as a warlock, traded as one in South Carolina and Pennsylvania and New York, colonies that reckoned the weight of a man's purse over that of his sins.

The colony of Massachusetts, however, was not so indulgent.

Governor Bradstreet, who had commanded Cowdray's capture, had also ordered the swiftest of trials and the speediest of convictions. These would have been followed by the hastiest of executions—had the Special Magistrate not persuaded the governor to countenance a delay. A *slight* delay. Just three days, which Anson Kendall might use to discover how to save his wife's soul. For Cowdray had laid a bewitchment upon her, a spell that only the warlock knew how to unmake. And no matter how many stones it took, Anson had sworn to learn the secret.

Three days ago, Cowdray had been defiant. He had laughed as the first stone was placed on his chest and had declared the second "a goose's feather." But three days without water, under the ever-increasing weight of the stones, had left his eyeballs bulging, red as grapes, and his tongue as thick as an ox's. Three days of unrelenting torture had curbed his pride. Anson had permitted himself the luxury of hope.

But as night had become day, and day had passed to night and back to morning again, and stone upon stone had been added, a terrible certainty slumped Anson's shoulders, as unbearable as the weight crushing the unholy vault of the warlock's chest.

"You will never tell," he whispered, allowing himself to finally realize it. He watched the man struggle for each breath, cracked lips moistened only by trickles of fresh blood. There was nothing Anson could offer him now. He could not promise to spare Cowdray's life; he could not promise him ease or even respite from his suffering. The worst had been done—more than the worst—and Cowdray had not broken.

Anson sank back, releasing a long breath. It was nearly midnight. Over the gallows field the rising moon hung like a ghostly pearl set in battered pewter. A bitter wind whistled off Massachusetts Bay, rattling the winter-bare branches of the hemlocks. The air smelled of smoke and snow-sodden soil and mud-damp stone and blood.

He could hear a woman sobbing. The shudders and heaves were tinged with a note of frenzy. It was Cowdray's whore—a dark poxy slut with red hair who had accompanied him from South Carolina, heedless of the dangers of entering Massachusetts. One of his witches, no doubt. Young and foolish. The others of his coven—it was rumored that there were hundreds—had wisely stayed away.

Anson gestured to his son, who stood with several of Governor Bradstreet's men, warming themselves around a bright leaping bonfire. James Kendall was thirteen, tall as a man but not yet so broad in the shoulders; the sleeves of his black coat hung down over his hands. He was at his father's side in two steps. He was a diligent boy.

Anson spoke so softly that his son had to bend down to hear him.

"Another stone. The largest that remains," he said. "And quiet that damned harlot."

James swallowed, but did not speak. Then he nodded, once. He went back to where the men were standing, and Anson could hear them murmuring quietly among themselves. No warlock had ever withstood seven stones. No magistrate had ever commanded it.

Anson passed a hand over his eyes, pressed the aching orbs with his fingers. He heard rough words being spoken to the crying woman, and her answering screams of misery as she saw the seventh stone being lifted. There was the sound of a blow, a muffled thud as the woman was cast to the ground. His head was throbbing. He felt small and empty, keenly aware of his own cruelty. He knew, in that moment, that there was something important in him that he could not find anymore, something that he would not be able to find again, but he did not care. He was watching a house burning, and the screams of the whore were his wife's screams. Sarah could not be saved. All he could do was throw on more wood so that he might not have to suffer her suffering much longer.

It took three of Governor Bradstreet's men to hoist the largest of the flat stones they had retrieved from the banks of the Forest River. As they settled it carefully atop the others, Cowdray released a long, wheezing groan, a bitter note on a cracked pipe. His eyes closed, lids barely stretching over the grossly protuberant orbs, and then he was still.

Anson waited a few moments then leaned forward to confirm that the warlock was finally dead. But as he brought his face close, Cowdray's blood-red eyes flew open. He spat. Blood and spittle thick as porridge flecked Anson's cheek.

"More ... will come ..." Cowdray rasped, pushing out each word on a wave of pain and fury, like a woman birthing a child. "Cannot ... kill us ... all."

With the back of his hand, Anson wiped away the bloody spittle. Whatever part of his humanity had fled had taken his sanity with it, and now all was burning in the house of his imagination with his wife's living, breathing, dead body.

"Yes, I can," he said. "I will."

His own father, the great Determination Kendall, used to have visions—divine visions, gifts from Almighty God. Now, looking into the bloody depths of Cowdray's eyes, Anson was struck with a divine vision of his own, as sharp and staggering as a hammer-blow to his forehead. He saw bodies. Hundreds of bodies, thousands of them, slack and lifeless, witches and warlocks, swinging from gallows against skies aglow with flames and smoke.

Anson Kendall had never been a cruel man, and his father had despised him for it.

Determination Kendall had been an inquisitor of highest renown, in great demand throughout the colonies as a Special Magistrate for the Courts of Assistants who had witches to be tested and tried. Anson could not remember a time when he did not travel with his father (his mother having died in childbed), but the beginning of his service as his father's assistant—and his father's harsh assessment of him—he could trace with painful clarity to his eighth year. Lacking other assistants, his father had deemed him a big enough boy to turn the thumbscrews on a young witch. Oh, how the girl had screamed. Anson could not bear it. He fled the room in tears. Determination found him vomiting behind a hayrick.

"God hates a coward," Determination had sneered. It was the first time Anson had heard those words, but it would not be the last.

Determination's belief in the unredeemable evil of witches was brilliant in its purity. His ears listened for accusations of milk-souring and cattle-foundering and babe-smothering as if they were a melody that pleased him. He was deaf to sweeter notes; tales of nurse-women who used magical arts to succor the ailing, or cunning-men who read the weather to augur auspicious times for sowing.

Anson, though, had wondered. Perhaps such creatures could not be said to be in God's favor, but were they truly in Satan's service?

He never shared such doubts with his father, of course. Determination would have accounted them blasphemous; proof of a weak, unguarded mind tainted by close proximity to the evil they faced every day. He might begin to look for marks or blots on his son's body, for any special fondness for cats or rats or black dogs. And looking for them he would find them, and Anson might find himself in thumbscrews, facing the flames.

His father served a fierce and implacable God, the kind that sacrificed sons.

But Anson was a clever enough boy, and remaining beneath the threshold of his father's scrutiny was as simple as keeping his lips pressed tightly together. Determination's righteous mind was far too occupied with higher pursuits to even notice his son's persistent silence, far less attempt to prise out whatever seditious thoughts might lay behind it. What small free time he had was dedicated to penning his magnum opus, a treatise he called the *Malignia Veneficas Americae*. He wrote at night, by the weak flickering light of a tallow candle, after the subjects of that day's inquiries had been locked away to suffer 'til cockcrow.

His great addition to the scholarship of witchcraft was to delineate its schools. He detailed the unique practices of blood witches and earth witches and showed the ways in which they differed. He wrote of less common kinds of witches, those who could turn the Bible itself inside out to summon power—speaking the Lord's Prayer in reverse, or confounding sensible individuals with stories and follies that left them dazed and vulnerable. These last, Determination wrote, were the hardest to detect, for their sorcery was exceeding subtle and sometimes barely distinguishable from mere politics or persuasion. Much simpler to uncover were the blood witches, barbarous fiends who drew their power from the living, agonized blood of humans.

Witches like Aebedel Cowdray.

When they first heard of Aebedel Cowdray, Determination was at the zenith of his power and prestige. His treatise had been published to great acclaim. England's Witchfinder General himself, Matthew Hopkins, had proclaimed it a *novum malleum*—a new hammer in the never-ending battle against sorcerous criminality. Determination found himself in greater demand than ever, each day bringing a fresh batch of summons from villages and towns desperate for aid in their prosecution of local malefactors.

Travelling to answer one such, they had stopped for the night at an inn, where Determination had happened upon an old colleague, a German witch hunter by the name of Eisenbach. As old men will, the two had fallen into commiseration about the wicked ways of the world. Eisenbach had lamented particularly the New World's lax attitude toward *der hexenmeisters*, so different from the admirable strictness of his own native land.

"One need only look at Aebedel Cowdray to see how servants of evil are coddled in America!" Eisenbach had seethed, slamming down his tankard so hard that foam flecked his grimy sleeve.

Cowdray's name not being familiar to father or son, Eisenbach proceeded to outline the specifics of the man's notoriety, how he lived and traded openly as a warlock in the lower colonies, keeping homes and offices in both South Carolina and New York.

"He's a slave trader. His great success comes from the fact that he performs some sort of unholy rite upon his blackamoors. It makes them wonderful placid, far more than such beasts are by nature." Eisenbach leaned forward, relishing the telling as much as Determination did the hearing. "He does a thriving trade with the plantation owners in the Carolinas and the West Indies. They have thrown their fortunes in with his, and as they have no wish to see their investments ruined, he will never be prosecuted, howsoever rank his sins!"

Determination snorted with outrage. Eisenbach, baring his rot-pitted teeth in a grimace, had further inflamed him with tales of Cowdray's riches, of his fine velvet coats and his cuffs of silk edged with lace, of how the warlock had ruined scores of virgins and lured good married women from their hearths to dance with the devil in the full moon's light.

"And naught can be done about it," Eisenbach had concluded, eyes sparkling as he looked over his tankard at Determination. Determination had said nothing in answer, but Anson had always remembered that moment. His father, like God, would not be mocked.

Later, as they were preparing for sleep, Determination had been strangely pensive.

"The abomination's very name chilled me," he mused, as he removed his heavy boots. "As if I had heard it before. But I am sure I have not. And yet"—he dropped a boot to the floor with a thump—"I feel as if someone has walked over my grave."

But the morning brought them renewed vigor and work, for they were to interrogate a whole family of witches, sin-shackled from the centenarian grandfather all the way down to the new-born infant son. And with such pleasures facing him, and many similar subsequent pleasures, Determination put Cowdray out of his thoughts.

It was, Anson often reflected, surely the happiest time of his father's life.

It had been the happiest time in Anson's life as well, even though he was plagued by night-horrors so extreme that the brightest light of day did not completely dispel them. Even though he could never stop his hands from shaking. Even though the screaming of tormented witches had taken up residence in his brain, and sometimes the only way he could find peace was to cut his own flesh with a sharp knife, releasing the screams on a warm trickle of blood. Because it was at that time, in Anson's eighteenth year, that his father decided he must take a wife.

The Inquisitors Kendall, as they were coming to be known throughout the colonies, were amassing a respectable fortune. Anson must produce sons to carry on their good work. No one— least of all Anson—expected that it would be a love match.

It was certainly not love at first sight. Sarah Roarke—the young-est daughter of the modest, observant Roarkes of Salem—was not at all beautiful. But she was lively and spry, with a tendency to laugh more often than was theologically approved. When they were together, they never spoke of witches or sin or what methods of torture were best for small children. His hands shook less when she held them, and once, when they were allowed to sit up together after the rest of the household had retired, he fell asleep with his head on her shoulder and did not dream at all.

Money was settled on them from both sides of the family, and the newlyweds took a fine house on Port Street. Years passed and children followed: James, and then Abigail. Anson began to think of how he might use his growing stature as a householder to petition for a release from his father's service. He began to imagine himself pursuing a new career, one more suitable to his nature—binding books or keeping a coffeehouse.

But the demand for the services of the Inquisitors Kendall did not diminish; rather, they increased with each passing year. And each year, Aebedel Cowdray's name came to them more often, from the gossiping lips of the men who were his father's closest associ-ates. *The wickedest man in the New World*, he was called. *A blood-sorcerer whose hand no earthly authority can stay.*

It was an outrage. Unlike their usual targets, Cowdray was no crook-backed old woman who dabbled in herbs and spoke to her cats; he was a true demon, worldly and sly, infamous as a brute fornicator and worse. And yet, the law could not—or rather, would not—touch him. Cowdray's protected existence made a mockery of all their efforts. What good their prosecutions, if the worst of the sinners was forever beyond their reach?

Determination's outrage did not become obsession, however, until Old Mother Grax told them of Aebedel Cowdray's snuffbox.

Old Mother Grax was a hunchbacked hedgewitch accused of causing her neighbor's chickens to lay black eggs with serpents in them. The Kendalls hung her strappado to extract the names of her confederates; it was one of Determination's favorite methods of interrogation. By this time, Anson had well-practiced techniques for distancing himself from the horror of it. He would pretend that he was simply watching someone else's hands. He would imagine Sarah singing to him, as she did sometimes at night. She sang terribly, tunelessly and without rhythm, but it was the most beautiful thing in the whole world. He could lose himself in that remembered song, and it felt as if he was no longer even in his human body, and something else managed his brutal tasks. His father had accounted this a great blessing, believing that it was evidence of the Divine Spirit working within his son, but Anson had his doubts that the Divine Spirit could be so cold; distant and passionless as a frozen moon in a winter sky.

(Now, as he sat in the ladderback chair, watching Aebedel Cowdray die beneath seven stones, his father's words made more sense, and Anson did not doubt the presence of the Divine Spirit, nor that it was cold, distant, and passionless.)

Under torture, the old witch-women usually babbled about Beelzebub, tales Determination deemed deceitful and useless. But when Old Mother Grax, mad with agony, had promised she would tell them of Aebedel Cowdray's dark masterwork—a magical artifact he had been refining for decades—Determination had been intrigued. So intrigued that he did something his son had never seen him do. He eased the woman's torment so that she might speak more freely. The old witch's tale gushed forth.

According to Mother Grax, Cowdray had taken a small box of silver—a box such as might hold snuff—and he had sorcelled it to contain all of hell within its confines. Into this torment Cowdray could consign living souls stolen from human victims. Misery and agony being the true fuel of blood-sorcerers like Cowdray, the snuffbox thus represented a constant, ready supply of power. Power that would continue to grow as the pain and suffering of the imprisoned souls compounded.

Cowdray had been filling the box with souls taken from the African slaves in which he traded. Taking the soul killed some—those who were old or weak from strain or injury. But the young and strong could survive without souls, for a time. The ritual left them mindless, forgetful, directionless creatures—but they could work the fields, and they were placid and tractable, and as such they brought even higher prices than slaves with their souls intact.

"Monstrous!" Determination had whispered at the conclusion of this terrible recitation. He pressed her with questions in quick succession: where was the snuffbox? How could it be found? How could it be destroyed? But before she could answer any of these, Old Mother Grax's pain-ruddied face had drained of color. Her rheumy eyes focused on the wall behind them.

"Alas, he is here!" She moaned in sudden terror. "Do you not see his shadow? There, there! Ah, master! Forgive a foolish old woman! Forgive me, Lord!"

The Inquisitors Kendall had looked around themselves, Determination clutching at the great red cross he wore around his neck, but they saw nothing. No dark shadow, no hint of malice or magic. So perhaps it was only fear that caused Old Mother Grax to expire as she did, quite suddenly, great gouts of blood flowing from her nose down her wrinkled chin.

"Of one thing I am sure: Aebedel Cowdray will not long be satisfied with the souls of heathens," was Determination's first grim conclusion. "Ere long, he will seek souls of greater merit, those of white Christian men."

But, having decided to take the cause for his own, Determination was at a loss for how to proceed. Cowdray had carefully confined his business dealings to the middle and southern colonies. His main trading offices were in New York, whose governor—the indulgent sinner William Penn—had once released an old dame accused of maleficum with the infamous pronouncement, "You are at perfect liberty to ride on broomsticks, as I know of no law against it." Enticing Cowdray to leave such safe harbor seemed nearly impossible.

Thus, when the Inquisitors Kendall sought audience with Governor Penn—with the intention of exhorting him to do his Christian duty and send Cowdray to face God's justice in

Massachusetts—they expected little succor. But while the chance of success was slight, they knew it was greater than any they could expect further south.

They did not, however, expect their slim hopes to be dashed so thoroughly as they were when they were shown into Governor Penn's office, and were received not only by the governor, but by his honored guest—Aebedel Cowdray himself.

Cowdray was tall and well-formed. He had brilliantly white teeth and curling black hair and eyes the color of frozen seawater. He was dressed even more richly than all the tales about him had suggested. Every inch of his coat was embroidered with silken floss and gold wire, his stockings were snow-white and fine, and his sleeves dripped with lace.

"These are the Inquisitors Kendall?" Cowdray's gaze had encompassed them both, but Anson had felt the warlock's eyes hang upon him particularly. "It is said you gentlemen have some quarrel with me. But I have none with either of you. I simply wish to conduct my business."

"Business in partnership with the Author of Misery himself," Determination growled. He had clutched the cross around his throat tightly, as if wishing he could use it as a weapon. He cast a fiery gaze on Governor Penn. "You have read my letter, sir. You know the crimes this filth stands accused of."

"I have read your letter as well," Cowdray interjected, raising his clean-shaven chin haughtily. "Your claims are ludicrous, based upon the lunatic rantings of a poor old woman you tortured to death." He paused. "But it matters not. My slaves are mine to do with as I will. What I do with them ... magical or not ... is of no concern to a couple of hired Massachusetts murderers."

"You ... dare!" Rage made Determination stumble over the words. "We do the Lord's work, you abomination! And while your slaves are indeed yours, bought and paid for, well do I know that you will not be satisfied with them. Such souls must seem mealy bread to one as fine as you. You will soon seek stronger meat."

"How he rants!" Cowdray drawled, in Penn's direction. "Have you heard quite enough, my good William?"

"Quite enough," Penn said. Throughout the whole interview, he had been paying little attention, focusing instead on the signing of several documents that seemed to require his urgent attention. "Have them shown out."

"Your honor!" Determination cried. "This is unconscionable!"

"You gentlemen are a credit to New England," Penn observed, as his secretary moved to bodily usher them from the room. "Indeed, you have confirmed, with admirable thoroughness, every suspicion about our observant brethren that ever I have conceived."

This parlor witticism drew a dry snicker from Cowdray and a bellow of fury from Determination. The secretary had to push Determination toward the door. Anson followed. And as he was at the threshold, watching his father rebuke the secretary with hot words containing promises of hell and damnation, he was suddenly aware of Cowdray's presence at his shoulder, cold and dark and smelling of silk.

"Tell your father to have a care," Cowdray spoke in a voice so low that Anson could not tell if the words were really spoken aloud at all. "If stronger meat I do seek, I could look farther and fare worse than the tender morsels of your regard. Your wife's name is Sarah. Your children are James and Abigail."

Anson spun, a wrathful exhalation on his lips, but there was no one behind him. Aebedel Cowdray and Governor Penn stood together at the far end of the room. The governor had poured out little glasses of port and they spoke with civilized anticipation of the delicacies that awaited them at the dinner table. Neither man looked up as the Inquisitors Kendall were thrown into the street, and the door slammed behind them.

Anson had wanted to flee New York at that moment, on the very next coach that would take them back to the safety of Massachusetts. He did not dare tell his father of Cowdray's threat, for the old man was already inflamed to the point of apoplexy. Determination had insisted that they wait outside the governor's home, lurking like a pair of brigands, until Cowdray finally emerged well after midnight, sated with drink and food. Determination refrained from accosting the man physically, but as Cowdray began his walk home, Determination followed him, loudly censuring him with every step. There were few passers-by at that time of night, but those there were watched with amazement as Determination hurled imprecations at Cowdray's back.

"Hear me, Satan-spawn!" Determination roared. "You God-forsaken atrocity, abortion of Babylon's whore, misery of mankind! Your crimes are seen by the Lord God Almighty, and He will not long suffer you to walk upon the good earth that is His noblest creation! Today you are clothed in silk and finery, but you will be reduced to ash, consumed in the lake of fire that burneth eternal ..."

Cowdray had not hastened his pace, simply continued to stroll with perfect equanimity, even pausing once to admire the velvety darkness of the night sky. When finally he came to his house on Pearl Street—an even finer house than the governor's—he had turned his head and looked at Anson.

HE WILL CHOKE ON THE HATRED HE SPEWS. Cowdray spoke without speaking, his words ringing inside of Anson's head. THEN THE DECISION WILL BE YOURS, MOONCALF. A SON DOES NOT HAVE TO TAKE UP HIS FATHER'S BATTLES.

Then he closed the door behind himself.

Anson had pleaded with his father to come away. But Determination would not. He had planted himself in the street, screaming up at Cowdray's dark windows, until officers of the watch came and arrested them for disturbing the peace.

Before the year was out, Determination Kendall was dead.

He died suddenly in his fifty-eighth year, in a month where the full moon fell on the thirteenth day. He began vomiting toads and slugs and other black sickening vermin from his lips, and soon they were gushing forth in such volume that he choked on them, his eyes wide with terror. He died clutching the red cross around his neck, and it did him no good.

Anson was not a vengeful man. But he had loved his father as best as he could, and it was brutally unfair that he should be murdered thus—so casually, so remotely, seemingly with as little effort as was required to snuff the life of a fly. If nothing else, Determination had been a faithful and diligent servant of God—far more perfect than his son ever had been or could be. He had devoted his life to enacting God's will in every word he uttered and deed he performed. And it had earned him not even the meagerest scrap of regard. Instead, God had suffered Cowdray, the worst of sinners, to fill Determination's last moments with terror, suffering, and misery.

It was unconscionable.

Anson remembered Cowdray's last words to him.

A son does not have to take up his father's battles.

They were not words of advice. They were words of challenge. Cowdray thought him weak-willed and hesitant, just as his father always had.

Anson saw that there was only one way he could truly honor his father's memory. And that was to prove him wrong.

Anson went to work with a vengeance he never knew he possessed.

He saw that it was useless to attack Cowdray within the fortress of safety he had created for himself. Cowdray had powerful allies. Anson would need powerful allies as well.

Governor Simon Bradstreet had recently returned to Massachusetts after the dissolution of the Dominion, and it was to him that Anson proposed an allegiance of interests. He knew that Bradstreet would care little about Cowdray's sins—but the warlock's vast fortune ... well, that was another matter. The governor was in desperate need of funds to fight the French's unceasing harassment of the colony's frontier outposts to the north. Cowdray had no wife or kin. When he died, the disposition of his estate would be uncertain. If it could be so arranged that he be arrested in Massachusetts, and there tried and convicted and executed, his estate would escheat to the colonial government.

Bradstreet's face had lit with interest when Anson described the scheme. But just as quickly, he had frowned. "Ah, but you will ne'er draw him to Massachusetts," the governor muttered bad-temperedly, as if hope itself were an annoyance.

But Anson was resolved to prove him wrong. He went after Cowdray's business agents, members of his coven—anyone with even a remote association with the warlock who had the misfortune to stray into areas controlled by those sympathetic to the growing fame of the (now solitary) Inquisitor Kendall.

He had a hundred in gaol within a month, and all of them under torture. Those who knew the most about Cowdray's affairs died the most quickly, just as Old Mother Grax had, gushing blood from their noses and eyes. Anson gathered knowledge in drabs and snatches. He learned how Cowdray would steal souls by means of a black snake that would slither up to kiss the lips of a sleeping man. The sleeping man would rise in the morning, but he would never again wake.

Anson was heedful of the threat Cowdray posed. He sent his wife and daughter far away from Boston and told no one—not even Sarah's family—where they had gone. He kept his son James with him. The boy was ten, a good age to be apprenticed. The work was endless, and Anson needed hands he could trust. James had a clever mind. He did not blanch at torture. It was what his father said must be done, and he did it—not with the kind of pleasure Anson suspected Determination had taken in it, but because he loved his father and wanted to please him. This made Anson proud. His son was stronger than he had ever been.

The most useful piece of information they collected was about a shipment Cowdray was expecting. The warlock had made arrangements to take a bride. Little was known of her, except that she came from a good family in England, and she was very wealthy, and Cowdray had sent his fastest ship to bring her—and the large dower sum that accompanied her—to New York.

When Anson learned of this, he rejoiced. For here, finally, was a way to get Cowdray to Massachusetts.

He knew of a woman who, by all reports, was the best weather-witch in the New World. He promised her that she would not be tried if she would stir him up a sorcerous wind that would compel Cowdray's galleon off its course, and into one of the harbors in Massachusetts, Boston or Salem or anywhere in between. She was reluctant, for no witch or warlock desired to cross Cowdray—but the Inquisitor Kendall's reputation had become near as fearsome, and she was eventually persuaded. And Anson did keep his promise. He did not prosecute her. He did nothing until he felt the winds shift, heard the sailors of the harbor begin to talk of other ships, previously bound for New York, mysteriously diverted to the waters of Massachusetts Bay. He waited long enough to be certain that she had kept her end of the bargain, and then he killed her, cutting her throat silently in the night with his own hand.

He was his father's son. He knew the ways of witches, knew their occult methods of communication, knew that he could not take the chance that the woman would betray his plans to Cowdray.

Anson Kendall had always had blood on his hands, so much blood that it dripped from his fingers. Once, he had longed to wash it away. Now though, he cared not. What was a little more blood? What was it, really?

How Cowdray had found Sarah, and had delivered to her a comb of ivory and silver (with a note that said it was a gift from her most loving husband) Anson never knew, even to his dying day.

Anson did not receive word of what happened to Sarah until more than a week after Cowdray's fastest ship had been blown into Boston harbor, and Cowdray and his whore had travelled North under the cover of sorcerous guises to reclaim the treasured cargo. Cowdray's affianced, a petulant and spoiled girl, repined in the governor's home even as Anson and his son had lain in wait, with twice two-dozen of Governor Bradstreet's best men.

It had taken all of those men to capture Cowdray, and the warlock—summoning ferocious spirits from within the snuffbox—had left most of them dead. It was only young James' bravery—for he had knocked the snuffbox from Cowdray's grasp—that allowed the remaining few to finally clap the warlock in irons.

It was a great victory, but short-lived. The next day, Anson received a letter from his daughter Abigail, who had sent it upon the fastest post.

Abigail wrote of how pleased her mother had been with the unexpected gift from her husband. But upon combing her hair with the jewel of ivory and silver, beautiful as the moon, Sarah Kendall had fallen into a trance. Abigail's letters became shaky on the page as she recounted how the comb had become a black snake, slithering up Sarah Kendall's nose.

His wife was not dead. But neither was she alive. She breathed, but there was nothing in her eyes.

All the arts of the local priest, the local doctor, even the local herb-woman had been employed to save her. But from each, the judgment had been the same; her soul was gone from her body.

His wife, pure and kind and laughing, who had never done a cruel thing in her life, had been consigned to an eternity of torture in a magically-created hell with only the spirits of black heathens for company. The thought of it nearly drove Anson mad.

Or perhaps it *had* driven him mad, he thought as he looked at the blood dripping from Cowdray's fingers, as he looked into the man's agonized face. Only a madman could take such pleasure in pain, so much joy in revenge.

Anson Kendall sat in the ladderback chair, watching the warlock die. The moon had risen higher now, casting a pallid glow over the gallows field. He pulled Cowdray's snuffbox from within his coat. The masterwork of the warlock's evil was horribly beautiful—worked in chased silver, the scene on the lid depicted a vision of the devil dancing in hell, ringed by souls writhing in torment. The face of the devil had been worked to resemble Cowdray's own.

Anson opened the box. It was lined with *uchawi* wood, polished glove-smooth. He ran his fingertips along the inside, and they came away coated with a dark, powdery residue that tingled. He rubbed his fingers together. The box was open, but Sarah's soul was locked within it, within a world of suffering, and there was nothing he could do to save her.

Anson clicked the box shut. He tucked it back inside his coat and stood. He turned away from Cowdray. James didn't notice his father's rise; he was warming himself before the fire. In the light of the now-risen full moon, and the flickering gleam of the flames, his young face looked very old and very sad.

In that moment, Anson felt very keenly the pain of failing everyone he had ever loved.

Then, there was a cry—high-pitched, desperate—and a dark blur, a flash of red and bright silver, and Anson felt something slam against him from behind.

It was a body, a young lithe body. Cowdray's whore. He smelled her reeking carnal stench, the salt of her tears. Her body was warm against his. He felt something else then. Sharp pain. He saw his son turn at the sound of the harlot's cry, watched as astonishment and horror spread across James' young face.

She had stabbed him, Anson realized, as his knees buckled.

And he saw her hand, covered with his own blood, coming up to do it again. With the strength of reflex, he seized her wrist, pain screaming through his side as he wrenched the silver knife from her grasp. She squeaked like a stepped-on kitten as he jerked her arm up behind her, laid the knife against her throat.

James was at his father's side immediately, Bradstreet's men at his heels. But Anson forestalled them all with a small shake of his head. Instead, he jerked the whore around to where Cowdray was taking his last breaths on God's earth.

"You've taken everything from me." His side throbbed with pain. Hot blood trickled down his leg. "Here is one thing ... one miserable, wretched thing that I can take from you."

"I care not ..." Cowdray's voice was barely audible. But even through his agony, through the pallor of swiftly approaching death, Anson saw tenderness in the warlock's eyes. He pressed the knife harder against her throat, drawing blood. The girl's hand came up to clutch his; their blood mingled, sticky as raw honey.

Anson was certain that he would slit her throat. He wanted very much to slit her throat. He wanted to cause this demon pain, do the work that even God had scrupled to do.

But then, in the soft moonlight, he saw his son's face.

It was held, as it always was, carefully and blankly. But something—something divine or demonic—allowed Anson to see, for the first time, the horror hiding behind the boy's eyes. His son had always wished to please him, and he had concealed his disgust well. But it was there, just as strong as he himself had ever felt it. Killing the witch would do no good. It would not rectify the unfairness God had ordained for the world. It would not please Him. Nothing would.

He shoved the girl away. She stumbled forward, falling to her knees at Cowdray's side. She seized the warlock's bloody hand, held it tight.

And then Anson realized what a horrible mistake he had made.

Cowdray could lift his hand just barely, just enough to touch the blood at the girl's throat. His swollen purple fingers encircled her neck. He did not have the strength to hold her, but she did not resist—instead, she leaned into his grasp. There was magic dancing around Cowdray's fingers, magic drawn from the blood of the girl, and from Anson's own blood, mixed with hers. As the warlock began to speak, Anson felt magic beginning to burn within him— blood calling to blood. His body felt hot, as if he had coals in the pit of his stomach.

There was an unearthly scream from the warlock. But the sound was coming from between the girl's lips, and then it became words. Chanting, high-pitched and wild, in a bitter old language. Power, brighter than the full moon, brighter than the sun at summer's zenith, wreathed the pair of them.

Anson fell to his knees, agony burning through his veins.

"More stones!" he screamed to Bradstreet's men. "All of them! Now! For the love of Christ!"

But Cowdray's voice continued to stream from the whore's lips, even as one, two, three more stones were heaped upon him.

"I curse you, Anson Kendall," the girl mouthed, her eyes wholly black. "I curse your children, and your children's children, and your children's children's children. Every full moon, from this time until the end of days on earth, I will take the body of one of your descendents and I will use it to do all the evil—all and more—that you think you have thwarted. I will be the everlasting curse of your lineage. I curse you. I curse you!"

Cowdray voiced the final word in high church Latin—*maledictus*—and Anson felt the force of it like a bolt from a crossbow. It slammed into him. He shrieked.

And then he realized that James was screaming too, clawing at his own flesh.

James. His child. His *son*.

Anson staggered to his feet, ignoring the agony that was melting his bones, ignoring the force of magic that was lashing him with molten fury. Bradstreet's men were cowering in terror; from one of them, Anson seized a short sword.

"I curse you," Cowdray rasped in his own voice as Anson seized him by his blood-soaked hair.

It took several strokes to hack off the warlock's head. But as the last ragged sinew was severed, the maelstrom of magic calmed. Blood gouted from the warlock's ruined neck; the girl who had been his voice, who had channeled his magic through her own body, collapsed—dead.

The sudden stillness seemed even louder than the deafening thunder that had preceded it. Anson looked to where James lay on the ground—the boy was unconscious, but he was breathing. His son was alive.

Anson Kendall lifted the severed head in his trembling hand, intending to cast it away into the darkest well of shadow he could find. Only then did he see that the warlock's eyes were still open, glittering with moonlight and malice. And his lips were curved into a satisfied, mocking smile.

Maledictus, the dead warlock whispered.

— Part I: Waxing —

Chapter One

A Battle of Wills

SACRAMENTO VALLEY, CALIFORNIA
29 DAYS UNTIL THE FULL MOON

Will Edwards lay on his belly in a stand of dry grass, peering through field glasses at the old farmhouse nestled in the bowl-shaped valley. His bicycle rested where he'd dropped it, the click of its still-spinning rear wheel drowned by the susurration of cicadas. The day had been Indian-summer hot, but the sky was deepening purple and the chilled-ink shadows of late November were beginning to pool in the valley's hollows. Soon it would be time to fire up the electric generator, to power the lights that would make the farmhouse seem the only warm place for miles beneath a cold, waning moon.

Tonight, though, the lights would stay dark. Because Will was the only one in the family who knew how to coax the stinking old kerosene power-plant into operation. And he'd be damned if he lifted a finger to help any of them ever again.

In fact, there was only one reason Will had staked out this observation spot at the top of the hill. It was Thanksgiving, and it was rumored that Ben might be coming home.

Will had never really seen his brother Ben .... not that he could remember, anyway. Ben had left home before Will could even walk on two legs, and he'd never come home since, not even once. All Will knew of his brother was based on incomplete snippets of information overheard from his parents or bartered for from his older brothers. Ben had had a fight with Father. It had been a fight so bitter that he'd been sent away, far away, across the country to New York City. There he'd built a whole separate life for himself. He had studied at the famous Stanton Institute as a student. After graduation, the Institute had retained him as an employee.

These unornamented facts did not suggest much common ground between Will and his older brother—save for one still-smoldering patch. They both thought that their father was an insufferable bastard.

For Will had had his own fight with Father, on his eighteenth birthday, and it too was bitter enough to make him leave home (well, for three days at least—and not to New York, but rather to his buddy Pask de la Guerra's neighboring spread a few miles over).

On the surface, it was a fight about birthday presents. Which, when considered in such a way, sounded awful petty even to Will's mind. But of course it was about so much more.

He'd had no cause to complain about *quantity*, for Father had given him no fewer than three presents. It was the *quality* of these gifts that he objected to, for each one had turned out to be worse than the last. The first was mingy, the second superfluous, and the third ... well, the third one was downright *intolerable*.

The mingy present was a silver dollar, almost fifty years old, a sentimental piece Father had kept on his watch chain for years. It was a nice piece of money—if one wanted to buy a steak dinner. But it was not enough for anything else. Certainly not enough for a train ticket to Detroit. Not enough to get free of this place. And Father knew it. It was nothing more than a pointed—and cruel— reminder of Will's powerlessness. It was as if Father had presented him with a ball and chain and expected him to be pleased that the shackle was lined with velvet.

Next came the superfluous present. Advice. What eighteen-year-old boy needed more of that? And not only advice, but advice that came wrapped in a Latin test to boot. Laying a hand on Will's shoulder, the old man had asked, "Will, can you tell me the meaning of the phrase *Veritas vos Liberabit?*"

"The truth shall make one free." Will offered the translation with slight hesitancy, trying to remember if *vos* was singular or plural, certain Father was trying to trip him up with the pronoun.

But Father didn't seem to care about the pronoun, he had just nodded gravely, then released a heavy sigh. "It's a very simple motto and it sounds very good. But I'm afraid it does not accurately capture the actual cost of truth or freedom."

What the hell did *that* mean? It sounded like Father was rehearsing another political speech for Argus—probably trying to figure out how he could work in something about the blood of martyrs. Will must have made a noise of exasperation, because Father had dropped his hand, and Will was left hoping beyond hope that he was saving the best for last. Maybe he'd changed his mind about the letter Will had received from Tesla Industries.

But as it turned out, the last present had been the worst—the absolute *worst*—and Will still got so mad when he thought about it that he didn't think about it. And so he had run away to the de la Guerras' and lost himself in work on Pask's auto.

Mechanical tinkering always set Will's spirits at ease, and Pask's 1906 Baker Electric was always in need of some kind of repair. Pask—the grandson of Don Diego de la Guerra, an eminent *Californio*—had been wildly enthusiastic about the machine when he'd gotten it three years ago, but had since grown as tired of it as any toy. The more Pask neglected the Baker, the more it acted up—and the more it acted up, the worse Pask treated it, driving it with the unconscious negligence he might use toward one of his father's field hands.

The culmination of Pask's mistreatment of the Baker was slapping red and green paint on it for Homecoming, then—after he and Will had one too many nips of whiskey at the game—driving it into an irrigation ditch. Pask had vowed he would leave the half-submerged heap there to rot, but Will had convinced him to have a team haul it back to the de la Guerra's barn, where Will had spent the better part of a month disassembling and cleaning the electrical motor.

Will lowered the field glasses, catching a glimpse of his own hands as he did. He'd scrubbed them with pumice soap, but they were still seamed with grease from his most recent work on the Baker. At least the time he'd spent hiding out at the de la Guerras' had been well spent. It had given him the opportunity to execute the *coupe de grace* of his rebuild—retrofitting the jalopy with a nifty little power system of his own design.

He called it an Otherwhere Flume. He'd come up with the concept during his last year at the California Polytechnic. While it was, in the main, a standard Otherwhere Conductor (its design taken straight from his teacher Mr. Waters' third year *Otherwhere Engineering* textbook) Will had introduced several significant improvements. Mr. Waters had been astonished by Will's ingenuity, but Will had never quite understood his teacher's astonishment. The inefficiencies of the standard design were all so obvious. They stood out as prominently as wrinkles in a tablecloth. All Will had done was smooth out the cloth.

With the Flume installed, Will could conceivably drive the beat-up old Baker all the way to Detroit. It wouldn't be comfortable or fast ... but he could do it. And Will was in such a desperate state of mind that he was actually considering it. It had been almost a month since he'd gotten the fat letter from Tesla Industries, informing him that he'd been accepted into their apprenticeship program. A whole month, and the acceptance letter had said that they wanted him to get there as quickly as possible.

Tesla Industries was the foremost center for scientific research in the United States, and their apprenticeship program was world-renowned. They only accepted one or two candidates a year—usually college men—but Mr. Waters had been so impressed with Will's work that he had recommended Will for consideration.

And Will had been accepted.

The fat letter had arrived on Hallowe'en. The acceptance letter itself wasn't fat, but the boilerplate apprenticeship contract enclosed with it was a hundred and thirty-two pages. Will had been giddy with excitement. His father, however, had hemmed and hawed. He told Will that he would have to review the contract before he could give Will his permission.

And of course, I let him, Will thought bitterly. *Trusted him, like an idiot.* And wasn't that just like Father! To pretend he was doing you a favor, looking out for your best interests, when really he was just stalling for time, stockpiling ammunition to fortify his position, so he could ultimately deliver the devastating answer from a position of unimpeachable strength:

No, Will. I'm afraid I don't think it is a good idea for you to enter this program. There are many more suitable opportunities closer to home. I'm afraid I cannot give you my permission.

"Bastard," Will muttered. Just remembering the old man sitting behind his heavy desk, delivering that shattering pronouncement so smoothly and casually, made him want to punch something.

A cooling evening breeze blew up the hillside, and along with the smell of dry grass and aging lupines, Will caught the buttery, sugary odor of baked squash. His stomach rumbled traitorously, and his mind joined in the rebellion, suggesting that there would also be roast turkey and mashed potatoes and pies. Ma'am made such good pies. Gosh, he was hungry. He sure wished Ben would hurry up.

Will caught sight of a flashing glimmer, like a trout leaping from a still pond. He quickly lifted his field glasses back to his eyes.

An automobile emerged from the dark cluster of oaks that hid the road leading to the Edwards' homestead. But not just any automobile. Will recognized it instantly as a Pierce Arrow—a 66-QQ. It was the biggest one they made, the six-passenger touring style. The gleaming chrome trim against the elegant French gray enamel, the bright-polished dark wood of the spoke wheels, the smooth blackness of the Panasote top ... what a honey of a machine! And if all that weren't enough, it was next year's model, a 1911. It would have to have been special ordered—and it must have cost a mint.

The car came to a luxuriant surcease before the house's front porch. The driver was first out of the car on the right-hand side. An imposing, heavily built man, he wore green-tinted brass goggles and a long motoring overcoat that brushed the tops of his mirror-polished black boots.

Well, well. If it isn't the Congressman, Will watched as his brother Argus peeled off his dogskin driving gloves. *Celebrating his victory with a big new car, and so proud of it that he won't even stand for a driver.*

The really hilarious thing was that Argus had run his recent campaign as "California's Man of the People." The newspapers had been amply supplied with photos of him earnestly shaking hands with laboring types in grimy overalls. The voters of California had swallowed *that* bunch of guff hook, line, and sinker, electing him to the U.S. House of Representatives just the past September. Will found himself wishing he had a camera right now. Wouldn't he send those newspapers some pictures! *California's Big Goddamn Show-Off* would be the headline.

And I just bet he's going to insist on being called "the honorable" now, Will thought. *Pft! As if!*

He watched as Argus came around to open the door for the well-dressed woman in the front passenger seat; Lillie, his wife. Lillie's hat emerged from the car first, her face swathed in taupe gauze to protect her from the environmental hazards of motoring. She was also positively smothered in furs. Though the day had grown hot, they would have had to have left San Francisco in the chill of dawn to motor the entire eighty miles to the middle of the Sacramento Valley.

Argus left the passengers in the back seats to shift for themselves while he saw his wife to the porch. Argus had married into an obscene amount of money, and while he suffered no lack of success in his own professional and political ventures, he was always mindful to keep that particular slice of toast butter-side up.

How lovely it must be to be the honorable Argus Edwards! Everything in life handed to him on a silver plate. Well, there was one thing he wasn't going to get ... his baby brother, the gearhead squirt, sure as hell wasn't going to show up fawning over his new car, no matter how amazing it clearly was. No sir!

Fuming, Will watched the passengers emerging from the back seats. First out was another of Will's brothers, Laddie. Unlike Argus and Lillie, he was not kitted out in motoring togs, but wore his customary well-tailored suit. Upon getting out of the car, he was quick to open his gold cigarette case and light a smoke. He did this with the air of elegant desperation that he did most things.

Next, a very large older man unfolded himself from what must have been a very cramped middle seat. He quickly vanished beneath the shady overhang of the broad porch, where Will's mother had come out to greet the new arrivals, wiping her hands on her apron before extending them in welcome.

Will's heart sank as he watched the final passenger emerge from the automobile, for it was clearly not Ben. But disappointment gave way to curiosity as Will noted the many extremely fascinating ways in which the passenger differed. This "not-Ben" was a girl, about his age, with long wavy brown hair held back in a red satin schoolgirl's bow. When she removed her light canvas motoring duster, he saw that she wore a neat embroidered shirtwaist and a navy skirt trimmed in white cord.

Everyone else had gone into the house, leaving her alone in the quiet, lowering twilight. Breathing deeply, she stretched. It was a languorous, cat-like movement that made Will's heart thump. Gosh. She was even prettier than the car. Was she one of Lillie's society friends, maybe? Or what if she was here with Laddie, one of his empty-headed conquests? Oh, that would be just terrible, if Laddie had taken to preying on innocent schoolgirls now. Will was simply dying to find out.

But ... no! Will dropped his field binoculars and sat back in the grass. Ben hadn't come, and that was that. He'd promised himself he wouldn't give any of them the time of day, and he wouldn't. Wasn't like he was missing anything except a tedious evening with brothers he already knew ... his witchly Ma'am chanting her fussy little kitchen spells to make sure all the food stayed hot ... his Uncle Royce, who had the most disquieting way of appearing suddenly at one's elbow when one least expected it ... and *Father* ...

He stood up and righted his bicycle. He slung his heavy leather toolbag (he never went anywhere without it) across his back. Pask's doors were always open to him, and the de la Guerras would surely be fixing up a good dinner too. In honor of the holiday they'd probably even crack open a bottle of old Spanish wine. They'd get up a game of pinochle and listen to their brand new Teslaphone—they were the first in the whole county to have bought one of the updated models.

But then again ...

Will stood astride his bicycle, looking back down the hill. The girl had gone inside. He wondered what her name was.

It wouldn't hurt to find out.

Yes, that was it. He wanted to meet the girl. That was a fair reason for a red-blooded American boy. He wasn't going home to fawn over Argus' car, that much he promised himself. It wasn't because he could smell the pies all the way up here. And it *certainly* wasn't because there was still a small piece of his mind that he hadn't yet given his father.

No. It was to meet the girl.

Kicking off, he coasted down the grassy hill toward home.

Will left his toolbag on the screened back porch and crept in through the mud room just off the kitchen. He was hoping to avoid notice, and with the kitchen in such a state, that wasn't hard. Pots bubbled and steamed, china and silverware clanked. Potatoes were being mashed, vegetables creamed, gravy stirred. It was like the engine room of a battleship about to engage a hostile fleet. A dozen itinerant girls—charity cases from all up and down the West Coast that his soft-hearted Ma'am took in and employed—worked under her watchful eye. There were so many of them, and in such constant rotation, that it was flat impossible to keep their names straight. Will had adopted the tactic of calling them all "Maisy" and accepting whatever good-natured or sharp-tongued correction might ensue.

The final turkey had just come out of the oven (there were three birds in all, each twenty pounds if it was an ounce, each shot by Nate in the thick oak groves along the Sacramento River) and preparations were being made for the food's distribution to various destinations. One turkey would go to the German family who ran the farm, one would go to the charity girls, and the last—the largest—would be served to the family. The birds that had been roasted earlier were covered with large chargers laid over with folded wool blankets that shimmered slightly; his Ma'am's sorcerous handiwork would keep the birds at the perfect temperature indefinitely.

Surreptitiously lifting one of the covers, Will picked off a piece of turkey meat. Then, licking his fingers, he snuck up behind his mother—who had not yet noticed his arrival—and laid an indifferent peck on her cheek.

"Hi," he grunted.

"Will!" Ma'am whirled and seized him. She showered him with kisses as if she hadn't seen him in months. "I'm so glad you came back. Were you over at Pask's? I was worried about you!"

"Aw, what are you worrying about me for?" He didn't like to worry his Ma'am. And even though he was still a little mad at her for her implicit support of Father's birthday presents, her rosy round cheeks and the good-humored glint in her violet eyes made it hard to stay so. Even though her skin was wrinkled and her hair was losing the battle to remain chestnut-colored, she always seemed younger than the girls who surrounded her.

"You and your father had an awful bust-up," Ma'am said. She laid a soft, warm hand on his cheek—the one she called her "reading" hand. It possessed some kind of special magical sensitivity that Will had never really understood the extent of. She held it there for a moment until he felt compelled to shy away like an impatient colt. "But I figured you'd both do with some cooling off. If I'd really wanted you I would have Sent for you."

Will shuddered inwardly but said nothing. All the Edwards boys hated being Sent for by their witchly mother. It wasn't that it was painful (unless she was really mad)—it was just ... well, what fellow wanted his mother poking her nose into his head? Especially when you were eighteen?

And on the subject of thoughts he probably would have preferred his mother not intrude on, Will tried not to look at one girl in particular—the brunette girl who had arrived in Argus' car and was now helping out in the kitchen. She had been given a large white apron to put over her stylish costume and had been set to rolling biscuits.

"Some motorcar the Congressman has got," Will offered with casual malice. Ma'am smirked at the jibe, and then, just as abruptly, her face darkened.

"And did you hear that they've left Kendall at home with his nurse, just so Argus could drive that silly contraption?" Ma'am tossed her silver-threaded curls with outrage. "Lillie didn't want to bother carrying him on her lap the whole way. Can you imagine! That woman hasn't a scrap of mother-feeling in her. I've only got one grandchild, and I never even get to see him!"

Will suffered this tirade in silence. Ma'am dislike of her daughter-in-law was inversely proportional to her love of babies over an extremely wide range. But the absence of his infant nephew Kendall (who he remembered as red-faced and screaming at the indignity of being swaddled in an extravagant confection of linen and lace) was a matter of supreme indifference to Will. He was more interested in another absence.

"So Ben isn't going to make it?"

Ma'am shook her head. "I guess something came up." She quickly seized a nearby bowl as if its contents were in urgent need of stirring. Ma'am was never any good at hiding anything—especially hurt. When she was happy, her face looked young; but when she was sad, she looked very old. Desperate to cheer her, Will wrapped his arms around her and hugged her off balance, roaring like a bear. Ma'am whooped and tried not to spill the contents of the bowl.

"But I have a letter from him!" she added brightly, as if that made up for everything. Which it didn't, but Ben was great at writing letters: breezy, fascinating and suggestive. Ben wrote very interestingly about things that weren't very interesting. His letters were like cotton-candy. They were thrilling and sweet, and you could eat a whole lot, but when you got right down to it there really wasn't much there. And if you ate too much, you'd probably get sick.

Of course, Will had been able to form his opinions only from the bits and pieces of Ben's letters that other family members shared with him, because Ben had never written him. Not a single solitary word. Ever.

Will, on the other hand, wrote to Ben quite often, in care of the famous Stanton Institute in New York City, where Ben had been employed for many years. He wrote him about his life, his disappointments, his hopes. He came to think of his letters to Ben almost like a kind of diary. You wrote in it, you shared secrets with it, but you never expected it to give anything in return. Still, Will had asked Ma'am about it once, asked why she reckoned Ben never wrote him back.

"He's probably just thinking of what to say," she'd said. "Someday you'll hear from him."

Will doubted it. And Ben's failure to show up at Thanksgiving seemed only to confirm that suspicion. Even so, writing to Ben had become an ingrained habit, and Will was already thinking of what he would write about the girl who was rolling biscuits. Ma'am smiled slyly when she saw how scrupulously Will was avoiding looking at their guest.

"Don't you two remember each other?" she asked, adopting a very proper tone. "I guess it *has* been a long time. William Edwards, this is Miss Jenny Hansen. Miss Jenny Hansen, this is my youngest son, William."

Jenny Hansen smirked, dusting flour off her hands so she could extend one in his direction. Suddenly, Will felt even more suckered than he had by Argus' car. At least Argus' car wouldn't laugh at him.

"Jenny Hansen?" he squeaked. Holy Moses. He *should* have lit out for Pask's! He wondered if there was still time to escape.

"Of course he doesn't remember me, Mrs. Edwards," Jenny said, withdrawing her hand when Will failed to take it. "It's all those rocks I shied at his head when we were kids."

"I remember you, *Scuff.*" He used the nickname he'd given her years ago, a testament to her perpetually scraped knees. "It's just I remember you all scrawny and homely and knock-kneed, and now, well ..." Will trailed off irritably. Damn it, he'd meant it as a dig and it hadn't come out right at all.

"Hasn't she gotten pretty?" Ma'am put an arm around Jenny and pressed a little kiss to the side of her forehead. "She and her dad came down from San Francisco with Argus and Laddie."

Will's mouth went dry. So *that* was who'd been crammed in the middle seat of Argus' car—of course! Mr. Dagmar Hansen, one of Ma'am's oldest friends. How could he have failed to recognize him? He was, after all, probably the largest man Will had ever seen in his life.

It was one thing to see a cute girl and want to get her number; it was quite another to discover that the cute girl was Jenny Hansen, and that her enormous father was on the scene to keep a sharp eye on her interests. Or a sharp eye on anyone else who had his eye on her interests.

"Will, take these out to the table," Ma'am said, shoving a bowl of mixed nuts into his hands. "Then go say hello to Mr. Hansen. Jenny, finish up those biscuits and then you can run along too, we've got plenty of help ..."

Ma'am's last words were lost as Will made his escape from the kitchen. He sullenly deposited the bowl of nuts onto the groaning table, then braced himself to be sacrificed upon the altar of the Edwards' family gaiety. His entrance into the family room would be heralded with baying cries of welcome; the joyous cries of predators having sighted a small animal they could harry. Will's brothers took harrying Will very seriously. They had elevated it to an art form. A late baby, Will was much younger than all of them—Laddie was the closest to him in age, but even he was a whole decade older than Will—so they all felt justified in taking a very stern fatherly tone toward him at the drop of a hat. Having all suffered under their Father's stern paternal tone, they found it great fun to use on their baby brother. It was like being trapped in a house with multiple Fathers, each of whom could whip him.

The large family room was a ground floor suite just off the garden, originally designed for a resident mother-in-law. There were no mothers-in-law in the Edwards family, but it was said the suite of rooms had been inhabited once by a superannuated Grandpap—the one Nate had been named for. But that old man died long before Will was born, and of him Will knew only that he'd come from up the mountains, and had brought a lot of cats with him, the descendents of which still hunted mice under the grain bins in the barn. After his death, the suite's sitting room had been set up with sofas and tables, lamps and a piano (usually plied by one of Ma'am's charity cases, as none of the Edwards family were at all musical)—all the comforts required for a cozy family evening. Books were conspicuous in their absence, but that was because all the books were kept in the next room, Father's study. The high walls of that sumptuous cave were lined with them, floor to ceiling.

But the door to the study was closed, which meant that Father was presiding within. In the family room, Laddie and Lillian were making themselves comfortable. The only liquor in the Edwards' house was Father's old scotch kept under lock and key, so Laddie had withdrawn his own capacious silver flask and was mixing up impromptu cocktails for himself and Lillie. It was whispered among Ma'am's girls that Lillie was "fast"—she drank and smoked and wore cosmetics ("And not just powder either!" Will remembered one girl's shocked assertion.) And while Argus was her husband, rumor had it that Laddie was the only one who could keep her in line. Will wondered how a fast, unmanageable wife was supposed to fit into Argus' expansive political plans; but on the other hand she *was* rich, and her family well-connected, so maybe that outweighed everything else.

"Good afternoon, William!" Laddie drawled, tapping a cigarette against the gold case. "Turned yourself in, have you?"

Laddie was unquestionably the handsomest of the Edward boys, dark and slim and elegant. As usual, he was dressed exquisitely—not in honor of the holiday, but because looking good seemed to be the sole moral imperative he upheld.

"Hullo," Will mumbled. "Where's Argus?"

"He's in with the *men*," Laddie said archly, nodding toward the library door. By "men," of course, Laddie meant Father and Mr. Hansen and Uncle Royce. It was clear Laddie did not include himself in that description, nor Nate (whom Will had completely failed to notice brooding in the corner). And certainly not Will.

Will wondered where Ben would stand in that equation. Ben would likely stand outside the equation entirely. Not a man, not a boy ... Ben was like a different species.

"We waited for Ben at Union Station," Laddie said. He had the most disquieting talent for knowing the drift of his brothers' thoughts, and voicing them when they otherwise would not have. "But he wasn't on the train. I suppose he decided against it at the last minute. I must say, I was really hoping for a reconciliation, at least a temporary one. Watching them fight it all out again would have been *such* fun."

Will said nothing. Ben's fight with Father was legendary within the family for its rancorous protraction, and in comparison, Will's own fight with Father was merely a candle held up to the sun. Ma'am had traveled to New York a few times, hoping to effect a reconciliation, but even she had ultimately given up. Ben now existed within the family only on paper, in the extended letters he wrote to everyone but Father and Will.

"Of course, I hear you're doing your best to step into Ben's shoes and give us all a wonderful show," Laddie said, as he handed a freshly-mixed cocktail to Lillie. "I hope you thought up some really good cutting remarks while you were hiding out at Pask de la Guerra's house. I'm expecting nothing but the best."

Will didn't say anything. He knew that the best defense against his brothers was surly silence.

"Speaking of Ben, I had a letter from him just the other day," Laddie said. "Full of the most scandalous gossip about people I've never heard of. He managed to make it more fascinating than scandalous gossip about people I know intimately. I call that quite a skill."

"Hi, Nate." Will turned his attention to his brooding brother in the corner. Nate's arms were crossed and he was staring at the floor, frowning deeply. Nate loved only one thing—horses. Everything else he hated. He hated being inside, he hated wearing clothes that weren't soiled with manure, and he especially hated being taken away from his chores for something as unproductive as a family gathering.

Nate did not answer, didn't even look up. After a pause, Will said, "Sorrel mare again?"

Nate nodded, keeping his dark steady gaze fixed on the carpet at his feet. "One of the hands left the bar off the stable again. I swear to God, if I find the man who did it, I'll have his hide for a new pair of mucking boots. She got down into the south pasture and ate a bellyful of clover and now she's got the slobbers."

"I thought clover was good for them," Lillie said, but her tone indicated that she couldn't be less interested if she tried.

"Most horses tolerate it fine," Nate allowed. "But one bite and that poor sorrel goes crazy. We have to put up hay for her special with no clover in it."

"My goodness, I wish Cook would take that kind of care with our dinners!" Lillie smirked sidelong at Laddie. "I believe she goes out of her way to miss the bones in the fish she serves us."

If he was Argus and Lillie's cook, Will mused, he'd probably put extra bones in their fish in the hopes that they'd choke on one. But he refrained from giving voice to this sentiment.

"And no matter how much care Nate takes with that sorrel mare, she still gets into the clover every time," Laddie looked at Lillie over the rim of his highball glass. "One might come to the conclusion that she hasn't the slightest idea what's good for her."

"Stupid beast," Lillie said, giving the words strange emphasis. Will had no idea what to make of it. Laddie, on the other hand, knew exactly, and he and Lillie punctuated whatever opaque joke they'd made by clinking their glasses together. Will had never really understood what kind of relationship existed between his two brothers and this woman. Honestly, he was kind of glad he didn't.

"She's not stupid," Nate flared, but not at anyone in particular. Once he'd said it, he turned his eyes back to the carpet and sank deeper into his own thoughts, from which, Will knew, it would be nearly impossible to pull him. Of all his brothers—the brothers he knew, the brothers who were more to him than mere abstraction—Will felt most akin to Nate. They both understood what it was to live with an overwhelming, obsessive interest—Nate for horses, Will for mechanical devices. How those obsessions were received, however, could not have been more different. Because while Nate's passion was in neat alignment with the family's interests (or, more to the point, *Father's* interests, as his renown as a breeder of the finest Morgans on the West Coast was largely due to Nate's zealous efforts) Father had been able to find no similar value in Will.

"Have you seen Jenny?" Lillie pinned Will with her suggestive green eyes. They were indeed, Will noticed, faintly rimmed with kohl. She rattled the ice in her glass, which was Laddie's cue to quickly take it from her hand and begin mixing her another.

"Yes, I saw her," Will said carefully. There was a trap in that question, and he wanted to be ready to jump out of the way.

"She was *so* excited to see you," Lillie purred. "The little chatterbox was positively bursting with questions about you on the way out."

"Questions about *me?*" Will frowned, determined not to reveal his interest. If they suspected he cared, the information was sure to be withheld.

"Oh yes," Lillie said. "But honestly, Will, you mustn't get your hopes up. She really has to hold out for a partner in a brokerage, at *least*." She lowered her voice a conspiratorial shade. "Her father has done all right by her, given that he's just one corked boot out of the mountains. He's put her into Miss Murison's, you know, and everyone there seems to just love her. They find her so sprightly and queer and interesting. And so full of *opinions.*" She dangled this last word in front of Laddie with a tantalizing smirk; he rolled his eyes and released an extravagant sigh.

At that moment the door to Father's library opened, and the men came rumbling out. First through the door were Argus and Uncle Royce, engaged in brisk, close conversation about a political rally scheduled to be held in San Francisco that Sunday—a rally Argus was going to give a speech at, or sell peanuts at, or something. Mr. Hansen and Father followed behind. Mr. Hansen moved with the slow dignity of the rich, amiable, and well fed, still smoking one of the cigars that the "men" had clearly been enjoying in the library. Father limped alongside him with his customary stiffness, his game leg (injured in a long-ago riding accident and never properly healed) making a faint scuffing sound on the carpet. Mr. Hansen and Father were of a height, but where Father was stick-slim, Mr. Hansen loomed like one of the enormous hundred-year trees his fortune had been built on, the old giants that took fifteen men to saw down.

Father and Mr. Hansen saw Will at the same time. When Father saw Will, his face changed. The look that passed over it, Will decided, was disapproval. It was a subtle shift, but Will was always aware of it. Mr. Hansen's face, on the other hand, brightened in a broad smile.

"Why, look who's here! Will!" Mr. Hansen clapped a heavy hand on Will's back, and Will had to struggle to keep his feet. Mr. Hansen was a very old and dear friend of Ma'am's—and just as Ma'am had always wished for a daughter, Mr. Hansen had always wished for a son. It was the one thing Will could say for himself, that of all the Edwards litter, Mr. Hansen probably would have picked him for his own.

"How you been keeping?"

"Fine, Mr. Hansen," Will said.

"You seen my girl Jenny? She came out with me special. That girl has the biggest crush on you—"

"Dad!" Jenny screeched from across the room, having entered just in time to hear these intolerable words issue from her father's lips. Her face was beet red. "I said *had* a crush. *Had.* When I was ten years old! For pity's sake!"

Mr. Hansen stuck his tongue out at her, a bizarre expression for a titan of commerce. With a smile, he gestured for Will to follow him out to the verandah, where he could finish his cigar. The evening had cooled, and mellow golden light hung over the back garden, Ma'am's pride. Late-season chrysanthemums nodded over the neat river-gravel pathways, their scent mingling with the smell of cigar smoke. Mr. Hansen breathed appreciatively. "Your mother," he sighed.

Then, turning his attention back to Will: "So, congratulations are in order. I hear you graduated at the top of your class!"

Will shrugged indifferently. He'd graduated from the California Polytechnic High School in June, but his pride in the accomplishment had been overshadowed by the disappointment he'd suffered since. When he'd come home at the beginning of the summer, after three years living almost three hundred miles away from home in the school's dormitory in San Luis Obispo, he'd felt like an independent man. Now he just felt like a bitter, thwarted boy.

"Still going on to study engineering?" Mr. Hansen rubbed a flake of tobacco from his lip then spat into a flowerbed. Even though he was now one of the richer men in San Francisco—a town that did not want for rich men—he still retained the manners of his early years in a rough-and-tumble logging camp in the Sierras. "Lots of opportunity in that line for a wide-awake young man."

"I think there is," Will said. He did not add the rest, *even if some others around here don't.* His father might not think so, but Will was capable of tact when he chose to exercise it. Mr. Hansen was a good, honest man and Will wanted his respect. He wished he could talk to Mr. Hansen about the apprenticeship he'd been offered. If Mr. Hansen was his father, Will betted he'd let him go to Detroit.

"Yes, it *is* a fine little machine ... it will be just the thing for weekend outings when my duties allow me to return home from Washington." Argus' voice boomed from inside the house. "Of course, I wouldn't *dream* of taking it out to Washington with me.

Taft, you know, ordered a pair of last year's models for state cars—
official automobile of the White House—and it wouldn't do for a
freshman Congressman to show up the president." A pause, during which Will imagined Argus taking a deep, ego-inflating breath.
"It's got a six stroke engine, so my mechanic tells me. He also told
me something quite astonishing about its disbursement, but I can't
quite remember what it was he said. It's quite low, or quite high,
whatever it's supposed to be."

"Dual valve six, sixty-six horsepower, 714 cubic inches of *dis-
placement*," Will muttered to himself. He did not mutter low enough
for his words to escape Mr. Hansen's notice; the man chuckled and
ground the stub of his cigar under his heel. He bent his head toward
Will's and spoke in a conspiratorial tone:

"Just between you and me, he had to have that same mechanic
start the car for him before we left San Francisco. I don't know what
he thinks we'll do when it's time to go back. Ask for your help, I
reckon."

Will didn't smile. "Well, why shouldn't he? I *am* the Edwards
family mechanic, after all."

Mr. Hansen clapped him on the shoulder sympathetically.
Apparently he'd heard about the fight between Will and his father,
because he did not ask for details.

"Cheer up. Things may turn out differently than you expect.
You're eighteen. You've got a lot of life ahead of you. You've got
plenty of time."

"It doesn't feel that way," Will said.

"It never does," Mr. Hansen grinned. "But you know what they
say. Haste makes waste." He paused, sniffing the air. "And hunger
makes the best sauce. You'd think that mother of yours would have
dinner on the table by now! Let's see what's keeping the old girl."

Indeed, dinner was about ready to be served, and everyone was
milling just outside the formal dining room, waiting to take their
seats. There were to be ten at the main table; the charity-case girls
(under the efficient organization of Ma'am's current right-hand

girl ... what was her name, Maisy?) had taken their turkey and side dishes out to the bunkhouse. The German family who oversaw most of the farm's operation had likewise retired to their own quarters, where they would feed not only their own large clan of sons and daughters, but also those ranch hands who hadn't gone into Sacramento or Stockton for a long weekend carouse. They would have a merry evening, and there would be dancing later. Will half wished he was eating with them.

But he was eating in the big house, in the high-ceilinged formal dining room, surrounded by fussy antiques. Father and Ma'am had bought the house over thirty years ago, fully furnished in the overblown fashion of those days, and they had never quite gotten around to redoing it. The formal dining room (used only for occasions like this) was painted in a sepulchral shade of blood red, with garish gold trim and swagged velvet curtains. The black walnut dining table, which had been brought around the cape on a clipper ship, could easily seat thirty (with all the leaves in) and weighed at least ten thousand pounds (so Ma'am swore, whenever she tried to move the damn thing).

Tonight it was laid with crisp ironed linens and the best crystal and china. As a finishing touch, Ma'am had lit the room with magic, fashioning softly glowing spirit orbs that hovered over the table like soap-bubbles, trembling gently with each breath of air. Will remembered how she'd used to make these on summer nights when he was much younger. How she would gather magic between her hands, shaping it like bread dough, murmuring rhymes to intensify the glow.

Of course, the delight of seeing the room lit with spirit orbs was diminished by Will's realization that she'd probably made them because he hadn't started up the generator—and no one had dared ask him to. He rather wished someone had, just so he could have had the pleasure of telling them no. But then again, the dining room did look pretty in the soft golden light; it was much less harsh than the bare electric bulbs.

Ma'am had outdone herself. The smell of food made Will's mouth water, and the beauty of the table took his breath away. He felt a twinge of sadness, followed by a little flicker of anger. Why had Ben let Ma'am get her hopes up, anyway? She wouldn't have gone to such lengths if she hadn't thought he was coming home.

Will's thoughts were interrupted by a soft plucking at his elbow. He tensed; he knew that pluck. It was Uncle Royce. Damn him, couldn't he at least have the decency to wear heavier shoes?

Will turned in time to see his uncle's back retreating in the direction of the grand entry alcove—an unspoken indication that Will was to follow. Will always had wondered what would happen if he simply did not follow Uncle Royce when the man summoned him in such a perfunctory fashion. But he'd never actually attempted the experiment. Like Father, Uncle Royce maintained an air of command. Both brothers expected to be obeyed unquestioningly, and as such, no one ever questioned that they should follow. It was the only trait they had in common; otherwise one would never guess they'd shared the same parents.

Uncle Royce was a mantic consultant in San Francisco. He lived in an old butter-yellow house on Nob Hill—a house, in fact, that was more famous than he was. After the cataclysm of 1906, every home on Nob Hill had burnt to the ground. All except one—Uncle .oyce's butter-yellow house. It was the talk of the town in the months after; a popular song had even been written about it. Will had always suspected Laddie's hand in that. Laddie moved in circles that included musical people, and Uncle Royce had been so amusingly vexed by hearing the jaunty air spilling out of every Victrola from the Mission to the Bay, that if Laddie *had* had a hand in it, it was a matchless coup. All the brothers enjoyed vexing Uncle Royce. All of them, apparently, except one.

"I've had a letter from your brother Ben," Uncle Royce said in a low voice, once they were in the entryway. "He says you're still upset about Detroit."

Will recalled the furious, impassioned letter he'd written to Ben after his fight with Father. Of *course* he was still upset. But at the moment, he was more astonished by the fact that his brother had mentioned him—that he was a topic of discussion. Did Ben mention him to other members of the family, too? Did he tell them what he wrote in his letters? The very idea sent a chill of embarrassment through him.

"He is worried about you," Uncle Royce continued, when Will did not speak. "He thinks you might do something foolish."

"Foolish?" Will snorted. Like try and drive Pask's jalopy two thousand miles cross-country, as he'd imagined he might? But of course he didn't say this, because that *did* sound foolish. Instead, he drew himself up and attempted to speak with manly dignity. "Uncle Royce, all I want is to go to Detroit and take the apprenticeship that Tesla Industries has offered me—and honestly, if I can figure out a way to accomplish that, foolish or not, then Ben is right to be worried."

Uncle Royce closed his eyes wearily. When he opened them, though, his gaze was keener than before.

"William. Like it or not, your father is completely correct. Tesla Industries is the wrong place for you right now."

"Why?" Will pounced on the words before they were out of his uncle's mouth, for they were the very same words he'd heard from Father.

Uncle Royce paused, clearly formulating a careful response. When he finally spoke, however, all he said was, "Do you recall a book I once gave you for your birthday? *The Adventures of Pinocchio*?"

As if he could forget! Uncle Royce's birthday presents were a grim joke among the brothers. He always bought the most unwelcome gifts, as though he studied the boy and purchased the things he was least likely to enjoy. For Laddie it was always sporting equipment. For stay-at-home Nate, theater tickets. For Will, who never could stand reading—books. And what books! Uncle Royce had a knack for finding the queerest and most disturbing children's books in existence, of which, in Will's opinion, *The Adventures of Pinocchio* ranked near the top.

"Which part are you suggesting I recall?" Will lifted a cool eyebrow. "The Fairy with the Turquoise Hair, or the Terrible Dogfish?"

"The Land of Toys," Uncle Royce replied pointedly. "Where boys are lured in by their own base impulses and transformed into asses."

"Base impulses!" Will barked. "I'm not chasing a showgirl or going to work for a whiskey manufacturer. I want to work. To *learn*."

"Whether it's a desire for whiskey or a desire for learning, when you use it as an excuse to hurt everyone around you, then it's a base impulse," Uncle Royce hissed.

"Will! Royce!" Ma'am's voice shrilled from the dining room. "What are you waiting for? Come in and sit down, we're all ready to eat!"

"*I* haven't hurt anyone," Will returned furiously, hardly registering his mother's call. "*I'm* the one that's been hurt. *I'm* the one whose future is being ruined—"

"Oh, for God's sake, there really is no talking to you," Uncle Royce interrupted, exasperated. He thrust a hand inside his coat pocket and pulled out an envelope. Will's eyes narrowed suspiciously as he looked at it.

"I've been asked to give this to you," Uncle Royce said. "It's a letter. From Ben."

Will blinked astonishment. A letter from *Ben*? For *him*? He reached out to snatch it, but before he could, Uncle Royce lifted it away.

"You're on a dangerous course, young man," he said. "Don't say I didn't warn you."

Seizing the letter, Will tucked it safely away.

"Will, you come sit by Jenny," Ma'am said when he came in, as if putting him next to Jenny would make up for the fact that he'd be sitting next to Father as well. Neither Will nor his father so much as looked at each other as they passed their plates around. When Will's was passed back to him, mounded with good food, he could only pick at it. While everyone else ate cheerfully, their end of the table was suffocated in grim silence.

Between bites he could barely taste, Will snuck sullen looks at his father, just waiting for the old man to broach a subject, any subject. Having just spoken with Uncle Royce, he was once again struck by how different the brothers were. Uncle Royce was compact, with dark hair and dark eyes and a fair complexion that didn't turn at sun or wind. Perhaps Father had once been pale like that; but even though he had always left the hard labor of the horse farm to his hired men—and later to Nate—he was as bronzed as if he spent every day in the saddle. His hair might once have been dark, but now there was as much silver in it as a Reno mine.

"Well, Jenny." Father cleared his throat, which Will always understood to mean that he was preparing to say something tedious. "How are you liking Miss Murison's? I am told it is quite a good school, as girls' schools go."

"I enjoy it very much, Mr. Edwards," Jenny said, the picture of politeness. Elbows off the table, back straight, eyes on Father like he had asked her the most fascinating question in the world. Whatever else could be said of Miss Murison's, it had certainly had a civilizing influence on the scuff-kneed girl Will had once been friends with.

"Are there any subjects of particular interest to you?"

"I am most interested in applied mathematics," Jenny said. "Quantitative analysis, statistics, that kind of thing. Lately I have been studying the works of Louis Bachelier. Have you ever heard of him, Mr. Edwards?"

Father's brow knit thoughtfully. "I can't say that I have."

Jenny's face fell ever so slightly. "Oh well, very few people have." Then, as if remembering some particular of training from Miss Murison's, she gave a pretty giggle and picked up her fork with an elegant movement. "Quantitative analysis isn't everyone's cup of tea, I suppose."

Father did not comment, but cut a slice of turkey into a precise shape and dabbed it into the gravy. After a long silence, Jenny attempted another conversational sally, this time towards Will.

"I was wondering, William," she began, rather formally, "when I was helping your mother in the kitchen, I happened to see a very large wooden crate behind the house. What's in it?"

Will glanced daggers at his father. It couldn't have been a more perfect—and dangerous—question if she'd been coached to it. Because the big wooden crate contained Will's third birthday present.

"It is a new electric power plant," Father answered. "The one we currently have is underpowered and antiquated. This new one is large enough to power the house and the barns and all of the outbuildings. It is, by all accounts, an exceptionally fine piece of equipment. We expected that Will would find it fascinating."

Will pushed potatoes around on his plate. The fact that Father was right—that the power plant was top of the line, and under other circumstances he would have been thrilled at the prospect of setting it up, rewiring all the old farm buildings, making the genie of electricity dance beneath his fingertips—cut no ice.

"Oh sure," Will muttered. "Just what every boy wants for a birthday present."

"But you've always been interested in machines," Jenny ventured.

"I tell you what I'm not interested in," Will said, feeling heat rise up under his collar. "I'm not interested in getting stuck here in California as the Edwards family *mechanic*."

"That wasn't the intention of the gift," Father said mildly. The conversation was drifting onto treacherous shoals. Will didn't care. In fact, he was glad of it.

"I know *exactly* what the intention of the gift was," Will said. "It was supposed to make me feel better about not going to Detroit. And like I said before, there's nothing that's going to do that."

"Detroit?" Jenny asked. "What's in Detroit?"

"You know Tesla Industries, right?" Will said.

"Of course!" Jenny said. "Who doesn't? All the kids in San Francisco are just mad for their wireless musical cabinets. Teslaphones beat Victrolas all cold, not having to buy discs."

"Teslaphones are just *toys* compared to what Tesla Industries is really doing," Will snapped his fingers for emphasis. "Tesla Industries is the leading center of Otherwhere research in the country—in the whole *world*. They've got an apprenticeship program that only accepts a tiny number of applicants every year. One of my teachers at the Polytechnic put me up for it ... and they offered me a slot."

"That's wonderful!" Jenny gasped and clapped her hands together.

"Yeah, isn't it?" Will shot an acid glare at his father. "At least, it would be, if I could go. But it's been decided that it's not in my best interests, you see. I've got a power plant to rig up, after all—"

"Really, Will, do we have to go over this again?" his father said wearily. "Now? At the dinner table?"

"We can talk about it anywhere you like. All I want is one reason for not letting me take the apprenticeship."

"I have already given you several—"

"One *good* reason," Will spoke over him.

Father lifted his hand wearily, raising a single finger. He looked at Will long and hard. "Traveling two thousand miles away from home and putting yourself under the complete control of a man like Nikola Tesla is idiotic."

"He won the Nobel Prize last year!"

"I didn't say he wasn't a *genius*," Father said. "But even geniuses— *especially* geniuses—can surround themselves with the wrong kinds of people. His company's policies regarding secrecy and privacy and the abdication of rights on the part of his contracted employees are completely outrageous. Did you even *read* the apprenticeship contract, Will?"

Will was hot with indignation. "Of course I did!" he said, even though he actually hadn't, as that document had been a hundred and thirty-two pages long and printed in very small type. But he had very diligently skimmed it.

"Then perhaps you simply failed to notice that they do not allow you to have any contact with your family? Indeed, with anyone outside the program at all?"

"Surely they're doing research that could make them millions of dollars, Mr. Edwards," Jenny said, wide-eyed. "Of course they must be secretive. They have to protect their intellectual property, don't they?"

"I suppose they do, Jenny," Father said, apparently surprised at suddenly finding himself in a two-to-one battle. Will was surprised too, but grateful. "But I would be shocked if their apprentices were made privy to work of such extraordinary value. Rather, I suspect some form of indoctrination—"

"Indoctrination!" Will blazed. "What do you mean?"

"I mean, *William*," Father said, in a warning voice, "that corporations—all organizations, as a matter of fact—must compel the loyalty of their workers. In the army, they call it basic training. Tesla Industries probably draws future employees from their pool of apprentices. And so they swear them to this absurd secrecy in order to make them feel like part of the group."

"Well, what's wrong with that?" Will said. "It sounds wonderful to me! I would be happy to stay as an employee of Tesla Industries."

"Of course you would!" Father said. "That's the whole point, Will. Organizations of this type do not give you a choice. You will be happy to be an employee because they will make you happy. They will make you part of a machine. Your ability to think for yourself will be reduced to what is good for the company."

"Yes, unlike here, where my ability to think for myself is reduced to what's good for the *family*," Will shot back.

Father sighed. "Will, I know how intelligent you are, and how talented. But as I have said, I do not believe Tesla Industries is a good place for you. Not right now."

"Mr. Waters can vouch for the program personally!" Once again, Will attempted to invoke the name of Herman Bierce Waters, M.E., Vice Director of the California Polytechnic, whose strong recommendation had gotten him the apprenticeship. "He would hardly do that if it wasn't completely trustworthy!"

"Mr. Waters' assessment is immaterial," Father said, icily. Then, clearly searching for a way to pour oil on troubled waters, he said: "How about a compromise. If you will wait until the spring, we will discuss it again then."

"They probably won't even want me anymore by then! Besides, what's going to be different in the spring than now?"

"Lots of things. The foaling will be done and—"

"The *foaling*?" Will was furious now, and everyone at the table was riveted to the awkward scene. "If you're going to make up excuses, can't you at least make one up that doesn't insult the intelligence you claim to believe I possess? Nate's always taken care of the foaling, and besides that, he's got two dozen *rancheros* to help him—and even the greenest one is more use than me! There's only one reason to wait until spring—so you can keep me under your thumb, wiring up your goddamn electrical plant, long enough for the offer to expire!"

"There is only one reason you need concern yourself with, young man!" Father roared in return, all patience lost. He slammed the table with his fist. "Because I am your father and I say so!"

"Oh, Wordsworth, please don't yell," Ma'am said. She always called Father by his despised middle name when she was annoyed with him.

Frowning, Father returned his attention to his dinner plate, responding as he always did when *he* was annoyed, in a tone mild yet palpably acerbic: "As you wish, my goddess."

"And you, Will"—Ma'am glared down the table at him, a look sufficient in intensity to make him curl back in his seat—"your father has made his decision. You're needed here. We'll discuss it again in the spring. If they want you now, they'll want you then. Honestly, a few months isn't going to make a bit of difference—"

"It makes a lot of difference to me!" Will said, standing abruptly and throwing his napkin down with a melodramatic flourish. "But as usual, what's important to me is the last thing anyone in this family concerns themselves with!"

"William, sit down." This, from Uncle Royce. It was the last straw.

"Ben has the right idea," Will snarled. "About all of you. No wonder he didn't come home."

Will stormed off to the barn. He climbed the ladder to the hayloft, then threw himself down on a pile of old feed sacks in a narrow, awkward corner—no good for storing hay—that a much younger Will had appropriated as his own secret fortress.

Everything was just the same as he'd left it when he'd gone away to school three years ago. There were still dozens of dogeared dime novels (now thick with dust) shelved on a pair of milk crates stacked atop each other. There were a lot of *Vanguard Girl* adventures. Also the *Rover Boys*, *Pluck & Luck*, *Diamond Dick*, several numbers of the *Tip Top Weekly*, a few *Brushfork Banditos*—and dozens of editions of the most popular of the pulp series, the *True Life Tales of Dreadnought Stanton*.

Oddly enough, of all the books on the shelves, only one was actually his. *The Adventures of Pinocchio*, the gift Uncle Royce had given him on his eighth birthday. He'd hated it from the minute the woodcarver Master Cherry hit the wood with the axe and the wood shrieked in pain. But apparently Father had thought there was something important in Uncle Royce's gift; enough that he felt compelled to read it to Will. It was a trial for them both, and perhaps one of the only things they'd ever agreed on—they both hated that book as much as Uncle Royce seemed to find it admirable and instructive.

All the other books were Jenny's, brought out to the farm with her during the summers she'd come to stay. Like every other American kid below the age of dull maturity, she had adored dime novels, detective magazines, adventure serials ... anything with a generous helping of adventure and danger. She had been particularly partial to the Dreadnought Stantons, and there were at least four or five new ones of those every year, each more lurid and hair-raising than the last. Jenny found them especially interesting because they were about a real-life person—the warlock Sophos of the Stanton Institute in New York City.

When he and Jenny were kids, the first thing she always did when she came to visit was show him the new books she'd brought. She'd always hoped Will would share her excitement over them.

But Will never could. Reading had always been difficult for him—so difficult that a specialist doctor in Sacramento had been consulted. The doctor had said that Will suffered from a condition called "word blindness." Will had (and still did) thought the diagnosis silly, for he could *see* the words just fine. It was just that they tended to slip and slide around, as if he were trying to pick a ball bearing out of a bowl of peeled grapes.

As he'd grown older, Will had learned how to muscle his way through a text—he could hardly have kept up with his classes at the Polytechnic otherwise. But even now, he found reading a tedious, headachy chore.

Not wanting to forestall her own enjoyment, but still wanting to include Will in it, Jenny had come up with the idea of reading the books to him aloud. And this Will *had* enjoyed very much, because Jenny had a flair for the dramatic. In this way he and "Scuff" had passed many a fine hour.

But he wasn't a kid anymore, and there was really only one thing up here that now interested him. Reaching past the books, he felt around behind them for the half-empty bottle of rye whiskey he'd hidden up here long ago. Like everything else, it was covered in a layer of dust, but he ignored this as he pulled out the cork with his teeth. He took a pull, finding it no mellower than it had been when he was fifteen, but the harsh burn of the alcohol nicely reinforced his feeling of being unfairly treated and all-around hard used.

"Did you even read the terms of the apprenticeship contract, Will?" he mimicked Father's voice to himself. He took another swig. "Bastard!"

He threw back a few more angry mouthfuls, but getting plowed was not really what he wanted to do. He suddenly remembered the letter in his pocket—a letter from Ben! He drew it out quickly. It was thin and light in his hand, but at least it was something. First, he examined the seal. Will wouldn't put it past Uncle Royce to have read the letter before handing it over. But the seal seemed intact, and if it had been steamed the ink would have smudged.

He tore it open quickly. To his surprise—and dismay—it contained only a single sheet of paper. It was a very fine piece of stationery, bordered and engraved with a rampant eagle which had clasped, in its claw, a two-sided scroll. One side of the scroll read "*Ex Fide Fortis*" and on the other side, "From Faith, Strength." Beneath the eagle were the words:

THE STANTON INSTITUTE
NEW YORK CITY

A beautiful piece of paper, clearly swiped from Ben's employer. But it hardly seemed worth the swiping, for Ben had only written eight words on it:

Dreadnought Stanton 32: "The Warlock's Curse." Page 153.

Will puzzled over this for a moment. He knew what the writing referred to, of course; Volume 32 of *The True Life Tales of Dreadnought Stanton*. Ben didn't even have to give the volume number. While *The Warlock's Curse* had always been one of the lesser known installments, the fact that Edison Studios had recently selected it as the basis for the first-ever Dreadnought Stanton photoplay had caused it to skyrocket in prominence. The motion picture was to debut with great fanfare on New Year's Day, and all the movie magazines were filled with news of the production, which was rumored to be the most lavish and expensive Edison had ever undertaken. Even Walnut Grove, the small town nearest the Edwards' ranch (which didn't even *have* a moving picture theater) was plastered with handbills from rival theaters in Sacramento and Stockton advertising the film's premiere.

The Warlock's Curse was among the many volumes that Jenny had left behind. He pulled it from the shelf and blew dust off it. On the cover was a picture of a young man's face drawn in two halves—one half that of a nice all-American boy, the other half twisted and sneering, demonic. The picture gave away just about all there was to the plot—the kid on the cover had inherited a family curse or something, and Dreadnought Stanton had to defeat the evil spirit who possessed him.

Will quickly turned to page 153. It was a page of illustration, showing a magical sigil, but with no other explanation. Will flipped back a couple pages and was laboriously scanning the text to try to figure out what part of the story the illustration was in support of, when a voice called from below:

"Hey, you up there?"

It was Jenny. Goddamn it! But of course she knew where to find him, this was where they'd played together as kids. Still, it annoyed him that she assumed she'd find him here—as if nothing about him had changed or ever would change. Why did everyone treat him like that?

"What do you want?" he growled forbiddingly. But Jenny had already climbed the ladder to the hayloft and was settling herself in next to him, taking care with her tidy costume. A shining curl had escaped from the thick mass of hair piled atop her head. Her very presence here seemed outrageous. It was one thing for her to come up here when she was a girl, with scuffed knees and freckles. But now she dressed like a woman and smelled like a woman, and it was a clear violation of every secret hideout code ever written.

Will quickly tucked Ben's letter into the pulp novel, and shoved them both inside his coat. Jenny didn't notice, too busy eyeing the dusty bottle of whiskey in his hand.

"Thank God!" She seized it and wrenched out the cork before Will could protest. "I was hoping you'd have a drink. And I wasn't about to squeeze in between Laddie and Lillie looking for one. Those two are like the stones of the pyramids, you can't get a piece of paper in between them!"

Will did not comment, but watched Jenny take a long swallow of the rye. She only gagged on it a little, then wiped her mouth with the back of her hand.

"And of course, after you stormed off, your father felt it was his duty to make small talk with me. You ever try to make small talk with your father? Especially when he's mad?" Jenny shivered at the memory. "Your family tires me out."

"You too?" Will said. Jenny took another snort, then capped the bottle and settled back comfortably, looking around. "Hasn't changed much," was her conclusion. "You've still got my books!"

"Yep, it's like I'm still twelve years old," Will said bitterly.

"Boy, I sure liked the Dreadnought Stantons." Jenny looked over the titles, smiling. If she noticed the absence of Volume 32, she didn't mention it. "You remember the fight we had over those? I wanted to be Admiral Dewey and you gave me a bloody nose."

Will rolled his eyes. It had been a ridiculous fight. Jenny had been reading him an especially patriotic Stantonade in which the great Sophos was called upon by Congress to investigate the magical theft of a jeweled sword presented to Admiral Dewey by President McKinley. They'd both been so excited by the action in the book that they'd quickly dispensed with Jenny just reading it and went on to playing it out. It had been great fun—until Jenny demanded to play the role of Admiral Dewey. She said it was only fair, because Will had gotten most of the other good parts. But he found the idea so preposterous he'd been forced to object to it just on principle. She called him a nincompoop. He told her to both "go soak her head" and "dry up."

Perhaps it was the contradictory nature of these two statements that had made Jenny shove him. Will had shoved her back. And then there had been hair-pulling and fists started to fly, and finally Jenny ran to his mother, crying, her nose bleeding. Ma'am, who tended to be quite democratic about such things, did not scold Will for hitting a girl, or even for hitting someone younger than him. Instead, she had given Jenny a clean rag to staunch the bleeding and then told her if she wanted to be Admiral Dewey she had to keep her guard up. Additionally, she confided that, like the Spanish Pacific fleet, Will had a tendency to leave himself open on the right. Jenny was an apt pupil; the next time she and Will got into a scuffle, she walloped him handily.

"Yeah, I remember," Will said, watching as Jenny smoothed her serge skirt over her thighs. Her button-top shoes peeked out under the ruffled hem of her silk petticoat, and his eyes wanted to linger on her slim ankle. He looked away, clearing his throat. "Now, I've bought you a drink. So why don't you go ahead and get lost? I'm sure Ma'am will wonder where you've gotten to. Sorry I can't offer you any Sen-Sen, but there's peppermint growing just outside the barn door if you want to chew some ..."

She frowned at him. "What do you have against me, anyway? We used to have lots of fun together. You got a girl or something, afraid she'll get mad at you for sitting with me up in the hayloft?"

"No, I don't have a girl," Will said. "I'm twelve years old, remember?"

"Oh, cut it out. You're being mulish, and it doesn't pay," Jenny snapped. "You and I have more in common than you think. Probably more now than we ever had when we were kids."

Will smirked indulgently. "What do you figure we have in common?"

"Everyone expects too little of us," she said quickly. "You always hear people complaining about how horrible it is when others expect too much of them. But it's worse the other way around. Isn't it?"

Will pondered this, then nodded in slow agreement. "But you're an heiress. Why *should* anyone expect anything of you? You don't have anything to prove. You don't have to make a living. You just have to sit back and let everyone treat you like a queen."

"Treat me like a set of silver being polished up for a shop window, you mean," Jenny grumbled. She reached for the bottle of whiskey again, but Will quickly tucked it away, mindful of her father sitting at the dinner table just a few hundred yards away.

"Miss Murison's is pretty good ... as *girls'* schools go ..." Jenny parroted derisively. "I've only learned one thing in that 'girls' school' that's worth more than two pins—and that's excellent French. Without it I could never have read Monsieur Bachelier's thesis. You would love it, William, it's on the use of Brownian motion to evaluate stock options." She paused, sighing dreamily, as if she were discussing the latest moving picture star. Then she frowned again. "Of course, when I try to discuss Bachelier's work with my mathematics tutor, all he wants to do is stare into my eyes."

"Gee, you got it rough," Will deadpanned. "Math tutors staring into your blue eyes. How can you stand it?"

"I *can't* stand it!" she countered sharply. "And don't you dare poke fun, William Edwards. You don't understand what it's like to have no one—not one single person—take you seriously. Your teachers, Mr. Tesla ... they all think you're a genius. *Everybody* takes you seriously."

"Not everybody," Will muttered. Not the one person who mattered.

Jenny heaved a sigh. "Well, that's how parents are," she said. "How *fathers* are, at least. I couldn't say about mothers."

Jenny had lost her mother when she was three years old, and despite the fact that Ma'am was a loving witchly godmother, it wasn't the same. Will hastened to change the uncomfortable subject.

"That's how *people* are," he said. "They're unpredictable, they don't make decisions rationally or logically, and they usually don't make much sense. It drives me up a tree."

"I suppose that's why you like machines so much, right?" Jenny mused. "Because they do what you expect?"

Will nodded, surprised. She leaned forward.

"But you see, I like things that do what you *don't* expect," she said. "For instance, when most people think about mathematics, they think of boring equations—you know, like two plus two equals four. But there are other equations, William. Equations that seem just as simple, except when you put in different numbers, the strangest things come out. They seem so boring on the surface, but then when you realize how incredibly, beautifully complex they are it's just ... wonderful."

Will was transfixed by how radiant her face had suddenly become. He recognized that kind of rapture. He smiled at her, and she smiled back, and through some unspoken agreement, they decided to be friends again.

And now that they were friends again, Jenny leaned toward him and dropped her voice low.

"William," she said, "I've got a proposition for you."

"Miss Hansen!" He feigned outrage. "I'll have you know, I'm not that kind of fellow!"

Snorting, Jenny punched him in the arm.

"You want to get out of here, right? I mean, get to Detroit, get to your apprenticeship, everything?"

"Yes," Will said. "More than anything."

"All right, then hear me out. Don't say anything until I'm done." She took a deep breath, then seemed to lose her courage. "It's just that I've been thinking about it for a while, but until I heard your situation it never quite gelled, you know?"

"No, I don't know," Will said. "Spit it out. What are you talking about?"

Jenny drew another deep breath. "All right. You know my mother died when I was very young. And you know that she came from money, and she left a bundle. That bundle was put into trust for me and my sister." She paused. "Now, in Claire's case the money goes to ... her support."

Will said nothing, but nodded. He had heard about Jenny's older sister Claire. She was a victim of the Black Flu epidemics, and was, according to his brothers' whispered gossip, horribly disfigured and deformed. She lived in an asylum somewhere, they said.

"In my case, however," Jenny continued, "I come into my money free and clear when I'm twenty-one. Or"—she paused meaning-fully—"when I get married. Whichever comes first."

She let the silence hang for a long time. Will didn't say any-thing, and Jenny evidently interpreted his silence as a failure of comprehension.

"We get married, dummy!" she said.

"Yes, Jenny," Will said. "I got it. You couldn't be any clearer if you whitewashed it on the side of a barn and then set the barn on fire. However, I was waiting for you to explain exactly how you think we can do that, when neither one of us is old enough."

"We are most certainly old enough!" she said. "By law, the groom has to be over eighteen and the bride over fifteen. Well, you just turned eighteen and I'm almost eighteen myself—"

"You still have to have your parents' permission if you're under twenty-one," Will pointed out. "How do you reckon we get that?" Will imagined asking Father for permission to marry Jenny. The image was terrifying—but not as terrifying as asking Mr. Hansen the same question.

"Oh, pshaw. Who doesn't lie about their age? You look twenty-one, especially if we clean you up and put you in a suit."

Will was skeptical. "What makes you think a hot marriage license will cut any ice with your mother's estate attorneys?"

"You leave that to me," Jenny said. "I have ... connections. As long as I've got a marriage certificate I can get the estate released. And I've got money to start us off. Dad's always giving me cash for dresses and chocolates and junk like that, and I've saved it up."

Will was beginning to feel slightly horrified. It was clear that, far beyond just "thinking" about this scheme, Jenny had put a lot of actual planning into it.

"Jenny, come on. Even if you got the money it would just be a matter of time before the ruse was discovered. What then?"

Jenny waved a hand. "Who cares? Possession is nine-tenths of the law. Once I have the money, they'll have to chase me down to get it back. What better place for me to lay low for a while than Detroit? And even if they find me, and try to sue me for the return of the funds, it'll take years to wind through the courts. By the time anyone makes any kind of judgment I'll probably be twenty-one anyway, and it won't matter!"

Will stared at her. "You're really serious, aren't you?"

She nodded.

"And you don't feel like it's kind of a dirty trick? On your dead mother and your living father?"

"What do either one of our fathers have to do with anything?" Jenny countered acidly. "I thought from your performance at the dinner table that you'd be all too happy to be shut of yours."

"Easy for you to say!" Will lifted his eyebrows. "My father isn't likely to hunt you down and beat you to a pulp."

"Oh, Dad's a big pussycat," she sniffed. "You know he likes you. He'll be thrilled having you for a son-in-law."

"But it won't be *real.*" Will's head was spinning. "And what if you fall in love with someone for real and want to marry *him*? You'll have to divorce me—"

"Or kill you," Jenny grinned. "Then I could be a widow. No shame in that."

"I don't much care for the way you think, Jenny Hansen."

"All I'm saying, William, is that it's high time we both showed everyone that they shouldn't underestimate us. Everything else is just ... logistics."

Will grinned slightly. "And after all, you *do* have a crush on me—"

"I do not!" Jenny screeched, eyes wide with indignation. "When I was ten, I was impressed that you could whistle through the gap in your teeth. Can you still do that?"

Will puckered and whistled. But the gap in his teeth was long gone, and the sound was puny and unimpressive. Jenny waved dismissively. "You're clearly not half the man you once were. So we've got to keep it just business. But look, it can work. We can do this."

"And what do you get out of it?"

"I get to be a married woman who makes my own choices about things." She spoke with strange fierceness. "That's all you need to know. You have to promise me not to ask any more questions than that."

Will thought about everything she had said. He couldn't really be considering it. It was crazy!

"We sure couldn't go into Walnut Grove to get a license," he mused. "The clerk there has known me since I was in short pants, and he'd have to send the paperwork to Stockton anyway, since it's the county seat."

"Stockton's where we need to go." Jenny's quick certainty gave Will the impression that she'd written away for the information weeks ago. "Most local offices are closed the Friday after Thanksgiving, but since Stockton is the county seat the offices there have to stay open. But I bet you the clerk will try to go home early. And if we don't get there tomorrow we'll have to wait the whole weekend and that would ruin everything."

Will nodded, stroking his chin thoughtfully.

"Maybe I could get the Baker off my friend Pask. It's only a few hours drive to Stockton from here."

Will knew the road like the back of his hand. He and Pask often drove down to Stockton to take in moving pictures and moon over unapproachable girls at dance halls. And the weather had been dry for the past few weeks, so no worries about getting stuck in the mud ...

"Will he loan it to you?"

Will made a face. "Just how do you figure we'd return it? No, I'd have to buy it from him outright. I guess he'd sell it to me. You said you had money?"

Jenny nodded. "Cover your eyes."

"What?"

"Just do it!"

Will covered his eyes, peeking through his fingers. Jenny hiked up the hem of her skirt. In her stocking garter was tucked a wad of banknotes so fat he wondered how they stayed put. He was so shocked he forgot he was supposed to be keeping his eyes closed.

"Jiminy Christmas!" he gasped. "Just how many dresses and chocolate bars does your dad think you need, anyway?"

"I've been saving for a long time," she said. "And supplementing it … creatively." She did not elaborate as she let her skirt drop. She pressed the wad of cash into his hand.

Will looked at it with astonishment. It had to be almost a thousand bucks! He didn't say anything.

"Well?" she spoke with some impatience. "Are you in?"

"Yeah," he said finally, tucking the money into his pocket. "I'm in."

The resolve in his voice was apparently insufficient, for Jenny narrowed her eyes and stared hard at him for a moment. Then, with great deliberation, she spit in her palm and extended her hand.

"Shake on it," she demanded.

Without hesitation, Will spit in his palm, and they pressed their hands together, damp and sticky. Jenny grinned broadly.

"That's that, then. I'm going back in to help your Ma'am with the cleaning up. Meet you back here tomorrow morning?"

"Before dawn," said Will.

"Wear your best suit," Jenny said as she slid down the hayloft ladder. "I won't marry you if you look like a hobo."

After she was gone, Will withdrew the wad of banknotes from his pocket. He stared at them, sudden delight rising within him. The more he thought about the plan, the more he liked it. He could be in Detroit, working at Tesla Industries, before the end of the month! Tucking the money back inside his coat, he hurried down the ladder, glancing at his wristwatch, wondering if he could make it over to Pask's place before too late …

"Hey, Will." The voice came from over near one of the stables. Nate's voice. Will froze, wondering how long his brother had been there. Knowing Nate, he'd lit out for the stable almost as quickly as Will had—he didn't like to be too long away from the horses.

"Hey, Nate." Will didn't think his brother had overheard any of the discussion between him and Jenny; they'd been speaking quietly, and Nate was not the type to listen in on conversations. He just wasn't interested in them. Nate was standing by the sorrel mare's stable, visibly fretting. The mare had a crazy look in her eye and her velvety muzzle was flecked with foam.

"Given her a purgative," said Nate, eyes fixed on the glossy Morgan. "I may have to have Ma'am look at her."

"Nothing Ma'am likes more than taking care of sick things," Will observed. "Nice, helpless little things."

Nate didn't turn from the ailing Morgan. "You talking about horses, or you talking about yourself?"

"Take a wild guess," Will said. "I have to go, Nate. See you around."

"I guess I know horses pretty well." Will had turned to go, but Nate's words stopped him. "Sometimes they can be pretty stubborn. Like this mare, we've tried and tried to keep her out of the clover, and she just keeps going after it. It's not good for her, but I guess she likes the taste."

Will released a long breath, clenched his fists. Even though Nate's lectures were milder than most, he still recognized one when he heard it, and he still resented it. He said nothing.

"Well, we'll keep trying to keep her out of that pasture." Nate's voice was slow and resigned. "But she'll probably keep going back to it, and one day it may kill her. That'd be a darn shame, because she's a really nice horse."

"Yep, it would be a darn shame," Will said. "I got it, Nate. Horses are stupid and stubborn and smart people like you and Father have to figure out what's best for them."

Nate looked pained.

"I never said you were stupid," he said. "This mare isn't stupid. She just doesn't understand. That doesn't make her stupid."

"But I'm not a horse, Nate." Will clipped the words. "I am a human being. I can think things through, predict the consequences, make informed choices. I can do that for myself. I don't need any-one to do it for me."

Nate drew in a deep breath, let it out. Then he nodded.

"I guess," he said. "If you say so."

He pushed back from the stable, and turned his gaze onto Will, and for the first time it was like he was really seeing his younger brother. It made Will uncomfortable. There was something about Nate's direct, unshifting gaze that made one feel as if he knew too much.

"I had a letter from Ben the other day," Nate said, scrutinizing Will. "And I think I figured something out. I think I figured out the difference between Ben and the rest of us—well, me, Argus and Laddie anyway. We all believe everyone is doing the best he can. Even Father." He paused, thoughtfully. "*Especially* Father. Even when we don't understand the things he does, we believe that he does them for reasons that are good. I believe it, I know Argus does, and Laddie too—as much as Laddie believes anything. But Ben ... doesn't. Ben doesn't believe it at all."

Nate blinked once, then asked, with real curiosity, "What do *you* believe, Will?"

"Sure, I believe Father does what he does for reasons that are good," Will said, quickly and caustically. "Good for *him*, that is. He just doesn't concern himself about whether they're good for any-one else."

Nate absorbed this gravely. Then he sighed. "I don't think that's true. Can't prove it one way or the other, of course. But I guess I'm willing to take him on faith. You and Ben aren't."

Will was silent for a long time. First, the words made him numb—but almost instantly, that numbness kindled into hot fury. Take him on *faith*? *Really*? He should just ... surrender? Kowtow to someone else's high-handed notion of what was right for his life?

"Thanks for the advice, Nate." He was so angry he almost choked on the words. "But you can keep it. Good luck with the mare. Honestly, I hope she gets in the clover again. I hope she kills herself on it. At least that way she'll die doing what she wants. She may be just a dumb animal, but even a dumb animal deserves a choice."

Then he got on his bicycle and pedaled furiously to Pask de la Guerra's house.

Chapter Two

A Sheep in Will's Clothing

28 DAYS UNTIL THE FULL MOON

Early the next morning, Will met Jenny behind the barn. They walked in silence through the misty half-light to a grove of oaks along the wide slow Sacramento River. It was a cold morning; frost made the fallen leaves a sparkling carpet of orange and red and yellow that crunched under their feet as they walked. The air smelled of distant smoke, from farmers burning off the last of their fields.

The clearing where Will had parked the Baker was another place they'd used to play. Jenny smiled in recognition, raising her gloved fingers to push aside a tattered strand of sisal dangling from a thick branch—the remnant of a long-gone rope swing.

But when she laid eyes on the Baker—on the sloppy red and green paint, and the streaks of mud that still lingered from its dunk in the irrigation ditch—pleasant nostalgia gave way to outrage.

"Just how much of my money did you spend on this heap?" she circled the Baker with a frown, eyeing the cracked leather of the folding top.

"Pask took five hundred."

"Are you *kidding*? That's more than half the price of a brand new Model T!"

"As it happens, Pask does not operate a Ford franchise," said Will, archly. "And this automobile cost almost four thousand when it was new."

"This *automobile* has not been new in a long time." Jenny's frown deepened as she examined the auto's stubby bonnet, the unique hallmark of its type. "And honestly, William ... an *electric*? Who buys an electric out here in the sticks?"

Will felt secretly smug. She was right, of course; an electric *had* been an unwise choice for Pask's family, living as they did in the middle of California's Central Valley where electricity wasn't always available. But that inconvenience had been one of the motivating factors behind the improvements Will had made. He couldn't wait to show her what the "electric" could do.

Jenny seemed to be waiting for him to argue back at her. When he did not, she concluded: "Well, I think your friend Pask is a swindler. But if this flivver will get us to Stockton in time, I guess it's worth it."

Remembering that there were bills remaining from the money Jenny had given him, Will began pulling them out of his pocket. Jenny stopped him with a hand.

"No, keep it. If you're going to pretend to be my husband you're going to have to do all the paying. It won't look right if I do it."

Jenny stowed the two bags she'd brought with her—a little calfskin handgrip and a canvas laundry bag—under the front seat. Noticing Will's puzzled glance at the laundry bag, she said: "There wasn't time to make sandwiches. But I figured we'd get hungry, so I got a couple of the pies and some of the leftover turkey meat from the icebox."

Will had already stowed his own bag the night before. He was bringing nothing but his tools. Everything else he could pick up in Detroit, but his tools—instruments of all sizes, from wrenches and come-alongs to delicate watchmaker and jeweler's sets—were like extensions of his hands, and he could not imagine being without them.

Jenny began doing up the buttons on her light canvas duster. "I talked with Dad last night. I told him one of my friends from back East was stuck at Miss Murison's over the holiday, and I was going to go back to keep her company. I told him you'd offered to hitch up the buggy and take me over to the station to catch the early train. He won't miss me until he's back in San Francisco on

Monday. With any luck, we'll be in Detroit before anyone thinks to look for us." She climbed into the car, tucking her skirts tight around her legs and fussing with her hat. It was an enormous hat, swathed all around with heavy gauze, just as Lillie's had been. It must have made the trip from San Francisco in the Pierce Arrow's trunk, for there certainly hadn't been room for it in the back seat. "How about you? After that show last night, won't your folks suspect the worst when you go missing?"

"Oh, I always run off to Pask's house when I'm mad," Will swung the steering tiller up and climbed into the driver's seat. "He promised to cover for me. If my parents call over, he's going to tell them that I've barricaded myself in their barn and nothing short of an act of Congress will get me out."

Jenny lifted an amused eyebrow. "Well, I certainly hope you didn't tell him to say exactly *that*," she said. "After all, I'm sure your brother Argus is just itching to draft some maiden legislation."

Will smirked as he lowered the tiller over his lap and reached down to press the ignition switch. The car made no sound as it started, but the needles on the two half-moon dash gauges—one for volts, one for amperes—jittered and rose. He moved the controller—a knife switch by his left leg—into the car's first forward speed, and the Baker slid noiselessly into motion.

The service road was rough and badly rutted, and Will had chosen it only because it would take them to the main road without passing the house. A crisp breeze rattled the branches of the oaks, sending a flurry of bright yellow leaves swirling before them. Will expected that Jenny would pull her heavy motoring veil down over her face, but instead she just closed her eyes and inhaled deeply. The chilly air made her cheeks flush pink.

"I always love starting a trip," she sighed. "It's like ... oh, I don't know, sharpening a pencil for the first time. It's very satisfying. I'm so glad you're coming with me. I knew you would."

"What made you so sure?" said Will. "You couldn't have known how much I wanted to get away."

"Actually, I did," Jenny admitted. "Your mother wrote my dad about the fight you had with your father, and I happened to catch a glimpse of the letter. So I figured you might be amenable." She paused. "And if you hadn't the guts, well, at most I would have wasted a little time. Maybe I would have asked one of your brothers instead."

The very idea made Will bark a laugh. "Like who? Laddie? San Francisco's most eligible bachelor? As you've pointed out, he and Lillie are like the stones of the pyramids."

"Why didn't she marry *him*?" Jenny wondered. "I can't even imagine marrying a man like your brother Argus. He takes up every particle of air in any room he's in."

"Laddie has no ambition," said Will. "Argus has enough for both of them. You're a girl, you tell me. I guess girls marry ambition."

"Girls like Lillie do," Jenny said. "Girls who have none of their own, that is."

"You don't think she has ambition?" Will said. "Seems to me she's got plenty and then some."

"Yes, but she only cares about being the social queen of San Francisco," Jenny sniffed. "That's not the kind of ambition I'm talking about."

"What other kind of ambition can a girl have?"

"Oh, forget it," Jenny snapped. "Let's stop talking about them. I had quite enough of those three on the way down from San Francisco. Now, as far as which other Edwards brother I would marry, if you were unavailable ... I was thinking more of your brother Ben."

"You've never even met him!"

"I've seen your Ma'am's pictures of him. He's not bad looking."

"A fine thing for my future wife to say," Will grumbled. "Besides, when it comes to being unavailable, Ben's got all of us beat." Thinking of Ben reminded Will of the letter in his coat pocket, and its simple, mysterious reference to *The Warlock's Curse*. "Honestly, sometimes I wonder if he really exists at all."

"What does he do out there in New York? He has a job at the Stanton Institute, doesn't he?" Jenny asked. "Does he actually work for *the* Dreadnought Stanton, help him retrieve artifacts and quiet restless mummies and all that, just like it says in the books?"

"I don't know," said Will. "From what I've heard, his position is more … administrative. I heard Laddie once call him a functionary. Argus says he's wasting his life in service to an outdated ideal."

"And your mother and father? What do they say?"

"They don't say anything."

Jenny knit her brow. "Dad says your family's strange," she said, but did not elaborate. She reached up and braced herself as they rounded a sharp curve, where the service road angled to skirt the farm's southernmost pasture. In the east, the rising sun was casting its first bright rays over the tops of the Sierra Nevada mountains, and in the chilly pinkish light Will could see the sorrel mare—Nate's despair—standing by the split-rail fence, happily munching on clover.

Will smiled with secret satisfaction. The last thing he'd done before he'd met Jenny that morning had been to throw open the mare's stall and shoo her out of it. She'd found her way to where she wanted to be. Good for her.

Even a dumb animal deserves a choice.

Will and Jenny did not speak much after they turned onto the main route south to Stockton. The morning was clear and fine, and the sky was painted with colors bright as the label on a produce box.

The silence went beyond their lack of conversation. Except for the creak of the Baker's leaf-springs and chassis, and the crunch of its rubber tires on the small gravel of the dirt road, the machine was perfectly silent. The Otherwhere Flume Will had installed emitted only a faint hiss, like the sound of a mighty waterfall heard from very, very far away.

"We're not going to have to stop and charge up the battery, are we?" Jenny asked. "Can we make it all the way to Stockton?"

"We sure can," said Will. "It's not an electric. Or rather, it is an electric motor, but it doesn't use a conventional electric battery. This car is powered by an Otherwhere Flume." When she gave him a blank look, Will added, "It's my own design. I based it on a classical Otherwhere Conductor, but I made several improvements."

"I'm afraid I don't know the first thing about Otherwhere power," Jenny said. "I did read an article once about how it's going to revolutionize civilization, or end tyranny, or increase global grain yields—something like that." She paused, knitting her brow thoughtfully. "Or maybe that was an article about steam tractors. I can't quite remember."

"I don't know about ending tyranny or increasing grain yields," Will said. "But I do believe Otherwhere power will revolutionize civilization. And I know Mr. Tesla thinks so too."

Jenny nodded. "So how does it work?" She lowered her voice and leaned slightly toward him. "An Otherwhere isn't ... *magic*?" The last word was spoken with a distinctly apprehensive edge. But then, remembering who she was speaking to, she hastily added, "That's not to say anything against your Ma'am, of course ... you know I haven't a thing against Old Users ... it's just some do, and ... oh, I'm sorry."

After stammering all this out, she sank back into the seat, red-faced and embarrassed, and pressed her lips tightly together.

Will said nothing. He'd had this exact same awkward interaction dozens of times, always with others close to his own age. They would *seem* to take the fact that his mother was a witch in stride—until, in some unguarded moment, their true feelings would slip out. Their distaste, their resentment—their fear. This was always followed by a clumsy apology. It was like clockwork.

But he hadn't expected it of Jenny.

Of course, he couldn't really blame her. They were both members of what the newspapers had dubbed the "Malmantic Generation"— the first generation to live under the shadow of the Black Flu.

The first case of the gruesome malady—typified by greasy tar-colored eruptions and blazing fever—was reported in 1878. By 1880, the epidemic had engulfed the globe. The wildfire quickness with which the disease emerged and spread was horrifying. But stranger, and even more terrible, was the fact that it only affected children. *Infant* children. Not every child caught it, but few families were spared the heartbreak of at least one case. Will's own sister, Catherine—born a few years before him—had lived only a few days before succumbing. And while Jenny's older sister, Claire, had survived the illness, it had left her a lifelong invalid.

Over the next ten years, hundreds of thousands died and the lives of millions more were ruined. The turning point came when scientists at a company called Sanitas Pharmaceutics made a key discovery—the Black Flu was not a strain of influenza. It was not any kind of virus or bacterium at all. Rather, it was an allergic reaction, triggered by the passage of magical energy through the channels of the body. And while some degree of allergic sensitivity was found in *all* children born after 1878—the scientists could not find a single individual born earlier who showed signs of it.

The scientists could not explain this strange sharp demarcation. They could only give it a name and a date: *The Great Change of 1878.*

Learning the true nature of the malady had made it possible to develop a medication to combat it. Stopping the allergic reaction merely required blocking the channels through which magical energy flowed in the body. Creating a chemical compound that produced this effect was not difficult. It was called the Panchrest, and it successfully brought the Black Flu to heel. In less than two years, the worst was over.

But the Black Flu had shredded the civic fabric, and that was not so easily mended. Before the Great Change, magic had been woven into society at every level. It was called upon for small daily conveniences and grand splendid achievements alike. Magic, it was often said, had built America. And in the decades preceding the Great Change, the uses of magic had become ever more industrial and expansive—so vast that no one could have imagined any limit to them.

But then the Malmantic Generation had come along. They could not use magic as their parents and grandparents had. Those who even attempted it would suffer bouts of violent illness, the result of their inborn allergic sensitivity. And the more magic they used, the sicker they would become.

People born before 1878—like Ma'am—came to be called "Old Users." They suffered no ill-effects from channeling magic. There was nothing stopping them from using it as they always had—and so they did. Why shouldn't they? They had grown up in a world steeped in it. They were used to its conveniences, and they were unable to comprehend the fear and resentment they engendered in the distinctly different species of human that was destined to replace them.

But now the century had turned. The Malmantic Generation—the first generation of the twentieth century—was coming into its own. The youngest members were already well into their thirties. What form would those fears and resentments take, Will wondered. Would the day come when his Ma'am would be truly *hated* for what she was, even by her beloved goddaughter?

Jenny broke what had become a long silence. "You sore at me?"

Will had slowed the Baker to a crawl. They had come to a place where irrigation runoff from the hill above had made the road soggy.

"You asked if Otherwheres are magic," Will finally said, as he looked down along the running board to gauge the softness of the mud as he brought the Baker across it. "Otherwheres are just different dimensions of our own reality. Back in the day when witches and warlocks were more common than they are now, Otherwheres were mostly accessed using magic. But now we access them using science. So ... nothing to worry about. All right?"

"All right," said Jenny, relaxing visibly. "But I still don't quite get what an Otherwhere is, exactly."

"It's a different plane of reality, a different ... shade." Will struggled for the right words. "Scientists believe there must be an infinite number of them. Some Otherwheres are very much like the world we know. Some are very hostile places, where human beings can't even exist because the laws of physics are so different. Exploring Otherwheres has always been dangerous for just that reason. You don't know where you're going to end up, or if you'll be able to get back."

Jenny tapped a fingernail against her chin. "I wonder if anyone's ever tried using Monsieur Poincaire's hyperbolic geometry to mathematically map this infinity of universes," she mused. "It seems perfectly suited to the job. And it might be kind of fun."

Will emitted a low whistle, looking at her sidelong. "*Fun?*" He pulled down the bill of his tweed touring cap against the glare of her blinding intellect. "I'm beginning to think that math professor of yours was staring into your eyes out of pure confusion."

Jenny snorted derisively. "It's all just numbers, William."

"Well, let's get back to my Otherwhere Flume, which is what you asked me about. It all starts with finding an Otherwhere compatible with our own universe's physical laws. Maybe Poincairian hyperbolic geometry could be applied to finding one, but that's neither here nor there. Because over two hundred have already been found, as the result of decades of risky exploration. They're called the Golden Dimensions. They're uninhabited and mostly physically identical to our own universe."

"Wait, there are some that are *inhabited?*" Jenny's eyes became big as plates. "By who?"

"I'm an engineer, not an anthropologist," Will shrugged. "Anyway, over the years, bright industrialists have built power plants in these Otherwheres. Coal plants, steam—whatever unique generating resource is available. There's one Otherwhere that's filled with enormous waterfalls; they've put in hydroelectric turbines just like they have at Niagara Falls."

Jenny was rapt.

"Anyway, all that power is transmitted from the Otherwhere into *our* world. That's what an Otherwhere Conductor is. It's the power of a whole coal plant, or hydroelectric plant, or steam plant, whooshing through an infinitesimal transdimensional portal into our own reality, where we can put it to whatever use we like." He paused. "Hey, could you dig out some of that food? I'm starving."

Jenny reached under the seat for the bag she'd packed, and from it, withdrew a whole apple pie. It was clearly a condemnation of the quality of pie to be found in San Francisco that Jenny expected to be able to break his Ma'am's pie into neat wedges. But the flaky pastry crumbled in her hand, and she frowned at the pie filling on her dainty brown leather gloves.

"Great," she muttered. "Now my gloves will smell like pie. Here."

Resting one hand on the tiller, Will took the ragged hunk of pie in his other and quickly devoured it, licking the sweet sourness of apple and cinnamon from his fingers then wiping his hand clean on his trousers. Jenny eyed him with mild disdain as she used a corner of the laundry bag for a similar purpose.

"No wonder you want to go to Tesla Industries!" Jenny said as she tucked the bag away. "But what I don't understand is why everything isn't powered by Otherwhere Flumes, or Conductors, or whatever? This car runs beautifully! It's quiet, and not at all dirty or smelly. And as long as there's power coming from the Otherwhere, there's nothing to stop us, isn't that right?"

"Not a thing," said Will, knowing that it wasn't entirely the truth. But he liked the glow of Jenny's admiration, and thus he had no immediate interest in explaining Old Randall Rudge.

Of course, Old Randall Rudge had to be explained eventually, but Will preferred to wait for that discussion until it became necessary.

They were passing through acres of almond orchards, the trees stretching out in neat rows as far as the eye could see, when the Baker began to slow. Glancing at the dash, Will watched the ampere gauge plummet to below five, and knew that it was futile to continue; he steered the auto off to the side of the road and brought it to a stop beneath a brilliantly colored billboard advertising the premiere of Edison Studios' moving-picture version of *The Warlock's Curse*. The enormous advertisement was dominated by the sharply handsome features of the idealized Sophos of the Stanton Institute. The famous warlock's eyes were rendered particularly prominently; large and green-glowing, rimmed with blackest movie-idol kohl.

Given that they were driving along the well-traveled main road between Sacramento and Stockton, they had already seen several such billboards—and each time, Will had wondered about the letter from Ben.

"What's wrong?" said Jenny. "Why have we stopped?"

Will took his hands off the tiller and leaned back in his seat. Pushing his motoring cap back on his head, he looked at his wristwatch.

"It's noon," he confirmed. "Old Randall Rudge in New Jersey runs his experiments every day at this time, and he draws down just about all the power the system has." He turned to Jenny apologetically. "I have a charging system for a secondary battery all worked out in my head. If I'd had time to set it up, we could have just switched over to battery when the Flume was low."

"What are you talking about?" Jenny tucked back a thick tendril of hair that dangled before her eyes; that particular curl had already escaped its pins several times, Will had noticed.

"The biggest problem with my Flume actually lies with the Otherwhere it draws power from. If I were a high-and-mighty industrialist, I could own my own power plant. But I'm not, and I don't. So I have to buy a license from someone who is, and does. That license entitles me to a slice of the output of a single power plant."

"So, what happened? You didn't pay your Otherwhere bill?"

"No, I'm all paid up through the end of the year," Will said. "But the particular high-and-mighty industrialist from whom I bought my license has demonstrated that he doesn't particularly care how many licenses he sells."

Jenny made a sound of understanding. "Oh! So when your Mr. Rudge, for instance, runs his experiments, it drains the pool for everyone. Why, I just call that bad business!"

"Profiteering is what we licensees call it," said Will. "We've all complained about it, but there's not much we can do."

"You know the other licensees?" Jenny said.

Will nodded. "We circulate a newsletter by post."

He got out of the car to stretch his legs. The morning had warmed up and the air smelled of smoke and sunshine. Judging from the white mile-markers they'd been passing—and the increasing numbers of driveways stretching off from the roadside—he figured they were only about ten miles out of Stockton. They had plenty of time. He reached back into the car and retrieved another chunk of pie, leaning on the hood of the car to eat it.

"We all banded together and made Old Rudge promise to limit his experiments to an hour a day." Will brushed crumbs from his sleeve. "Boy, what an hour that must be in New Jersey!"

"Sounds like you've had this license for a while," Jenny said.

"Almost a year," Will said. "I got it for a project at school, and I've been tinkering with it ever since, hooking it up to various electrical devices, perfecting my Flume. I finally decided to drop the whole thing into Pask's car because—" He stopped, suddenly feeling kind of sheepish. But Jenny was two steps ahead of him.

"Because I bet the license isn't cheap and your folks don't give you as much pocket money as the grandson of a de la Guerra gets," she concluded. "If he liked the car with the Flume in it, he'd have to renew the license, which meant you'd get to keep tinkering with it. Right?"

Will blinked at her. "You sure you don't have some witch in you?" he said, thinking of the uncanny perceptivity his mother's magical skills gave her.

Jenny shuddered. "No, I don't have any witch in me," she said. "So we have to just sit around here waiting for Old Rudge to finish his experiments in New Jersey?" She crossed her arms. "We *do* have a wedding to get to."

"Can't be helped." Will bent down to peer under the chassis, idly examining the axles and leaf springs. "It's the curse of a shared resource."

"So, what if we had our own Otherwhere?" Jenny asked. "All the power from one coal plant whooshing straight through your Flume, without anyone else tapping into it? Could we drive fifty miles an hour? A hundred?" Her eyes gleamed.

Will paused to consider. "The chassis probably wouldn't stand that kind of speed for long," he concluded. "Especially over these roads. But you could build one that would. And with the right kind of roads, you could really fly. A hundred miles an hour would be nothing if you had thousands of horsepower. Someday, I bet you'll see machines that can do it."

Jenny was silent for a long time, lost in thought. When she lifted her head to look at him, there was awe in her eyes.

"Why, William, you're a bona-fide *genius*."

"Lay off," he muttered, blushing. "People have been fooling around with Otherwhere Conductors for years. I just figured a way to get around a few things. My shabby Otherwhere license was the least of my worries. Getting around the Connection Drop Problem, that was the hard part."

"The what?"

"Like I said, people have been fooling with Otherwhere Conductors for years. But you don't see them in automobiles like this one because of a technological hurdle called the Connection Drop Problem. See, it's easy enough to open a connection to an Otherwhere, but it's always been impossible to maintain that connection reliably. The connections drop seemingly at random—and usually at the most inconvenient moment possible. But everyone knew that it couldn't just be random—something had to be causing it. People have been trying for years to figure out what that something is. They've looked at fluctuations in barometric pressure, at global temperatures, all sorts of things, but no one could figure it out. But I did. And once I figured it out, I built the Flume and ..." He trailed off, spreading his hands as if further explanation was unnecessary.

Jenny leaned forward, elbows on the dash. "So, how did you do it?"

"You ever hear of Röntgen rays?"

"Röntgen? He won that big prize from the dynamite mogul, didn't he?"

"The Nobel, yes. Ten years ago. When I was at the Polytechnic I started getting interested in Röntgen rays. I learned that they were all around us, just as a general background state. It was supposed that they'd be at a higher level when sunspots flared up. I wondered if there was a correlation between these sunspots and the Connection Drop Problem."

"And was there?" Jenny asked.

"Several observatories around the world have been watching sunspots since 1849," Will said. "They have almost a hundred years of data on them. So I wrote away and requested copies."

"So that was data about sunspots," she said. "But how did you get the data about dropped Otherwhere connections?"

"Tesla Industries," said Will. "They've been working on this problem for years. They maintain a steady-state Otherwhere connection, and they've been keeping records on it. Every time it's randomly knocked off line, they make a note of the date and time. My teacher at the Polytechnic, Mr. Waters, knows one of the lead researchers there. He got me a copy of those records—but it sure took some doing! Tesla Industries is pretty secretive."

"And once you had both sets of data, you simply had to apply a Bayesean Linear Regression and *poof*!"

"Well, no." Will admitted. He had no idea what a Bayesean Linear Regression even was.

"So how did you compare the data?"

"I didn't." Will shrugged. "Before I had a chance to, another one of my teachers—a planetary scientist, he'd heard what I was working on—pulled me aside in the hall and shared an early draft of an article he'd been asked to review for a journal. It showed how Röntgen rays from the sun are stopped by the atmosphere surrounding the earth. Some believe that a kind of magnetic field is involved."

Jenny threw herself back in her seat, exasperated.

"Oh, now you're just being horrible," she growled. "I've heard of shaggy dog stories, but never shaggy engineer stories! So what are you telling me about Röntgen rays for, then?"

"I'm just trying to demonstrate to you that nothing in life is ever as easy as you think it's going to be," Will said loftily.

Jenny snorted. "Believe me, William Edwards, I don't need *you* to tell me that. Now, are you going to tell me what you discovered, or just keep playing around?"

Will grinned. "I discovered that I was on the right track, but with the wrong ray. It was *cosmic* rays that I should have been looking at. We get about eight to ten solar flares every day that shower the earth with cosmic rays. They're strong enough to disrupt a connection."

"So ... what do you do about it?"

"I've managed to create a pretty effective shield using the principles of magnetism. What makes my Otherwhere Flume different from a regular old Otherwhere Conductor is that I've added an electro-magnetic field generator to deflect stray cosmic rays. It's powered out of the Otherwhere itself, so the system is entirely self-sustaining. Which reminds me ..." Will wanted to check and see if Rudge's experiments would have any impact on the strength of his electro-magnetic field generator. Circling around to the back of the car he opened the trunk and took a reading on a small dial. He was so absorbed in thought he didn't notice that Jenny was standing next to him.

"That's it?" she asked in astonishment. "It's ... a cigar box!"

"That just houses the workings," Will said. It was a good sturdy wooden box, and Will had liked the colors of the label. He had especially liked the picture on the inside of the box's cover, and he realized suddenly that Jenny would probably like it too. Lifting the lid, he grinned as he showed it to her. She put a hand over her mouth and giggled.

"The Hero of Manila!" she read, examining the old picture of Admiral Dewey.

But the intricate workings of the device within quickly drew her attention away from the brightly colored image. She bent down to get a closer look.

"I would have guessed it to be much bigger!" Jenny said. "Your Mr. Waters sure must have been impressed."

"He never actually saw the prototype," said Will. "I just built it this past summer." Will checked the thick silk-wrapped cord that connected the box to the Baker's motor. He made sure the Flume was securely seated in the cradle he'd built for it, then closed the trunk. Jenny was scrutinizing him.

"But before you graduated, you showed him your schematics and all that, right?"

"No, I never drew anything up." Will dusted off his hands. "Mr. Waters wanted me to, but I didn't see the need. I knew how I was going to build it. He got the concept, just like you do. And his friend at Tesla Industries, the lead researcher who got me their data on cosmic rays—a man named Grigory Grigoriyev, one of their leading Otherwhere Engineers—he gets it too. He's has asked to have me on his team special. I can't wait to show him what I've done!"

Jenny's eyes widened in horror.

"You're not going to *show* it to him, are you?"

"Well of course I am!" Will's eyebrows shot up. "What's the good of building something this swell if you can't share it?"

"What's to keep them from stealing it from you?"

"Naw, that's Edison you're thinking of, and he's in the moving-picture business now." Will gestured at the billboard looming over their heads. He came back around to the front of the car and peered at the dials to see if the ampere gauge had come up at all. "Mr. Tesla is a straight shooter. Mr. Waters says so."

"William Edwards!" Will turned at the sound of command in Jenny's voice and found her planted right behind him. She was not physically imposing—he'd always been taller than her—but the ferocious intensity in her blue eyes was enough to make him want to draw back. Reaching up to seize his shoulders, she held him fast.

"Now listen," said Jenny, in a firm, bell-clear tone. "I want you to make me a promise, right this very second, or our deal is off."

"P-promise?" he stammered. "What do you want me to promise?"

"I want you to promise me that you will not share your invention with anyone at Tesla Industries until it's protected by a United States patent. I will take care of it all—the filing, everything. I'll get it patented for you."

"Get it patented for me?" Will was incredulous. "Jenny, what do you know about patenting anything? You're seventeen!"

"And you're *eighteen*, and you've invented the most incredible thing I ever heard of in my entire life!" She countered. "I know that if you don't protect your rights, you'll lose them." Jenny paused. "You've made a great discovery. Don't you know how great?"

"Yeah, but—"

"Look, haven't I done okay so far?" Jenny lowered her hands, and her voice became pleading. "Haven't I got everything all planned? Haven't I got us a crooked lawyer?"

Will didn't say anything.

"You're a genius, William," she said softly. "And geniuses need people to protect them. Just promise me. Please?"

"All right, Jenny," he said. "I promise."

Jenny squealed with satisfaction. Raising herself up on her tiptoes, she pecked him on the cheek. "You're going to make a perfectly wonderful husband."

"But I'm not going to Detroit just to sit around!" he added plaintively. "I want to show everyone at Tesla Industries what I can do!"

Jenny shrugged indifferently as she climbed back into her seat and rearranged her duster. "I'm sure you can find plenty to show them that doesn't involve giving away your best invention right out of the gate. You just have to play them along a little bit."

Will looked at his watch. Old Rudge's hour was over. He started the car and put the controller into reverse. Power whooshed through the Flume like a distant breeze.

Both of them lost in thought, they drove on in silence, Dreadnought Stanton's brilliant green eyes following them blankly.

Chapter Three

For Better or Worse

Stockton, located at the mouth of the San Joaquin Valley, was called "The Chicago of the West." Will's father had often sniffed at this appellation and observed that one could quite accurately gauge the intellectual smallness of any given city by the bigness of the city it compared itself to. Will, however, loved Stockton—and not because of its hotels or restaurants or shops or any of its other urban attractions. He loved it because it was the most industrialized city in California, a city of mills, factories, foundries and shipyards, all surrounding the mighty man-made channel that led to the Pacific Ocean. Things were *made* here.

Sometimes, Will would make Pask park out front of a factory just so he could watch the activity going on around it—the bustling hive of workers, the raw materials going in and finished products coming out.

Pask, however, never had much patience for these protracted observations. He and Will came to Stockton to whoop it up, not to watch the forward march of American industrial progress. He preferred cheap whiskey, moving picture theaters, dances and vaudeville.

Will and Pask had come down at the beginning of the summer, on Pask's dime, to attend a big to-do—organized by the town's business elite—celebrating the opening of the brand new Hotel Stockton. With his parents away in Europe, Pask had been invited to attend as the de la Guerra family representative. He and Will had had an excellent time swanking it up on the glassed-in rooftop garden, eating the boosters' canapés and downing their liquor.

As Jenny and Will drove along Pacific Avenue, the town seemed to swell around them. They turned down El Dorado Street to Weber Avenue, navigating around horse-drawn carts laden with goods headed for the wharf. Will slowed the Baker as they passed the Hotel Stockton, thinking its newness might impress her, but Jenny didn't give it a second look. She had her eyes peeled for the San Joaquin County Courthouse a couple of blocks down—a massive building of white stone with fat frondy palm trees planted out front and a heavy clock tower cupola that seemed much too large for it, like a very big hat on a very small man.

Will parked the Baker aslant the concrete curb. They climbed out and hastily shed their motoring overcoats. As he stuffed his under the seat, he was aware that Jenny was eyeing him critically.

"I told you to wear your best suit!"

"This *is* my best suit!" Will returned. That just seemed to alarm her further, so he added, "And it's just about new!" This was also true; the suit had been obtained just a few months prior for his graduation exercises. However, it had been ordered from a catalog, so it didn't really fit him properly. The trouser hems brushed his anklebones, revealing bright red home-knit socks, and the grease-marked cuffs of his blue twill workshirt jutted out beyond the jacket's sleeves.

"Oh, it'll just have to do." Jenny fussed with his tie then took his arm. "Come on!"

Inside, the building smelled of varnish and marble and bureaucracy. The shield of the State of California was inlaid on the floor of the main foyer, lit by light from the cupola above. The ringing officialness of it all made Will suddenly nervous.

"Hey Jenny, I don't suppose you've researched what happens if we're caught?" He bent so he could speak low in her ear. "Getting a marriage license under false pretenses, I mean. It's probably just a misdemeanor, right?"

"For me, anyway!" said Jenny, brightly. "For you, it could be a lot worse. Especially since you're intending to take me across state lines. I'm sure you've heard of the Mann Act? I'd advise you to keep any immoral purposes to yourself."

For not the first time, Will found that he wasn't entirely comfortable with Jenny's sense of humor. But he pressed his lips shut and watched as she corralled a cleaning lady for directions. He thought of Detroit. He needed to get to Detroit and this was going to get him there. That was all that mattered.

The county clerk's office, they were informed, was on the second floor. Jenny's heels clicked and echoed as they climbed the wide marble stairs. The building was mostly deserted this day after the Thanksgiving holiday, but as Jenny had predicted, most of the offices were open—not *enthusiastically* open, perhaps—but open.

The second floor, far less grandiose than the first, smelled of legal-sized paper and red ink and wooden filing cabinets. The walls above the half-paneling were painted the dull shade of green that municipal governments seemed to order by the hogshead. They walked down a hall lined with closed doors, pebbled glass windows gold-stenciled with the names of the departments within, finally entering the door marked "Licenses."

The room was not large, and the dozens of tall wooden filing cabinets that lined the walls made it seem even smaller. Behind a counter that spanned the length of the room, a desk was centered, its in-box stacked high. And behind that desk, a clerk—his feet propped up, a cigarette in his mouth—deeply absorbed in the newest of the Dreadnought Stanton serials. Will was beginning to feel like the Sophos of the Stanton Institute was following him around.

"We've come for a marriage license," said Will, his voice sounding too loud in the silence. "We'd like to get married, please."

The clerk took them both in at a glance, but said nothing.

"I'm twenty-one," Will volunteered, probably too quickly.

"And I'm eighteen," Jenny added, with similar haste. The clerk ground out his cigarette and smiled at them both wearily. Reaching behind his desk, he pulled out a handful of forms.

"All right. These have to be filled out in triplicate. There's a desk with a pen and ink over there. Bring 'em back to me when you're done. You have the twenty-eight bucks?"

Will nodded, glad that Jenny had thought to leave him the cash. Having Jenny fish the money for their marriage license out from her stocking garter might have made the clerk just the tiniest bit suspicious.

Together, they went over to a stand-up desk and filled out the papers using the dip pen that rested in an inkwell built into the table. It was not a good pen, and Will's hand was shaking slightly. He cursed as he kept blotting the forms.

"Should we give them our real names?" Will whispered to Jenny. He was getting flustered; embarking upon a course of misdemeanory wasn't his natural sphere of expertise.

"Of course we have to have our real names on there," Jenny whispered back. "My lawyer may be crooked, but he's not crooked enough to get my mother's estate released to 'Susie Smith'!"

"All right, all right … what's your middle name?"

"Elaine."

Will wrote their names side by side. It looked so formal: William Wordsworth Edwards and Jennifer Elaine Hansen.

"William *Wordsworth*?" Jenny smirked. "Really?"

"Named after my father, same middle name and all," said Will. "It's a family joke. Ma'am hates Wordsworth."

Jenny shook her head. "Your family sure is strange."

When they were done, they brought the papers back to the clerk, Will trying to control the tremor in his hands. Perusing them, a slight frown passed over the clerk's face. He looked from Will to Jenny.

"You live up near Walnut Grove, and you live in San Francisco?" His brow wrinkled. "But you two came all the way out here looking for a license?"

Will and Jenny looked at each other. Jenny was the quickest. "I have family in Stockton," she said. "We're visiting them."

"You want to give me their name and address?" the clerk countered. Jenny gulped; the clerk narrowed his eyes. "I didn't think so." He paused, then looked hard at Will. "And I don't suppose you brought anyone to vouch for you? For your ages, particularly?"

Will's whole body went hot, then cold.

"Well, no," he said. "I mean, we're both old enough. What would we need someone to vouch for our ages for? The very idea!"

"I've got my Vanguard Girls card!" Jenny offered, quickly fishing a pasteboard card out of her wallet. The Vanguard Girls was the nation's leading organization for the advancement of young women. She showed it to the clerk. While it bore the stamped signature of the organization's founder—Mrs. Amanda Haynes Reader—it had nothing about Jenny's age on it. Perhaps Jenny had hoped the card would affirm the unquestionable moral rectitude of its possessor.

The clerk looked over the card—out of politeness merely. Then he handed it back to her. "I'm afraid that doesn't cut any ice with the county, miss."

"Sir, the truth of it is ..." Will leaned forward, tried to draw the man into his confidence, "Well, we've got some explaining to do."

The clerk looked at Will curiously but said nothing. Jenny also looked at him, but he put his foot on top of hers and pressed down, indicating that she should keep her mouth shut. Will leaned forward further and lowered his voice to the barest whisper.

"My girl here is ... well, she's in an *embarrassing way*, if you know what I mean. And we've got to break it to her dad. If I can't show him a marriage license, he's going to take after me with a shotgun."

"And rightfully so," the clerk said. But it was clear his interest had been piqued. Will had often noticed that men who read dime novels liked a little scandal.

"I want to do what's right, sir," Will said. "And I'd be much obliged if you'd help us out in this matter." Without quite knowing what he was doing, or what the ramifications might be, Will reached into his pocket for one of the bills Jenny had given him. He didn't realize that it was a hundred until he was sliding it across the counter, but by then it was too late to take it back for something smaller. The clerk barely glanced at the note before putting his hand over it.

"All right, circumstances being what they are ... and it's the holiday ... I'm going to grant you the certificate today." He pulled out a stamp and a pad and stamped all the documents, signing his name at the bottom of each one. "You need to take these over to Judge Lawson to get them officiated. He'll be none too pleased to see you given he's probably nursing a hangover. He lives just off Fremont Square, a few blocks up from here." The clerk wrote out an address. "He'll do the service, and his housekeeper and her husband can be your witnesses. Then you bring the signed papers back to me, and it'll all be square. But you'd better make it quick, I'm going home at four."

Will glanced up at the large clock above the door; it was already well past three. He touched the brim of his cap to the clerk and took Jenny's arm.

"C'mon!" he murmured to her. "If we want to be married today, we'll have to run!"

They dashed to the judge's house, a fine expensive home that looked out onto a neatly groomed park. He was not, as the clerk had imagined, nursing a hangover; he had solved that painful inconvenience by getting drunk again. This meant that it took several tries for Will and Jenny to explain the nature of their visit, and then additional time to convince him that yes, it was indeed necessary to complete the transaction even though, technically, the day might be considered a holiday. Once the judge had been convinced of this, there was an additional amount of convolution when he learned that Will and Jenny did not intend to solemnify their vows with a visit to a priest; as a result, he insisted on reading some lines from the Bible to lend an air of sanctity to the proceedings. Throughout all this, Will shifted nervously; Jenny, to her credit, stood calm and cool and collected, with the air of one who believes that her plans will succeed. Will kept looking at the clock on the mantel; it was

ten minutes to four by the time the judge pronounced them "man
and wife."

The housekeeper and her husband, who had served as witnesses,
invited Will to stay for cake and sherry, but there was no time to
waste. Offering quick thanks, they ran back to the county recorder's
office, making it to the door just as the clerk was taking out his keys
to lock it.

"I guess you just made it!" The clerk took the papers from them
and looked them over. "I halfway didn't think you'd get old Judge
Lawson to stay awake long enough to sign these." He stepped inside
the office and stamped all three copies. Two of these he threw into
the teetering in-box to be dealt on Monday; the third copy he
handed to Will.

"There now, it's official." He took Will's hand and shook it heartily. "Congratulations, son." He tipped his hat to Jenny. "I hope you'll
both be very happy."

Will and Jenny staggered out of the courthouse, both of them
feeling a bit dazed. It was another warm afternoon, and the brightness of the sunlight and the gentle hush of the palm trees that
fronted the courthouse made everything seem very strange. By
mutual silent agreement, they sat down on the courthouse's marble
steps, gazing together at the license in Will's hand. They both stared
at the paper for a long time, at its official red stamp and firm black-
ink signatures. Finally, Jenny took it from him, folded it neatly, and
tucked it inside her purse.

"Congratulations," Will said to her.

"You too," she returned.

"So now what?" he asked. "Straight to San Francisco? That's over
eighty miles, and it's kind of late in the day to be getting started."

"I'm tired," said Jenny. "And I'm hungry."

"We're going to have to find someplace to sleep, then." Will
stretched out on the stairs, putting his hands behind his head. "We
could just bum it."

She stared at him in angry horror. "William Edwards, I am not
going to spend my wedding night sleeping in a public park!"

"Well then?" Will propped his head on his elbow and looked up at her. "What's it going to be?"

Jenny didn't say anything, but chewed her lip anxiously. Every detail of Miss Murison's training was clearly militating against the very thought of checking into a hotel with a boy—even if they were just friends. So, she was beginning to understand the temperature of the soup she'd gotten herself into, was she? Her mostly misplaced virginal hesitancy gave Will a moment of unkind satisfaction. Sitting there with her, in the failing light of a November evening, the scope of their mutual impulsiveness was beginning to dawn on him too, and he didn't want to be the only one suffering from it. But then again, fair was fair. He'd agreed to this as well, and they'd sworn a partnership on a spit-shake. It was too late for second thoughts or recriminations.

"All right, how about this," he spoke with careful casualness. "The Hotel Stockton is just up the way, and it's awful nice."

Jenny nodded, but did not speak.

"We'll get a couple of rooms, then we'll go find dinner, and see a show or something. There's lots of places I know from coming here with Pask. Okay?" When Jenny didn't answer, he nudged her ankle with the toe of his shoe. "C'mon, Scuff. You're not going to go all soft on me now, are you?"

She looked up at him, but still did not speak.

"There's always something good at the Yosemite Theater," he said. "Last time I was here with Pask, we saw an old warlock who could sorcel up fireworks that would make your eyes pop."

Jenny remained silent.

"And look, I even got money. My *own* money, I mean. I'll treat you." He dug the silver dollar out of his pocket, the one his father had given him. He flipped it at her and she caught it, looked it over.

"Another birthday present from my father," said Will. "So as you can see, he's not only a bastard, he's a cheapskate too."

Jenny turned the silver dollar over and over in her hand, examining it for a long time before she finally spoke.

"But don't you understand, William? This is a *wonderful* present." She looked up at him. "Don't you know what this is?"

Will shrugged. "It's just an old silver dollar."

"No, it's more than that. It's more than just what a dollar can buy, or the silver in it, or the beautiful engraving of Liberty enthroned beneath thirteen stars. It's a trade dollar."

"So?"

She tilted her head and looked at him. "Haven't you ever heard of Gresham's law, William?" It was a purely rhetorical question, for she continued on immediately: "It refers to the tendency for bad money to drive good money out of circulation. Gold and silver fluctuate in value depending on how much of them are on the market at any given time. In the 1870s, we had all those big silver strikes in Nevada, and silver flooded the market. That made silver into bad money ... because there was more supply than there was demand. Because there was less gold and more silver, people spent silver and kept gold. Do you follow me?"

"Sure," said Will, though he wasn't entirely sure why they were taking the journey in the first place.

"Now this coin," Jenny continued, holding it up to the light, "was created by a man named John Jay Knox—a San Francisco banker. He knew that there was a great demand for silver coins in Asia, especially China. So Mr. Knox created these—purely for export, mind you. Trade dollars."

"But they started to show up in circulation here in the States, because silver producers—who still had far too much silver on their hands—could have their silver minted into trade dollars. And they didn't bother sending them overseas, they just dumped them into the market. Over time, as more and more silver was found, and the price of silver decreased, their value just kept going down. At one point, the value had fallen so far you couldn't get even eighty-six cents for this dollar! And employers, wise to this opportunity for arbitrage, began buying them at a discount and using them to pay their workers—Gresham's law at work!"

After this, she fell into a silent contemplation of the coin, so entranced that Will finally had to snap his fingers in front of her face to get her attention. When her blue eyes rose to meet his, they were sharp and bright.

"So the point of your story," he summarized, with a wry smile, "is that I should like this coin because it was created out of greed and became less and less valuable over time?"

"No," she said. "I'm saying that you should respect it because it is fascinating. Because it makes you think about everything money really is. Money is the ability to do things—but only if you believe in it. And more importantly, if *other* people believe in it. What makes a silver dollar with eighty-six cents of silver in it worth eighty-six cents ... when a pennyworth of paper printed by the United States Treasury is worth an actual dollar? Why will one give you more power to do things than the other?"

"I have no idea," Will said. "Hey, weren't we going to go find a hotel or something? Or are we going to spend our wedding night talking about John Jay Knox and the price of silver in China?"

Jenny grinned as she flipped the dollar back to Will.

"Don't you dare spend that," she said. "It's a very special thing, and someday you'll be glad you have it."

Will shrugged as he tucked the silver away. He didn't believe her, but it was nice to see Jenny smile again.

"The Stockton sounds good to me," she said. "But no magic. It gives me the creeps. I want to go dancing."

Will grinned. "Now that's more like it, Mrs. Edwards."

Chapter Four

Dancing with the Dorians

The Hotel Stockton rose up behind a galleria of shops that ran along Weber Avenue. It boasted the most modern accoutrements, including refrigerated air, a glass-enclosed rooftop garden, and a fine restaurant overlooking the deepwater channel to the Pacific.

When Will and Jenny went to see about rooms, Will was surprised when the deskman greeted Jenny with warm recognition.

"Miss Hansen! How lovely to see you again! Are you in town to see your sister?" The man looked sidelong at Will. "Is your father joining you?"

"No," said Jenny. "I'm here alone." She paused, catching herself. "I mean, I'm here with my husband." She took Will's arm and hugged him close. "We've just been married today."

Will thought the desk clerk would float to the ceiling, he was so entranced by this notion. He actually clapped his hands together with delight.

"Oh, how lovely! Many, many congratulations!" The man beamed at them. "This calls for a celebration. I will put you in one of our best suites." He snapped his fingers for the bellhop, but the only luggage they could produce was Jenny's calfskin handgrip and Will's leather toolbag.

They and their meager belongings were shown upstairs to what was certainly one of the hotel's most impressive suites. There were three rooms—sitting room, bedroom, bath, all enormous. Like the rest of the hotel, they were done up in the old mission style, with heavy fumed-oak furniture upholstered in soft sueded leather, creamy stucco walls accented with bright glazed tile, and hammered bronze light fixtures with mica shades. Along one wall, behind curtains of silk, tall French doors opened onto a broad pillared balcony. No sooner had the bellhop left than a porter arrived, bearing a bottle of French champagne in a tub of ice and two crystal flutes on a silver tray. "With the hotel's compliments," he said, tipping his red cap smartly after he'd laid these out.

Will sank down onto one of the leather sofas. "Is that it? Or should I be expecting the mayor to walk through the door with the key to the city?" He paused, watching as Jenny unpinned her hat. "Call it a guess, but I think you've stayed here before."

Jenny laid her hat aside, setting the hatpin neatly atop it. "I wasn't lying when I said I had family in Stockton. My sister Claire is here, at the Stockton State Hospital, just up California Street. Dad and I have been here a half dozen times since the hotel opened, visiting her." She tried to open the bottle of champagne, but the cork was too slippery and her hands were shaking too much. Will took it from her and buried it back in the ice.

"Nix on the booze," he said. "We should eat something first."

"Right." Jenny glanced at herself in a nearby pier mirror, made a face. "I'm going to get cleaned up."

While Will waited, he cursorily examined the appointments of the room—lifting a knick-knack or two—then stepped out onto the balcony, leaning on the rail to look out over McLeod Lake and the deepwater channel beyond. As he was gazing at the bustling commercial piers and heavy freight steamers, an idea struck him. The room also had a telephone. Hurrying back inside, he picked up the receiver and spoke to the hotel operator. She said that, yes, she could certainly get him a line to Detroit. It would be well past dinnertime there, Will knew, but Mr. Waters had always said that Mr. Grigoriyev kept odd hours.

Pressing the smooth cool rubber of the receiver against his cheek, Will listened silently as the operator contacted several of her sisters across the United States, intricately negotiating a connection across many different exchanges.

Finally, heart pounding, he heard the cracking, distant, quiet sound of a deep, basso "This is Grigory Grigoriyev speaking." Will waited for the operator at the far end of the line:

"You have a call from California, from a Mr. William Edwards. Connecting you now."

Will was about to say "hello" when the voice on the other end of the line boomed with expansive warmth:

"William Edwards! I thought we would never hear from you! Waters has spoken so very highly of your skills."

"I'm glad to speak to you as well," Will said, feeling a rush of relief at the warmth of the man's greeting. "I wanted to telephone and apologize for the delay. I would like to accept the apprenticeship you have offered me. I can come to Detroit immediately."

"This is wonderful news. You certainly are not planning to come by train?"

Will—who, up to that point, had been thinking only about getting to San Francisco and Jenny's crooked lawyer—hadn't given more than a passing thought to how he was going to get to Detroit. But of course he'd have to take a train. How else could he be expected to get there? He was so puzzled by Grigoriyev's statement that he stammered:

"Well, I do have an automobile," he said. "It runs on a new type of power source of my own design. It could make it all the way to Detroit."

A sound of mildly scoffing indulgence crackled across the line. "Yes, Waters has told me about this 'Otherwhere Flume' you have been working on. I must remind you, Mr. Edwards, continuous power delivery is hardly revolutionary. It has been around for decades."

"No it hasn't," Will blurted—then, realizing how impertinent it must have sounded, added: "Not *really* continuous power delivery, I mean. There's always been the Connection Drop Problem."

There was a silence over the line.

"No one has found a way around the Connection Drop Problem," said Grigoriyev.

"I have," said Will. He let the silence hang. He'd promised Jenny not to reveal more, and, besides that, he liked giving this man something to look forward to.

"If that is the truth, then it won't be long before you're not an apprentice anymore, and are rather a highly paid employee," Grigoriyev cleared his throat—a rough, rattling sound over the long-distance lines. "You must come at once and bring this Flume of yours. But don't bother with the automobile, you'll find we've got plenty of those in Detroit."

"We can be there in a few days," Will said.

"We?" Grigoriyev must have said the word quite loudly, for it crackled over the line like fireworks. "What do you mean, 'we'?"

"Well, I won't be coming alone." Will fingered the thick silk-wrapped receiver cord. "I'm ... I'm bringing my wife."

"*Wife?*" Grigoriyev bleated. "Mr. Edwards, you never mentioned anything about a wife!"

Will didn't quite know what to say, so he said nothing.

"Didn't Mr. Waters explain our position on privacy to you?" Grigoriyev said. "Haven't you read the terms of the apprenticeship contract? It is a strict matter of Tesla Industries policy, dictated by Mr. Tesla himself. Our apprentices live on the Compound, in private dormitories, and must uphold the strictest modes of conduct and sanitation. You are simply not allowed have a wife!"

"I can't very well leave her behind, Mr. Grigoriyev!" Will suddenly realized that in this situation that would be exactly what Grigoriyev would demand he do. He covered with a quick lie: "She has no family out here and no one to stay with. She must come with me."

There was another long pause. Finally, Grigoriyev spoke again.

"I'm sure this is a very expensive call for you, Mr. Edwards, so for the sake of your wallet we will not discuss the matter any further. I will simply have to find some way to make this right." He didn't sound very happy about it. "Mr. Edwards, please keep in mind that at Tesla Industries we put a priority on secrecy and discretion—

as well as a pure, sanitary mode of existence. Your wife will have to respect that. I take it she is ... *well-behaved*?"

"Of course, Mr. Grigoriyev!" said Will, putting some outrage into the answer. Grigoriyev made a sound that might have been a grunt of satisfaction or disbelief. There was a brief silence.

"She's not fat, is she?" Grigoriyev asked.

"Not at all," Will said, and his answer must have been a bit warm because Grigoriyev then asked, with an even more intense note of alarm, "For God's sake, *you're* not fat, are you?"

"No, sir. I'm not fat."

"Chubby at all?"

"No, I'm a perfectly normal size." Will heard Grigoriyev release a long sigh of relief.

"Thank goodness. Mr. Tesla might have overlooked it, given your brilliance, but he wouldn't have liked it. This will make things much easier. Now, you must not take the train. It is far too dirty and slow. We must have you here immediately. Where are you now? Don't you live somewhere near San Francisco?"

"I'm in Stockton right now," said Will. His head was spinning from the speed at which the man changed subjects, and the oddness of the subjects themselves. "But I will be in San Francisco on Monday. I have ... business there."

"Excellent. After your business is done, you must go to Berkeley, to the College of Mechanics. There's a graduate student in the physics department who goes by 'Massy.' Ask for him. He will send you through the Dimensional Subway."

Will's heart leapt. He'd heard about the Dimensional Subways. They were still experimental, but it was said that they had the potential to completely replace the old-fashioned magically powered transportation portals called Haälbeck Doors—the use of which, for members of the "Malmantic Generation," was an invitation to a sickening bout of magical allergy. A vast network of Haälbeck doors still existed, but they could be used safely only by older businessmen, men born before The Great Change, whose ability to use magic was unimpaired.

The older generation's use of Haälbeck Doors (not to mention a million other kinds of magic) was the source of great hard-feeling among their younger counterparts. Up-and-coming businessmen begrudged their seniors their access to swift, easy magical transportation across the country. Some even went so far as to deem it a "Mantic Trust." There had been increasingly loud demands that the government take steps to bust this trust, to "level the playing field" for the younger professionals.

Will couldn't care less about the political posturing—he left that stuff to Argus—but he knew that Dimensional Subways and other scientific advancements like it were going to be critical in settling the issue. Will was thrilled at the prospect of seeing it in action.

"That will be fine," said Will, but Grigoriyev had already rung off without a goodbye.

Will gently replaced the receiver in its cradle, simultaneously elated and disquieted. He hadn't even imagined that the presence of Jenny, playing the role of wife, might give Tesla Industries a second thought about him. Gee, maybe he *should* have read the apprenticeship contract more carefully. But all that writing had been so tiny.

What if they decided that they couldn't take a married apprentice at all? That it was too hazardous to their jealously guarded security? Or worse, a threat to their "pure, sanitary mode of existence" (whatever the hell that meant). Wouldn't *that* be a piece of irony? Just like that story where the wife sold her hair to buy the husband a watch fob when the husband had already sold his watch to buy her a comb. Will never had liked that story.

And then there was the fact that Jenny had actually started to take an interest in his work. She had made him promise to patent his Flume! What would Mr. Grigoriyev think of that kind of meddling?

Well, no use worrying about it. He was a married man now, even if the role was purely fictional. And his purely fictional wife wanted to go dancing.

It being the Friday night after a holiday, there was no shortage of dances. After a good hearty dinner, Will took Jenny to a place he knew, one he and Pask had haunted on many a Saturday night—the Tivoli Concert Hall on El Dorado.

The admission fee was twenty-five cents for a couple. The inside of the dance hall was cavernous and echoing, and had always reminded Will of a gymnasium. At one end of the hall was a small stage, where a ten-piece ensemble played marches and two-steps and slow drags.

Dozens of couples were already dancing under a ceiling hung with small electric bulbs inside colorful Chinese paper lanterns. Even more couples milled above the dance floor, on the darkened mezzanine balcony, sipping soft drinks judiciously made hard by the addition of flask-carried liquor.

Jenny gazed around herself with wonder as they entered. Looking down at her, Will felt a sudden thrill of pride. He'd never come here with a pretty girl on his arm. All in all, it was a much nicer feeling than he'd expected. He could get used to this.

"You've never been here before?" he asked her, before immediately realizing what a dumb question it was. Jenny said she'd been to Stockton with her dad, and he certainly wouldn't have taken her out dancing.

"I've never been to a place like this at *all*," Jenny breathed, wide-eyed. "The girls at my school all try to keep up with the newest steps ... but none of us have ever actually gone to a dance hall!" She watched the dancers swirling across the polished wood floor, the girls in frothy white gowns of embroidered linen and lace. She looked down at herself ruefully. "Gosh, I'm not even dressed right."

"It won't matter once we're moving." Will pulled her toward the floor. "Come on."

They had to push their way through to get a good place, but they were soon moving together smoothly, her hand on his shoulder, his hand on her waist. Will had an extensive experience of female waists—in the context of the dance floor, anyway—and he discovered that Jenny's was comparatively very fine; firm, smooth, and warm.

"You must come here a lot," she said. "The coat-check girls all know you. I heard them giggling."

Will grinned ruefully. "Pask and I have given them plenty to giggle about." When Jenny blushed at the implication, he added quickly, "Not like that! I mean, we just tease them, that's all. Give them a hard time." Damn it, that was the wrong choice of words. He felt his face getting red too.

"I have simply got to get some new clothes." Jenny quickly changed the subject, looking not at Will's face but instead at a particularly lovely gown spinning past them. "I haven't a stitch beside what I'm wearing."

Will's face remained red, and he said nothing. Jenny looked at her hand, resting on the breast of his suit jacket. "You'll need new things, too," she mused.

Will shrugged. "I don't need much. Besides, I think I'll be getting a stipend from Tesla Industries eventually. Maybe I can hold out until then." He struggled to recall his diligent skimming of the apprenticeship contract—hadn't there been something in there about money?

"We'll figure it out," she said, giving his chest a confident pat. "Meanwhile, I'll just keep track of how much I spend on you. We'll settle it all up when we get divorced. Don't worry, I'll give you easy terms."

"Oh, really?" Will smiled down at her. "I hope you'll keep in mind that I'm providing *you* a service as well. Keeping you safe from mashers, showing you the sights of Stockton, driving the car. There's got to be some value in that."

"With a car like Pask's, you're virtually ensuring you never get put out of a job, William," Jenny smirked.

"Why do you always call me William?"

"It's your name, isn't it?"

"Yes, but everyone else always calls me Will. Or sometimes Bill."

Jenny made a face. "I don't like 'Will'," she said. "It makes you sound stubborn and perverse. Or like a legal document associated with death. And Bill is even worse. It makes you sound unpaid and unwelcome, something to be dodged. I like William. It's a beautiful name. Though you'll notice I don't include Wordsworth in that estimation."

"And what about 'Edwards'?" he said, softly. It seemed a more serious question than the ones that had gone before.

Her face was impassive. "I'll be 'Hansen' again, eventually."

"But you'll never be 'Miss' again. You'll be a *divorcee*. Doesn't that bother you? You act like you don't care."

Jenny shook her head sharply, forestalling further conversation. And Will realized that it *did* bother her, and she *did* care, but while she'd planned out the tactical logistics to a nicety, the emotional logistics had yet to be worked out. And until such time as they could be, she was determined not to think about them at all.

They slowly made their way off the floor after the song ended. It was hot, and the band was launching straight into an up-tempo castle walk—a popular favorite—and a stampede of couples rushing onto the floor made it hard to pass. As they were moving toward the refreshment counter, they passed a cluster of very distinctive young people. Each one wore clothing of unbroken black—the boys even wore black shirtfronts and black collars and black ties. But it wasn't their bizarre outfits that distinguished them; it was their sickly, sallow complexions, seemingly smudged with purple bruises. The girls emphasized this ugly contrast by heavily ringing their eyes with black kohl. They smoked black cigarettes in ebony holders, blowing the smoke upwards in elegant arcs. Jenny stared back at them as she and Will stood in line for drinks.

"Dorians," she whispered to him.

Will nodded, sparing the group an amused look. The black-clad youths were devotees of the British writer Oscar Wilde, specifically his famous Lippincott's serial, "The Picture of Dorian Gray." They fancied themselves living the American version of *La Vie Boheme*. To achieve the dark, wan, sickly look that they seemed to associate with that Bohemian life, they used—or rather misused—magic. The special cigarettes they smoked—"Golden Bat" brand, which came in an exquisite green and gold package—had been specially charmed to have a variety of effects on the smoker. They were as stimulating as the cocaine that came in medicine bottles, and they bestowed a distinctive glamour on the hair and eyes, lending both a dramatic, fascinating gleam. The final effect derived from the first two; the charm placed upon the tobacco was sufficient to induce the mildest form of magical allergy—too little to cause any real harm, but poisonous enough to give the users an "interesting" pallor.

"They're all over the place in San Francisco." Jenny's tone was intensely disapproving. "They're like a plague."

"And now they've spread to Stockton," smirked Will. "Can Fresno be far behind?"

But Jenny clearly didn't think they were funny. She stood glaring at the Dorians so hard that eventually one of them—a girl—noticed and raised a plucked eyebrow, and blew a thin plume of glowing smoke in her direction. The purplish smoke curled in the shape of a bat—a hallmark of the expensive cigarettes.

"People shouldn't use magic that way," said Jenny, and this time instead of whispering she said it loudly, so her voice would carry. "It's not healthy, and it's an insult to everyone who's really suffered and—oh, it just makes me mad!" Will might have had to break up some kind of fight had Jenny not turned and started shoving her way toward the door. Will didn't catch up with her until she was already retrieving her canvas duster from one of the giggling coatcheck girls.

"Come on, Scuff. They're just a bunch of *poseurs*. What's got you so upset?"

"I'm tired," she said flatly. "I want to go back to the hotel."

When they got back to the hotel, however, Jenny's mood had not improved. She tore the hairpins out of her hair and slammed them down on the side table.

"As if the Black Flu epidemics were just some kind of ... joke!" she muttered, as she went to her grip for a boar's-hair brush. She sat on the edge of an ottoman and began to brush her hair; the action seemed to calm her. "Some kind of fashion statement! Almost a million people, all over the world—dead! And that doesn't even take into account all the millions more who have suffered. Mothers, and fathers, and—" She closed her mouth and brushed with a vengeance. Will sat on a chair watching her. Her hair gleamed in the electric lamplight.

"And your family isn't helping matters any!" she said, out of the blue.

Will raised his hands, startled. "What has *my* family got to do with the Black Flu? I lost a sister to it myself, you know!"

"Your brother Argus," she hissed. "California's Man of the People—he based his whole campaign on an anti-immunization platform!"

Will groaned. He couldn't think of anything he wanted to discuss less than politics—especially his brother's politics. But the question of mandatory Panchrest immunization had divided the nation—and it was true, Argus' passionate partisanship on the issue had swept him to victory.

The Panchrest—the life-saving medication that had halted the Black Flu epidemics—was able to stop the deadly allergy because it blocked the natural magical channels in the human body. It "gummed up the works," so to speak. And the effect was irreversible. Those who took the Panchrest were rendered immune to magical allergy—but also unable to work any kind of magic at all.

This was a matter of little concern to the members of the Malmantic Generation; since the strange generational allergy was discovered, it was clear that magical practice was outside the reach of humanity's new breed. However, there was the question of the Old Users, and the disquieting advantage they enjoyed. Their ability to use magic without impairment was an ever-increasing source of concern.

And so, some had begun to argue that the Panchrest should be administered, preventively, to every United States citizen—young and old. Supporters trumpeted the scheme of mandatory immunization as a critical necessity to public health—but their deeper motivations were just as clear. Mandatory immunization would bust the "Magical Trust." Older businessmen would have no magical advantage over their younger comrades. No longer could they take advantage of Haälbeck Doors, or a hundred other little charms that they currently employed to their mercantile advantage.

The political faction Argus had aligned himself with—the Anti-Immunizers—argued that the government had no place interfering with the ability of the older generation to conduct their business. They argued that legislating such a fundamental rearrangement of the human system was unconstitutional. And they argued (probably most persuasively, in Will's opinion) that as the Panchrest had been developed very quickly, in response to the national emergency of the Black Flu epidemics, that no one really knew what its long-term effects might be.

But it was clear that Jenny didn't share any of these concerns. The fire in her eyes was as clear a sign of that as if she were wearing an "Immunization Now!" button on her lapel.

"If those ... *poseurs* ... were forced to take the shot, they wouldn't be able to flaunt their bad behavior," she said. "Your brother is on the wrong side of that issue. I tried to get him to see it on our drive down, but he didn't want to listen."

So that's what Lillie had meant by "full of opinions." That must have been one heck of a ride down from San Francisco. If there was one thing Will knew about "California's Man of the People," it was that he had no interest in listening to opinions that weren't his own.

Will couldn't help smiling at the thought of Jenny bracing Argus on the issue, and this fanned the flames of Jenny's annoyance. She threw her hairbrush back into the grip and stormed into the bedroom, unbound hair streaming behind her in a glorious halo.

"I'll sleep on the couch," he called after her back, unnecessarily.

"Darn right you will," she said, slamming the bedroom door.

Chapter Five

Ben's Letter

Even though the couches in the suite were deeply cushioned, Will was too tall to sleep on any of them comfortably. At around 3 a.m. he gave up the attempt and stretched, resigning himself to wakefulness. He went out onto the balcony and looked over the channel. The waning moon cast a pallid light over the water, and despite the late hour, barges were being loaded to make the trip down river to the Port of San Francisco.

On the sidewalk below, he saw a group of young people walking together, heading home. They moved in a somnolent procession, as if on their way to a funeral—it was the same group of Dorians who'd made Jenny so mad at the dance hall. One of the girls was shading herself from the moonlight with a black parasol. It was a ludicrous, pretentious display—but also strangely evocative. And for some reason, it reminded Will suddenly of the mysterious letter from his brother Ben.

Hurrying back inside, Will went to the hall closet where he'd hung his suit jacket. From the pocket, he retrieved the copy of *The Warlock's Curse* with Ben's letter tucked inside. Sitting down at the leather-covered writing desk, he withdrew the letter, spreading it out flat.

A single sheet of stationery. He read the words on it again:
Dreadnought Stanton 32: "The Warlock's Curse." Page 153.

Will flipped through the book to 153, back to the illustration of the magical sigil. He'd thought about that sigil during the drive down, trying to recall what role it had played in the book. All he could remember was that it was part of the magic the villain had used to unlock a magical artifact—a journal or a box or something like that. And in the book, for the magic to work, the sigil had to be traced in blood.

Will carefully read the relevant sections of text, and they confirmed his recollection. He sat back in his chair, annoyed. Clearly, it was Ben's intention that he trace the sigil in blood, and that would unlock some kind of hidden text. Which might seem very nifty if he were still twelve—but *really*? First Ben didn't send him letters at all, and now that he did, he had to bleed to read it? Besides that, Will had nothing to draw blood with.

Sighing heavily, he looked around the room, and noticed Jenny's hat sitting on the small side table. He took the hatpin from it and tested its edge; it was quite sharp. He winced as he jabbed it into his thumb. Squeezing a drop of blood, he rubbed it between his thumb and forefinger then carefully sketched the sigil on the page.

No sooner had he finished than the blood-streaks faded, and letters appeared, shimmering as if they'd been written in silver ink:

Dear Will, the first line read. *Happy birthday.*

Will squinted, pain needling through his head. The words were small and cramped, and they seemed to waver like heat rising on a hot summer day.

Sorry to have to subject you to a bit of unpleasant magic, but this stationery I borrowed from the Sophos' office was the best way for me to ensure that this message wouldn't be intercepted.

First of all, I want to say that I have always enjoyed your letters. Yes, I did get them. And I'm sorry I never wrote back.

Will hmphed. That was a good way to start, anyway.

I would have written you back if I could have, but it was impossible. I made a promise to Father and Mother and Uncle Royce. And honestly, it's not the promise I care about so much, but if they knew I broke it ... well, you never would have heard from me at all. So I had to wait until the time was right, when I knew you'd be ready to break off from them for good and all.

Your last letter, written after your argument with Father, told me everything I needed to know on that score. Even though you don't really know me, little brother, I know you. I know that you're going to Detroit, I know that you won't let anything stop you. And I just wanted to say that I will help you any way I can. Father has no right to stop you. It's your life.

Just reading the words lifted Will's spirits. It was the only morsel of encouragement he'd received from anyone in his family, and he hadn't realized just how sweet it would be.

Now, if you need traveling money, Father always keeps a few hundred dollars in cash at the back of the bottom left drawer in the desk in his study. If don't feel right about stealing from him, rest assured that you need take only enough to get you to Detroit. I've opened an account there on your behalf, at the National Bank. I've put in all the money I can spare. It will be enough to get you set up. I will send more when I can.

Will flipped over the page.

Now, I'm sorry to say this, but don't for one minute think that this is going to be easy.

Will took a deep breath, swallowed. He looked out the window for a moment, letting darkness soothe his eyes before continuing on.

You know as well as I do that Father and Mother don't like being crossed. They will spare no effort to bring you home, if for no other reason than they told you that you couldn't go. So be careful. Remember, Mother has eyes all over the country. She hears from every one of those damn girls she has ever taken in. You know she's taken in a lot of girls over the years. And it's not just her girls, it's her girls who know other girls. For God's sake, just watch out for girls in general, won't you?

Will smiled. He thought of Jenny's hair, how it had flowed behind her as she stormed off to the bedroom. He didn't need his brother to tell him to watch out for girls.

Now, the good news is that Tesla Industries will protect you. They value secrecy above everything. Once you are safely settled with them, they'll keep Father and Mother at bay. So just get to Detroit and you'll be fine.

I will come and see you when I can. For now, I can only write. One page every night, front and back—every night the charm resets, allowing me to write you something new. This paper is the safest way for me to communicate with you, but I'm afraid you mustn't write me back. Communication that goes out using the Sophos' stationery is not monitored (for it is assumed that the Sophos' letters do not need to be) but he is alerted when new messages arrive—and I guess I don't need to tell you it wouldn't go particularly well for me if he were to find out I was using his office supplies to communicate with my long-lost baby brother.

Running out of room. One sheet just isn't enough, but it will have to do.

Be sure to read this letter again after midnight.

Your brother always,

Ben

Chapter Six

Claire

Will woke the next morning to the sound of Jenny bustling around softly. She was holding her hat on her head, looking around with annoyance.

"What on earth has become of my hatpin?" she muttered. Will sat up slowly, muscles cramped from his resigned surrender to the longest of the too-short couches. Reaching over to the writing desk, he retrieved the hatpin and handed it to her guiltily, first checking to make sure it wasn't streaked with blood. She gave him a curious look as she took it, but said nothing.

"Are you going out?" Will asked.

"I won't be coming back to California for a long time." She pinned the hat to her head, then checked its angle in the mirror. "So I'm going over to the hospital. I'm going to say goodbye to my sister."

Will rubbed sleep from his eyes. "I'll drive you over if you like."

"It's not far by streetcar," said Jenny, clearly intending to put him off. Then an idea seemed to hit her. He could fairly see it forming behind her eyes. "Why don't you come with me?"

"Why would you want me to come with you?"

"You ... you might be able to help me with something very important." Her eyes were now fairly blazing with inspiration, and she looked quite resolved. "Yes, you simply must come. But we will take the streetcar ... I don't want to drive up in front of the hospital in Pask's broken-down old machine." She placed a hand on his wrist. "Will you come? Please?"

Will had originally thought that her outing would be the perfect opportunity for him to sneak into the bedroom and get some proper sleep. But a hand on the wrist! Who could resist that? He found himself recalling what his brother had written him about girls.

Walking down Weber Avenue toward the streetcar stop, Will pondered what he knew about Jenny's sister Claire. He knew that while the Black Flu killed many babies outright, in some children the mutations progressed slowly, deforming and disfiguring the victim over many years. What little he knew of Claire's particular situation had been relayed by Laddie, who had a twisted fondness for such dark gossip.

"Claire is an absolute hideous *wreck*," Laddie had said in the sinuous whisper he reserved for the most shocking horrors. "Have you ever seen pictures of the Elephant Man? Well, imagine him all black and oily and covered with oozing sores. She can't breathe without some kind of bellows to inflate her lungs. They keep her locked up and feed her raw meat every few days. She tears it apart with her black razor fangs. I imagine it's quite grisly."

Will certainly didn't believe the part about the raw meat or the fangs. His technological interest had been piqued, however, by the bellows system Laddie had described. He'd been quite interested in knowing how such a system would work. Would it be automatic, or triggered by the victim's own muscle impulses? Now, however, walking with Jenny, his own morbid curiosity made him feel ashamed. He'd never thought of Claire as a person, just a monstrosity. He certainly hadn't thought of her as someone's sister. But she was Jenny's sister, and Jenny loved her.

The Stockton State Hospital was large and white, with eyebrow arches and two deep enfolding wings. As they walked through the main gate, Will noticed the tangle of electrical wires that ran into the building from overhead poles. A system of bellows like the one Laddie had mentioned would certainly require electrical power, multiplied by however many patients were kept alive on them. It struck him that if the machines ran on electricity, he could surely power one of them with his Otherwhere Flume. It might be an improvement over being tied down in a hospital. Patients might be able to go home and live with their families.

"You don't have to come in if you don't want to," said Jenny, breaking through his thoughts. But Will was really interested now. What if he could find a way to improve the lives of people like Claire?

"I might as well," he said.

At the reception desk in the lobby, they were greeted by a sister in a simple religious habit of charcoal gray, the large red cross around her neck the only spot of color. As Jenny spoke to her quietly, Will idly gazed at the pair of pictures hanging on the wall behind the reception desk—a picture of a very old man hung next to that of a much younger one. Will recognized them both immediately. The older man was Brother Scharfe, famous as the founder of the Scharfian Fellowship—a strictly observant religious sect best known for its operation of sanatoriums for the "Cursed" (as the church so charmingly termed the survivors of the Black Flu) all over the United States. Despite their tendency toward unkind terminology, they were the undisputed experts in the treatment of victims of the Black Flu, and as such had been contracted to run many state hospitals, especially those with large numbers of long-term patients.

The younger man in the second picture was even more famous. He was Brother Scharfe's successor, Brother Phleger. One could hardly pick up a newspaper or watch a newsreel without catching a glimpse of his smooth, handsome, muscularly Christian face, strikingly disfigured by a sickle-shaped black blot across his cheek—the legacy of a childhood bout of Black Flu supposedly overcome by his precocious faith in Christ's redemption. A fiery polemicist, he was at the forefront of the Mandatory Immunization movement. He regularly thundered from the pulpit on the necessity of the legislation to America's continued claim to be a Christian nation.

And even if one didn't read newspapers or watch newsreels, one could hardly miss seeing his uniquely marked face on the hundreds of thousands of little religious tracts carried by adherents to back doors all across the United States. Will's family's home was a prime target for such missionaries, for it was well known in their area that Mrs. Edwards was an unapologetic, still-practicing witch.

Ma'am never could abide these black-coated Bible-thumpers. While she was genuinely nice to anyone who came to her door looking for a handout—overly so, some might say—she would chase Scharfians off with a broom.

"Come on," said Jenny, taking his arm, as the sister rose to escort them to Claire's room. Will was surprised at how tightly Jenny clung to him.

If Will was worried about being too obvious in his interest in the bellows that kept Claire alive, he found that he needn't have been. Even someone with no interest in machinery at all would have found it impossible not to stare.

It was enormous, and—in Will's instant estimation—far louder than it needed to be. It would be dead easy to muffle the sound of the chugging air-pump at the mechanism's heart. But perhaps the Scharfians didn't believe in such finicky niceties. As Will had expected, thick electrical cords looped down from the ceiling to the machine—but they weren't even hard-wired in, they'd been screwed, via some kind of adaptor, into a light fixture. It was a very inefficient and inelegant setup—not to mention a fire hazard.

The machine was so huge it entirely dwarfed the small human figure, wrapped in a colorful knitted afghan, who sat huddled beneath it.

"Good morning, Claire!" Jenny yelled as she briskly crossed the room. Adding to the oppressive clamor was the distorted screech of organ music from a wireless Teslaphone, which had been turned up to maximum volume to contend with the sound of the bellows. Jenny went over to the tall wooden cabinet and snapped the Teslaphone off, muttering something Will certainly couldn't hear. Then, going to her sister, Jenny folded the blanket back from Claire's head. Will froze.

For once, Laddie hadn't been exaggerating.

Claire was so deformed by bony protrusions that her form was only vaguely human. Her blackened skin was encrusted with oozing lesions, the most severe of which were swathed in clean white bandages. Her throat was monstrously distorted not only by the ravages of the Black Flu, but by a silver tube that had been surgically inserted into her throat. The tube was connected by a flexible hose to the large bellows that rose and lowered with a mechanical clack and hiss. Her whole body seemed to distend and contract as the bellows worked her lungs for her.

Will knew he shouldn't stare, but he couldn't help it. It wasn't even Claire's deformities that transfixed him. It was her left hand. Somehow, her left hand alone had escaped the ravages of the Black Flu. It was a beautiful hand, absolutely unblemished, neatly manicured, mockingly perfect.

Lifting his eyes, Will realized that Claire was looking at him. Her eyes were sunken and red-rimmed, gummed with thick yellow ooze. Jenny, who had fetched a washcloth and some water from a nearby table, began wiping the crusted matter from her sister's eyes, her movements both tender and matter-of-fact.

"There you are, now you'll be able to see a bit better. Let me get your tapper."

The "tapper," as Jenny called it, was a small self-contained device with a single bakelite key on a lever of brass. No sooner had Jenny positioned Claire's smooth perfect hand over it than her sister began tapping rapidly. A speaker on the device issued a series of loud tones, both long and short. Will recognized it immediately—a Morse machine. Learning the code had been a fad at his school, especially with boys who aspired to a career in the military.

You're back soon, Claire tapped.

"Yes, I wanted to see you," Jenny said. She did not translate for Will, and Will wasn't sure whether it was because she wanted the conversation to remain private, or whether she didn't think it was worth relaying.

Dad with you?

"Not this time."

Who's he?

If Will hadn't known Morse code, he wouldn't have had any idea that they were talking about him; Jenny did not look his way and Claire did not move, except the tiny motions of her finger.

Jenny stood, returning to Will's side to take his arm. He hadn't realized he was standing quite so far back in the room until she pulled him forward. "This is William Edwards. William, this is my sister Claire."

Will nodded to Claire. Claire swiftly tapped:

He needs a new suit.

Jenny smirked, but did not comment. "I've told you about him, haven't I?"

Boy you liked once, yes?

Jenny blushed, but didn't look at Will. "He's an old friend," she said, and released his arm quickly. Will stuffed his hands in his pockets and retreated.

Why are you here?

"To say goodbye." Jenny took a deep breath, straightened. "I'm going away. I'm finally going to do it. I'm going to take care of what we talked about."

There was a long silence, filled only by the noise of the bellows. Finally, Claire tapped one short word.

No.

"Claire, you know I have to at least try. And don't worry, I'm going to make sure that the operation doesn't—"

No.

Will had a strange feeling that Claire would have screamed the word if she could have. Something about the way the bellows revved suddenly, as if reacting to sudden tension in her body.

Jenny sank to her knees before her sister, and spoke very softly.

"Claire, I can do this. I have to do this."

No. Claire tapped again. And again, and again. **No. No. No.**

She was still tapping it when someone entered the room. Jenny stood, turned quickly. She was white as a sheet, Will saw.

"Miss Hansen!" The older woman who had entered the room wore the white coat of a doctor over a neatly tailored skirt. "I didn't think we'd see you back so soon!"

"Good morning, Dr. Smyth," said Jenny, putting all of Miss Murison's haughtiness into the greeting. "Yes, I didn't expect to be back so soon either. But the situation is quite unusual. I have been married, and I have brought my husband with me."

"Husband?" Dr. Smyth blinked. She looked at Will, her eyes appraising him. "Why, your father didn't mention—well! It's a pleasure to meet you, Mr—"

"Edwards," he said. "William Edwards."

"I am Dr. Margaret Smyth, Superintendent of the Hospital. I am also Claire's personal physician."

"My husband and I made a special trip to Stockton to see you. We wish to ask you one more time to reconsider your decision regarding my sister's operation." Jenny gave Will a sidelong glance. "My husband is in agreement with me that the surgery should not proceed. I wanted to make it very clear that it's not just me who objects."

"What surgery?" Will tried to whisper in Jenny's ear, but Jenny nudged him with her elbow and he was silent. Dr. Smyth just shook her head.

"I'm sorry, Miss Ha—I mean, Mrs. Edwards. I am well aware of your concern for your sister, but your father has power of attorney over her affairs. He recognizes that the surgery is our policy, and a condition of her continued treatment at this institution. He has given his approval, and no amount of opposition from yourself—or, I'm afraid, your new husband—can be considered."

Will felt Jenny stiffen beside him. "I know very well that my father has power of attorney, and that he's given his approval," she said, heat creeping into her voice. "But I also know that you have the power to delay the surgery based on medical advice. And that's what I—what *we* are asking you to do."

"Of course I would delay the surgery if I harbored even the slightest concern for Claire's health." Dr. Smyth spoke with officious briskness. "But I do not. The surgery is very simple and straightforward, and it has already been scheduled. There is nothing for you to be worried about."

Jenny drew a deep breath, then leveled a dark gaze on the woman. When she spoke, her voice was sterner and more frightening than Will ever imagined it could be.

"Let me make myself perfectly clear, Dr. Smyth," she said slowly. "The matter is by no means as simple and straightforward as you believe. I am in discussions with the Consortium regarding this matter, and a great many other matters as well. If you proceed with the operation against my wishes, I can promise you that they will be very, *very* disappointed."

Dr. Smyth stared at Jenny for a moment, open-mouthed. She seemed to struggle for words. When she finally did speak, her voice was unsteady.

"Of course," she said. "That ... that is a different matter." She looked between Jenny and Will, and Will was surprised to see there was actual fear in her eyes. "Perhaps there is more to consider than I first thought. Perhaps postponing the operation would be in Claire's best interest. I believe we could wait another six months. But after that, we will have to reassess the situation."

"Thank you for your consideration," said Jenny, icily. Will stared down at her in astonishment. What on earth was she doing? What was this "Consortium" she was talking about? He felt like they were kids again, and Jenny was acting the part of some villain in a melodrama.

No no no no ...

Across the room, Claire was still tapping the word, again and again, a quality of misery in the repetition. Dr. Smyth looked over at her, but there was no sympathy in her eyes.

"What is wrong, Claire?" she called. Claire's finger stopped abruptly, and the speaker on the tapper fell silent.

"I'm afraid you walked in just as my sister and I were in the middle of a disagreement," Jenny said, going back to Claire's side. "We were arguing about the Teslaphone. Personally, I don't like how it's always blaring."

Dr. Smyth raised her eyebrows as she looked at the Teslaphone cabinet. "Oh, someone turned it off?" she said. "That won't do. Brother Phleger is delivering a special sermon this afternoon. Of course all our patients are looking forward to hearing it." She went over and switched the Teslaphone back on. The sound of the screeching organ music had given way to the smooth, oily tones of a preacher:

"This is your Brother Dolphus Phleger, speaking to you from Justice, Illinois, where the New Faith Seat of Praise is being raised in honor of our great Lord's holy name. His will be done!" He blurted this last bit like he was spitting a curse. "You just heard our own little Sanctity Snow—'God's Special Snowflake'—on the all-electrical organ, her playing today inspired by the message of courage and strength I want to deliver to all the valiant souls who will be participating in this Sunday's rally in San Francisco ..."

"We keep our patients' Teslaphones on so they will never miss a word of the Good Brother's teachings," Dr Smyth commented. "And of course, all our patients just love that dear little Sanctity Snow."

Turning from the machine, she inclined her head toward them both. "It was a pleasure to meet you, Mr. Edwards. Congratulations on your marriage, Jenny. I hope you will both be very happy together. Rest assured that Claire will continue to receive the best treatment our institution can provide."

Jenny frowned, pressing her lips together as Dr. Smyth left the room. "All the best treatment!" she blazed, once the doctor was gone. She was stomping over to turn off the Teslaphone—now resounding with Brother Phleger's rich, syrupy baritone—when Claire tapped:

Leave it.

Jenny froze, but did not turn. Brother Phleger was saying something profound and resonant about the moral decay of the United States, and how it was the duty of upright citizens to oppose injustice and tyranny in all its forms.

You two really married?

Jenny still did not turn, but nodded.

Don't do it, Jenny. Please. Too dangerous.

"I have to. You know I do." Jenny ran across the room, pressed a kiss to her sister's blackened, tear-glistening cheek. "I love you, Claire. Goodbye."

Then, grabbing Will's arm, she fled.

She fairly dragged Will along the halls and corridors until they were outside the hospital's tall front doors. Then, sinking down on the front steps, she buried her face in her hands and broke down in tears.

Will was confronted with the age-old masculine conundrum of just what, exactly, one was supposed to do with a crying girl. He had the feeling that taking her in his arms and holding her close might help—but then again, it might not. In the end, he just sat next to her and patted her back softly, uncertain as to whether or not that was sufficient.

Then he remembered probably the only valuable thing his father had ever taught him—always carry a clean handkerchief. Pulling it from his pocket, he handed it to Jenny and she took it gratefully, daubing her eyes then blowing her nose lustily.

"I'm sorry. I wish you hadn't come with me. I thought having you there would make Dr. Smyth more reasonable. She always is when my dad's around. But I still had to threaten her just as much."

"What was that all about?"

"I just bought my sister six more months."

"What was the procedure?"

"It's called a salpingectomy. It is the surgical sterilization of a female human, rendering her incapable of reproduction."

"Sterilize her? You mean like ... gelding a horse?"

"The procedure is just a *tiny* bit different," Jenny said with faint contempt, "but I suppose that's close enough for a rancher's son."

Will drew back in shock. "Why, that's *awful*!"

"It's compulsory for all the patients here. Especially the ones like Claire, the ones they call *magically cretinous.*" She spoke the term with distaste. "Dr. Smyth says it makes patients easier to care for, and removes even the slightest possibility that their contaminated genes could be passed along."

"But surely ... I mean, she never could be a mother, could she?" Will tried to be tactful, but as soon as the words were out of his mouth he wished he could take them back.

"You don't know that for sure!" said Jenny, fiercely. "No one does! And with science and money, who knows what could happen? You made an incredible power source out of a cigar box! How can they say for sure that Claire couldn't be healed someday?"

Will didn't know what to say. He took Jenny's hand in his. Her skin was cold. He held her hand in both of his, rubbing it to warm it.

"Why was Claire so upset, Jenny?" he asked. "Why did she keep saying 'no'?"

Jenny's eyes widened, then became keen and wary." You understood what she was saying?"

Will nodded. "Sorry. I should have said something. I didn't mean to eavesdrop."

"So that's why you jumped out of your skin when she said I liked you." Jenny gave him a wan grin. "*Once* liked you."

"When I could whistle through my teeth," remembered Will. "Why was she so upset, Jenny? What are you going to do?"

Jenny, who had been letting Will hold her hand without demur, now snatched it away. She stood up. Where there had been tears in her eyes, now there was just anger.

"You promised not to ask me about that," she said. "Don't do it again."

Will didn't say anything for a long time. "She said it was dangerous," he said finally.

"You just let me worry about that," said Jenny.

Will took a deep breath. "I need to tell you something," he said. "I got a letter from my brother Ben. I finally read it last night. He wants to help me get to Tesla Industries. He's opened an account for me at the National Bank of Detroit and put money in it. He says it's enough for me to get started on. For *me* to get started on."

Jenny stared at him. She was breathing hard, as if about to launch into a furious tirade, but she said nothing. Will shifted uncomfortably under her piercing gaze.

"Anyway, once I get to Berkeley, and the Dimensional Subway, I'm set." He looked at the handkerchief in Jenny's hand. She was clutching it so hard her knuckles were white. "I don't know what you're thinking of doing. But if you're thinking of doing it because of me, you don't have to. We could get the marriage annulled. Things could go back to the way they were."

"You think I want that?" Jenny whispered.

"I don't know what you want!" said Will, through clenched teeth. "You've made me promise not to ask."

"And you haven't even been able to keep that promise!" She bit the words. "Listen to me, William Edwards. Your plans are *not* the only ones I'm concerned about. You may think I'm just part of your plans. But it's the other way around. You're part of *my* plans, and I need you."

"Well maybe I don't want to be part of your plans, have you thought about that?" Will replied sharply. "Especially when you won't even tell me what they are!"

"I *have* told you!" she said hotly, voice rising. "I want to file your patent. I want to see that your work is protected." Then, in a culmination of pique, she threw the handkerchief at him. "And I want my share of the profit!"

He couldn't help but smile at that. He picked up the handkerchief in two fingers, grimacing at its dampness. "Well then," he said. "We'd better get going. But no more crying, because I only have one handkerchief."

"Unless ... you're trying to ditch me?" she said, and suddenly her voice was small and uncertain. "Are you trying to ditch me, William? Don't you want me to go to Detroit with you?"

"Of course I do!" Will said, jumping to his feet. Then, aware that he'd spoken too quickly, cleared his throat. "I mean, if you want to."

"I do," she said softly.

The sun was sinking swiftly behind Mount Diablo as the California Navigation and Improvement riverboat *H.J. Corcoran* steamed out of Stockton. It was an all-night trip to San Francisco (with many stops along the way to pick up passengers and freight), fifty cents per passenger and a dollar for a sleeping cabin.

Will paid for the cabin, but he knew it would be far too small for both of them to sleep in decently. And it would seem suspicious for a young married couple—who would presumably have no scruples about decency—to buy two. Thus, when the hour got late, Will left Jenny to sleep in the cabin and went down to the hold make himself as comfortable as he could within the Baker's close confines.

Automobiles were common enough now that Will hadn't had any difficulty convincing the stevedores to load Pask's machine on alongside the horse teams. The hold, loaded with produce bound for sale in the San Francisco markets, smelled of San Joaquin River mud and the dray horses' pungent leavings. A chill, low-hanging fog blanketed the dark water, and Will shivered as he wrapped his motoring duster close.

There was no light in the hold, save a low-burning kerosene lamp that swung in a brass gimbal. So Will switched on the Baker's headlamps and went to sit in front of the car. Consulting his wristwatch to ensure that it was past midnight, he pulled Ben's letter out of his pocket. To his astonishment, he discovered that the text had entirely changed.

Dear Will:

First, I've got to tell you something important that I forgot to write in my last letter. The minute Mother figures out you've really gone, she's going to Send for you, and the longer you don't answer the madder she's going to get ... and you know, when she's mad, the Sends hurt worse. So you'd better know what to do about it.

There's no nice way to put this ... you have to be willing to hurt yourself. The only way to really break a Send is with pain. And it can't be just a pinch. It's got to hurt and hurt bad. Stab a pin into your leg, burn a match against your arm, something like that. It will break the Send and give her second thoughts about Sending for you again.

Will absorbed this information, brow wrinkled. What did that mean, "give her second thoughts?" Would breaking the Send hurt Ma'am as much as it hurt him? Will didn't like that thought at all. Ma'am's Sends were annoying, but they weren't worth hurting her for. Shaking his head, he continued to read.

Now that's out of the way, I want to get to the business at hand—and that's telling you the truth—the real truth, as opposed to whatever our parents may have told you. Or, for that matter, what our brothers have told you, for you are no better off trusting any of them than you are trusting Father. He's made each one of them into a perfect little replica of himself. Parts of himself, anyhow.

First of all, I wasn't "sent away." I left when I was thirteen—by mutual agreement. They probably told you I was intractable. I wasn't. I simply wanted something Father didn't want me to want, and as you have discovered, in our family, that's on a par with being a boy who tortures cats or sets barn fires. But I imagine what you're most interested in is why I fought with Father. Because of all the secrets that have been kept from you, I'm sure it's the one that's been kept most carefully.

Here, Will began reading more quickly.

The fight happened just after you were born. Father and Uncle Royce called all of us boys into Father's study. Uncle Royce closed the door and he locked it. I remember Father had you in his arms—he was holding you so gently. You wouldn't imagine it, but he was always very good with babies. Mother wasn't there—she was sleeping, I think. You were a late baby—she was over forty when she had you—and the birth had been very difficult.

Now, it gets a little strange.

Will lifted an eyebrow. As if it wasn't strange already, this story told on a magical sheet of paper, filled with family secrets that he wasn't supposed to know!

It was Uncle Royce who made the bizarre announcement. He said that in order to forestall the possibility of any of us contracting Black Flu, we were all going to be inoculated with Panchrest immediately. That very night.

Can you understand just how bizarre this announcement was, Will? First of all, one doesn't "catch" Black Flu. It's the severest form of magical allergy, but it is no more contagious than hayfever. Also, the very concept of Panchrest inoculation was unheard of at the time. These days, of course, the question of mandatory immunization is a topic of intense national debate—with our own brother Argus making political hay out of his Anti-Immunization stance, which I find ironic in the extreme, given what happened that night. My point is, in 1892, when this happened, there was no talk of using the Panchrest preventatively. There was no discussion of "busting the Mantic Trust" or any such foolishness.

But Uncle Royce told us that we were all to be inoculated that night. Father did not speak, but simply sat behind his desk, five hypodermic syringes lined up before him. One for each of us.

Argus, Laddie, and Nate submitted without protest. And you, of course, could not struggle, for you were only an infant.

When it my turn came, however, I refused. I knew how the Panchrest worked—by irreversibly blocking the magical channels in the human body. Taking the shot would render me incapable of ever practicing magic. And I had been planning a career in magic all my life. I'd never made any secret of it. Little brother, there was nothing I wanted more than to be a warlock.

I could have been one, too—a real one, as powerful as an Old User. There were only two of us boys who could—Argus and me, both of us born before 1878, the year of The Great Change. And as I'd just seen Argus take the shot, at that moment I was the only one left.

Magic has lineages, Will. Sure, Mother was just a hedgewitch, and her magical lineage wasn't especially powerful or distinguished. But it was hers. And it was ours. And it was mine. And Father wanted to take it away from me.

When it became clear that I was going to kick up one holy hell of a fuss, Uncle Royce sent the other boys out of the room. Of course, they all stayed right by the door to listen through the keyhole. So then it was just Father, Uncle Royce, and me. And you, of course.

I told them both to go to hell.

Secretly, I believed Uncle Royce would help me. I know you don't like him, Will. None of the brothers do. But he's always been more like a father to me than Father ever was. And at least he tried to comfort me—unlike our own father, who could only stare at me with the coldest eyes I've ever seen.

Uncle Royce told me he knew people at the Stanton Institute. He promised me that he would find a way for me to study there. But what good would that do me? I kicked and screamed. I fought. I wasn't going to let them take magic away from me. But it was two on one, Will. And they were both strong.

Uncle Royce held me down in a chair. Father gave me the shot.

And that was the end of me.

No more room. I wish I had thought to nick two sheets of stationery from the Sophos' office. Maybe I'll revive the old art of writing crossways lines next time. But for tonight, I guess that's enough.

Your brother always,

Ben

Will sat back, exhaling a gulped breath he hadn't been aware of was holding. It congealed in the cool night air, swirling in the harsh beam of the Baker's headlights.

My God, thought Will. It was monstrous.

How could Father and Uncle Royce have *done* that to him? And then, in all the years that followed, maintain that everything had been Ben's fault?

He could hardly believe it of his father. Father may have never appreciated Will's passion for Otherwhere Engineering—but other than opposing the apprenticeship he'd never done anything to actively thwart it. He'd never done anything to Will like he'd done to Ben—destroying all his hopes with such utter thoroughness. It would be like blinding him and chopping off his hands.

Will folded the letter and carefully returned it to his pocket, letting his hand rest over it for a few moments. Then he crawled into the Baker and turned off the lights.

But he knew there was no way he'd be able to sleep.

Chapter Seven

The Rally

The *H.J. Corcoran* was scheduled to make two stops along the San Francisco wharves—the first at Pier 27 to unload the cargo, and the second at Pier Three to unload passengers. The second stop, at the Ferry Terminal building at the foot of Market Street, would have been more convenient, but Will and Jenny had to get off at the first, because it was the only place where the Baker could be unloaded.

They drove south along the Embarcadero, the piers a hive of activity even before dawn on a Sunday, making their way to Market Street and the financial district where, Will supposed, Jenny's crooked lawyer was to be found. As they drove, Will saw evidence of the catastrophic earthquake and fire that had occurred just four years prior. But the city seemed determined to put the horrible memory behind itself as quickly as possible. Razed blocks sat side-by-side with fresh new construction.

Driving along Market Street was a novel challenge for Will. He'd never driven on such a busy thoroughfare. He had to contend not only with streetcars and horse-drawn carts, but also with barking traffic cops. He was relieved when Jenny directed him to turn off onto Fourth Street and park the machine in an alley.

The Emporium, one of San Francisco's biggest department stores, was just around the corner on Market, and they had a whole bank of pay telephones. Jenny used one of these to call her crooked lawyer at home. Will leaned against the wooden telephone booth, listening as Jenny asked for a Mr. Sawtelle. She briskly assured him that it was a matter of extreme urgency, and that yes, she was aware that it was Sunday, and a day of rest, but that nonetheless, he must come down to his office and meet her immediately.

Hanging up the receiver, Jenny slid open the glass-and-mahogany door and stepped out of the booth. "Mr. Sawtelle wants to finish his breakfast," she informed Will, "but I got him to agree to come down. He'll be here in an hour."

Will would have been happy to get some breakfast himself, but Jenny had other plans for their spare hour—plans involving a ride up the elevator to the second floor of the Emporium, where the ladies' clothing department was housed. Will trailed after her, supremely superfluous, until Jenny parked him on a wooden bench next to a couple of other similarly superfluous husbands. Both men grunted a sympathetic greeting before returning to their conversation. Will stared. The store was already having a Christmas sale! And the store was packed with holiday shoppers apparently unaware of just how ridiculous this was.

"I just hope we can get down to the Presidio in time," said one of the men. "The match gets underway at two-thirty."

The other man consulted his watch. "Pshaw. You got plenty of time."

"Sure, if the rally doesn't jam up all the traffic," the first man fretted. "They're expecting hundreds."

"Church gets out at eleven," the second man noted. "And you know those good church folk, they all want to get home for lunch. I'll lay you a nickel they quickstep it through their speeches at the courthouse, burn their effigy or whatever it is they're going to do, and clear out by one."

"I sure wouldn't mind hanging around and watching," said the first man. "Apparently it's going to be a big hoop-dee-doo!"

Will saw Jenny out of the corner of his eye, darting purposefully through the ladies' department with two shopgirls in tow. Jenny moved with the calm assurance of thorough practice; she had merely to gesture to something and a shopgirl would pick it up and add it to the mounded pile she carried. Finally, she and the shopgirls disappeared into a fitting room. When they emerged, Jenny was wearing a very serious suit of dark grey wool with a black velvet collar that made her look years older than she actually was. But she had not entirely abandoned her commitment to remaining fashionable; the suit's severe effect was softened by a lacy, ruffled shirtwaist of blush pink, and the skirt was of the up-to-the-minute "hobble" variety, with a wide band of black velvet near the hem that restricted her stride to a wibbling mince.

She had also obtained a new hat, even more excessively large than her last. It featured an entire bird's wing in the front, rising up from the brim.

"How about it?" she said, doing a half-turn in front of him. "Do I look like a serious married woman?"

Will was opening his mouth to reply when one of the salesgirls, who had been following Jenny like a baby duckling, marched up and briskly handed him several neatly wrapped parcels (the clothes Jenny had changed out of) as well as an enormous hat-box containing the now clearly disgraced hat she'd worn in to the store. Laid atop the boxes was a neatly penned receipt. When Will saw it, all thoughts of replying to Jenny's question vanished.

"Good lord!"

"Don't worry, I have an account here," Jenny said. "The bills go to Dad."

"How can anyone spend that much on a hat?" he wailed as he followed Jenny out of the department. The two men watched in sympathy as he went.

Emerging from the Emporium, they crossed Market Street, dodging drays and autos alike. Jenny led him about a half block down to O'Farrell, and came to a stop outside of a very grand structure—the Union Trust Building. It looked like a Greek Temple. Will, having expected something quite a bit seedier, was surprised.

"You wait out here," said Jenny. "And keep a lookout."

"Keep a lookout for what?" Will protested. "And what exactly am I supposed to do if whatever it is I'm supposed to be looking out for shows up? Hoot like a barn owl? Throw the hat box at them?"

"Fine, if you won't let me be nice about it, I'll be rude," she said. "You look like a Sacramento Valley bumpkin and I'd be embarrassed to bring you into Mr. Sawtelle's office."

"Bumpkin!" Will would have thrown his hat to the sidewalk in outrage, but his hands were quite full. "Well, I like that! Won't your Mr. Sawtelle want some proof that you have a husband?"

"This is all the proof I need," Jenny said, half-drawing the marriage certificate out of her purse. "Signed and sealed by the county clerk in Stockton." As she tucked the certificate back, Will noticed another envelope in Jenny's purse—heavy, cream-colored, with a professional logo printed on it.

"So you expect me to just stand out here on the sidewalk?"

Jenny sighed. "For heaven's sake, do I have to think of everything?" She pointed across the street to a coffee shop. "Go have a piece of pie. I'll meet you there in a half-hour."

Glad of the chance to lay down his burdens, Will hurried across the street. He was delighted to discover that what had looked to be just a regular old coffee shop was actually an automatic restaurant. He'd heard about these "automats" from his more citified friends at the Polytechnic—all the offerings were arrayed behind tiny glass doors and accessed by deposited nickels. With the loose change in his pocket, he bought not only a slice of pie, but also some coffee and a bowl of oxtail soup. He enjoyed figuring out how the automat worked, peering in through the little cubes to see the waitresses bustling in the kitchen beyond. He was disappointed to discover that the food was not delivered in some more clever way, via chutes or pneumatic tubes or something. He finally sat down and ate his pie, which was fine, but not much compared to his Ma'am's.

He was just finishing the last bite when he became aware of a commotion in the street outside. At first it was hard to separate from the late-breakfast din of the café, but then he recognized the unmistakable sound of brass horns and drums. The jaunty march drew the attention of several of the automat's patrons, and they went to the front window and peered down Market Street.

A parade was coming up the street—and though Will could only see the first few marchers from where he was standing, it seemed like it must be a large one. Traffic down Market Street was grinding to a halt and distant passersby were clogging the sidewalks to watch.

A small brass marching band came first; not any kind of a formal band in uniform, these men wore Sunday suits and hats. There were a few trumpets, a handful of trombones, even a couple of tubas. And one large drum. Instead of bringing up the rear, the drum was right up front, where the marching band conductor would usually be, clearing a path with its thunderous *thud-thud-thud.*

Will stepped out onto the sidewalk, joining dozens of others to get a better look. As the small band passed, Will could better see the hundreds of marchers following them. They were led by a half-dozen matronly ladies—full-figured, stalwart, clad in their best Sunday dresses and huge flowered hats—bearing a wide banner before themselves:

SAN FRANCISCO CHURCHES UNITED FOR
MANDATORY PANCHREST IMMUNIZATION

"They're marching up to the U.S. Courthouse on Seventh," someone in the crowd nearby said. "They're coming from the revival at the new Scharfian Temple. Brother Phleger gave a sermon by Teslaphone this morning, and I hear it was a doozy!"

Most of the marchers waved small American flags, but a few dozen carried neatly lettered signs. Most of these bore the official slogan of the movement—"Immunization Now!"—but a few other variations had been interspersed for variety's sake. Several signs read "Keep America's Children Safe," with America's children (as a class) represented by a picture of "Little Sanctity Snow," the cherubic, white-ringleted musical prodigy whose divinely inspired stylings on the electrical organ accompanied all of Brother Phleger's Teslaphone jeremiads.

Some marchers had the special job of handing out literature to those gathered along the curb to watch. A pamphlet was shoved hastily into Will's hands. It bore the now familiar photo of Little Sanctity Snow, and a coy headline that read "Stamp out the Allergy—*for Good*." Will noticed it also bore the logo of Sanitas Pharmaceutics—the manufacturers of the Panchrest—at the bottom. He shoved the pamphlet into his pocket.

A distinctly different group—younger and more boisterous—followed the first contingent of marchers. At the vanguard of this group walked a handful of sharp-looking young men in business suits, carrying a banner of their own:

LEVEL THE PLAYING FIELD—FAIR IS FAIR!

The signs carried by the young men in this group were much different than the ones which had preceded them. There were no pictures of angelic (and presumably endangered) children. Instead, their signs were painted with cartoons of rich fat old men, lifting magical charms aloft with self-satisfied arrogance. Little stars and swirls around their heads graphically signified their use of magic. Each sign bore the exact same words: "Bust the Magical Trust!"

So these were the representatives of the Malmantic Generation's business class, thought Will. The professional men under the age of thirty who keenly resented the magical advantages—charms and potions to enhance attention, boost financial acumen, extend vitality, charm the tongue for keener negotiations—which were still available to members of an earlier generation. As it was the city's financial district that they were marching through, these young men attracted the crowd's most enthusiastic cheers and whistles.

The young businessmen were followed, at some length, by two very large men, dressed in matching shirts of bright red satin decorated with silver spangles. They were broadly mugging for the crowds, and the other marchers had clearly given them a wide berth so they might command the greatest amount of attention. Between them they carried an effigy of a well-fed man dressed in a politician's suit, swinging from its neck by a noose. Pinned to its shirtfront was a placard: "Argus Edwards, California's *Traitor* to the People."

Will put a hand over his mouth, not sure if he was stifling a gasp of horror or a belly laugh. Criminy, it looked just like Argus! So *that's* what he and Uncle Royce had been sweating their brains over at Thanksgiving. Oh gosh, what he wouldn't give to see his brother's face right now!

"Will!" Someone seized his arm, startling him—but it was just Jenny, her cheeks pink with excitement. Her blue eyes sparkled. "I got the money! Can you believe it, I got it!" Reaching inside her purse, she pulled out a crisp new envelope. She was just opening it to show him the contents when a loud call came from a ways down the sidewalk:

"Jenny?"

Jenny and Will turned at the same time—and at the same time, they gasped.

Standing on the corner at the far end of the block were Argus and Mr. Hansen.

Argus, surrounded by a large number of his political cronies, was clearly taking his responsibility to look stern and disapproving very seriously, so he gave Will little more than a quick glance. But Mr. Hansen's brow furrowed in confusion and he began walking toward them, pushing his way through the dense crowd.

"Jenny?" he called again. "Will?"

"Dad!" squeaked Jenny. "Oh no, how could he—quick, William! We have to get to the car! If he catches us—"

Her words were cut off as Will took Jenny's arm and began pulling her along the sidewalk in the opposite direction.

"William!" she cried, stumbling. The stupid, fashionable hobble skirt made it impossible for her to move any faster than a mincing trot.

Will swore under his breath. Glancing back, he saw that Mr. Hansen had escaped the press of the sidewalk and was running along the curb of Market Street, knowing he'd be able to move faster. Will slowed. He didn't want to run away from Mr. Hansen. It just seemed so ... low.

Jenny sensed his hesitation. "Goddamn it, William! We have got to get out of here—I mean it!"

The panicked urgency in Jenny's voice was like a bucket of ice over his head. His heart raced. Picking her up, he threw her over his shoulder and began to run.

"*Jenny!*" Mr. Hansen's voice was a breathy roar. "Jenny, Will, *please* ... stop!"

Will shouldn't have been able to outrun a turtle—much less a still-powerful father-in-law—with Jenny weighing him down, but he too made a break for Market Street, just as Mr. Hansen had, darting in among the crowd of marchers. Cries of pointed disapproval rang from all sides, but their bodies made an effective screen.

Just off Market Street, Will glimpsed a small alleyway between two of the buildings. Hoping Jenny's father hadn't seen them turn down it, he slid Jenny off his shoulder, and they stood listening as Mr. Hansen called for them. They listened as he continued past them, and kept listening until his calls grew softer.

When they could no longer hear him, they hurried back to the Baker. As the two men in the Emporium had predicted, the march had proceeded with admirable efficiency. The streets had already cleared, and Argus was nowhere to be seen.

Will refrained from saying anything until they were in motion. Then he exploded.

"What the hell, Scuff?" he yelled. "You said he'd understand!"

"I meant *someday*," Jenny yelled back with equal heat. "If he caught us now, before he had a chance to cool off and accept the situation, there'd be hell to pay!" She kept glancing back, as if expecting her father to appear at any moment.

Will jammed the controller forward into the next higher speed. After they had put several blocks behind them, Will looked over at Jenny. She was frowning unhappily, and she looked tiny beneath her huge winged hat.

"They all must have come back to the city early." Her face was closed and dark, and her earlier happiness over her success was gone without a trace. She knew that she had hurt her father, and Will could see that it stung.

"Well, of *course* Argus came back early," muttered Will. "If he got wind that someone was going to hang him in effigy, he wouldn't have missed it for the world."

"Dad will see," said Jenny softly, striking a tightly closed fist against her leg. "I'm going to show him and then he'll understand. He'll understand everything."

Then she didn't say anything else for a long time.

They drove down to the Ferry Terminal Building, where they could catch the ferry that would take them to Oakland, where the Berkeley campus was. Given that Mr. Grigoriyev had said that the Dimensional Subway would take them straight to Detroit, it wasn't worth making arrangements for transporting the Baker. They both agreed (Will more reluctantly than Jenny) that it was time for them to part ways with the crummy old machine.

Using tools from his leather bag, Will carefully removed the Otherwhere Flume and tucked the cigar box safely inside his vest. It was bulky and the corners poked him, but it was safer there than rattling around in his bag of tools. Jenny withdrew her little calf-skin grip from under the seat. In their escape, Will had neglected to retrieve her packages from the automat, but he supposed she didn't dare comment on that.

Even though the Baker was a beat-up old wreck, Will felt a twinge of regret. He and that car had had some fine times. He gave it a last fond pat. Jenny sniffed.

"Honestly," she said. "It's a rotten heap and the one good thing about it you just took out. Which, strictly speaking, I own, since I bought the car."

"Don't push your luck," Will growled, lifting the toolbag and settling it over his shoulder. Leaving the Baker behind made him keenly aware of how little he truly had. His Otherwhere Flume, his toolbag, his cap, the clothes on his back—and an angry father-in-law hot on his heels.

A quick ferry ride to Oakland, followed by a quick streetcar ride, and they were on Berkeley's leafy campus. Will knew the campus layout by heart—before he'd been accepted into the Tesla Industries apprenticeship program, Berkeley had been one of his top choices of colleges. He'd often scrutinized the campus map, noting with special interest the South Hall, which housed one of the very first physics laboratories in the United States.

And even though he was going to Tesla Industries, Will felt no less excited as they entered the ivy-covered building and climbed the polished wooden stairs to the second floor.

Entering the physics lab, Will was reminded of the similar lab he'd worked in at the Polytechnic. Bunsen burners sat atop soapstone work surfaces; cabinets and shelves were crowded with apparatuses, tools, etched reagent bottles. He breathed in the wonderful smell of science—tangy and bitter and profoundly *rational.*

In a far corner of the room a heavyset young man stood hunched over some kind of experimental setup that was emitting random, infrequent clicks. Curious, Will crossed the room to get a closer look. The sound of his steps was swallowed by the soft asphalt floor tiles.

The clicks, Will discovered, were coincident with the flash of a phosphorescent tube and the galvanic jerk of a pen on a scrolling piece of paper. The paper was also being marked at regular intervals by a chronometer. Nearby was a barometer; as the chronometer ticked off a marking, the heavyset young man indicated the barometric pressure reading near to it.

Will was so fascinated that he didn't even look at the young experimenter taking the measurements. The clicking device seemed familiar.

"A Geiger counter!" he blurted, when the recognition finally hit him.

It was only then that the two young men actually looked at each other, and when they did their surprise was compounded.

"William Edwards!" the young experimenter cried.

"Tom!" said Will. There was a round of hearty handshaking and backslapping. "Are you the one everyone calls 'Massy'?"

"Yeah, the fellows gave it to me as a goof." Massy sheepishly patted his belly, which had indeed gained in mass since Will had last seen him. "Too much time in the lab, not enough with the kettle bells."

"Jenny, this is Thomas Masterson," Will said. "He was a senior at the Polytechnic when I was just a raw frosh. He showed me around."

"Pleased to meet you," said Jenny, extending her hand. "I'm Will's wife."

"Wife!" Massy's eyes widened, and he stared at Will. "But you just graduated, didn't you? You move fast!"

"You don't know the half of it," Will said. "I'm on my way to Tesla Industries. I've been accepted into their apprenticeship program."

"You're going to Fort Tesla? With a *wife*?" Massy shook his head, as if he didn't know which fact was more astonishing. "Boy, they must really want you!"

"You know, I'm standing right here," said Jenny, rather sourly. Massy gave her a courtly bow.

"I'm sorry, Mrs. Edwards," he grinned. His eyes traveled over the gear they both carried—Will's toolbag, Jenny's little grip—then back up to them. "So, using my exceptional powers of deduction, I reach the following conclusion. Given that Tesla Industries thinks you're so swell, they've decided to impress you by offering you the use of the Dimensional Subway to get to Detroit. Am I right?"

"On the nose."

"Fine and dandy," Massy said. "Happy to oblige. But you'll have to wait until I take my next reading. I've been taking them every fifteen minutes for the past month—it's been one hell of a job, even with someone relieving me at night."

"What are you recording?" Will asked, peering at the pens on the paper.

"Studying the correlation between cosmic rays and barometric pressure," Massy said. "You know how some researchers think that the Connection Drop Problem is associated with barometric pressure, right? Well, it's my theory that it's not the barometric pressure, but the fact that more cosmic rays get through when the pressure is high. In other words, I'm starting to get the idea that it's the cosmic rays that cause the random connection loss."

"You don't say." Will shoved his hands in his pockets, doing his best to remain casual. He glanced at Jenny, but she was pointedly ignoring the conversation, instead looking out a window onto the smooth green lawn outside the South Hall.

"I certainly do! I've been taking readings for a month now, and the preliminary results are very interesting. I've already decided to do my master's thesis on it."

Will cleared his throat. He looked at his shoes for what seemed quite a long time before an inspiration struck him.

"So how are you accounting for the terrestrial radiation?" he asked.

Massy shrugged. "I'll just factor it out using the Princeton averages."

Will sucked in air through his teeth.

"What?" said Massy, immediately on guard.

"Hell, Tom, I don't like to mention it if you've already been taking readings for a month—"

"What?" Massy roared.

"This building has a granite foundation," said Will. "Noticed it when I came in."

"So?" Annoyance laced the graduate student's voice.

"Haven't you heard about the comparative analysis of granite they did down at Stanford?" Will asked. "They found extremely high radiation in some California granites. Who can say how much radioactivity the granite foundation in this building is giving off?"

"God damn it!" Massy blurted. "Granite? You're saying my whole set of readings might be screwy because of granite?"

"It's not so bad." Will strove to sound soothing. "You just have to figure out the exact level of terrestrial radiation you're dealing with. Do some comparative studies of different granites, that kind of thing."

"That'll add months!"

"Oh well, it's not like you know of anyone else who is working on this," Will said. Then he added, somewhat pointedly: "Do you?"

"No, no one," said Massy. "But still—"

"Then what are you worried about? Take all the time you need. Get your numbers right. It'll make defending your thesis that much easier, right?"

"Yeah, I guess," said Massy. He didn't sound happy about it, but he sounded convinced, and Will exhaled a silent sigh of relief.

After taking his reading, Massy led them out of the laboratory and down the hall. He walked ahead of them both, muttering curses under his breath as he did. Jenny leaned close to Will.

"Good work," she said, elbowing him in the ribs. "You're sneakier than I thought."

"I am *not* sneaky," Will whispered back, hotly. "California granite *is* radioactive."

"Well, thank goodness, because otherwise your Nobel Prize is going to have Thomas Masterson's name on it. Now, I don't like to say I told you so—"

"Then don't."

"Fine. But I will say this. The sooner we get your Flume patented the better!"

Will said nothing, but suddenly felt a strong agreement with her. The thought of anyone else getting credit for the discovery he had made—even Massy, who he liked—was flat out infuriating.

Massy came to a stop at a very simple door, certainly simpler than one would expect for what lay behind it. It actually appeared to be a broom closet that had been retrofitted for its special purpose. On the door some wag had tacked up a sign printed by New York City's Transit Commission, warning travelers against swearing and spitting. On a hook screwed into the wooden doorframe hung a clipboard; it held a sheet to record the Subway's use. Using a stub of pencil tied to the board by a piece of dirty string, Massy quickly wrote down their names. Then, pulling out a key he wore around his neck, he unlocked the large wooden cupboard on the wall.

Within the cupboard was a tangle of wires. Will could see glass fuses as well as a board of numbered wheel dials and a very large knife switch. A list of locations was thumbtacked to the inside of the cupboard door. Massy peered at this list, running his finger down it until he found the numerical code for Detroit. He carefully set the dials, then threw up the knife switch. There was a low hum, and the door ... *smudged.* It didn't shimmer, or glow, it just seemed to lose focus. Will blinked to make sure it wasn't his eyes, but it wasn't.

Fascinated, Will rubbernecked over Massy's shoulder into the open cupboard. Even a glimpse of the arrangement of the wiring board might help him understand how it all worked. It was a piece of Tesla Industries technology that was still extremely experimental, and they had never published any information about how it actually worked. But Massy quickly closed the cupboard and locked it.

"Now, it's really quite easy," he said. "You just walk through this door, and you'll be in the Otherwhere. In front of you, you'll see another door. The distance to the second door is proportionate to the actual physical distance between here and the place you're going, so I'd say that makes it ... oh, about fifty feet. So you walk that fifty feet to the second door, you open it, and you'll be in Detroit."

"And it's not going to make us sick?" said Jenny. The brisk, businesslike tone in her voice told Will she was scared.

"That's the whole point, there's no magic in it," Massy said. "Not a bit. It's powered by electricity. It goes through an Otherwhere where the wind never stops, so they've rigged up a whole bunch of windmills to generate electrical power."

"And what about that Connection Drop Problem everyone's always talking about?" Jenny said. "What if that happens while we're in there?"

"Unlikely," Massy said, stroking his chin. "If it did, you might get stuck in there. But someone would get around to resetting the system. Eventually."

Jenny looked at Will with naked alarm on her face.

"Never fear, Mrs. Edwards," Massy chuckled. "You have a greater chance of getting struck by lightning."

"Are you referring to the probability in a given year, or over a whole lifetime?" she snapped at him. "Because I will have you know they are orders of magnitude apart!"

Massy was taken aback by this outburst.

Will put a steadying hand on Jenny's arm. "Actually, it's probably more on the order of me personally getting hit by a meteorite within the next fifteen minutes," he offered. Jenny's eyes turned inward, and he could almost see the calculations flickering behind her eyes as she factored in a multitude of estimated variables, including the area of the Earth's surface, the density of human habitation, the size of Will's head ...

"About one in twenty-trillion," she concluded with a sigh, after just a few seconds. "That's much better."

Massy was silent for a long moment, looking between them. Then he released a whistle of admiration. Will felt a strange thrill of pride at having a wife—even a fictional one—who could be calmed by mathematical analysis.

"I guess I can see why you married her!" said Massy. "If Tesla Industries wasn't men only, they might take you both."

Jenny frowned at him, chin lifted regally "I'd say thanks for the compliment, except I can't see how either one of those statements qualified."

"All right, all right," Massy said, throwing up his hands. Catching a glimpse of his wristwatch, he startled. "Hey, I got to get back and take my reading! Get on through, you two. And whatever you do, don't stop in the middle." He directed this advice at Will particularly. "Don't you dare go Otherwhere exploring. You get lost in there, and no one's going to come in and find you."

Readjusting the satchel on his shoulder, Will took Jenny's hand and opened the door.

"Oh yeah, and watch out for Jepson! He's a no-good son-of-a—" But the rest of Massy's words were lost as Will closed the door behind them.

All at once they were in a hot, arid desert under a bright burgundy-colored sky that roiled with clouds the color of pomegranate juice.

Powerful winds assaulted them. The force of the gusts plastered Jenny's skirts against her legs and she had to seize her hat with both hands to keep it from being flung into the distance. Will squinted against the clouds of red dust that the wind kicked up. The windmills Massy had mentioned were clustered around the portal at intermittent distances, tall and black and stark, blades whirling like electric table fans.

The second door was, as Massy had said, about fifty feet distant. Like the door they had just come through, it looked like it belonged to the inside of a broom closet. Jenny grabbed Will's arm and pulled him toward it.

"Come on!" she yelled, above the howling wind.

But Will could not move. He was frozen with awe. He was in an actual Otherwhere. An entirely different dimension. He could hardly believe it. He scanned the horizon, trying to freeze the wonder of it in his memory.

But then the Flume tucked inside his vest began making a strange sound—a high-pitched hum. He slapped a hand to his chest. The cigar box was getting warm. Hot actually. Very, very hot—very, very quickly. The hum became a squeal, loud and piercing. Then a screech. Will's heart began to race. Leaping forward, Will dragged Jenny to the opposite door, threw it open, and pushed her through.

Chapter Eight
Detroit

Slamming the door behind him, Will stumbled across the polished floor of a dark and quiet room. He fell against the far wall, toolbag clattering on the floor at his side. There was the smell of burning wire and rubber; Will clawed at his chest, frantically reaching inside his vest to pull out the cigar box. Once he got it out he dropped it; it was hot as hell, smoking and sputtering. When he opened the lid, blue sparks leaped out, followed by little orange tongues of flame. Pulling his handkerchief out of his pocket he slapped desperately at the mechanism until the fire was out, then peered disconsolately inside the box.

"Damn," he muttered.

"What happened?" Jenny breathed, alarmed. She was caked with fine red dust from hat to hem.

"I have no idea. I think—something to do with Critical Interactive Resonance, maybe?" His mind was already navigating the tangle of melted wires, trying to imagine what could have happened, and what he'd have to do to fix it ... *if* he could fix it. "Never even thought about what might happen if I took the Flume into a different Otherwhere ..."

"Well, it is clear you are thinking about it now," Jenny said loudly, trying to break through his absorbed concentration. "Please, share."

Taking a deep breath, Will turned his gaze away from the ruined Flume and onto her dust-streaked face.

"Every Otherwhere, being a different dimension, has slightly different laws of physics from our standard universe." He spoke slowly, thinking through the problem as he did, drawing conclusions with every word. "The Otherwheres we use are compatible enough with ours to allow us to exist within them. But the physical incompatibility between Otherwheres can be quite substantial. Substantial enough that if you bring two of the wrong ones into contact with each other—"

"I'm guessing you're about to say *boom*."

Will frowned. "Not *boom*, exactly. More like *schloop*, as the two Otherwheres collapse in on each other. Then maybe *boom* after that. I don't think anyone would live long enough to find out."

"Oh, *wonderful*." Angrily, Jenny began brushing red dust off of herself. "Not only is my lovely new suit simply *ruined*, but I almost got *schlooped* in an Otherwhere. So much better than taking the train." She looked at the cigar box in Will's hands. "Can it be fixed?"

Will released a long sigh.

"No." He ran a glum finger over Admiral Dewey's scorched face. "It's ruined. I'll have to build a whole new one from scratch."

Jenny's face lit up with rather more happiness than Will thought was appropriate. He glared at her as he climbed to his feet, tucking the ruined Flume back inside his vest. "What are you smiling about?"

"Don't you see?" she said. "This takes care of all your problems with Tesla Industries! They wanted you to show them your Flume ... and now you can't! It burned up! You'll have to build a new one from scratch, and that will take weeks."

"It'll take a couple of days."

"It will take *weeks*," Jenny repeated, with emphasis. "Or to be more precise, it'll take as long as it takes for me to file your patent. So you can stay in Tesla's good books and still not get robbed blind. Problem solved!"

Will considered this. He shook his head.

"You think like a criminal, Scuff," he said finally.

"I think like a *businesswoman*," said Jenny. "There's a difference. Now, where exactly do you think we are, anyway?"

The answer to that was simple enough; they were in a classroom filled with desks. One wall was lined with high windows, through which they could see the dark night sky. The sun had just been setting when they'd left California—so here was one clear indication that they'd emerged, as expected, many hundreds of miles to the east.

Another wall of the classroom was dominated by a large chalkboard, scribbled from edge to edge with complicated equations. Glancing over them, Jenny could not keep from rubbing out an incorrect variable and replacing it with another.

"Show off," said Will. Jenny stuck her tongue out at him.

Passing into the hall, their impression that they were in some kind of school or university grew stronger. The classrooms were numbered, and banks of wooden lockers lined the walls. Given the late hour, the building was completely abandoned and quiet, and their steps rang on the linoleum floors as they set off in search of an exit.

"Hey!" A yell rang from the far end of the hall. "You kids! What are you doing in here?"

A janitor in well-worn overalls was approaching them, an old man with an extravagantly bushy walrus moustache. He wielded his pushbroom like a weapon, eyeing the trail of red dust they'd both left.

"What the hell do you think you're doing? Look at this mess! You think I'm just here to clean up after slobs like you?"

"Well, you *are* the janitor," Jenny pointed out.

"We just came through from California, along the Dimensional Subway," Will quickly interjected. "Sorry about the mess."

"I may be the janitor"—the man pointed the words at Jenny—"but that don't mean I get paid to do my job twice. I already cleaned up this wing and I don't mean to do it again!"

"Clearly, a man who takes pride in his work," Jenny muttered. Will stepped on her foot.

"Sir, I'm supposed to meet Grigory Grigoriyev," he said. "Is this Tesla Industries?"

The old man's eyes widened, and then he barked an incredulous laugh that resounded through the silent halls.

"As if the *great master* would allow a Dimensional Subway inside Fort Tesla!" he sneered. "Boy, you don't know much about Tesla Industries, do you?"

"I hope to learn more soon," said Will. "I've been accepted as an apprentice there."

"Ah." The old man drew out the word, as if suddenly understanding something. "That explains it. You're an awful lot younger than most of the apprentices. And what are you doing, bringing a girl with you?"

"You know, it gets awful tiresome, being referred to like a poodle," Jenny said, crisply.

"A mouthy girl, too," added the janitor. "What is she, a suffragette or something?"

Will put a hand on Jenny's arm. "This is my wife." The conversation was not only becoming too familiar, the kindling flame in Jenny's eyes suggested it might imminently come to blows. "Could you just tell us where we are, and how to get to Tesla Industries?"

"You're in the Detroit Institute of Technology," the old man said. "Just because that hincty Russian is a pal of the dean here, he thinks he can give people free use of the place." He pushed his broom emphatically through the dust Will and Jenny had trailed. "Make extra work for other people is what he does. Vagrants popping in and out at all hours. I don't get paid to welcome guests, not even ones all the way from *California*."

"Oh, for heaven's sake," said Jenny, digging in her purse. She pressed a coin into the man's hand. "There. Now you *have* been paid. Can you please tell us what time it is, and how we can get ahold of Mr. Grigoriyev, or, failing that, how we can get to Tesla Industries? In fact, can you provide us with any useful information? Or are you only capable of regaling us with your complaints?"

The janitor looked at the coin. With a deliberate gesture, he lifted it to his mouth and bit it. Then he tucked it slowly into his pocket. When he spoke, he addressed his answer to Will, as if Jenny didn't exist.

"It's getting on eleven," he said. "You could try dialing Grigoriyev up, but I expect the switchboard at Tesla Industries is closed for the night."

"We'll call him tomorrow," said Will. "In the meantime, can you direct us someplace nearby where we can stay the night?"

"*Sure* I can." The old man smiled pleasantly in an unpleasant way. "You just go out those doors over there, walk along Adams until you get to Brush. Go down Brush a few blocks. You'll find a swell hotel just across the street from the Michigan Central Depot. The Hotel Acheron. Tell 'em I sent you."

Touching his cap to the surly janitor, Will hurried Jenny out of the building.

Walking out onto the night street, they were surprised to find that it wasn't dark. The streets were lit with a high, harsh light that made the shadows of the buildings seem even darker, and gave the street a strange, unreal feeling, sharp and contrasty, as if they had stepped into a silver nitrate photographic print.

"The moon isn't full, is it?" said Jenny, puzzled.

Will shook his head, and pointed up the street toward a very tall, slender scaffold, supported on all four corners by steel guy wires. "Those must be moonlight towers. I've read about them—they're how Detroit lights their streets. Up at the top is an array of electric arc bulbs, so bright you're supposed to be able to read your watch by them at midnight." He gazed at his wrist to confirm the report. Jenny took his arm and pressed up against him.

"I wish they'd thought to install heat lamps instead," she said. And indeed, once Will's interest in the moonlight towers waned, he noticed just how bitterly cold it was. Soot-grimed snow was piled up in the gutters, and a biting wind sliced them both to the bone.

"I always wondered why women made such a fuss about furs," Jenny said through chattering teeth. "What I wouldn't give for a mink or a sable right now!"

Cold as it was, when they got to the Hotel Acheron they both hesitated before going in. Surrounded by seedy saloons, it fulfilled every qualification of the worst kind of flophouse, clearly catering to traveling salesmen and their hangers-on.

"Maybe it's not so bad," said Will, shivering. "It's probably nicer on the inside."

Unfortunately, it was worse. The walls of the lobby were stained with old damp and the room smelled of mold and urine and harsh tobacco shake. Jenny stood in the very middle of the lobby, as if unwilling to get too close to any of the greasy-looking walls, as Will went to speak to the night-man.

The night-man was gaunt, his rat-like features deformed by what must have been a protracted childhood bout with Black Flu. The entire left side of his head, from eyeball to ear, was engulfed in a coal-black mass of protuberant cauliflower-textured flesh, shiny and moist-looking.

"By the hour or by the night?" He did not even look at Will, but rather leered at Jenny. His left eye—sunken like a dull ochre bead within the massive doughy growth—glittered suggestively. Pulling silver from his pocket, Will slapped it down on the counter, hard.

Laughing softly, the night-man pulled himself painfully from his chair—he also wore a heavy leg brace supporting a twisted, misshapen leg—and retrieved a room key from the pegboard behind him.

The room they were given was on the third floor, and reaching it required navigating not one but two puddles of fresh vomit. The room had peeling wallpaper with a pattern that suggested leering demonic faces; a swayback bed with a rusted iron frame; and a window that opened onto a brick wall. It was lit by a single, weak electric bulb, and there was a small, disgustingly filthy handsink in the corner. Will didn't want to say anything to Jenny, but he would bet that the grim parade of down-on-their-luck men who'd occupied this room before them had used that sink for very specific purposes that had nothing to do with the washing of hands. The room was freezing—if possible, it seemed almost colder inside the room than it had been out on the street. Will discovered that the radiator was cold to the touch; someone had turned off the valve. He turned it on and was greeted by the welcome hiss of steam.

"It'll warm up soon," he said, glad to find one note of comfort in the otherwise cheerless room.

"At least there's a b-blanket," she chattered, climbing into the bed without even bothering to take off her shoes. "Only one though." She eyed Will with some hesitation. Her next words were colored with false bravado. "Well, I suppose there's nothing else to do. Come on, pile in!"

When he lifted an eyebrow at this, Jenny made a noise of exasperation. "I can't let you freeze to death, can I? And we've both got all our clothes on." Making her face grave, she crossed her heart with her index finger. "William, I promise I won't take advantage of you."

Without a word, Will climbed into bed beside Jenny and wrapped a corner of the blanket around himself.

"I say, this isn't a bit like California, is it?" said Jenny, as they shivered against each other.

"Not at all," he said. "Thank God."

Opening her purse, which she had kept clutched close to herself, she withdrew the envelope she had gotten in San Francisco. He wasn't sure if she was doing this for his benefit, or if she just wanted to confirm that she still possessed their ill-gotten gain. He watched as she pulled out ten pieces of paper. Each one was a gold certificate. Each gold certificate bore a face value of $10,000.

Will's heart leapt into his throat, and it took some doing to choke it back down.

"Jenny ..." he finally managed. "Jenny, that's ... that's ... a *hundred thousand dollars*."

Jenny nodded.

Will sat up straight. If his marrow wasn't chilled before, it sure as heck was now. "You've been walking around with a hundred thousand dollars in gold certificates in your purse?" He clapped a hand over his mouth, wishing he hadn't spoken the words aloud.

"You're right, it would be an awful shame if some random purse snatcher got ahold of them." She placed the certificates back in their envelope, then, instead of returning the envelope to her purse, she slid it down the front of her dress. She patted her bosom. "There. Better."

"Better?" Will squeaked. "You don't thwart purse snatchers by inviting rapists, Jenny!"

She laughed softly. "There are a lot more random purse snatchers than random rapists, my sweet darling William. And besides, I've got you to protect me from them."

Will stared at her, speechless once again.

"Sleep tight," she said, leaning over to press a kiss on his cheek. She recoiled abruptly, with a frown. "Oh! You're so bristly. I wish you'd at least brought a razor."

Then Jenny cuddled up under his arm and pulled the blanket tightly around herself. She fell asleep immediately, her face relaxing into an expression so placid that Will found it almost unholy.

He leaned his head back against the bed frame and stared at the grimy orange bulb hanging from the cracked ceiling. Under other circumstances, finding himself cozied up in a bed with a warm, beautiful girl would have significantly discomfited him—especially since the couple in the next room had begun noisily rattling their rented bedsprings and he could hear every particular of their exertions through the thin walls. But all he had to do was imagine what any of the low-lives in this hotel would do if they knew that a couple of kids from California were carrying around $100,000 worth of gold certificates—cash-on-demand, payable-to-the-bearer, no-questions-asked gold certificates. Gee, that was as good as a cold shower and then some!

Suddenly, Will wished he *had* thought to bring a razor, but not for shaving.

Knowing that he wouldn't be able to sleep a wink with all those gold certificates stuffed down Jenny's dress, he pulled the letter from Ben out of his pocket. Glancing at his wristwatch to check the time, he was somewhat disoriented when he found that it was just after ten ... but then he remembered that meant it was ten in *California*. He was in Detroit. Removing his watch, he carefully set it forward by three hours.

Then, he unfolded the letter, wondering idly if the Sophos' magical letterhead reckoned midnight on Eastern or Pacific time. It must have some mechanism for adjusting, he decided, for he found that the words on the paper were new.

Dear Will:

You know, writing you these letters is very odd, because each time I feel like I have to go farther back in the past to explain the previous letter. In the last letter I told you about the fight I had with Father, and why I went away. But then I realized that, to really understand why that happened, you have to understand Catherine.

Of course, you know that you had a sister, and she died of Black Flu eight years before you were born. You probably have some idea how hard Mother took it—but you don't know, not really. Because you were the one who pulled her out of it. You being born allowed her to live again. You gave her back her sanity.

Anyway, Catherine. I was six years old when Catherine came and went.

Before Catherine, I had a mother, and she loved me. She was the first one who taught me magic. She showed me all sorts of wonderful little tricks—a child's magic. She taught me silly things—how to turn the down of a baby chick bright blue, how to make a flower bloom with a touch.

Oh Will, I loved her so much. I thought she made the moon rise and set. For six years, I had a mother. But after Catherine, she was gone, and I would never have her again.

It is believed that the children who die most quickly from Black Flu are those with the greatest inborn magical powers. Catherine died within three days of being born, the allergic reaction tearing through her like wildfire. It is possible that she was magically afflicted, for it all happened during a full moon, which surely made matters worse. Magical afflictions are at their worst during a full moon.

I can't tell you how horrible it was. I remember looking into her crib and seeing her tiny, black, disfigured hands grasping for something, clutching. I was afraid of her, Will. I was afraid that she would try to grab me and hold onto me like a tick or leech. That's what she looked like. A fat black grub. Something that would get under your skin and burrow. Even to this day, remembering her makes me sick. That's an awful thing to think about your baby sister. I've never told it to anyone until now. I certainly never told it to Mother, but she knew. She always knew what we thought in our heads, Will. And that's what made her start to hate me. She hated me for the way I felt about Catherine.

And she stopped looking at me.

Do you know what I mean when I say that? You probably don't. I doubt she ever punished you like that. You were her joy, her life, her sun. But believe me when I say, it was the worst punishment she could ever give, worse than any whipping. After Catherine, she fed me, and put me in clothes, but she never looked at me again. In her mind, I was erased.

Of course, it wasn't just me. Everyone in the family suffered. Mother completely surrendered to misery and grief. She drank, Will, did they ever tell you that? She drank, she raged, she was violent. Witches are terrifying when they go mad. Have you ever seen her when her eyes go all black? It was all Father could do, taking care of her, and even he didn't always manage. Someday, when this is all over, ask him what really happened to his leg. They probably told you it was a fall from a horse. It wasn't.

That was about the time when Uncle Royce started staying long weekends at the house to help with us boys, and help Father. The other boys resented him coming in, because they'd all figured out how to shift for themselves, in their own ways. Argus has always had a soft spot for Laddie, and will always keep him under his wing. Nate has always felt more brotherhood for horses than humans. But no one wanted anything to do with me. No one except Uncle Royce. He thought I was worth paying attention to. I don't blame him at all for what happened. I would lay down my life for him to this day.

I am very sorry for the tiny writing.

Your brother always,

Ben

Will wasn't aware that he'd fallen asleep until he woke in a blank panic, from a bad dream he could not remember. His first impulse was to feel for the gold certificates to make sure they were safe. Then he remembered they were down the front of Jenny's dress. Damn it, he wished she'd never even shown them to him!

Throwing off the thin blanket, he climbed out of bed. Whatever the dream had been about, it had left him antsy and profoundly uneasy. The steam radiator had heated up and then some; the small room was now hot as a Turkish bathhouse, and the damp heat had caused a decade of unpleasant odors to ooze from the walls. He loosened his collar, sweating. Going to the door, he rattled the knob, reassured himself that it was securely locked. He paced under the grimy orange light of the single bulb. The night was dead still. He was surprised at how quiet it was. Even in the middle of California there was always *some* sound filtering in—but here they were in the heart of a huge city, with a train station right across the street, and the silence was so perfect it almost hummed.

He paused by the side of the bed and looked down at Jenny. She was sleeping peacefully, her face soft and lovely. That one curl, the one that always escaped from her pins, curved across her cheek. He was reaching down to gently put it back in place when pain, sudden and sharp, bent him double. He clutched at his head as nausea knifed through him.

William Wordsworth Edwards!

Will staggered back from the bed, moaning involuntarily.

It was Ma'am. Sending for him.

The amount of pain associated with one of Ma'am's Sends was directly related to how mad she was. And boy, was she ever *mad*.

What on earth do you think you're doing?

Each needle of pain that flared inside his head was associated with strange visions: fires, earthquakes, tornadoes. Monstrously destructive forces of nature. Will cringed at the force of magic flowing through his mind.

What have you gotten that sweet Jenny Hansen into? Where have the two of you gone? If you've laid a finger on her, boy, I will murder you!

Will gritted his teeth and tried to hold his mind closed against the onslaught. He breathed deeply and steadily. He knew that while the magic was very painful, there wasn't as much force behind it as it seemed. Ma'am would never use enough magic to cause real damage. This was a beating with a wooden spoon, intended to frighten more than harm.

Pask de la Guerra tried to cover for you, but he told us everything in the end. Where did you get the money to buy his car? It didn't come from your father's cash, so where?

Trying to block his mother's keening inquisition from his mind was like trying to plug his ears against the sound of a bandsaw.

Mr. Hansen cabled us about your appaling behavior in San Francisco. He said you picked up Jenny and ran away from him! Can you imagine what he thinks?

So the cat was out of the bag. Or rather, the cat was in the bag, along with a whole bunch of other angry cats. Will had known that he was going to have to face the consequences of their elopement, but somehow he'd hoped they might take a little longer in arriving.

Where are you?

The question was blasted with more force than anything that had come before it, and it almost compelled Will to scream the answer aloud.

Don't think about Detroit, he commanded himself. Then he realized that he was thinking about Detroit. God, he hoped it wouldn't leak through to Ma'am.

I expect you're on your way to Detroit.

Will muttered a curse, but then realized it hardly required mind-reading to guess his destination. And his family would follow him—and even if they didn't care about getting him back, they would care about getting Jenny. Their only hope was to get to Tesla Industries, hide behind the company's powerful veil of secrecy. That's what Ben had advised him, Will remembered. Ben had said it was his only hope.

Young man, I hope you realize that your father and I—not to mention Mr. Hansen!—aren't just going to take this kind of foolishness lying down!

Suddenly, Will remembered something else Ben had written.

You've got to be willing to hurt yourself.

Will staggered over to the steam radiator. He held Ben's words in his head like a shield against Ma'am's keening.

It's got to hurt and hurt bad.

If you don't contact us immediately and tell us that you're bringing Jenny home ...

Steam at atmospheric pressure was 212 degrees Fahrenheit. Will remembered this random fact as he pressed his forearm against the hot steel. Tears sprung to his eyes as fresh pain, stronger pain, surged through him.

And, miraculously, the screeching in his head subsided almost instantaneously. It vanished with a whimper, like a barking dog squirted with a hose.

Exhausted, Will sat on the floor, cradling his burnt arm. He wondered if he'd hurt Ma'am. He didn't want to. He just wanted her to stop shrieking at him.

Suddenly, he felt angry. He and Jenny had every right to do what they'd done. It was Jenny's money, and she got to decide what she wanted to do with it! And he got to make choices about his life too, just like Ben had said in his letter.

Still cradling his arm, he crawled back into bed next to Jenny. He breathed in her smell of long-ago hyacinth soap, new wool, gritty red Otherwhere dust.

"We've made it to Detroit," he murmured to her, closing his eyes. He knew she wouldn't hear. Maybe he said it for his own benefit. "I don't know what you're planning, and I don't want to know. You get to make your own choices just like I get to make mine. That's what Detroit means. It's like what you told me about that silver dollar. It's more than just what it is. And we're here."

Finally, arm aching, Will fell asleep.

Chapter Nine

Signed in Blood

The next morning, a firm knock on the door startled Will from a deep sleep. Dislodging his arm from beneath Jenny's head, he noticed she'd drooled all over his sleeve. The honeymoon was over, he thought blearily. He'd sure gotten the short end of that stick.

The knock came at the door again, louder, and Will stumbled across the room. Before opening the door, he rolled his not-drooled-on sleeve down over the arm he had burned the night before; the place where he'd pressed it against the hot radiator was shiny red, edged with small blisters.

Waiting on the doorstep was a strange disheveled man. He was in his mid-fifties, Will guessed, with thick, wild, uncombed hair and an air of notable distraction, as if there was something just outside his field of vision that he was desperately trying to see. But his clothes, despite being untidy, looked well-made and expensive; he did not seem to be one of the hotel's seedy traveling salesmen.

"Can I help you?" Will asked, rubbing his eyes.

"I'm Grigory Grigoriyev," the man announced in a very loud voice. He had a pronounced Russian accent, yet he clearly strove to speak with precision. "You can call me Grig, everyone else does. I have come to collect you and your ... wife." He said "wife" with special emphasis.

"Oh! Mr. Grigoriyev! I mean ... Grig." Will stood up straighter and attempted to look respectable. "I'm sorry! I ... I wasn't expecting you."

"I asked for you specially, you know!" said Grig, sounding oddly put out.

"Yes, I know," said Will. "Mr. Waters told me."

"Waters is a good man." Grig spoke with great intensity, as if his pronouncement on the character of Will's mentor at the Polytechnic was to be the last statement he would ever make on the subject. He looked past Will, frowning. "Is your wife in there?"

"Yes," Will said. "But she's not awake yet." Then, aware that the conversation had proceeded quite a ways without an answer to the obvious question, "And if you don't mind my asking, how did you find us here, anyway?"

"*Jepson* told me," Grig spat the name with venom. "That lazy good-for-nothing janitor who sent you here. He's always sending people here who don't know any better. The owner buys him beer for his trouble. But it's not *his* trouble. It's the trouble of the people who have to stay here. This place is not clean. It is the kind of place one goes when one does not want other people to hear screaming."

Will wasn't quite sure what to say to that disturbing description. He chose a safe route. "I would appreciate any assistance you could give us in finding a better place, sir. We're very anxious to get settled, and I'm very anxious to get started."

"We have taken care of all of that," said Grig. "You, of course, cannot live in the dormitory on the compound, as would otherwise be customary. So we have obtained an apartment for you and your wife. It is a good place near where you will be working. Very clean. It is the same building I, myself, live in, so we will be able to walk together. We have seen to every particular. Mr. Tesla won't stand for anything else."

Will was relieved. "All right," he said, happy for once to place his fate in someone else's capable hands.

"I will wait for you and your wife downstairs," Grig said, attempting one last time to look past Will into the hotel room. "I will drive you both over. Please don't be long."

Will closed the door and found that Jenny was awake.

"Who was that?"

"That was my mentor, Mr. Grigoriyev," said Will. "Except I'm just supposed to call him Grig. The janitor told him we were here. He's waiting to give us a ride to our new apartment."

Jenny's shoulders slumped in relief. "If I never see this place again it will be too soon," she said, with a shiver.

Grig waited for them in front of the hotel, leaning against a handsome burgundy-colored Atlas Model H, staring up at the building as if it were personally offensive to him. As Will and Jenny emerged, he turned his scrutiny on them, paying particular attention to Jenny. They must have made a strange looking pair: Will with his lumpy toolbag and ill-fitting suit and Jenny in her modish new outfit still caked with red Otherwhere dust.

In the bright light of morning, their motoring dusters were just as insufficient against the winter chill as they had been the night before. Grig, who was wearing a heavy woolen overcoat, helped Jenny into the back seat and, with pronounced chivalry, arranged a motoring blanket over her lap. He then gestured for Will to get into the front seat as he climbed into the driver's seat on the right. It was a gasoline machine, so Will was rather surprised that Grig hadn't left it running; he'd have to go around to the front and crank-start the car, never an enjoyable task. But Grig did not. He just toggled a switch, and the car engine cranked and roared to life.

"Hey, an electric starter!" Will exclaimed. "Nifty!"

"Child's play," Grig sniffed. "And yet the automobile manufacturers around here want nothing to do with it! Henry Ford especially. He has a significant lack of imagination." He steered the car away from the curb, adding: "We have had some gratifying interest from the men at Cadillac, however."

The streets of Detroit were made of tightly laid red brick, bright and cold and clean. The main thoroughfares were immaculately kept, with snow and manure piled along the gutters for later removal. Grig turned the car up Woodward, and as they passed the famous Campus Martius and the grand City Hall, he noted their existence with bland indifference. Clearly, he considered this the extent of his duties to provide a civic welcome, for he offered nothing more. They turned onto a broad causeway that ran northwest with ruler-straight precision. Will caught a sign, held the words in his mind: *Grand River Avenue.*

Grand River Avenue was the widest street he'd ever seen, much less ridden on, with two lanes of traffic in each direction and street-cars clank-clanging down the middle. The bulk of the traffic lumbered along slowly—heavy, horse-drawn wagons that kept to the side. But it was the automobiles—dozens upon dozens, more common here than anywhere Will had ever seen—that gave the avenue its air of hectic modernity.

Grig did not speak again until after they had been driving for quite some time, and then it was to comment apologetically: "The Compound is rather a ways from downtown, I'm afraid." But even though they drove and drove—a mile, two miles from the city's downtown core, the urban congestion hardly thinned. And Will didn't notice the distance, or even Grig's comment on it; there was so much to take in. He'd thought Stockton, California's hub of manufacture and commerce was impressive—but Detroit!

About three miles up Grand River Avenue, they turned onto a narrow side street lined with newly built homes. Grig brought the automobile to a stop before a building that bore a small brass sign that read "Winslow Street Apartments." It was a new building, so new that its white stone walls had not yet become grimed with factory smoke.

The tiled apartment entryway was neat as a pin. Grig led them into a common sitting room, which was decorated with a few brightly colored religious icons. A small window garden of care-fully tended geraniums and flowering winter cactuses ornamented the bay sill.

A woman was waiting for them there. She was small and spruce, with a smooth unreadable face. Across her lap was spread a knitting project of inexpressible complexity.

"I have brought them, Mrs. Kosanovic!" Grig announced in a loud voice, as if reporting a military victory.

Mrs. Kosanovic carefully laid her knitting aside—all fifty needles and eighty-five skeins of it—and rose with regal slowness. She shook Will's hand gravely, and inclined her head in Jenny's direction.

"We are pleased to have you," she said, her voice tinged with an accent similar to Grig's. But it was clear that Grig did not intend the greeting to be an extended one, as he glanced impatiently at his pocket watch and made a noise of extreme discontent.

"Ten already! For heaven's sake, this will not do! We must go, Mr. Edwards. Your wife and Mrs. Kosanovic can see to the details of the apartment. Come!"

Jenny hopped up to kiss Will goodbye, the very picture of an attentive new wife. But as she straightened his tie, her true intentions were made clear. "They're going to ask about the Flume," she whispered low in his ear. "Remember—two weeks to rebuild it, at the very least! Understand? You made me a promise!"

"Promise," said Will, taking advantage of the ruse to give Jenny a peck on the cheek. She blushed as she turned away.

"He must have a coat," Mrs. Kosanovic stated flatly. "Niko will not be pleased if he catches the influenza. Give him one of yours, Grig." Will was surprised at the tone of command in the landlady's voice. He was even more surprised at Grig's meek compliance. Gesturing for Will to follow, Grig led him upstairs to the second floor, where he opened the door to an apartment at the front of the building overlooking the street.

Will was surprised that Grig's apartment seemed utterly unlived in. There was nothing in it other than the furnishings, which were solid, new, and unassuming. A couple of suitcases rested by the door, and as Grig fetched him an overcoat from the closet, Will noticed that there were far more empty coat hangers than coats. Will's curiosity got the better of him.

"Why, it looks like you just moved in as well!"

"For the past decade, I have lived in the dormitory on the Compound with the apprentices. It is standard practice for all of Mr. Tesla's research associates." He handed the coat to Will, who shrugged it on gratefully. "But given the unusual circumstances

surrounding your arrival, he felt it best that I take up residence
here."

Will was shocked, but said nothing—*could* say nothing, as he
was entirely at a loss for words. The man who was to be his mentor had been required to uproot his life, for *him*? Just because he'd
showed up married? Gee! He really hadn't expected the company's
reaction to be this extreme. And what would happen if they found
out it was all a ruse? Will shuddered inwardly at the thought. Well,
they could never know. That was all.

It was a short walk from the apartment building to Will's first
glimpse of "Fort Tesla"—or at least, of the heavy, fifteen-foot-tall
fence of black wrought iron that surrounded it. A neatly trimmed
boxwood hedge was planted along the fence's inside perimeter, its
dense evergreen foliage reaching to the top of the iron bars and
confounding any attempt to see the buildings within.

"The Compound covers a full twenty acres," said Grig, as they
walked along Sullivan Street toward the main iron gates—huge,
ornate, rendered in a strikingly modern style. The design featured
geometrically-dissected circles, lightning bolts, and broadcasting
towers—symbols of the technological advancements upon which
Nikola Tesla had built one of the greatest fortunes of the new century. The gates were huge, to allow for trucks to pass in and out of
the compound, and faced directly onto a long street.

"That is Piquette Avenue," Grig said, gesturing down the street.
"There are many car factories along that way." As he was saying
this, Will noticed a young man standing on the corner behind a
hand-lettered sign propped up against a hydrant. Grig added loudly,
"And some lazy bums should go and bother them, instead of us!"

The young man, being thus addressed, smiled slightly, but said
nothing. He was slender and wiry, dressed in an irregular assem-
blage of seemingly scavenged workingman's clothes. He had coal-
black hair and dark eyes. His sign read "One Big Union" and featured a hand-drawn picture of an alarmed-looking black cat.

"Mornin', Mr. Grigoriyev." The young man spoke with a bright,
brassy twang, eyeing Will. "Fresh meat for the grinder?" He tried to

hand Will some literature, but Grig slapped it out of his hand with a venomous curse and pushed Will along the sidewalk toward the gatehouse.

"Damn Wobblies! That one has taken it upon himself to serve as our own personal social conscience. I don't know why he has decided to enlighten our little corner of the world, but Mr. Tesla despises him."

At the gatehouse, Grig exchanged some words with the gatekeeper. And then, less than twenty-four hours since he'd left California, Will was inside "Fort Tesla."

Inside the Compound, space seemed to expand. The access roads and sidewalks, laid out with geometric exactitude, bisected fields of open parkland, dotted with trees.

"I am sure I do not need to recite the history of Tesla Industries to you," Grig began, as they walked briskly along a precisely angled pathway, "but the recital to our new apprentices has become second nature to me, so I beg your indulgence. I myself began with the original company—Tesla Electric Light and Manufacturing—when Mr. Tesla formed it in '86. It was his pioneering work in wireless broadcasting, developing the World Wireless System, that secured his fortune and gave him the ability to build the model industrial compound you now stand within.

"To your left, you will see the Teslaphone manufacturing plant." Grig gestured to the building as they passed it. It was very large, with small high glass windows that sparkled in the bright morning light. The factory hummed with activity, and through the open doors of the building's large loading bay Will could glimpse hundreds of factory workers in pristine white uniforms. "Naturally, it is the closest building to the main gate, for it is kept in constant operation."

Behind the plant, deeper within the enclosure, were many more tidy little buildings, neatly tucked in among the groomed parkland. Will's attention was captivated by one building in particular, which appeared to sit right in the very center of the compound—an appearance reinforced by the fact that a broad paved roadway ringed it like a moat, with smaller roadways radiating outward like spokes from a hub.

"That is the executive building, where Mr. Tesla has his personal living quarters and laboratory," Grig said. "A lovely building, is it not? It was done by Stanford White, designer of the famous Wardenclyffe tower on Long Island, the first of the many thousands of Tesla Towers across the United States that make up the World Wireless System." Grig ended the exposition with a curt wave of his hand. "You will likely never go in there."

Grig made a special point of indicating the apprentices' dormitories as they passed them, and his tone suggested that it was still a matter of some irritation that Will would not be living in them.

"As I believe I have mentioned, all of the other apprentices live within the Compound," he said. "And, of course, during the term of their apprenticeship, they are not allowed to venture outside these walls except under the most extraordinary of circumstances. But Mr. Tesla has arranged for the ample satisfaction of every wholesome need a young man could possibly have. We have a very good cafeteria—all vegetarian, of course, Mr. Tesla would no sooner allow dead animal flesh through the gates than he would a woman. Over there is the moving-picture theater—no Edison films, as Mr. Tesla has no wish to further line the pockets of an unethical cad. You'll be pleased to learn, however, that Mr. Tesla has agreed to bend the rules for the new Dreadnought Stanton film. If he hadn't, our young men surely would have rioted. We have a lovely little Buddhist temple we use for our daily meditation exercises. And of course, we have a barber ..." Grig gave Will's shaggy hair and stubbly cheek a reproachful look. "You could certainly do with a visit to the barber, Mr. Edwards."

Finally, Grig came to a stop before a long low building, set back from the sidewalk in a neatly trimmed bower of foliage. Affixed to the door was the number three, rendered in bright thin silver.

"This is my building," said Grig. "Which is to say, it has been given to my team for our exclusive use. Here you will be working."

When they stepped inside, it was clear that this really was Grig's building, for everyone greeted him with great deference, starting with a man Grig introduced as Mr. Hahn, the department's secretary.

"Good morning, Mr. Grigoriyev," Mr. Hahn said, taking Grig's coat and showing Will where to hang his. "I will let Legal know that you have arrived."

Then Grig led Will into the main room of Building Three. Instantly, Will knew that despite every questionable thing he'd done to get to Detroit—lying to his parents, scheming with Jenny to get her inheritance, running away from Mr. Hansen—it had all been worth it. He'd made the right choice. Before him was the biggest, best equipped physics lab he'd ever seen. There seemed to be literally acres of the most up-to-date, advanced scientific equipment, and it all gleamed as if it had just been unwrapped. The lab in Building Three made the lab in which Will had worked at the Polytechnic—even the lab at Berkeley—look like a couple of cracker-barrel country stores compared to the Emporium on Market Street.

A dozen young men were working at desks around the room. They were all very trim and neat, wearing freshly pressed suits beneath their rubber aprons and sleeve protectors. They all looked as if they took full advantage of the Compound's barber on a regular basis. And while the workroom was enormous, all these young men occupied just one half of it. The other half held but one desk, several worktables, and an absolutely enormous machine that was clearly in an ongoing stage of construction. Stopping before it, Grig laid a tender hand on its side.

"This is my project," he said, stroking the machine's metal flank as if it was a living thing. "You will be primarily assisting me on my work with this. I haven't come up with a name for it." He peered at Will appraisingly. "Good at coming up with names, are you?"

Will shrugged. "Never really tried it." He paused. "What does it do?"

Grig smirked and laid a finger alongside his nose. "Doesn't do anything yet. It's what I hope it will do that's important. But if I start explaining that to you now we'll never meet the rest of the apprentices."

Briskly, Grig led Will from one desk to the next. All the other apprentices were much older than Will—some in their mid-twenties, even. This confirmed the rumor that Tesla Industries usually recruited college men for their apprenticeship program. Most welcomed Will with polite indifference. There was only one really friendly greeting, and that came from a young man who Grig introduced as Mr. Courtenay. Mr. Courtenay had an exceptionally messy desk. It was stacked high with papers and dissertations and theses. Interspersed among these were several expensively-framed pictures of Marie Curie. As the friendly young man pumped Will's hand, he said, "Quick—why is the sky blue?"

Will knit his brow, taking a moment to try to grasp the relevance of the question. Was he trying to impress Marie Curie or something? Finally, Will suggested, "Because it's not red?"

"Critical opalescence," the young man said eagerly, digging into his pile of papers and withdrawing a dog-eared thesis that he shoved into Will's hands. "I've just been reading up on it, and it's *fascinating*. Feel free to borrow anything else that catches your fancy, I'm happy to share."

"Mr. Courtenay—we call him Court—is a great appreciator of the work of Mr. Einstein," Grig commented as they left his desk and proceeded on their tour. Will clutched the bound document against his chest, overwhelmed but encouraged.

His next encounter, however, was less encouraging. In fact, the young German to whom he was introduced—Mr. Roher—was downright hostile.

"So. You are to be Grig's pet engineer." Roher did not bother to rise from his office chair or even take Will's outstretched hand. He was short and quite fat, and his face was so unpleasant that it made Will wonder if this was why Grig had asked if he were fat. Two unpleasant fat men in one department would certainly not be an ideal situation.

"Max is a theoretical physicist, so naturally he looks down on us humble engineers," Grig chuckled.

"It was not my intent to insult engineers, Mr. Grigoriyev," Roher said, lifting an eyebrow. "Only *pets*."

"Now, Max," Grig said, with an indulgent sigh. "Do try to be a bit more accommodating. Mr. Edwards will be taking the desk next to yours, and it won't do to get off on the wrong foot."

Rolling his eyes, Roher threw down his pen with pronounced annoyance. "Babysitting? Really?"

"I believe you will find everything you need," Grig said to Will, ignoring Roher's outburst. "Anything you don't have, you can request from Mr. Hahn." He smirked. "Or you can always ask Mr. Roher, of course."

"Don't bother asking me anything," said Roher, picking up his pen and glaring down at the papers he'd been working on. But Grig laid a soft hand on his shoulder.

"Just a moment, Max," he said. "I want you to see this. Mr. Edwards has been working on something that I think you will find very interesting. It is his improved Otherwhere Conductor that I was telling you about. Mr. Edwards, I believe you call it a Flume?"

Will's heart leapt into his throat. He considered lying, saying that he'd left it at the apartment ... but that would only forestall the inevitable. He reached into his vest where the lumpy cigar box still rested.

"About that ..." Will began. "There's been a problem."

Will laid the cigar box on the desk and lifted the lid, revealing the tangle of burnt wiring within. "I'm afraid bringing it through the Dimensional Subway was a mistake."

An infuriating smirk curled Roher's lips as he peered inside the box. Grig's face, however, remained impassive.

"I expect it was the result of incompatible Otherwhere Embedding," Will offered. Roher poked at the wiring with a disdainful finger. "I guess it resulted in an episode of Critical Interactive Resonance."

"Of course it was, and of course it did," Roher sniffed. "You could easily have protected the mechanism against an overload of that type, you know. There's a very handy little gizmo you'd do well to familiarize yourself with, Mr. Edwards. It's called a *fuse*. Maybe you can get one of the dollar-a-day line workers in the Teslaphone plant to explain the concept to you."

Will reddened with embarrassment, but refused to rise to the bait. Quietly he shut the lid on the Flume.

"Never mind," Grig said. "There's plenty of time. You can rebuild the prototype, of course?"

"Yes," Will said. "It will take me ... a couple of weeks, probably. But I can get started right away, if you'd like me to."

"No, that won't be necessary," said Grig. "I've seen and heard enough to know that you can, and that is sufficient. At the moment, I have a far greater need for your personal assistance on my own project. I think you will find it very interesting."

"Would you like me to throw this away for you?" Roher smirked, tapping the scorch-marked lid of the cigar box. "If there's one thing I am glad to help you find, it's the ashcan. I imagine you'll be needing to use it quite a lot."

Clenching his teeth, Will continued to pointedly ignore Roher's barbs. He was growing unhappier with his assignment of desk mates by the moment.

Mr. Hahn, Grig's secretary, came up behind them.

"Mr. Grigoriyev, Legal just rang. They're ready for you to bring Mr. Edwards over."

Grig sighed. "Paperwork. The bane of human existence. Come, Mr. Edwards. We shall make this quick."

Emerging from Building Three, they discovered that it had grown colder and the sky was clotted with gathering snow clouds. Will was once again glad for the overcoat his mentor had lent him. They walked briskly to another building. It was not numbered; instead, a sign by the front door read, in thin modern letters of chrome, "Corporate Offices".

After negotiating receptionists, assistants, and even an elevator, they arrived at a large corner office. The placard on the door read "George Jovanovic, Chief Counsel"

The office's occupant was an older man, balding, with a round belly and skinny legs. He wore a very flashy vest, which did not surprise Will, for it was his experience that only balding men with round bellies and skinny legs—or lawyers—ever went in for vests like that.

"Pleased to meet you, Mr. Edwards," said Jovanovic, shaking Will's hand heartily. Then he wagged a finger at Grig. "Is it true you've already been showing him around Building Three? Before he's signed his paperwork? *Tsk tsk, Grig.*"

"Oh for heaven's sake, let's just get this over with," Grig muttered, taking a seat. "Never were we so plagued by lawyers in the old days! We all have much more important things to do, Mr. Edwards included."

"The formalities must be observed!" The lawyer sounded hurt on behalf of the formalities, as if the formalities were a small kitten constantly being abused. Retrieving a freshly-typed stack of papers from his desk, he slid on a pair of half-moon glasses and peered down at them.

"Now, Mr. Edwards, we sent you the boilerplate apprenticeship contract with the acceptance letter, but given your irregular circumstances we had to make a few adjustments." He looked at Will over the top of his glasses. "Am I to understand that you brought a *wife* with you?"

Will nodded. Jovanovic's eyes lit with amusement as he touched a place on the page. "Good thing we took out the celibacy clause then, isn't it?"

"Celibacy clause?" Will said.

"It was all very clearly stated in the boilerplate we sent you," Jovanovic said, and Will's embarrassment burned afresh. "All interns must agree to remain pure and chaste for the term of their association with Tesla Industries."

"Mr. Tesla believes that by refraining from intimate physical congress, one can channel one's mental activities to a higher plane." Grig stated all of this with textbook flatness. "Meditation is also involved."

"In any case, we have stricken that clause." Jovanovic smiled again. "I trust you will meditate a little bit harder, Mr. Edwards, to make up the difference."

Jovanovic turned over the sheaves to another place on the contract.

"Another irregularity ... as the result of your matrimonial state, arrangements have been made for you to live off the Compound. I'm sure Grig has told you how exceptional this is. I have revised the language surrounding punishments for leaving the Compound, items of that nature ... but I have also added some new language about not leaving the Compound unless you are accompanied by Grig. He will walk you to and from work every morning."

Will looked at Grig, raising his eyebrows. Grig gave him a soothing smile, much as he had given Roher.

"It is a peculiarity of Mr. Tesla's," he said mildly. "He fears for the mental purity and physical cleanliness of his workers, especially his apprentices, who are younger and more impressionable. He would like our program to be ... well, he thinks of it rather like a monastery. A monastery of brilliant young men, working toward the achievement of science's noblest aims."

Will absorbed this. Finally, drawing a deep breath, he said, "Mr. Grigoriyev, Mr. Jovanovic—I didn't come to Detroit to see the sights. I came to work and to learn. I swear to abide by any restriction."

Both Grig and Jovanovic seemed amply pleased by that response. Jovanovic, particularly, smiled even more broadly.

"Well! That is the kind of attitude we like here at Tesla Industries. We needn't bother going over the rest of these changes, then. It is good to know that you understand that we have your best interests at heart. So, let's get these signed, and you and Grig can get back to work." Retrieving the signature page from the end of the stack of papers, he laid it on top then squared the papers neatly. Then he opened his desk drawer and withdrew something small wrapped in a sanitary cardboard wrapper. From the wrapper he extracted a small steel razor blade that glinted in the light.

"You expect me to sign in *blood*?" Will wanted to be accommodating, but he could not keep the surprise from his voice. He was aware that many companies, especially old-fashioned ones that still trafficked in magic, required such a soul-binding signature on contracts of importance. But Will hardly expected it from a company with the kind of modern, progressive reputation that Tesla Industries had.

"I assure you, Mr. Tesla would prefer that our contracts not be signed using bodily fluids," said Jovanovic. "But it is a corporate necessity that I have prevailed upon him to accept. You may cut your finger yourself, or I can do it for you. I promise you, I am quite good at it."

Will remembered Jenny's admonitions."I think perhaps I should look these over," he said, haltingly. "May I sign them tomorrow?"

Grig and Jovanovic exchanged glances. Jovanovic's cheerful demeanor clouded.

"We *did* send you the boilerplate with the acceptance letter," he said. "And you *did* have ample time to review that, didn't you?"

Will gulped. "Uh ... sure. Of course. But the changes ..."

"The changes really are insubstantial," Jovanovic interjected curtly. "And you have already seen the inside of Building Three."

"That is my fault," said Grig. "You mustn't hold Mr. Edwards responsible—"

"Nonetheless, he has already seen more of Tesla Industries than Mr. Tesla would allow anyone to see without signing a non-disclosure agreement, at the very least." Jovanovic pointed out. He sighed before adding, "Also, there is an additional complication."

"An additional complication?"

"I don't know if Grig has told you, but there have been urgent inquiries about you. Inquiries which give us very significant legal pause."

Will's blood chilled. "Inquiries?"

"Your professor at the Polytechnic, Mr. Waters, telephoned me yesterday, asking about you," Grig hastily explained. "Your people back home are demanding that you be returned to them immediately. It seems that not everyone is pleased about you taking this apprenticeship."

Will flushed, humiliated. Goddamn it. He knew his parents were looking for him, but he hadn't imagined they would contact Mr. Waters, contact Tesla Industries—suggest that he should be dragged home like a truant schoolboy playing hooky in the pool hall! It was just plain mortifying.

"I'm eighteen years old!" Indignation burned under Will's collar. "I have every right to come here. My people back home don't have anything to say about it."

"Absolutely you do," Grig said encouragingly. "That's the spirit!"

"By signing the contract, you empower us to respond to these inquiries on your behalf, should your parents decide to pursue the matter more ... forcefully," said Jovanovic. "Once you formalize your legal relationship with Tesla Industries, we will handle everything."

"Fine," Will said, snatching the shining little razor blade.

Jovanovic took out a dish and a bottle labeled "Haycraft Leech Saliva"—a substance that would allow the blood to flow as freely as regular ink. The lawyer put several drops from the bottle into the dish and passed it over the desk to Will. Will cut his finger and let the drops fall into the dish. Jovanovic gave Will a steel-nibbed pen. Will signed the contract. Once he was finished, the lawyer blew on the signature to dry it, then squared the papers.

"We'll have a copy certified for you, Mr. Edwards," he said. Then he went to his desk drawer and withdrew another small, glittering thing. He showed it to Will—it was a small pin, like a tie tack, enameled in black and red with the lightning bolt design that featured so prominently in all of Tesla Industries designs.

"Your Tesla Industries Identification Badge." The lawyer pinned this to Will's lapel, smoothed the fabric. "Take care with that, Mr. Edwards. It's a mark of distinction." Then he dusted his hands and nodded at Grig. "He's all yours."

"Excellent," Grig said, beaming. "Let's get to work."

And work they did. In his first day, Will ate a vegetarian lunch in the gleaming white cafeteria, copied several dozen pages of Grig's notes—still not quite succeeding in comprehending the exact nature of the project he was working on—rewired a faulty magnetometer that none of the other apprentices had had time to fix, and was informed by Roher that he'd decided to nickname Will "Blockhead."

The short winter day purpled into frostbitten evening. Near dinnertime, Grig had been called into an urgent conference with Mr. Tesla. In his absence, Court was tasked with giving Will a more thorough tour of the Compound. Will was disappointed in Court's perfunctory discharge of these duties, especially the slapdash tour of the power plant with its massive Tesla Coils. Court was much more interested in getting to the end of the tour—a secret spot where the apprentices went to smoke. Pushing aside some branches in the tall laurel hedge, his guide led him to a cleared-out hollow, made more comfortable by the addition of some empty crates that bore the mark of a scientific instrument company in Chicago.

"Smoking is absolutely forbidden inside the Compound," Court warned, as he pulled out a paper packet of cigarettes. "You just let Niko catch you at it and see what happens." Lighting up, he blew smoke over the hedge. He offered Will one, but Will waved it away—he'd never picked up the habit, and if Tesla didn't like it he didn't want to. "But don't worry, Grig watches out for all of us. He's like a mother hen. You're lucky to have gotten on this team. We're the best in the whole compound."

"So there are other groups?" Will asked. Court nodded.

"Three total," he said. "Mr. Tesla has a mania for the number three. He does everything in threes, or multiples thereof. If you ever have to help Grig with a report intended for Mr. Tesla, make sure you never send it up with an even number of section headings." He looked regretful, as if freshly reliving some painful section-heading related mishap. Then, having worked through the trauma, he took another drag on his cigarette and continued.

"Now, my personal area of expertise is geophysics," Court said. "I was recruited because Tesla's big project right now is using the resonant frequencies of the earth to transmit electric power wirelessly."

"Sounds interesting," said Will, carefully. Even with Court, who had been friendly and open, he didn't feel safe venturing more than that. He'd been at Tesla Industries less than a day, but already he was feeling wary and overwhelmed, like he was sure to give the wrong answer at any moment. Will was not used to being around people who were as smart—and likely smarter—than he was. It was … well, it was *terrifying*, that's what it was.

Court, perhaps sensing this anxious disquiet, peered at his face in the gloom.

"You really are just a kid," he said wonderingly. "What are you, fifteen?"

"I'm eighteen," Will said curtly. "And I'm not a kid."

"Clearly not, since you've got a wife." Court smirked. "You do realize that they're bending over backward for you, right? You must be hot stuff."

Will snorted with amusement. If only Court knew how far from "hot stuff" he felt like at the moment! But he didn't say this, and after a moment of silence, Court took the hint and changed the subject, leaning in closer to whisper, "So what's your wife like? Pretty?"

Will frowned at him, waved cigarette smoke away.

"Fine, fine," Court sighed, leaning back. "You're not the kind to kiss and tell, huh? Not going to have any sympathy for us poor souls trapped behind these iron fences? Well anyway, everyone here is positively furious that you've found a way to get around the celibacy requirement."

"Roher already hates me," Will said.

Court shrugged. "Roher doesn't hate you because of that. He hates you because you're younger than him and quite possibly more talented, if they want you so bad. Roher's more interested in physics than he is in sex." Court rolled smoke in his mouth, blew a perfect ring before adding: "And someone who's more interested in physics than sex is a dangerous person to have hating you."

"From his response to my work, I can't see why he'd hate me," Will muttered, still stinging from the embarrassment of not having thought to put a fuse into his Flume. Adding to the humiliation was the fact that Roher had been absolutely right. A simple breaker would have stopped the overload in its tracks. "Apparently he thinks I'm an idiot."

"The more Roher acts like you're an idiot, the more he thinks you're a threat," Court offered sagely. "You and he share similar specialties, except he's more theoretical while you're more practical. He's one of the new high-energy physics boys. He's been trying to figure out how to entangle the output of multiple Otherwheres to generate amplitudes of current far greater than any we're now capable of. But he hasn't been able to get past the Connection Drop problem. And you're working on that, right?"

Will nodded. Court smiled broadly, clearly amused.

"That's why Grig called him over to look at that cigar box of yours. Grig's always looking for ways to get Roher to work more collaboratively with the other apprentices, and he knows Roher is just dying to pick your brain. But Grig gives the kraut too much credit, I'm afraid. Roher's too proud. He'll never ask for your help in a million years. He'll just sit and stew about the fact that you've figured it out and he hasn't."

Will said nothing. It was nice to imagine that he had something over on Roher. And really, Roher's intransigence might be the one thing protecting him from having to share the secrets Jenny had made him promise not to spill.

But any further confidences between Will and Court would have to wait for another time, as Grig's voice, calling their names, rang through the frosty night air. Court hastily ground out his cigarette and waved out the fumes. Emerging from their hiding place in the laurel, they hurried back to Building Three.

The first thing Will discovered was that at Tesla Industries, work did not follow any kind of regular schedule. The apprentices worked as long as Grig worked, and Grig worked as long as Tesla worked. Thus, it was not until nearly nine, after Grig had returned from yet another meeting with the reclusive genius, that he finally said, "It's been a long day, Mr. Edwards, perhaps you'd like to get some rest." They left the other apprentices still hard at work over their desks; Roher shot Will a sour glare as he followed Grig out.

They walked the short distance back to the apartment under the pale artic glow of one of the nearby moonlight towers. Will was exhausted and his head was spinning and he wanted nothing more than to sleep. When he went inside, Mrs. Kosanovic was waiting in the common room. Her incredibly complicated knitting project seemed only to have expanded in complexity. As Grig climbed the stairs to his apartment, Mrs. Kosanovic called to Will.

"I have given you and your wife Number 20. It is on the second floor, down the hall. You will find her there. Also, a telegraph boy delivered this." From her pocket, she retrieved an envelope from the Western Union Telegraph Company. Before giving it to him, she added: "Collect." Will fished in his pocket for a few pieces of silver.

The telegram was addressed to Jenny, and whoever had stuffed the envelope had left it unsealed. Will paused as he climbed the carpeted stairs. He had promised himself he'd respect Jenny's wishes and not pry into her affairs, but curiosity got the better of him. Sliding the typed telegram from he envelope, he read:

Received your message. Hart has been informed of your arrival. Waste no time. Hetty.

Well. That didn't tell him much. He tucked the telegram back and moistened the gum, pressing the flap shut.

Number 20 was a corner apartment at the back of the building. He felt rather silly knocking at the door of what was supposed to be his own home, but Mrs. Kosanovic hadn't given him a key. Jenny flung open the door.

"You're home!" she said, hugging him and pulling him inside in one movement. She must have had a bath, for her hair was damp and she smelled of steam and Ivory soap. "I thought you'd never come!"

"I didn't know if I ever would." Will looked around the apartment. It was furnished exactly as Grig's had been, with solid, new, unassuming furniture. The high ceilings were ornamented with elegant plaster reliefs, and the hardwood floors were polished to a gleam. Will emitted a low whistle.

"Wow," he said. "Swell."

"Isn't it?" Jenny chirped, as she gestured him to follow her down a short hallway. "I even managed to get two bedrooms. That was heck to square with Mrs. Kosanovic, let me tell you!"

"How'd you manage?"

Jenny shrugged dismissively. "I just told her we had to have a nursery." She patted her stomach. "I suggested that the need was urgent and impending."

Will threw up his hands. "They're already upset enough about me being married!"

"You're the one who came up with the story in Stockton," Jenny reminded him. "And besides, I don't plan on being pregnant long. Grieving a miscarriage will be just the thing to make that landlady leave me alone. I can already tell she's the nosy type."

"Jenny Hansen, that's awful!"

"That's Mrs. Edwards to you," Jenny corrected him. "And the word you're looking for is *brilliant*." She showed him one of the bedrooms through an open door.

"That one's mine." There was no doubt that she had commandeered the best for herself. The bedroom was large, and looked out over the back garden. "The bed is a dream."

There was no way for Will to confirm the accuracy of Jenny's assessment, because all he could see of the bed was piled high with department store boxes. Clearly, she had managed to keep busy during his day at work. Jenny gave him no time to ask about them as she steered him across the hall and into the second bedroom.

"This one's yours."

The second bedroom was much smaller and its window overlooked the alleyway that separated the apartment building from its neighbor.

Will raised an eyebrow. "Gee, thanks."

"There's still power in firsties," Jenny countered, referring to the old games of marbles they'd used to play. "Besides, just wait until you see all the wonderful things I got you downtown!"

"Yes, I notice you've been spending your inheritance again," said Will.

"Oh no, I didn't spend a *dime* of my own money." Jenny's blue eyes were wide with innocence. "You'll be happy to know that the gold certificates have been safely deposited, so that's one less thing to worry about. Now, sit"—she patted the bed—"and close your eyes."

Will did. Jenny placed something smooth and heavy in his hands. Opening his eyes, he beheld a small case of fine leather.

"It's your wedding present," Jenny smiled. Her cheeks were pink and she looked slightly embarrassed. "Or, well, maybe a first day at work present. Something like that."

Opening it, Will discovered that it was a shaving kit—a very nice one. The straight razor had a handle of polished tortoiseshell and a gleaming steel blade. A whole panoply of grooming implements were neatly tucked in as well: brush and cup, soap and strop, comb and scissors.

"There's everything you need to grow a perfectly lovely moustache," Jenny said. "You'd look good with a moustache."

Perhaps it *was* time to grow a moustache, Will thought, remembering what the lawyer had said about his family's "urgent inquiries." He stroked his upper lip thoughtfully but said nothing.

"Also, I took care of your clothing problem." She opened the closet, and inside hung three suits so new the creases hadn't hung out yet. Will stood to examine them, and noticed a pair of uncomfortable-looking shoes sitting on the closet's top shelf. He turned as he heard Jenny pull open a dresser drawer.

"A half-dozen shirts," she said, showing him the drawer's neatly folded contents. "White, of course. I don't trust men who wear striped shirts. And linen cuffs and collars. I got you wing collars, is that all right?"

Will didn't answer. Office shirts were not his customary attire, and he'd certainly never developed a preference for any of the dozens of types of collars available. It was staggering how he could go from having nothing to having everything—right down to the linen wing collars—provided for him within the space of a day.

"I once asked you if you had any witch in you," he said finally. "I take it back. I should have asked if you had any quartermaster."

Jenny laughed. "If there's one thing the daughter of a rich man knows how to do, it's shop," she said. "And believe me, I wasn't just shopping for you."

For the first time, Will noticed that Jenny was wearing a pretty new gown of chestnut colored wool. As she led him out to show him the rest of the apartment, she stopped at the hall closet to show off her most prized new acquisition: a fur coat, plush and warm, the very same color as her own rich brown curls.

The kitchen was of the modern antiseptic type: white walls, black and white checked floor tile and glass-fronted cabinets. Jenny clearly hadn't found time to shop for groceries, for the icebox contained nothing more than a half-eaten sandwich, wrapped in wax paper. Just off the kitchen was a breakfast nook with high windows that looked out over the small back courtyard. Whatever time Jenny hadn't spent buying clothes or depositing gold certificates she had apparently spent here. The table was spread with papers—evening newspapers (turned to the financial sections) and a large leather-bound volume on the subject of patent law, bearing the fresh stamp of the Detroit Public Library.

"By the way, what do you mean all this didn't cost you a dime?" Will asked.

"I certainly don't intend to touch those gold certificates for our day-to-day expenses!" said Jenny. "I stopped in at the National Bank of Detroit. It turns out your brother Ben was as good as his word." She went to her purse and pulled out a small wad of cash. "That's what's left. From here on out, until I get your patent done, you're footing the bills."

"Just like a good husband," Will smiled.

"Like a good *client*," Jenny corrected. "You've retained my services. And I promise you, it will be an investment that pays off a thousandfold."

Will counted the money. There wasn't much, just over two hundred dollars. Then he was surprised at himself. When did he start thinking of two hundred dollars as 'not much'? The apartment and most of his meals would be taken care of by Tesla Industries. As long as Jenny would be satisfied with the shopping she'd already done, it was plenty of money to go on. He shook his head as he tucked it away. He'd been hanging around secretive heiresses too long.

Thinking of heiresses and their secrets made him remember the telegram Mrs. Kosanovic had given him. Taking it out of his pocket, he handed it to Jenny without a word. She quickly opened it, scanned it, nodded. Then she opened her calfskin grip and tucked the telegram inside. For the moment the little suitcase was opened, Will saw several other envelopes and bundles of paper inside, neatly secured with rubber bands. She saw him looking and quickly closed the grip and tucked it under the table.

"So, tell me about your first day. Did they ask about the Flume? Did you tell them anything?"

"They asked," said Will, taking a seat at the kitchen table. He stretched, rubbed his face. "I showed them the burned out wreck, told them what happened."

"Told them you'd build a new one?"

Will shrugged. "They said I needn't bother. Grig said there was plenty of time. He wants me to work with him on his project."

Jenny's eyes narrowed, and she frowned in deep thought. Will was surprised by this reaction.

"*Now* what's wrong?" He threw up his hands. "You wanted me to stall them, and they've been stalled. I thought you'd be pleased!"

"No, something's not right," Jenny interjected, concerned. "They were all very excited to get their hands on you and that Flume. But now you're here, and the Flume isn't working, and they don't much care. Doesn't that strike you as odd?"

It didn't particularly, and Will was about to say so when Jenny released a little squeal of alarm. She put a hand over her mouth.

"Criminy," she whispered. "They're heading you off at the pass."

Will was utterly lost. "What?"

"What if they've already been working on something similar? Maybe it isn't finished yet, maybe they're not ready to submit it for a patent ... and if you got there first, all the work they'd put into it would be lost. So they *deliberately* sent us through the Dimensional Subway, knowing that it would destroy your prototype."

"That's a lot of what-ifs," Will scoffed. "It's also possible that they simply didn't foresee what would happen, just like I didn't."

"Maybe so," allowed Jenny. "But then again, if that's the case, why didn't they set you to work rebuilding your Flume immediately? They were so interested in it before."

Will couldn't explain that. He thought about Roher—Court had said that the two of them were pursuing the same lines of research. Could Roher have come up with something like the Flume? But if Roher already had the answers, why would he have taken such an immediate dislike to Will?

Jenny took a deep breath. "Whatever the explanation, it's a good thing I got these while I was downtown." She showed him a box full of drafting paper, mechanical pencils, India ink, rulers and protractors. "The man at the scientific supply house said it was everything you'd need to draw up schematics for a patent."

"More than enough," said Will, looking over the extravagant collection. Jenny set the box in his lap.

"Good. We'll start tonight. We'll have to work fast!"

"Jenny, I'm exhausted!" Will protested. "A fellow needs his rest! Besides, drawing up schematics can't just be done in a couple of nights."

"The papers have to be submitted before the end of the year to be technically filed in 1910 ... and of course all the offices will be closed the week before Christmas. So we have to send everything off by the end of next week at the latest."

"There's no way!" Will wailed.

"Where there's a Will there's a way!" she said, clearly very pleased with her own brilliant wit. She put a mechanical pencil into his hand. "I'll go put on a pot of coffee."

It was almost 3 a.m. when Will finally stumbled into bed. As exhausted as he was, there was one last thing he had to do before he turned off the light. He pulled out Ben's letter, and discovered that news—especially in the Edwards family—traveled fast.

Dear Will:

Earlier today, I was notified by the bank in Detroit that the account I funded on your behalf has been drawn upon, which means you have arrived. Which is wonderful, and I extend my sincere congratulations. However, I don't know what to make of the bank's report that it was a woman—claiming to be your wife and producing a marriage certificate to prove it—who came in to withdraw the funds.

I am left wondering just what the holy hell is going on. Who is this mystery woman? Is she part of a ruse you cooked up to avoid detection? If so, I guess I'm glad that you're following my advice to "be careful"—but why, exactly, do you feel the need to be careful with me?

Here there was a break in the line of the text. It was clear that Ben had resumed the writing after some passage of time.

Well.

Just got a letter from our mother.

She has explained the situation to me, and I guess I don't need to tell you that she is in an all-fired rage. Clearly, you followed my instructions on how to block her Sending, for the fact that she's been unable to reach you is one of the major points of her fury.

What could have possessed you to marry Jenny Hansen? Don't you know that's just added insult to injury? It was one thing for you to go to Detroit against our parents' wishes, but at least that was just a family matter and they might have pursued it quietly. But now you've brought D.L. Hansen and all his money into the mix! Don't you know how many detectives a timber fortune can buy?

Let me put this plain. You must send Jenny home. Telegraph Mr. Hansen immediately, tell him where his daughter is, then get the hell out of the way. And while you're at it, telegraph me too, and let me know that you've done it, because I won't be able to rest until I know that you have.

If you value my advice even a little, please do exactly as I say.

Your brother always,

Ben

Will folded the letter away. He lay with his arm over his eyes, the pressure soothing his headache.

He considered the situation. If he telegraphed Mr. Hansen as Ben suggested, and let him know where Jenny was, it would indeed take care of many of the problems currently facing him—Jenny's worrying secrecy, her taskmaster ways, the resentment of his fellow apprentices. It might even placate his parents into calling off their attempts to drag him home.

A little charge of fury made him frown. Why did his parents insist on seeing his actions as those of a spoiled child, instead of those of a man trying to choose his own destiny? Really, they were the ones who had forced him into this stupid corner. If Father had just let him go to Tesla Industries as he'd wanted, none of this would have happened. He wouldn't have had to make this bargain with

Jenny. He wouldn't be forced to make this horrible choice—between protecting his own best interests and being disloyal to her.

He felt very low.

But wasn't that the true measure of a man, he thought? That he held to the bargains he made, no matter what? And he *had* struck a bargain with Jenny. They'd spit-shaked on it, and she'd held up her end of the deal in every particular. If he sent her back he would be acting just like the spoiled child everyone thought he was. A spoiled child who'd made a childish mistake and was now trying to avoid a whipping.

No. He couldn't give Jenny up, no matter how many problems it would solve for him. It would be disloyal and unfair. They'd find a way to make this work. Lay low, avoid anyone who might be looking for them. D.L. Hansen might be rich, and Father and Ma'am were surely implacable—but he and Jenny, they were *smart*. He would stick by her like she'd stuck by him.

"For better or for worse," he concluded, and then almost immediately fell asleep.

Chapter Ten

The Scientist's Apprentice

Will's first week at Tesla Industries was a blur. Having grown up on a farm, Will was no stranger to hard work and long days, and having struggled his way to the top of his class at the Polytechnic, he knew how taxing intense mental activity could be. But the level of effort required of him at Tesla Industries was orders of magnitude beyond anything he'd ever experienced.

His first challenge had been simply comprehending what Grig's enormous uncompleted machine, hunkering like a steel behemoth in one half of Building Three, was built to *do*. Grig, always running from meeting to meeting, had shoved reams of schematics and wiring diagrams into Will's hands (as if that should be sufficient for Will to decipher the machine's function) but it wasn't until after lunch on Tuesday that Grig finally had time to explain it to him.

"As you know, Will, one of the great challenges we Otherwhere Engineers face is the limited number of Golden Dimensions," Grig began. Will nodded, knowing well enough that only about two hundred such dimensions—Otherwheres with physical laws sufficiently compatible with their own native dimension to allow for safe exploitation—had been discovered.

"But what if we could create entirely *new* Otherwheres?" Grig said softly, eyes sparkling. "Create them to our own specifications, from the ethereal scratch? Create them, and then when we are through with them ..." He kissed his fingers to his lips. "Poof. Destroy them."

"Create dimensions?" Will blinked. "Actually ... create them?" He cast his mind back through the schematics Grig had given him—and in an instant all of the functions that had seemed so puzzling when regarded out of context made perfect sense. Sure, he thought. Of course. That's what the machine *had* to do.

Seeing the light of understanding on Will's face, Grig smiled."Clearly, the thrilling possibilities are not lost on you," he said. "So, have you thought up a name?"

"What?" Will said absently, still working through the incredible implications in his mind. Custom building a dimension to one's own specifications! As long as the basic physical laws remained compatible, one could specify everything one wanted in it—including limitless amounts of energy, without even the need to build any kind of power plant ...

"A name!" Grig broke through his thoughts. "This machine needs a name! I told you that yesterday."

Will certainly didn't want to admit that he hadn't understood what the machine was supposed to do until just two minutes prior. He licked his lips and threw out the first name that came to mind:

"The Dimensionator."

Grig was silent for a long time, rubbing his chin thoughtfully. Will heard a snuffled snort from where Roher was sitting across the room.

"I don't know," Grig averred. "I'm not sure if Mr. Tesla will like it."

Will's heart sank to his shoes, but then inspiration struck him. Remembering the conversation he'd had with Court, he lifted a finger and said:

"The *Tri*-Dimensionator."

Grig's eyes widened.

"Oh, yes!" he breathed. "That's *it*."

"Now *that* was brilliant," Court said, the next time they were able to sneak off to the little hideout in the laurel hedge.

"Tri-Dimensionator! Maybe you should have gone into advertising instead."

"Nothing doing," Will snorted, not even looking up from the dissertation that he'd brought out with him. Grig had asked him to write an abstract by the end of the day, and it was hard slogging. "Thanks for the advice."

"No problem," Court said. "Listen, I've got a way you can pay me back. I need to use your mailbox."

"My mailbox?"

Court rubbed the back of his head sheepishly. "Sounds silly, doesn't it? Here all the other fellows are jealous because you have your own apartment and a warm willing wife waiting in it. But what I'm really jealous of is your *mailbox.*"

Lowering the dissertation, Will looked at him quizzically. "I don't follow you."

"There's a book I need," Court said in a low voice. "And I can't have it sent here. Can I have it sent to you? I'll tell you a secret about Roher if you say yes. Something that will help you knock the wind out of him."

"I don't know," Will said, though the idea of getting dirt on Roher sounded especially attractive. "I don't want the mailman gossiping to my landlady about delivering me a stack of Tijuana Bibles."

"Oh for God's sake, it's not *pornography.*" Court snorted smoke out through his nose. "Trust me, there are two things that I know how to get ahold of inside this high-security prison—the finest of smokes and the bluest of literature. But there's one thing I can't get ... and that's what I need your help for."

"So, what is it?"

"Well, you know I'm a geophysicist, right? That's what Tesla and Grig keep me around for. But what I'm really interested in is The Great Change of 1878. You know about the Great Change, right?"

"Not much," Will said. "I know that no one really knows why it happened."

"Apparently, there is one man who does," Court says. "And he wrote a book explaining it. It's called *The Goês' Confession.* It's scarce as hen's teeth, and it's almost impossible to get a copy. Apparently there's some mysterious 'Agency' that destroys the books whenever they can find them. But whoever they are, they can't destroy them all, and there's a whole underground network of people who keep printing them so the truth can be known."

"I don't get it," said Will. "What truth? What Agency? What's a Goês?"

"Gee, don't they teach you Greek out there in California?" Court said. "The whole thing is a goof on the Stanton Institute. You know what a Sophos is, right?"

Will shrugged. "Yeah, it's a title. Like a president or something."

Court made an exasperated sound. "In Greek, Sophos means wise man. A Goês is the opposite of a Sophos. A charlatan, a fool. But you know the old saying—only the truly wise man knows he is a fool."

"All right," said Will. "So some fool wrote a book confessing something. So what?"

"This book reveals the truth about The Great Change. What really happened."

"So what really happened?"

"I'll let you know after I've read it," Court said. "Which I can only do if I give my friend of a friend who's managed to get a copy an address that isn't ... well, you know. *Monitored.*"

"Come on, I'm sure they don't open your mail here," Will scoffed. Court raised his eyebrows significantly but said nothing.

Will paused, brow wrinkling with concern. "You don't think they'll be opening *my* mail, do you?" And the minute he said it, he realized that it wasn't his mail he was worried about.

"Of course I don't, dummy," Court said. "If I did, I wouldn't be asking to use your mailbox. So how about it? Deal?"

"Deal," said Will, absently. But despite Court's reassurances, he resolved once again to remind Jenny to be careful.

And he did remind her that night as they sat up late at the kitchen table, each working feverishly over their own project. He laid down his mechanical pencil, leaned back in his chair, and looked at her.

"What?" she inquired sharply, after he'd stared at her in silence for a long time.

"Court doesn't think they'll watch our mail," he said. "But you'll be careful, right, Jenny?"

"What are you talking about? Who's Court?"

"Another one of the apprentices. He's a good guy. He wants to use our mailbox to have some stuff sent to him, because Tesla Industries monitors the mail the apprentices get."

Jenny snorted, shook her head. "Your Mr. Tesla sure runs a tight ship." Then she returned to her work without another word. She was scrutinizing the stock pages of *The Detroit News*, making neat little notes by issues that seemed of particular interest to her.

"They're looking for us, you know." Will did not need to say who.

"Of course they are." Jenny didn't bother to look up.

"I mean *really* looking for us. They've already contacted Tesla Industries. Everyone's furious. And now they've got all your dad's money on their side—"

"My dad can go soak his head!" Jenny snapped. She kept her eyes on her papers, but he saw her expression soften and grow slightly wistful. "Darn it." She was silent for a long time. "I only need a couple of weeks, William. Once your patent is filed, I'll go away and they won't make trouble for you any more."

"That's not what I mean!"

Jenny sighed. "Yes it is. Or at least it should be. I may be helping you with your patent, but I know I'm hurting you just as much. If I weren't here, your parents wouldn't be half as mad as they are."

Will rubbed his tired eyes. "What have we done that's so wrong?" He found himself thinking back on the conversation he'd had with Nate in the barn. Nate had said Will should try to take his father on faith. "Why can't they have faith in *us?*"

"It's not that our parents are bad, or mean, or unkind," said Jenny, softly. "They just don't understand. They *can't* understand. Things were different for them. They lived in a different world, and they're trying to hold us to those standards. We have to teach them. It's our job to show them, even though it's hard, even though it may make them … hate us." She paused, biting her lip at the thought.

"Your dad won't ever hate you," said Will.

Jenny seemed oddly unconvinced. "I'll wire him tomorrow. I'll tell him I'm coming home."

"Jenny!"

She answered the alarm in his voice. "I'm not really going to go! It's just to stall for time. I'll tell him I'm coming home, but only if he makes your parents promise to stop bothering Tesla Industries about you. It takes days to get to California by train, and that'll keep everyone out of our hair for at least that long."

"And when you don't show up at the station?"

"All we need is a head start," she said. "I'll work harder between now and then to make sure I have everything I need to write up the description. If I have to go before you're done with the schematics, I'll find a way for you to send them to me." She reached across the table and placed her warm little hand on his wrist, pressing it encouragingly. "Like I've said, William, I have plans, and you're a part of them. But it just wouldn't be fair if my plans spoiled yours. They won't. I promise."

Will contemplated this. It satisfied the strict business requirements of their deal, but he did not find it very satisfying otherwise. In fact, the thought of Jenny leaving—going off into the cruel world by herself, with no one to watch out for her—was downright disheartening. He laid his larger hand over hers.

"Can you at least tell me what Claire meant when she said that you were doing something dangerous?"

Jenny drew a deep breath. Withdrawing her hand from beneath his, she lifted her head to fix him with a steady gaze. Will was struck by how her eyes—the color of the summer sky when she was cheerful—could become the color of tempered steel when she was annoyed.

"Why don't you think of it this way?" she offered. "The word Claire should have used was *risky*. And yes, what I'm doing is risky." She laid a hand on the stock pages. "But everything in life is risky. That doesn't mean it's dangerous. What I'm doing is not going to cause either of us any harm. All right?"

Will sighed. Nothing she'd said made him feel better. Picking up his mechanical pencil, he leaned back down over his work.

"All right," he said, as he began drawing again. "Just promise me one thing. Promise you'll ask me for help if you need it. Remember what you said? Geniuses need people to protect them."

This made her smile softly, and blush, but she said nothing more.

Chapter Eleven

Working with a Will

Dear Will:

I am in receipt of your telegram confirming that you've sent Jenny home. Good for you. You've made a wise choice. I've had a very interesting letter from Mother describing the hullabaloo you've caused back home. She says Jenny made it a condition of her return that everyone had to stop bothering Tesla Industries about you. Loyal little wife you've got there! Sometime you'll have to tell me what the hell you two were thinking. Didn't I tell you to watch out for girls?

Mr. Hansen got Mother to agree, but apparently Father was a lot more pigheaded about it. So now she's almost as mad at Father as she is at you. She knows it was his pigheadedness that drove you to take such desperate measures—and while it was her duty to support him, she can't figure out why he was so riled up about you going to Tesla Industries in the first place, or why he cares so much now about getting you back.

Well, anyway. Leave them to hash it out amongst themselves. You're at Tesla Industries, and the parents won't be bothering you anymore, and I hope things can really get started for you in earnest. I am still hoping to come visit you, as I promised. It is very difficult to get away at the moment because we at the Institute are all working very hard on the promotion efforts for the new Dreadnought Stanton moving picture that Edison Studios is putting out.

It occurs to me that you've probably wondered just what it is I do at the Stanton Institute. Especially since it is a magical institution, and I've described at length how my ability to practice magic was taken from me at a young age.

My work isn't especially glamorous (if you'll excuse the pun). I'm what is called a Jefferson Chair, but that really reflects more of how my position is funded as opposed to what I actually do. My official title is Senior Mantic Research Associate. I compile detailed reports on magical artifacts of particular power or interest for Sophos Stanton. He uses my research—and the research of many others like me—to decide what artifacts he needs to take into the Institute's safekeeping. Of course, his retrieval of said artifacts is usually not quite as dramatic as is portrayed in the pulp novels. Most of the time, in fact, we just buy them. But it's a good day's work, especially when we can take something particularly dangerous or malign out of the hands of those who might seek to use it for nefarious purposes.

Anyway, I will send you details about my arrival when I can. I am looking forward to seeing you in person. It's been such a long time, and we have so much to discuss.

Your brother always,

Ben

All the other apprentices at Tesla Industries got Sundays off. For them it meant a day of rest on which they could enjoy a special vegetarian meal in the cafeteria, a few extra hours of meditation in the Buddhist temple, or participation in a Tesla-approved gathering of unquestionable moral value. While the other apprentices—especially Court—grumbled about the dullness of their Sundays, Will would gladly have traded places with any of them, because it would have meant he didn't have to deal with Jenny coming into his room at the crack of dawn to shake him awake.

"Good morning!" she chirped in his ear. "Let's make the best use of this day, shall we?"

Growling, Will rolled over and turned his back to her. "Let's just leave me the hell alone, shall we?" he mumbled sleepily. "*We're* not doing anything but sleeping."

Jenny gave him a firm shake. "This Sunday and next Sunday are the only two full days we've got to work before the patent has to go in," she reminded him. "Come on, get up."

Will found that he couldn't care less. He was exhausted. In the past week, under Jenny's merciless whip hand, he'd averaged little more than three hours of sleep a night. He had just drifted back into a peaceful slumber when a torrent of cold water came splashing down on his head. He leapt out of bed, spluttering. "Jesus!"

Jenny had retreated to the other side of the room, water glass in hand. She was trying to look firm and resolute but he could tell she was also trying not to giggle. He glared at her.

"It's like living with Genghis Khan!" he yelled at her. "Can't I take one stinking day off? Just a couple of stinking hours, even? Please?"

"No," she said. "You can't. This has to get finished, and it has to get finished before the end of this year. Remember? Plans?"

"Right," Will sighed. "Plans." He wiped water from his face. "Fine. I guess a couple weeks without sleep never killed anyone. Just made them *wish* they were dead."

Jenny's smile returned, brighter than ever. She handed him a towel.

"C'mon, there's fresh coffee," she said. "And I've got an idea that will make the time just fly."

After shaving and dressing and downing two strong cups of coffee in succession, Will felt almost ready to face the morning, even though the sun hadn't yet risen and the apartment was still pitch-dark. Arranging his implements before himself—t-squares and protractors and mechanical pencils—he winced as Jenny switched on the light that hung over the kitchen table.

As he was rolling up the sleeves of his old blue workshirt, he heard her gasp. He steeled himself to defend his sartorial rights—Sunday might be just another workday, but damned if he was going to dress up like it was!—but then he saw that she was looking not at his shirt, but at the burn on his arm.

"William! What on *earth* did you do to yourself?"

Will looked down at the place where he'd pressed his skin against the steam radiator to break Ma'am's Send. It did look pretty alarming, luridly red and puckered. It was funny how burns actually looked *worse* after they'd had some time to heal up. He pulled the fabric back down over the ugly scabs, shrugged.

"Nothing," he said quickly. "Just an accident—down at the lab." Time to change the subject. "So, what's your great idea to make the time fly?"

"I'm going to read to you, just like old times!"

"Great," said Will, unenthusiastically. The only book they had in the apartment was the fat leatherbound volume of patent law she'd picked up from the library. Or maybe she was going to read him the stock reports. "Better put on another pot of coffee."

"Oh, don't worry, this will keep you awake." To his shock, she held up a book with a brilliantly colored cover ... showing a boy's face, bisected into halves of good and evil. The copy of *The Warlock's Curse* that he'd brought with him from California—the book he had used to unlock Ben's first letter.

He struggled to hide his discomfort. "Where did you find that?"

"I found it when I was tidying your room. I *do* tidy, you know." She looked over the book. "And anyway, it's my book, isn't it? It's one of the ones I left up in your hayloft." She turned to the inside front cover where eight-year-old Jenny had scrawled her name in large, blocky letters. "Why'd you bring it with you, anyway? You didn't bring anything else."

Will shrugged. "I brought my tools, didn't I?" It was a trick he'd learned from Father ... when you didn't want to answer a question, the best tactic was to answer without *giving* an answer.

Jenny hmphed. "Well anyway, I'm glad you brought it. It's just about the most hilarious one there is. And I promise I'll do all the voices like I used to."

The True Life Tales of Dreadnought Stanton books were not supposed to be hilarious—they were supposed to be dramatic, moving, thrilling—but the effort they expended to be the latter was exactly what made them the former. When they were children, Jenny used to read the books without irony, delivering each dire pronouncement or witty quip with breathless appreciation. In the years that had passed, however, she'd developed an exquisite knack for pricking the inflated bombast and poking fun at its deflated remains.

"Chapter One: Down on the Farm!" she announced, after she'd Voice-Of-God-ded her way through the prologue, which was as tedious and irrelevant as prologues in a Dreadnought Stanton book usually were, written in a distant third person and reminding the reader that the *True Life Tales of Dreadnought Stanton* were, indeed, based on tales drawn from true life as it was lived in those United States, and that readers wishing to assert their status as patriotic Americans should read each and every one of them diligently and repeatedly, and also buy them as gifts. "Oh boy, here we go. I can't remember, is the villain in this one a stone-stupid animancer or a bloodthirsty sangrimancer? Sangrimancer, probably. They're the ones who come up with the best curses." She paused. "You know, just for once I'd like to see Dreadnought Stanton go up against another credomancer. Now *that* would be a book I'd buy as a gift."

Will smiled. "C'mon, Scuff. You know credomancers are always the good guys," he commented, rubbing out a stray mark with a gum eraser.

Indeed, it was a formula so pat and unswerving as to be unworthy of comment. Credomancers—warlocks who wielded the power of faith—were represented by the series' titular hero as unfailingly decent, noble, patriotic, and wise. The other kinds of magical practitioners were cast, by contrast, in predictably repetitive shades of unflattering light. Animancers—witches or warlocks who drew power from the vital spirits of nature—always had a mental capacity on par with a brick. A very *small* brick. When they were the villains, it was usually because they couldn't even begin to comprehend the terrible forces they were attempting to control. And it was, of course, Dreadnought Stanton's duty to enlighten them.

Sangrimancers—blood sorcerers—made much better villains. They weren't stupid, rather they were utterly depraved, usually in some wonderfully lurid fashion. But no matter who the villain was, the Great Credomancer, Dreadnought Stanton, Sophos of the Stanton Institute, always won the day with good manners, clean morals, and American ethics.

"*It was blooming spring, and young farmboy Dick Smith stood at the edge of a freshly plowed field, dreaming of the bountiful harvest that would reward his diligent efforts.*" Jenny stopped, unable to even get through the first sentence of the first chapter without rolling her eyes. "For pity's sake, why are the heroes in these things always named 'Dick'? I swear, I've read a hundred of these things and it's nothing but Dicks as far as the eye can see—"

"Just get on with it," Will interrupted, reddening. Jesus, this was going to be a long book. "And keep your thoughts to yourself on the plowing part, if you please."

Lips twitching mischievously, Jenny continued, in a very serious tone:

"*But little did he know the terrible fate that was about to descend upon him, the result of a dire family curse laid upon his ancestors,*" she read. "*Young Dick's shining eyes were filled only with dreams of prosperity, of his crops that would laden the tables of American citizens from sea to shining sea, providing bountiful sustenance to support the great efforts of a nation on the march.*" She peered at the sentence more closely. "Is 'laden' really a verb?"

"Sure, if Dreadnought Stanton says it is," Will lifted an eyebrow. "I can't believe you're even questioning it."

In this fashion they proceeded to fill their Sunday with the tale of a standard-issue farmboy, who grew up in a standard-issue town in some standard-issue state, who was called upon to weather unimagined tragedy so that ultimately he might be delivered from it and learn a valuable lesson. The action proceeded swiftly. By the third chapter, it was revealed that young Dick had inherited a terrible family curse. One of the farmboy's fool ancestors had apparently annoyed a depraved warlock (a sangrimancer, just as Jenny had predicted) causing said depraved warlock to lay a curse on their lineage for as long as the gravid Earth should twirl 'neath the sun's beneficent splendor.

"Now *that's* a nice piece of writing right there," Jenny had commented dryly, tapping the line with her index finger. "Makes it sound like the Earth's about to have puppies."

The story really picked up on the first full moon after the poor sap's eighteenth birthday, when the curse kicked in. Suddenly, and without warning, poor Dick Smith found himself bodily possessed by the revenant spirit of this vengeful old malefactor. And that's when Jenny's dramatic talents started to shine, as she read the lines of the evil warlock with malicious relish:

"*Do you not see, you sad mortal worm, that your body belongs to me, and you are powerless to stop me from using it to wreak whatever dark magical havoc my unquiet mind can conceive?*" Jenny read the warlock's words in a low, sneering voice, and if she'd had a moustache, she would have twirled it. The warlock proceeded to make the poor farmboy do all sorts of horrible things, culminating in a particularly thrilling scene where he set fire to a barn and his spunky girlfriend—who was named Tessie—had to risk her life rescuing all the little baby lambs from the ravenous flames.

"Whew!" Jenny said, sitting back in her chair and fanning herself once Tessie and all the little baby lambs had escaped from the threat of being barbecued. But she did not rest long. "I wonder when Dreadnought Stanton is going to finally show up! We're almost to the end!"

"He's a busy man." Will sketched a careful line. "Give him time."

And indeed, Dreadnought Stanton arrived only in the nick of time, having arrived in the farmboy's standard-issue state for a bit of rest and fresh country air. *Poor Dreadnought Stanton,* Will smirked. *Goes out for some quiet relaxation in America's heartland—maybe do a little fishing—and all he gets are cursed farmboys setting barnfires and attempting to murder baby lambs.*

At least it didn't take long for the Sophos of the Stanton Institute to put things to right. As anticipated, Dreadnought Stanton quickly dispatched the evil spirit with a magical light show and a swirl of commanding Latin.

Concluding this passage, Jenny wrinkled her nose.

"I'd forgotten how weak the ending of this one was." She frowned. "Jeez, you'd think it would take more than three paragraphs to send that filthy fiend packing. Usually they put up more of a fight."

"They'll probably make it better in the Edison movie," Will suggested. "I hear the special effects are going to be top-notch."

"Maybe," Jenny said, but she sounded unconvinced. She quickly ran through the last few pages, which described how the farmboy and Tessie had thanked Dreadnought Stanton (who was probably more interested in getting on with his damn fishing, Will imagined), declared their undying love for each other, and then hugged some baby lambs.

"And they lived happily ever after," Jenny concluded as she closed the book. Her voice was husky from extended reading. Will glanced at his watch, then looked at it again in disbelief—it was almost seven! They'd been at it for twelve hours straight.

"I can tell you one thing, all that talk of baby lambs has made me hungry," Jenny said. Will's stomach was growling too—they'd sustained themselves on nothing but melodrama and coffee all day. Jenny slapped the book down on the kitchen table and jumped to her feet. "That's enough for today, William. Let's go get some food!"

"I'm not supposed to leave the apartment building without Grig," Will said. "I promised."

Jenny made a face. "What do you mean, you promised?"

Will pressed his lips together. He didn't want to tell Jenny about the contract he'd signed in blood. Not yet, anyway. He was pretty darn sure he wouldn't want to tell her tomorrow. Or ever, in fact.

"They would just prefer that I not," he evaded. "You know Mrs. Kosanovic is always watching us. Mr. Tesla likes to have control over his apprentices."

"He doesn't own you," Jenny said. "Honestly, William, you have to start thinking more like a genius and less like an indentured servant. Tesla doesn't bring together bright young minds like yours for his health. He does it because he stands to profit by it. He is not your friend. He's not your protector. He wants work and thought out of you, and he wants to profit from it. There's a big difference between accommodating him to achieve your ends and putting your neck under his foot."

Will was reminded of the young labor organizer he'd grown accustomed to seeing outside the Compound. Whenever the street-corner radical managed to gather a small crowd (which wasn't often) his speeches usually went along in a similar vein. It seemed dangerous to Will to get into the habit of thinking in such a way, even if it was just Jenny encouraging him to do so.

"If I'm going to break another rule," said Will loftily, "it's going to be for a better reason than sneaking out to get food."

"But this isn't just *food*." Jenny assumed a seductive, cajoling tone. "It's *chop suey*. When I was out walking yesterday, I came across a place that's open all night. Their egg rolls are as good as anything I ever ate in San Francisco, and you know that's saying something."

After a whole week of vegetarian meals in which unsalted mashed potatoes had featured prominently, the very thought of savory meat and rich oily fried noodles made Will's stomach rumble.

"Come on," Jenny said, going to the hall closet and taking out her new fur coat. "We'll sneak out the back. No one will know we're gone."

Tiptoeing down the rear stairs, they crept along the side alley and out to Winslow Street. The night was bitingly cold, and a few flakes of snow drifted down through the glow of the moonlight towers. Jenny, holding the warm fur close around herself, led the way with brisk little steps, heels clicking on the frozen pavement.

The restaurant wasn't far, just a bit of the way up Piquette. It seemed to cater specifically to the many late-shift factory workers in the area, and when they arrived it was crammed with an off-hour dinner rush. It was brightly lit and decorated with colorful folding screens and gilt carved brackets; large decorative knots of silk hung on the walls.

Will and Jenny were given a table in the back near the kitchen, and before long Will was ravenously devouring crispy egg rolls, greasy pork and vegetables over fried noodles, and thick, salty hot-and-sour soup. With each bite, Will felt strength returning that he hadn't even known he lacked.

"I just don't understand how Mr. Tesla thinks that men can work without meat," Jenny mused, reaching for another egg roll. "My dad used to say that two pounds of good beef and two pints of good beer would get better work out of any man than the fanciest French meal at Delmonico's."

The mention of Mr. Hansen—who believed Jenny was even now on the way home to California, and who was due for another sad disappointment—made Will sigh.

"You know, I really like your dad," he ventured. "I wish things didn't have to be the way they are."

Jenny played with her napkin. "You let me worry about my dad."

"You seem to like to have a corner on the worrying market," Will retorted. "Honestly, I'm getting kind of tired of it."

"Really?" she said, lifting an eyebrow. "In my experience, most people like to not have to worry about things."

"They like to not worry about things that don't matter," Will said. "But this *matters*, Jenny."

"There are a *lot* of things in life that matter," Jenny snapped. "But they don't all matter equally. Sometimes you have to put one before another."

"You, for example, put your sister before your father." In response to the flash of annoyance that passed over Jenny's face, he said: "You made me promise that I wouldn't *ask*, not that I wouldn't *deduce*." He paused, sipping his tea. "Whatever your plans are, they're clearly for Claire's benefit—and your father doesn't approve. You've put Claire before your father. QED."

"Well, just who else is going to?" she said through clenched teeth. "My father has everything he needs to look out for himself. Claire doesn't."

"She's got an inheritance, just like you do—"

"Do you think for one moment that anyone will ever let her use it the way she wants?" Jenny cut him off sharply. "My sister is as intelligent and conscious as you or I, William. But because of her ... infirmity ... she is not allowed to make decisions for herself, and never will be. They'll keep her in a prison and treat her like a moron, they'll cut her apart and take away even the *dream* of a normal life ... unless I help her."

"Help her how?" Will said quickly. But Jenny was not to be that easily caught. She just leaned back in her chair, crossed her arms, and glared.

Will suddenly found himself thinking about the book they'd spent all day reading. He grinned wanly, taking the last eggroll from the grease-streaked plate.

"You know something?" he said, biting into it. "You're Dreadnought Stanton."

"What?" she said, still frowning.

"You're Dreadnought Stanton," he said again. "You intend to come in the nick of time and set everything right, against all odds. Through the force of sheer will."

She narrowed her eyes at him and did not smile. "I promise you, it's going to take more than sheer will."

At that moment, the waitress came along with the bill, two crisp little half-moon cookies resting atop the Chinese-scrawled slip of green paper. When Jenny saw them, her stormy mood dissipated almost instantly.

"Fortune cookies!" she said, seizing one. "I thought they only had these in San Francisco." To Will's surprise, instead of eating the cookie, she crumbled it in her hand and extracted a little slip of paper.

"They have your fortune printed on them," she said, showing him the slip then turning it over to read it. Her brow wrinkled and her smile dimmed.

Will took the other cookie and broke it open, extracting his own small slip of paper.

"*The past is in your future*," he read. "What the heck does that mean, anyway? What does yours say?"

"Mine doesn't make any sense either," she muttered, tucking the little slip away into her purse. "These aren't as good as the ones in San Francisco. The last one I got there said *Who dares, wins*. I'm going to stick with that one."

As they were making their way through the crowded restaurant toward the front door, Will caught sight of a familiar figure through the front window. It was the street-corner activist who usually hung around outside Tesla Industries. It had begun to snow hard, and his threadbare outfit was dusted with white. He was talking with a man in a shiny, cheap-looking suit. The man was showing him something, some kind of flyer, and the dark-haired young man was shaking his head—and as he did so, he happened to catch sight of Will and Jenny. His eyes met Will's for just a moment. Then he quickly put his hand on the shoulder of his companion and turned him away from the restaurant window. He pointed down Piquette, and whatever he said made the man tip his hat eagerly and head quickly in that direction.

As soon as the man was gone, the organizer came inside the restaurant, hurriedly making his way toward them. He did not look at Jenny, clearly not expecting any kind of introduction, but rather spoke low hurried words into Will's ear:

"You seen that feller out front? He's showin' around flyers of you and your girl. You might consider going out the back way." Then he turned on his heel and left the way he had come. To the restaurant proprietor who had greeted his entrance with a dark frown, he touched the brim of his hat and said saucily, "Don't worry, brother, I ain't gonna steal nothing."

Will quickly spun Jenny toward the back of the restaurant.

"What on earth—" she began, but then fell silent as she saw the look on Will's face. He led her through the kitchen—to the bemusement of the busy Chinese cooks—and out the back door. When they emerged in the back alley, she looked at him curiously.

"They're still looking for us!" said Will through clenched teeth, pulling his cap down tight on his head. "There was someone outside the restaurant showing around flyers!"

"But *why*?" The snow was falling even more heavily now, powdering Jenny's fur coat with little puffs of white. "Dad thinks I'm on my way home! I told him I'd only come if your parents would leave you alone—and he said they agreed!"

Will nodded. Ben had even written that Ma'am had agreed to Jenny's terms. But he said Father ... Father had been *pigheaded*.

"They've double-crossed us," said Will, grimly. "They think they can get you home *and* get me back."

"Why would they do that?" Jenny said. "Why wouldn't they keep their word?"

"I don't know." Will set his jaw and glanced at his wristwatch. It was not yet nine o'clock. There was still plenty of time. "But I know someone who might."

Chapter Twelve

Harley Briar

Dear Will:

I am in receipt of your urgent telegram dated 9:30 p.m., Sunday, December 4th. And I'm sorry to say that I can't shed much light on why there are people still looking for you, even after Jenny made that deal with her dad. It does indeed seem like a double-cross, as you wrote in your wire.

I am absolutely certain that Mother believes that all efforts to bring you home have ceased. She gave Mr. Hansen her word that she would comply with Jenny's demands, and she wouldn't break her word to him for anything. So if there are detectives still looking for you, I would lay money that they're not working for our parents ... they're working for our <u>parent</u>, singular. <u>Father</u>.

Father has said he wants you back from Detroit, no matter what it takes. And you know how Father is when he gets a bone in his teeth.

I will see if I can find out anything more. Meanwhile, don't worry. It'll all come out all right. You'll see.

Your brother always,

Ben

After all the hard work they'd put in on Sunday, Will expected that Monday would be a particularly execrable specimen of its type. And indeed it was, as Grig was called into a private meeting with Mr. Tesla almost as soon as they'd arrived at Building Three, and didn't return all that day.

Roher always took Grig's absences as an opportunity to subject Will to torment and abuse. Will had sat on tacks no fewer than three times, found little doodles on his papers of stick figures being stabbed with stick daggers, and once he even discovered a "kick me" sign pinned to his back.

Probably the worst thing, though, was Roher's chair. It squeaked. A high-pitched, grating squeak. And Roher, aware of this fact, made it his business to constantly rock back and forth with tiny little movements. *Squeak, squeak, squeak*—it was like Chinese water torture.

Having suffered through a morning of particularly intense mistreatment, and particularly prolonged squeaking, Will finally cornered Court after lunch. "So what's the dirt you promised me on Roher?"

Court grinned as he pulled out one of his cigarettes. "You're not letting the kraut get to you, are you?"

"If he calls me 'Blockhead' one more time I'm going to set fire to his desk," Will vowed fiercely. "Which I don't suppose *you'd* care about, except the whole building might go up in flames, including your pictures of Marie Curie, and I don't think you want that."

Court's lazy smile disappeared. "Don't you dare threaten Marie!" He gestured Will to lean in close.

"Roher's got a *girl*," he whispered. "Passes notes to her through the fence almost every day. She's a cute little blonde number with braids. Wears them all pinned up on top of her head. I've seen the two of them canoodling through the iron bars, fingers entwined and all that. It's like Romeo and Juliet."

"I thought you said he wasn't interested in sex, just physics."

"I never said he *wasn't* interested in sex," Court said, as if he found the very idea preposterous. "Just that he was *more* interested in physics."

"Fine. So what do I care if he has a girl?"

"You may not care, but Mr. Tesla sure would," Court offered slyly. "You might just want to let Roher know that *you* know what everyone else around here knows—Grig included. Then maybe he'll lay off you."

Will pondered this, but said nothing more. And even when he went back to his desk that afternoon and found that each and every one of his steel pen nibs had been bent and blunted, he did not immediately act upon the information he had received. Instead, he just smiled to himself. Roher could just keep on playing his little games. For now. Because Will had learned something else from his father besides the value of a clean handkerchief—for an attack to be most devastating, it had to be delivered when the moment was right.

Afternoon stretched into evening. Grig remained closeted with Mr. Tesla, finally sending a message to Building Three that their conference would not be completed until well after midnight, and that the apprentices should retire. Which they did, in all haste, Roher singing a mocking "Good night, Blockhead!" as he'd strolled out. Will was left alone in the darkened Building Three to brood. Wasn't this a fine state of affairs, he thought irritably. Stuck waiting to be walked the whole three blocks home. He thought idly about getting started on rebuilding his Flume, just so he could have something to do.

No, it was just too absurd. There was no way he was just going to sit here. Grig's message had said the apprentices should retire. That could be taken to mean him, as well. Sure, it was a stretch to impute such a special dispensation to the brief text of the message— but it was a plausible excuse, and he could embroider it if need be. Snatching his coat, he left Building Three and headed for the front gate.

208 THE WARLOCK'S CURSE

He emerged onto the street in front of the huge main gates feeling both triumphant and apprehensive. He looked up and down the street for private investigators in shiny suits. Having deemed the coast clear, he was just beginning to turn toward home when he caught sight of the young labor organizer standing on the corner. Will knew he wouldn't get another chance to thank him for the good turn he'd done at the chop suey house—he certainly could never do it in front of Grig—so he quickly crossed the dark street to where the young man stood hunched and shivering, hands jammed deep in his pockets.

It was just 20 degrees out, but the young man had only a canvas overcoat, worn over several sweaters and a ragged muffler. As Will approached him, he was trying to light a hand-rolled cigarette with bare, trembling hands. Will remembered a packet of matches he'd picked up when he and Jenny were in Stockton. He'd grown accustomed to putting them in his pocket every day, along with whatever spare change he had, and his apartment key. Stopping in front of the man, Will fished in his pocket and handed the matches to him.

"Thanks, brother," the young man said, looking up. His eyes became slightly wary when he saw who'd handed them to him. But whatever inspired the wariness, he kept it to himself as he struck a match into bright flame. The sudden harsh illumination revealed dark circles under his eyes. Will was reminded of the Dorians he'd seen at the dance hall in Stockton, but he didn't guess labor organizers went in for such pretentious affectation.

The young man waved out the match and regarded the packet with interest.

"Hotel Stockton," he observed. "The private dick said you were from California. I hear tell it's mighty nice. Oranges and sunshine, right?"

"Plenty of sunshine, I guess," Will said. "But my family didn't have oranges. We had horses."

"Must have had money too," the young man said, narrowing his eyes as he inhaled smoke. "Poor folk don't send private investigators looking for their sons."

When Will did not say anything, the man held out the matchbook with a shrug.

"No, keep them," said Will. He paused, then added: "Thanks for what you did the other night."

No comment. Just another indifferent shrug as the man took a pull on the harsh tobacco.

"Hey, you want a cup of coffee?" Will asked. The young man peered at Will curiously, as if wondering if he'd heard him right.

"You sure you ought?" he grinned crookedly. "You sure your Russian nanny won't mind?"

"That's not a very friendly thing to say to someone offering you coffee," Will said. "Especially when he's willing to buy you a sandwich to go with it."

The young man grinned again as he stuck out his ungloved hand. Even through his own glove, Will could feel how cold the young man's skin was.

"We ain't never been properly introduced. Name's Briar," he said, drawing it out so it sounded like *bra-ar*. "Harley Briar. Labor organizer for the Industrial Workers of the World. But I guess you already knew that, right?"

"I knew one, but not the other," Will said. Then he added sheepishly, "You'll have to tell me a good place to go. Someplace ... you know, safe. I only know the chop suey house and I don't think I should go back there."

Briar shook his head. "Boy, you're on a short leash, ain't you? Private dicks holdin' one end and Tesla Industries the other. Hope you didn't sign any kind of contract with Tesla, by the way. Normally I don't concern myself with the problems of college boys, but his contracts are awful damn bad."

Will shuddered. He didn't want to think about the contract he'd signed, because the more he thought about it, the more he regretted it. He regretted not reading it in the first place, he regretted not having Jenny look over the changes ...

It'll all come out all right. You'll see. He remembered the words in Ben's letter. They were surprisingly comforting.

What was done was done. And after all, he was working at Tesla Industries. It would all come out all right ... somehow.

"C'mon," Briar said. "I know a fine safe place, and it's close t'hand."

Will followed Briar to a small, dingy café on Grand River Avenue tucked in among a clot of darkened mechanics shops. The inside of the café was very, very warm—they probably kept it this way, Will realized, because most of the men inside seemed to be as insubstantially clothed as Briar, with wads of newspaper sticking out of the collars of their thin shirts and shoes held together with twine. No one gave Briar a second look, but Will drew many appraising glances. Remembering the Tesla Industries pin he wore, Will turned his lapel under to hide it.

Will ordered two cups of coffee and two big club sandwiches, and as they waited for their food, he took Briar's measure. The young man was small and scrawny, but his hands—strangely stained and scarred—were large and looked very strong. When Briar noticed Will looking, he held them up for examination.

"I come from Kentucky," he said, turning them over. "My dad and brothers all coal miners. Beats the hands to hell. I got out of there when I was fifteen. Been kicking around all sorts of places since then." The coffee came first, and Briar poured lots of sugar and most of the cream into his.

"So, I've been wondering," Will said, stirring what cream was left into his cup, "I see you on that corner every day, but I don't get just who you're trying to organize. The workers at the Teslaphone factory are escorted out on autobuses, and the other apprentices aren't even allowed to leave at all."

"I started hanging around outside Fort Tesla just out of sheer cussedness," Briar smirked, warming his hands on the white china. "Just 'cause Niko finds us organized labor types so messy and upsetting. He thinks of us like a spot the dog left on the rug. But I'm only there mornings and night. During the day, while you're inside, I make the rounds." Briar paused, took a large swallow of his coffee. "Now, everybody knows about Detroit's auto factories, 'course, they're famous. And our boys have plenty to do with them. But I got a different angle. I work the *magical* factories. The three big ones between Woodward and Grand River ... CharmCo, you heard of them, right?"

Will nodded. "They make the charms that the old businessmen use. The ones that have all the young businessmen yelling about a Mantic Trust."

"They make all sorts of things," Briar said. "Strong charms for old men, weaker charms for young men, woman charms to tell pregnancy or stop it ... anything and everything. They run a nonstop line and they're rotten to their workers. All the magical factories are. See, except for a few old hands, all their workers are under thirty. And even if they're not working lots of magic, they're still working it steady, and that exposure builds up, worse than the Black Lung I saw back home." Now the sandwiches came, and no sooner had the waitress set the plate on the table than Briar attacked the food. When he spoke again, it was through a full mouth. "'Course, by the time they actually get sick, the factories don't want nothing to do with them no more."

The waitress was trying to hurry away, but Briar plucked the hem of her apron, and said, in a very courtly fashion, "I'd be much obliged if you'd bring me a cup of hot water, sister."

The waitress rolled her eyes and jerked her apron away.

"Bum," she muttered, but, eyeing Will's nice overcoat, she left and eventually returned with the hot water Briar had requested. Will watched as Briar opened the bottle of ketchup that was on the table and poured half of it into the cup. He winked conspiratorially.

"Good as tomato soup, free as the wind."

"Heck, I'll buy you soup—" Will began, but Briar cut off the words with an emphatic shake of his head.

"Nothin' doin'," he said. "I did you a favor and you paid me back. We're square. Grig Grigoriyev and all you brainy bastards inside Fort Tesla can say what you like about me, but I ain't any kind of a bum."

There was an uncomfortable silence, broken only by the sound of silver against china as Briar stirred his ketchup soup.

"You come a long way to work at Tesla Industries," Briar said finally, tapping the spoon against the cup's rim. "You're awful young. I guess they picked you right off the horse farm, huh?"

Will was eager to get to the main point. "Look, can you tell me what the man—the private detective—what did he say to you?"

"Well, he said he knew you and your girl were somewhere around Tesla Industries. He wanted to know if I'd seen you, if I knew where you two were holed up. Your father is offering a good reward." Briar signaled the waitress to refill his coffee cup. She frowned disdainfully and did not hurry to do so.

"My *father*?" said Will. "He said that? Exactly that?"

Briar nodded. "Exactly that. Said he'd been hired by your father in California. That surprise you?"

"No. It doesn't surprise me at all," Will muttered. It confirmed Ben's suspicions. Mr. Hansen and Ma'am had agreed to Jenny's terms—but Father hadn't. With Father, it was a grudge. Father was going to have his pound of flesh, come hell or high water.

"Bastard," Will whispered.

"What's he after you about?" Briar asked. "You two elope, maybe? You couldn't stand to leave her behind in California?" He paused, then added thoughtfully, "That's 'bout the only reason I can figure Tesla would let you live off Compound." Then he snorted with laughter. "Hell of a good dodge ... I bet half them college boys you work with wish they'd thought of it!"

"Wish they'd thought of it," Will affirmed, "and hate me because I did. Except I didn't. I just kind of ... lucked into it."

"That's the kind of luck to have," Briar said. "Dumb luck."

There was a sudden disturbance at the front of the café, as the door was jerked open with a loud tinkling of bells. A young boy—no more than twelve—poked his head inside and looked around wildly. When his gaze fell on Briar, he seemed to melt with relief.

"Harley!" he cried, rushing inside and over to their table. Undernourished and undersized, he wore ragged clothes and his face was streaked with oily grime. "Gee, Harley, am I glad to find you. You gotta come!"

Briar leaned back in his seat. "Gotta come where? What gives?"

"There's trouble over at Mayflower! Floor boss made Rico Selvaggi work a double. He's gone off the deep end!"

Briar paled, and was already half out of the booth before the boy had finished speaking, putting on his coat and hat. "There anyone else over there can help?"

The boy shook his head, his face anguished.

"Nobody," he said, then added caustically, "Nobody who ain't afraid of getting *canned*, that is. But I'll come, Harley!"

"Hell, no. Wrassle down Rico Selvaggi?" Briar slapped the scrawny kid on the shoulder. "You keep running. Get down to the Temple of Labor, see if anyone there can come. I'll do what I can in the meanwhile."

"You ain't goin' to take on Selvaggi by yourself, are you?" The kid's eyes were huge with the thought of it. Even Briar looked daunted. He looked at Will, body tense with haste. "You," he snapped. "You really want to pay me back? Hell, pay me *forward*? I need you to come with me. Selvaggi is a big mean son-of-a-bitch, and I can't handle him alone."

Will knew he shouldn't be out on the street—Ben had warned him against it. But the private investigators wouldn't be looking for him in the kind of places a labor organizer was likely to take him. All that was waiting for him at home were his unfinished schematics and Jenny's foot-tapping. And Grig wasn't likely to check on him until after midnight. Nodding, he slid out of the booth to follow.

As they jogged along the dark sidewalk, Will asked Briar, "What is 'Mayflower'?"

"Mayflower Tobacco Company. They're one of the big three magic companies I was telling you about. Magic ain't their primary business, they mostly just manufacture regular cigarettes. But they got a huge magical sideline making Golden Bat Cigarettes ... ever hear of 'em?"

Will grunted assent. He remembered them—the black-papered, magically-infused cigarettes that came in beautiful green and gold packages. The cigarettes the Dorians smoked to give themselves an "interesting" pallor.

"Mayflower employs about a hundred magical workers to charm the Golden Bats. I been talking to some of these fellows, and the boss at Mayflower caught wind of it, packed a couple dozen of 'em off to the breadline. Now he's making the men he *didn't* fire pull double shifts. A double shift is murder on the guys who are sensitive. And Selvaggi is *extra* sensitive."

They heard angry, unearthly screams coming from the Mayflower Tobacco Company a whole block before they reached the building itself. Inside the cavernous building, lit from high above by strong electric floodlights, dozens of cigarette rolling machines clanked away noisily. Before each machine, workers in stained white aprons, stood busily sorting and packing cigarettes as fast as the machines could spit them out into long square holding trays. These workers seemed to be carefully ignoring the screams of a man at the far end of the factory floor, where a large cluster of rolling machines was set off to one side, expelling cigarettes wrapped in black paper. The employees on these machines wore black aprons to distinguish them as magical workers, and while some of them kept to their business, many more stood around the packing table onto which the screaming man had climbed, kicking hundreds of black cigarettes onto the floor around him. He was a powerfully built man, and in his demented rage he'd torn off his apron and his shirt, and was standing bare-chested under the harsh light. To Will's horror, he could see tendrils of something black writhing beneath the man's skin like fat burrowing centipedes.

"Jesus," Briar muttered, charging forward.

"Get down from there, you goddamn anarchist!" The floor boss—identifiable by his soft white hands and expansive belly—screamed up at the man.

"Kresswell, it's your own damn fault!" Briar yelled right in the fat floor boss's face. "What the hell you thinking, making him pull a double shift? You know Selvaggi is sensitive!"

Kresswell glared at Briar with equal parts disgust and astonishment. "I don't give two shits if he's sensitive! He's hired to do a job and if he can't do it he can go find work somewhere else!"

"Yeah, I'm sure you'll make it real easy for him," Briar hissed, then leaped nimbly up onto the table beside the big man, who was muttering words to form some kind of spell. He ran his hands over his body, fingers desperately trying to trace charms onto his own flesh. Briar pulled Selvaggi's hands down, forcing them to his sides. The man struggled and bellowed.

"It hurts!" he shrieked insensibly. "God, it hurts ... I have to do something ..."

"Using magic will just make it hurt worse," Briar said in a low steady voice. "Come on, let's get out of here. I'll get you help ..."

"He's costing us hundreds, shutting down this line!" Kresswell cried. He glared around himself at the workers who were standing and watching. "And what the hell are you all doing? Get back to work!"

Briar was still trying to keep the man's hands down, keep him from casting magic. He looked down at Will, his whole body tense with the strain.

"Grab some of that rope." Briar nodded to hemp coil laying by one of the machines. "If we don't tie him up we'll never get him out of here."

"That's company property!" Kresswell said, advancing threateningly when Will moved toward the rope. "Don't you dare ..."

Will dug into his pocket and came up with a five dollar half-eagle—enough to pay for a whole spool of rope. He threw it at Kresswell, who fumbled and caught the money, eyeing it with astonishment.

"Where'd you get money like this?" he barked. "You steal this?"

But he made no further attempt to stop them as Will helped Briar tie Selvaggi's hands behind his back. The raving man moaned, sobbed, his fingers twitching as if to sketch the air. Together, Will and Briar lifted him down from the table. He was very heavy, and when they tried to help him walk, his feet dragged drunkenly.

Then things got worse.

A half-dozen men in dark heavy wool coats and low-pulled slouch hats appeared at the factory's far door. They were carrying truncheons and rifles.

All the color drained from Briar's face. "Hell. Company muscle. And they're itching to break heads. C'mon, Will, we've got to run."

Looping their arms between Selvaggi's bound ones, they dragged the man in the opposite direction, toward a small access door at the far corner of the factory floor. But the company men had already sighted them, and began to give chase, yelling.

Even though he was doing the most to keep the delirious man on his feet, Will found himself being dragged along as Briar dodged through dark alleys and backways. Stumbling and panting, they did not stop until the sounds of their pursuers had grown distant and dim.

Selvaggi collapsed to the frozen ground, moaning and shivering.

"Give him your coat," Briar commanded harshly. "He doesn't have anything else."

Without a second thought, Will hurried to comply, wrapping the warm wool around the man's trembling form. Selvaggi's flesh was burning hot to the touch, and the grubby, bruise-like trails of black under his skin seemed to throb, as if about to burst forth in a tarry gush. Once Will got the coat around him, Briar took a deep breath and muttered a few low words under his breath. Then he shook out his shoulders like a prizefighter, bent down, and picked the huge man up. He slung him over his shoulder fireman-style, his knees quavering but not buckling, and began walking toward Grand River Avenue. Briar smiled wanly at Will's gape of astonishment.

"I'm tougher'n I look, kid," he puffed. "We got to get him to Greektown or he's done for. Come on."

Luckily, the downtown streetcar on Grand River Avenue was not long in coming. The other passengers gaped as Briar slung the whimpering Selvaggi into the car, but Briar was interested only in the man's suffering, kneeling next to him, putting a soothing hand on his throat, murmuring more low, comforting words. Briar and Will hauled Selvaggi off the car at Gratiot Avenue, which Will remembered without fondness as being in the vicinity of the Hotel Acheron, the dive where he and Jenny had spent their first night in Detroit.

"Sorry to have got you mixed up in all this," Briar said as they dragged Selvaggi along Gratiot. "Good thing those thugs didn't catch us. That would have been tough to explain to your folks at Tesla Industries."

As they turned down Beaubien, Will noticed that the signs for the restaurants and shops they were passing were in Greek. They finally came to a narrow brownstone-style storefront with a hand-lettered sign in the front window printed both in English and Greek: *Dr. Lazaros Gore*. Still holding Selvaggi up, Briar had to kick the door with his foot instead of knocking. The door was opened by a tall, olive-skinned woman. She wore a nurse's uniform: a plain white shirtwaist and white cotton apron, stained brown in places with iodine. Her hair was neatly tucked up under a starched muffin cap.

"Oh, Harley," she sighed, stepping forward to help. In one swift movement, she wrapped her arm around Selvaggi and lifted him over the threshold.

"Good evening, Irene," Briar greeted her with odd formality. "This one's just lost his job, so you got yourself another charity case."

"I've got money," said Will, following Briar inside. "I can pay."

The nurse glanced back at Will, frowning. Then she looked at Briar. "Who is this swell fellow?"

"His name's Will Edwards," Briar said. "He was buying me dinner when this happened. He's a good egg."

Together, Briar and the nurse dragged Selvaggi into a receiving room just off the main hall. As they laid him out on a sturdy table, an older man entered from the back room, clearly drawn by the commotion. He was in gartered shirtsleeves and was holding a copy of the evening paper. Removing his reading glasses from his face, he looked them all over curiously. The old man's gaze lingered, though, on Selvaggi, as the nurse removed the coat Will had wrapped around him. The big man's bare, goosepimpled torso was swirling with moving bruises, yellow and purple and black. He looked as if he was being pummeled by invisible fists.

Laying his paper aside, the old man clucked his tongue unhappily. "Dear, dear, dear," he said, running his fingers lightly over some particularly swollen places on the man's skin. "He's positively riddled with Exunge. He's done far too much magic."

"Gee, you think?" Briar deadpanned. He'd taken up a position near the door and was watching the proceedings with dark eyes.

The doctor gave Briar a reproachful look. "I've seen him before, yes?"

"Yes," said Briar.

"But not this bad, before," the doctor said.

"He's got kids to feed," Briar said. "His wife died last year, he's one foot out of the poorhouse. What else do you expect him to do?"

The doctor sighed heavily. "Well, let us see if we can get him fixed up again. Irene, are you ready?"

The nurse nodded. She'd already assembled a small tray containing just one simple piece of equipment—a razor. Will watched with horrified fascination as she swiftly drew the blade across Selvaggi's chest, leaving three parallel trails of blood. The cuts were not deep, just enough to make the blood well up from the man's skin, quick and strong and black. Looking closer, Will saw that the man must have been cut like this before—many other light silver scars crisscrossed his skin. Irene placed one strong brown hand on his chest and began massaging the blood over his heart. Then the doctor, who was standing across the table opposite from her, placed a hand over hers. He closed his eyes and began murmuring something, a guttural kind of language that didn't sound like Greek.

Irene reached below the high collar of her white blouse, accidentally streaking it with blood, and withdrew a small two-chambered pendant. Will's eyes widened, for he knew what it was instantly.

He'd remembered seeing illustrations of them in the Dreadnought Stanton books. It was an alembic, a kind of power-channeling pendant that was unique to one—and only one—type of magical practitioner.

"They're ... *sangrimancers*," Will whispered to Briar, who snorted.

"Well, hell! I guess you *are* a genius, just like everyone says."

Will watched as the alembic in Irene's hand began to glow.

"I've never heard of sangrimancer *doctors*," he breathed, watching as the doctor and his nurse chanted in unison, passing the glowing alembic over the man's body, the allergic swelling beneath his skin subsiding and fading as they did.

"Seems there's a lot you ain't never heard of," Briar said. "Dr. Gore's the best in Greektown. And him and his daughter are the finest people you'll ever meet."

Will could almost feel the man's pain subsiding. The black substance, which Dr. Gore had called Exunge, was mostly gone now, leaving only faint smudgy traces. Breathing deeply, the man was soon asleep.

"All right, that should be enough," Dr. Gore said, withdrawing his hand from Irene's. He looked at his daughter with concern. "Are you all right, my dear?"

Irene had grown exceptionally pale, and now there were dark circles under her eyes—the wan Dorian pallor Will recognized. A sangrimancer nurse risking a bout of magical allergy to save a stranger from his? The very idea made Will's head spin.

"I'm fine," said Irene softly, withdrawing her hands and going to wash them. When she returned with hot water and bandages to tend to the man's wounds, Dr. Gore took them from her.

"I'll take care of that," he said. "You go lie down for a bit."

"No, I will—"

"Harley," Dr. Gore called over his shoulder. "Please talk sense into her."

Briar crossed the room in two strides and wrapped his arm around Irene's waist. She was much taller than him, and larger, but she leaned against him nonetheless. "Come on," he murmured fondly. "You gotta stay strong for the cause." Irene nodded, compliant, and as they left the room Dr. Gore eyed Will.

"So, I heard you say you had money," he said tartly, as he began cleaning the wounds on the man's chest. Will dug out all the spare change he had left after the evening's activities, regretting that he'd thrown a whole five-dollar gold piece at the odious floor boss. But the handful of coins seemed satisfactory to Dr. Gore. After daubing Selvaggi's chest with a towel, he washed his hands again with strong-smelling soap, then began laying on strips of bandage. The man's chest rose and fell with peaceful regularity beneath the doctor's deft, careful touch.

"Will he be all right?" Will asked.

Dr. Gore shrugged. "That depends on what you mean. This time, he will recover. But I've seen him so many times before. For someone like him, someone so sensitive to Exunge, using any magic is very damaging to the system. He will die young. So no, he won't be all right."

Will felt the terrible injustice of it—that this man had to put his life in jeopardy just so he could keep himself and his children out of the poorhouse. But despite his sympathy, Will was more curious about something Dr. Gore had said earlier. "What does that word mean, Exunge?"

"The tendrils of black you saw moving under his skin, that is Exunge," Dr. Gore said. "The substance represents the toxic residuals that are left after one works magic. If one works too much magic, it builds up in the system, causing illness. If too much builds up, death."

There was the sound of footsteps coming down the stairs, and Briar poked his head into the examining room. He punched Will on the arm.

"C'mon kid, I'll walk you back. Don't want you to catch hell with the wife."

Will's heart leapt, and he checked his wristwatch. It was almost midnight. Jenny probably wasn't worried yet—she was used to him working late—but what if Grig happened to check in at the apartment and discovered that he hadn't been home? He grabbed his coat.

"Thank you for your patronage!" Dr. Gore's voice called after them as they left. "Please try not to come again!"

Will hadn't a nickel left in his pocket after paying Dr. Gore, so he and Briar had to walk back, the cold night air urging them briskly along.

"Sangrimancer doctors," Will said again, still hardly able to believe it. "I always thought sangrimancers were evil through and through."

"Yeah, that's what all the Dreadnought Stanton books want you to believe," Briar scoffed, turning up his collar and jamming his hands deep in his pockets. "But those are kids books, and you're no kid."

"It's not just the Dreadnought Stanton books," said Will softly. "Everyone knows they torture people. I mean, they have to. They have to empower the blood they take with suffering, right? "

Briar lifted a thoughtful eyebrow. "Sangrimancers do draw power from blood charged by human emotion," he allowed. "Suffering, misery, despair ..." He paused, looked at Will. "But you don't have to torture a man for him to feel misery. I saw enough misery in the coalfields back in Kentucky—hell, I see enough of it in the factories here in Detroit, every day—to fuel magic bigger than you can imagine. Dr. Gore and Irene, they take that suffering and use it to help people. They take the suffering *out* of their patients' blood. And that's why I say they're the finest people you'll ever meet."

Will absorbed this silently.

"Sure, sangrimancy can be exploitative," Briar concluded, tucking his chin into his ragged muffler. "But it's also the only kind of magic that has the capacity not to be."

Will looked at him incredulously. "How do you figure that?"

"Sangrimancy is the only kind of magic where there can be conscious cooperation," Briar said. "In credomancy, one person can't have power unless they fool or manipulate some other person. And that other person can't agree to be fooled, 'cause that would defeat the whole purpose. In animancy, magic is drawn from spirits that don't have any kind of conscious thought ... natural spirits that can't agree nor cooperate, only respond according to their nature. Are you getting me?"

"But someone can agree to let a sangrimancer use his blood," Will said, with soft surprise. He'd never thought of it that way before.

"Bingo," Briar said. "So what them Dreadnought Stanton books say ain't necessarily false—'cause at it's worst, sangrimancy is the worst of all the kinds of magic. But they ain't true either, because at its best, it can also be the best."

Will took this in. "You'd think we'd hear about those kinds of sangrimancers once in a while," he murmured thoughtfully.

Briar snorted, breath congealing white. "Not in a Dreadnought Stanton book, you won't. Like I said, they're kids' books, for kids. When you grow up, you learn different." He paused, then added in a mutter, "It's just a goddamn shame that in this world, most people don't ever grow up at all."

Chapter Thirteen

The Goês' Confession

Dear Will:

No word from Mother about the private investigators, but no more urgent telegrams from you either, so I suppose things have settled down for you in Detroit.

The good news is I've obtained several days of leave from the Institute, and I will be coming to Detroit on December 16th.

I am very much looking forward to seeing you,

Your brother always,

Ben

"Good morning, Blockhead!" Passing behind him, Roher slapped Will on the back so hard that it made his pen gash the paper of the report he was writing for Grig. Will glared at Roher as the fat kraut sat down heavily in his desk chair, grinning and squeaking with renewed vigor.

But Will said nothing, just laid the ruined paper aside and replaced it with a fresh sheet. "Good morning, Mr. Roher," he said with what he hoped was quiet dignity.

"How's that Flume of yours coming?" Roher smirked, rocking back and forth. "You figured out what a fuse is yet?"

"Oh, lay off the kid," Court said in disgust, dropping a thick stack of papers on Roher's desk. As he passed Will's desk he gave him a conspiratorial grin, twirling a finger around his head to suggest imaginary blonde braids.

"You stay out of this, you nitwit," Roher glared after him. "You just stick to kissing your pictures of Marie Curie."

"She's smarter than you'll ever be!" Court catcalled back. "And a whole lot prettier, too!"

Will hoped that would be the end of that morning's unpleasantness, that Roher would quit talking and just stick to his stupid squeaking. But Grig was out of the office and Roher wasn't one to pass up a chance like that. Leaping out of his chair, he snatched something off his desk and came to Will's side, bending down over his chair. Will recoiled from the heavy body looming over him— usually Roher favored the ranged attack.

Without a word, Roher slid a paper over the fresh sheet that Will had intended to start working on. He said nothing for a moment, just let Will stare at it dumbly.

It was a flyer—a facsimile document clearly duplicated with the intention of issuing it to multiple offices—with two grainy pictures on it. The pictures were of himself and Jenny.

"Is that your wife?" Roher whispered in Will's ear. "She's real pretty, Blockhead. How'd you land a wife like that?"

The bottom of the flyer bore the logo of the Pinkerton Agency, the familiar wide-open eye with the text "We Never Sleep" written under it. The heading on the flyer was short but humiliating:

SOUGHT: TWO RUNAWAY CHILDREN

Will's face flushed with rage as he read over the text: *Loving families in California eagerly desire the subjects' return ... subjects are known to be in Detroit, Michigan ... subjects are in extreme danger ...*

Extreme danger—that was rich! Was there no lie Father wouldn't tell just to get his way? Cheeks burning, Will pushed the paper back in Roher's direction. "Mr. Tesla is taking care of it."

"Mr. Tesla is taking care of *you*," Roher continued, very softly. "But I'm sure he doesn't give a pin about your pretty little wife. In fact, I'm sure he figures your pretty little wife is nothing but a distraction. What if someone told the Pinkertons where she was at? What if they snatched her out of that love nest you share and hauled her home? You could move in here with us. Oh, it would be such *fun* having you around the dormitory."

Will turned, furious, but Roher had already backed away, laughing as he returned to his desk.

"Will and Jenny Edwards, sitting in a tree ..." he sing-songed. "R-u-n-n-i-n-g ..."

Something cold and dark overcame Will suddenly, a feeling stronger and more violent than he'd ever known. The feeling spread through his whole body, turning his limbs to ice and fire at the same me. He saw himself going over to Roher, grabbing him by his tie, bashing his face on his desk until all the papers were bloody.

But he did not move. Instead, he just sat at his desk, looking down at the flyer for a long time. Then he folded it and placed it quietly in his desk drawer. He looked at the blank fresh sheet of paper that lay beneath it.

For an attack to be most devastating, it had to be delivered when the moment was right. And it had to be delivered before it was too late.

Taking up his pen, he dipped it into the inkwell and quickly began to write.

Dear Mr. Tesla ...

Later that week, the book Court had asked to have delivered to Will's mailbox arrived, and when they were finally able to sneak away for a smoke so Will could give it to him, Court was so excited that he didn't even light up, just seized the package and began tearing at the paper like a kid on Christmas morning.

"Oh gee!" Court raised the book before himself, regarding it with solemn awe. "I can't believe I got it!"

Whatever the source of Court's excitement, it couldn't possibly be the result of the book's appearance. It didn't just look cheap, it looked hasty and furtive, as if it had been printed in someone's basement. It had a cover of rough brown paper, the kind of paper

one might expect to wrap pornographic contents. While the title—
The Goês' Confession—wasn't at all titillating, when Will saw the
book's subtitle, he experienced a strange thrill.

Veritas vos Liberabit.

"The truth will set you free," Court translated, seeing where
Will's gaze rested. But Will did not need a translation. He'd trans-
lated those same Latin words himself, for his father, on his birthday.
It was incredible that they should reappear again here.

Court opened the book eagerly.

"You're not going to read it *now*, are you?"

Court looked up, his face sharp with intensity. "Damn right I'm
going to read it now!" Will shrugged and left him to it, returning to
his work in Building Three. When, after five hours, Court had not
returned, Will grew curious. And when he snuck back out to look
for him, he found Court in precisely the same place he'd left him,
hunched over the book, pale and shaking as if he'd seen a ghost.

"That must be some book," Will commented. Court jumped with
a startled squeal. When he saw that it was Will, he held up the book.

"It's incredible," he whispered, his voice hoarse. "Will, it's the
most incredible thing I've ever read."

"All right," Will said, taking a seat on one of the scientific-equip-
ment crates. "Let's have it."

Court rubbed a hand over his mouth, eyes darting back and
forth. He was clearly trying to think of the best way to begin.

"So, I've always been interested in The Great Change because
there's a theory that it was geological," he said. "Like, some kind
of change in the geology of the Earth. But how could a geological
change result in a whole generation suddenly developing an allergy
to magic? That doesn't make any sense. That's why I wanted to get
this book. I thought it might shed some light."

"And does it?"

"It doesn't just shed light, it sets the whole world on fire," Court
whispered. "This book says that it *was* a geological change. A fundamental alteration of the very structure of the Earth itself." Court
paused, letting the implication sink in both for Will, and, it seemed,

for himself. "You see, there's a poorly understood geological structure beneath the earth's surface. It's called the Mantic Anastomosis.
It's a big web of a special kind of rock, and it's wrapped around
the earth like a net. Now, if you read old geology textbooks, they
explain that the Mantic Anastomosis was a kind of processing system for a substance called *geochole*. Of course that's the technical
name, but if you read the popular literature they used to refer to it
as Black Exunge ..."

Will must have gasped, for Court paused and looked at him.
"You've heard of Black Exunge?"

Will tried to seem casual. "It's, like, the toxic residuals of magic,
right?"

"Exactly," Court said. "When humans work magic, this toxic
substance is created. Now, in the old textbooks, they say that it was
the rock web that actually created the Exunge somehow. They didn't
really understand how even back then. But however it was created,
sometimes large pockets of this Exunge would build up beneath the
ground. And if it reached the earth's surface and came in contact
with a living thing, incredible and terrible things were the result."

"Like what?"

Court hitched closer.

"*Aberrancies*," he said in a low, thrilling voice. "Remember
reading about those in history class? How there used to be huge
monsters, giant jackrabbits and things like that? How they'd storm
across the plains, wreaking havoc? Aberrancies were created when
something living came in contact with Exunge. The Exunge had
some kind of mutational effect on them, made them swell up out of
control, grow huge and deranged."

Will blinked, his head spinning. He was thinking about Selvaggi,
and the dark tendrils that had swirled beneath his skin. Dr. Gore
had said they were Exunge.

"Now, this fundamental alteration to the earth's geological
structure changed the very nature of how Exunge was produced and
processed," Court continued. "Before The Great Change, the Mantic
Anastomosis generated and processed all the world's Exunge, on

a huge global scale. After The Great Change, human beings *themselves* generated and processed Exunge, on a tiny personal scale. If a human being worked magic, the Exunge that resulted from working the magic stayed in his body. The more magic he worked, the more Exunge was created."

It was exactly what Will had seen at Dr. Gore's house. Selvaggi had worked too much magic—and as a result, his body had become riddled with Exunge.

"But ... then, you're saying that all human beings born after The Great Change had an entirely different physical structure from their parents and grandparents?" Will asked.

"Isn't that the very definition of the Malmantic Generation?" Court lifted an eyebrow.

Will shook his head in astonishment. Yes, it was! He was beginning to see why Court was so excited by this book. "So how could something like this just happen?"

"It didn't just happen," Court said. "It was *engineered.* By a bunch of Russian scientists in the 1870s. They created something called Lyakhov's Anodyne, and this Anodyne somehow restructured the Mantic Anastomosis. And the crazy thing is, these Russian scientists developed the Anodyne because the Earth told *them* to."

Will blinked again, twice this time.

"What are you talking about, the *Earth* told them to?"

"Oh, this is where it gets really crazy," Court nodded. "See, the Mantic Anastomosis is not just a giant web of magic rock. It's a giant *living* web of *conscious* magic rock."

"Oh, hogwash," Will blurted reflexively. "With fried hog and a side of hog stew."

Court snickered. "I'm just telling you what the book says."

"So how did the Earth go about telling these Russian scientists to fundamentally change its own structure?" Will asked skeptically.

"Alcestis," Court said.

"Who?"

"Well, that's what she's called in the book, but that's just a pseudonym, based on a tale from Greek mythology. It doesn't give her real name, but you don't really need to know it. The important thing is that she was a real person. A witch. She had some kind of special psychic connection with the consciousness of the Mantic Anastomosis. So she became kind of an avatar for the earth—its voice, its human representative. Speaking on the earth's behalf, she relayed that the earth itself wished for the implementation of the Anodyne." He paused. "And so, they took her word for it."

Will thought through this.

"So." He attempted to summarize. "Before The Great Change, human beings could work magic without any kind of real limitation—all the toxic residuals would simply build up within the Earth. Of course, sometimes you'd get Aberrancies, big huge monsters tearing up the plains and stuff like that. But after the Great Change, people couldn't work magic without immediately suffering from the toxic residue that magic created."

"Sounds simple when you put it that way," Court said, as if trying to prompt Will to a conclusion. "But you haven't even mentioned the Black Flu."

Will narrowed his eyes, trying to figure out what he was getting at. "Some people are just naturally sensitive to Exunge," he murmured, remembering Briar's words. Then, awareness dawned on him instantly. "It's Exunge that causes the Black Flu! I mean, allergy to Exunge. It's not allergy to magic, it's allergy to *Exunge!*"

Court touched the tip of his nose with his finger and nodded gravely.

"But it was *children* who died in the Black Flu epidemics!" Will said. "They never worked any magic!"

"*Life* is magic," Court said. "Just by being alive, we humans work a tiny bit of magic. We work a tiny bit of magic, and create a tiny bit of Exunge. The children who were intensely allergic to Exunge ... they were the ones who got the Black Flu and died immediately. Those who were less allergic ... they lived longer, but became twisted, deformed wrecks."

Will thought of Claire—and of his own sister Catherine. Ben had written that the children who suffered the worst cases of Black Flu were thought to be those with the greatest inborn magical talents. Perhaps magic just flowed more freely through their bodies ... and after The Great Change, that physical anomaly would have been a death sentence.

"Alcestis must have felt like an idiot," Will commented wryly, after a long thoughtful pause. "I guess she was kicking herself for taking advice from the Earth, huh? A million dead worldwide will do that to a witch."

"Oh, it gets worse," Court said, shaking his head gravely. "Much worse."

"How can it get worse?"

Court took a deep breath. At this point in his exegesis, he had to fortify himself with a cigarette. He withdrew one and lit it, sending smoke curling up over his head.

"So, as you say, a million dead worldwide is definitely a cause for concern. And so in 1880, the same group of warlocks and scientists who had created the Anodyne—a kind of cabal, let's call them—convened a special summit. Alcestis and her consort—some guy the book calls Admetus, he isn't that interesting—traveled to New York City where the summit was being held. The cabal wanted her there to channel the spirit of the Earth so they could get some goddamn answers about just what the hell it was thinking."

"And what did the Earth say?" Will asked. "Oops?"

Court released a grim, graveyard chuckle. "No. The Earth said: 'Yeah, I know.'"

"*What?*"

"The Earth knew exactly what it was doing. The Earth knew what would happen. It *wanted* it to happen."

"What the hell are you saying?" Will whispered, horrified.

"See, when Alcestis made a psychic connection with the consciousness of the Earth, it infected her mind with all its alien hugeness and strangeness. But *she* infected *its* mind too. She infected it with human notions it had never experienced before. Paranoia, hatred, and fear—fear of death, especially. The consciousness of the Earth had no way of knowing about death before—not its *own* death, anyway. It had previously understood existence as eternal. By bonding with Alcestis' mind, it learned of death, and came to fear it."

Court paused, letting his words hang before saying, finally:

"And it came to feel that humanity was its greatest threat. It decided that it would be better off without us."

Will stared at him, open-mouthed. "You have got to be kidding," he said finally. "So why all the nonsense about Anodynes and witches and everything ... if the Earth had decided it wanted humanity eradicated, surely it could have found a more effective way?"

"Shh!" Court said anxiously. "Don't give it any ideas! But you're right, it seems like it would be pretty simple just to wipe us all out with fire and flood, and I have no idea why, if it feels that badly about us, it doesn't just do so. Maybe it doesn't understand its own strength. Whatever the reason, that was why it wanted the Anodyne implemented in the first place. As a weapon against humanity."

"But now that it had seen the actual results, it found them unsatisfactory. It was displeased by the fact they weren't worse. That it wasn't killing humans off faster. Apparently impatience was one of the human traits the Earth inherited from the witch Alcestis."

"Jesus!" Will blurted. "She's probably the one witch in all history we *should* have burned!"

"If it hadn't been her, it would have been someone else." Court spoke with an infuriating air of philosophical distance. "Anyway, the members of the cabal knew that they were in hot water. They had the whole spirit of the Earth sitting right there in front of them, casually telling them that it was very disappointed that all of humanity wasn't dying off as quickly as it would like. So what does this cabal do?"

"What *is* there to do?" Will said.

"Precisely," Court said. "All they could do was stall for time and hope that they'd figure something out. So they had to placate the earth. Humans weren't dying as fast as it wanted ... so humans had to be made to die faster. They struck a bargain with the Earth. They called it 'The Settlement.'"

"A Settlement—to *kill* people?"

"To kill very *specific* people," Court said. "All of them Old Users, the most powerful witches and warlocks of the last generation. They were still using huge quantities of magic under the old rules, and for the Earth, they were like cavities in a tooth—painful and annoying. So the Earth demanded that the cabal begin sacrificing these Old Users on its command."

"And *did* they?"

"Apparently so," Court said. "The book says there was a whole organization of warlocks created to do so. Fire to fight fire, I guess. They're called the Agency."

"They're the ones you said were destroying the books!" Will remembered.

Court nodded gravely. "I can see why they'd want to, given that this book doesn't make them sound very nice at all. See, the head of this Agency gets his orders directly from Alcestis herself. The Earth tells her who to kill—and she tells him."

"And if he refuses to comply?"

"Hell to pay," Court said. "You may not be a geologist like me, Will, but surely you know what the Earth can do if it wants. Natural disasters like Krakatoa, Tunguska, the great floods in Galveston ... all of these happened after the Settlement. And they all corresponded to occasions when the cabal failed to comply with the Earth's commands to the slightest letter."

"Just like I said!" Will lifted his hands. "The Earth doesn't need witches or Settlements. It can destroy us at its whim. So why all the complication?"

"Maybe it has something to do with love," Court said thoughtfully. "The witch infected the spirit of the Earth with human thoughts and emotions. Maybe the thing that's hurt us the most is also the thing that's protecting us."

"All right, now for the big question," Will said. "What does the book say we're supposed to do?"

"Do?" Court shrugged. "It's a confession, not a handbook."

"If it's a confession, then someone must be confessing," Will said. "And whoever it is must know what we're supposed to do. He must have some idea, at least. Who is the Goês?"

"I couldn't tell you," Court replied. "But if he was mixed up in this—and he must have been, if he knows the whole story the way he does—I don't know if I want to take any advice from him. But I have to give him credit for one thing. He chose the right name. Because he sure as hell is one big fool."

Chapter Fourteen

First and Last

That Sunday, Will finished the schematics.

He made the final ink stroke, allowed it to dry, and looked down at the completed pile. He was very proud of them. While working on them, he'd thought through what happened with his prototype, and had come up with several important improvements and design enhancements. He'd even added a fuse. It was a wonderful piece of work.

A work of genius.

He'd done it.

It was late afternoon, and he and Jenny were both sitting in their accustomed places at the table in the breakfast nook. Jenny looked tired; her face was drawn and sallow, and not only had the usual curl escaped from her hairpins, but it had been joined by a sinuous tangle of its fellows.

He was just about to tell her the good news when something very strange happened.

A voice spoke in his head.

SHE'S VERY PRETTY, MOONCALF.

The sound of it made him nearly jump out of his skin. It was like his own thoughts, but it was also just like when Ma'am would Send for him ... clear as spoken words. But it was not Ma'am's voice. It was a man's voice, tinged with a strange, broad accent like some two-bit British actor in a Teslaphone dramaplay.

He rubbed his face, ran his fingers through his hair. He was just tired. Exhausted. God, he was looking forward to a good night's sleep.

Jenny glanced at him. "What's wrong?" she asked softly.

"Nothing." He smiled. "Everything's perfect. I've finished."

Her eyes widened.

"Really?" she said. "You're done? *Done* done?"

"Done *done*," he said, pushing the drawings toward her. "They're all yours now."

"Oh Will, how wonderful!" Jumping to her feet, she raced over to hug him, and he hugged her back. He didn't want to let her go. Finishing the schematics meant something else. It meant she was going to leave. And, at that moment, he realized that he didn't want her to.

Flushing, she extracted herself from his arms. "You're tired," she said. "Why don't you get some sleep?"

He nodded. He was tired, so very tired. He walked to his room with heavy steps, his feet leaden and dragging. But just as he was falling asleep, the voice spoke in his head again:

SHE'S LEAVING YOU, MOONCALF.

The words made Will's heart race with panic, and suddenly he was wide awake. Rushing into the front room, he saw that it was true. Jenny was gone. He looked in the closet. She'd taken her fur coat.

Rushing back to his room, he looked out the window, and caught a glimpse of something small and fuzzy and brisk sneaking down the back alley.

DECEITFUL LITTLE CAT.

Throwing on his coat, Will rushed out to follow his wife.

Will caught sight of her waiting at the streetcar stop near Winslow Street. Factory men looked at her as they passed; Will felt sharp, surprising twinges of jealousy as they did. He glanced at his watch. The streetcar wouldn't come for another ten minutes, so he jogged up Grand River Avenue to wait at the prior stop. Thus he was already settled in the car—collar pulled up and hat pulled down, face buried in his chest, the very picture of a napping commuter— when Jenny climbed on. She took a seat at the other end of the car. He watched her beneath the brim of his hat.

She rode the streetcar all the way downtown, exiting at the Campus Martius stop. On a Sunday afternoon-becoming-evening, the streets were mostly still, save for a few late-afternoon shoppers, weighed down with wrapped packages, hurrying homeward. The downtown shops were all richly decorated for Christmas, drifts of tinsel sparkling in the colored light of fat electric bulbs. On a busy corner, a little group of carolers stood singing before a bucket, their hand-lettered sign proclaiming them representatives of the Detroit Scharfian Assembly, collecting donations for the ongoing relief of the Cursed nationwide.

While Shepherds watched their flocks by night,
All seated on the ground,
The Angel of the Lord came down,
And glory shone all around.

The sound of singing faded behind him as Will followed Jenny down Griswold Street, into the heart of the city's financial district.

Just past Fort Street, Jenny turned to enter a very tall office building, faced with glossy white terra-cotta tile. He watched through the front glass as she climbed into one of the elevators. The sweeping arrow on the dial above the elevator traversed the floor numbers in a half-moon sweep, and it did not stop until reaching its furthest extreme—Floor 23. The penthouse.

He entered the building and strode across the white marble floor. He did not press the call button, but simply stood before the elevator doors, watching as the movement of the arrow sketched the car's descent. When it had returned to the ground floor, the elevator operator opened the door. He startled when he saw Will standing there.

"Why, mister!" The elevator operator was a slight black man whose uniform included a bright red coat, gold-trimmed cap, and a smile that did not reach his eyes. "You gave me a scare. I didn't hear you ring, sir."

"What's on the penthouse?" Will said, taking a step forward. He did not enter the elevator, but rather positioned himself so that the operator could not close the door. "And the girl you just gave a ride up. What's she doing here on a Sunday, anyway?"

A slight furrow of his brow was the only indication that the elevator operator found these questions unusual or impertinent. He continued smiling, but his next words were less obliging than the first ones had been: "What are you, a cop?"

"No, I'm not a cop," said Will. He dug in his pocket for a couple of bucks and pressed them into the man's hand. "I work for the Bureau of Printing and Engraving."

The man rubbed the bills between his fingers as he considered his answer. Then he pocketed them.

"That's Miss Hansen," he finally said. "She's come here 'bout every day for the past couple weeks. She always rides up to see Mr. Hart in his office on the penthouse."

"Did you say Mr. Hart?" Will recalled the telegram he'd intercepted. *Hart has been informed of your arrival ... waste no time.*

"Mr. Atherton Hart, President of Hart Financial." The man eyed Will. "I guess you don't want me to run you up there?"

Will shook his head and stepped back. Exiting the building, he crossed the street to watch the door. He wrapped his coat tightly around himself against the chill evening wind.

Silly Mooncalf. Trusting a woman.

That voice again. Will rubbed his temples grimly. Why did he keep hearing it? Was some malign force speaking to him? Ridiculous—no malign force had any reason to be interested in him. The voice kept commenting immediately and directly on his present experience, reflecting his own confused feelings back to him in the harshest and darkest of mirrors. So was he cracking up? No, he concluded—he was just very, very tired. He needed to get some sleep.

Leaning against the wall of a dark alleyway, Will waited for a long time. As he waited, he felt illustrated eyes on his back—Dreadnought

Stanton's eyes. An Edison Studios advance-man must have recently passed this way, for the alley's brick walls had been freshly plastered with colorful advertisements for *The Warlock's Curse*. And that advance-man must have had Scharfian missionaries hot on his heels, for in several instances Dreadnought Stanton's mystical green gaze had been overlaid with the sterner visage of Brother Phleger, on less colorful handbills exhorting the faithful to attend an old-time revival that the good Brother would be conducting at the Detroit Scharfian Fellowship that Friday, December 16th. The sick would be healed, the faithless baptized, and the repentant welcomed home—all to the prodigal melodies of Little Sanctity Snow, "God's Special Snowflake," on the all-electrical organ.

Nonsense pasted upon nonsense.

By the time Jenny finally emerged from the building, the hour had grown late. She was not alone. A handsome young man in a suit of scrupulously modern tailoring escorted her to the curb, and stood waiting with her. Atherton Hart, no doubt. He was at least twenty-four, and looked like he'd stepped straight out of an advertisement for golf clubs. He had Jenny's arm, and was smiling down at her as he spoke. When she looked up at him, she smiled back.

Hart waited with Jenny until an autocab pulled up. He helped her into it, speaking a few words to the driver and sending her on her way. *He's sending her home,* Will thought, relieved.

Atherton Hart watched after the cab for a long moment before returning to the warmth of his presumably luxurious penthouse office. It could have been worse, Will told himself. He could have found himself following them both to a hotel. But he realized just how perilous the situation was. Jenny was only seventeen—almost as old as Will, sure, but she was a *girl*. A girl running around with no one to protect her, visiting men in penthouses, all alone, late at night. If something happened to her ... if someone took advantage of her ... he'd be to blame. He could never forgive himself.

Then a panicked realization seized him. Jenny was heading *home*. There was no way he could get there before her. She'd be terrified when she found him gone.

GOOD.

The voice in his head was bitter and sinuous. It made Will shudder. But suddenly, he realized that he agreed with the voice. Good. Let Jenny worry about him. Let her see what it was like to have someone run off and not tell you anything. *Good.*

Jerking his coat around himself, he began walking back along Griswold. He found that he recognized the area: he'd walked near here with Harley Briar when they had brought the sick man to Dr. Gore's. When he reached Gratiot, he turned up it, let his feet take him to Greektown, and knocked on the door of Dr. Gore's home. Once again, it was Irene who opened the door, surprised to find him on her doorstep. She was not wearing her nurse's whites now, but rather a pretty and proper Sunday outfit with a high collar. Around her neck, hanging from a thin gold chain, something shone—not the alembic Will remembered, but a little gold cross. When she finally did speak, it was not to him, but rather to call behind herself into the receiving room.

"Harley, it's for you."

Behind her, Harley Briar emerged. To Will's surprise, he was dressed up in a suit—a secondhand suit with frayed cuffs, but a suit nonetheless.

"Will?" Briar's face was both concerned and curious. "What the hell are you doing down here, kid? And how'd you know to find me?"

Will didn't answer immediately. He *hadn't* known Briar would be here. He'd just known that he was feeling sick and disoriented, and he'd ended up here. Maybe he'd been thinking of the man in the factory, Selvaggi.

"I don't know," said Will, his teeth chattering. "Sorry to bother you."

Briar and Irene exchanged glances as he turned to go.

"Wait," Briar called after him, before he'd reached the bottom step. "I'll get my coat."

Briar led Will to the Mechanic Street Bar, which was close to Dr. Gore's, and quiet and dark and warm. The air was blue with the smoke of cheap cigarettes. Will and Briar took seats at the far end of the long bar, crammed close together by the crowd of similar men in similar circumstances. Will didn't know what to say at first, so he drank thick walnut-brown ale until his body felt heavy and words began to suggest themselves.

"So you know Jenny? My wife?" Will said. "I think I'm falling in love with her."

Briar wiped foam from his lips. "You're already married, but you're just now falling in love with her?"

"It's a long story," Will said.

"I got time," Briar said.

"We needed to get to Detroit," Will said. "And she could get her hands on some inheritance money if she got married. So we got married. It was supposed to just be a business arrangement."

"That's all marriage ever is," Briar shrugged. "Usually a better deal for the husband, though."

"It hasn't been a good deal for me," Will said. "She thinks it's still business, but I think I'm falling in love with her. And I think ... I think there might be someone else."

Briar made a sound of sympathy. "That's rough. I can promise you, it ain't worth trying to change a woman's mind over something like that." He took a long drink of his beer before adding wistfully, "Ain't worth trying to change a woman's mind over much of anything, really."

Will nodded. He sure knew how strong Jenny's mind could be. Briar drained his glass, gestured for another round. While he waited, he took out his pouch of tobacco and began rolling a cigarette between his stained, scarred fingers.

"So, have you told her?"

Will shook his head. "I don't think I can. I ... I don't think it would be fair. She'd think I was trying to keep her from leaving."

"Wait, she's *leaving* you?" Briar shook his head with confusion as he tucked the cigarette between his lips. "You're in love with her

... but you think there's someone else ... *and* she's leaving you? I gotta say, kid, it don't look good."

"She's leaving me for other reasons," Will looked up angrily. "She's got plans. She's ... got some kind of project she's working on, and she won't tell me what it is. She's so secretive. And my father is looking for us, and she thinks that if she goes away, he won't bother me anymore. Because she knows that I want to stay at Tesla Industries more than anything." He paused, and added softly, "Almost anything."

"Now that sounds better," Briar said. "She cares about you."

The words, spoken aloud, warmed Will's heart. Or maybe it was just the fresh glass of beer that the barman had brought, which he seized and downed in one protracted swallow. He gestured for another.

"I'm worried about her, Harley," Will whispered. "I'm afraid she's doing things that are dangerous. She thinks she can do anything. She's so smart, she believes she can always think her way out. But what if she can't? What if she's in over her head?"

"What if you're in over yours?" Briar retorted. He half-stood, leaning over the bar to light his cigarette at a flickering gas jet designed for cigars of ages past. "Just 'cause she's a girl don't naturally mean she don't know what she's doing. Don't you trust her?"

"Of course I trust her," Will snapped back. "But that doesn't mean I trust anyone else. I know what the world can do to pretty girls."

"Oh you *do*, do you?" Briar's voice was amused. "You havin' such a vast experience of the wicked ways of the world and all."

Will ignored the dig. "Whatever she's mixed up in, it involves money. A *lot* of money. A hundred thousand dollars."

Briar's eyes widened, and he seemed concerned. "People with money like that *are* the most dangerous sort to get mixed up with," he allowed. "Money makes people do terrible things."

"She's mentioned something called 'The Consortium.'" Will recalled Jenny's threat at the Asylum in Stockton. "Have you ever heard of it?"

Briar shook his head thoughtfully, exhaling acrid smoke through his nose. "I've heard of lots of consortiums. Consortiums, conglomerates, syndicates, trusts ... don't have much use for any of 'em. What kind of consortium did she mean?"

Will shrugged; he had no idea. Of course he'd heard of business consortiums too, and if anyone was likely to be in one of them, it was that slick Atherton Hart fellow she'd gone up to see. But it was difficult to imagine why a doctor in a mental asylum would be scared of a business consortium.

Briar was silent for a long time, obviously contemplating Will's situation. He drew his glass of beer close to himself.

"Well, I'll tell you, Will," he said, turning the glass between his palms. "Telling someone you love them is a funny thing. It can make things a whole lot better or a whole lot worse, depending. But there's only one thing worse than telling them. It's not telling them at all. That's the only advice I got for you. Sorry."

It wasn't any more than Will already knew. But it was good to have a friend offer it to him. Nodding gratefully, Will raised his hand for another glass of beer.

By the end of the night Will and Briar had both drunk far more than they should have, and they had to lean on each other heavily as they staggered back to Dr. Gore's. Their path was lit by the glow of the almost-full moon, multiplied by the light of moonlight towers. The streets were ghostly bright.

When Irene found the pair of them collapsed on her doorstep, she sighed with indulgent disdain, crossed herself quickly, and let them in, directing them to the receiving room, where Will took the couch and Briar climbed onto the examining table.

The next morning Will felt much better, despite a hangover of monstrous proportions. Not wanting to wake the still-snoring Briar, he let himself quietly out of Dr. Gore's house, emerging into the wan cold light. He started back toward Fort Tesla, glancing quickly at his watch. He had plenty of time to meet Grig, and with luck, his mentor would never even suspect he'd been gone.

The activities of the night before seemed a strange blur to him. He remembered that there had been a voice in his head ... but that seemed unreal now, as if it was just a story he'd been telling himself. He couldn't even remember what the voice had said—he knew it had made sense at the time, but all he could remember now was harsh guttural gibberish. He laid it all down to sheer exhaustion. He'd been working so hard on the schematics. But now, he realized with a sudden thrill, that was all done with. The schematics were finished. No more late nights. He could live like a normal person.

Without Jenny.

He stopped dead in his tracks.

Could he really have fallen in love with her, he wondered? But the answer came to him instantly, so obvious it made him snort at himself. Sure, who wouldn't? Who *couldn't* fall in love with a girl like that?

Briar was right. He had to tell her.

As Will made his way up Woodward Avenue, he stopped before a storefront with holiday decorations more cheerful than most, the front window draped with chains of colored paper and strings of popcorn. It was a jewelry store—this much he ascertained from the display of rings and necklaces—small, and not particularly grand. They didn't charge him much to set the silver dollar his father had given him into a necklace, and they did it while he waited.

Then, standing before the shop in the rising sunlight, he opened the little purple velvet gift box in which the jeweler had nestled the newly-set necklace. The silver gleamed in the orange and crimson rays of dawn. It really *was* incredible, he realized. But it wasn't incredible for all the strange and detailed reasons Jenny had given him. It was incredible because Jenny's eyes had lit up when she looked at it, and her breath had been taken away in wonder.

He clicked the velvet box shut and slid it into his pocket. He would tell her on Christmas Eve. Surely she wouldn't leave him before Christmas. He would give her the necklace and tell her that he loved her. And he wouldn't care if she laughed. Actually he knew that he would care, very much, but he tried not to think about that.

Will reached the Winslow Street Apartments just as Grig was stepping out the front door, pulling on his leather gloves. They were accustomed to meet on the apartment's front steps for their work-day walk to Fort Tesla, so Will didn't understand why, when Grig caught sight of him, his eyes filled with alarm.

"Are you feeling well, Mr. Edwards?" Grig touched his arm with concern. "You look ... peaked."

"Fine, Grig," said Will. And it was true. He *did* feel fine. The little velvet box in his pocket made him feel fine. But as they walked to the Compound, he caught a glimpse of his reflection in a nearby window and was shocked at how haggard he looked—his cheeks hollow and sunken, his eyes ringed with dark circles.

But with the little velvet box in his pocket, Will found that his workday at Tesla Industries went very quickly. He was impervious to Roher's sallies and squeaks. As he bent over a soapstone workbench, wiring up an important subsystem of Grig's Tri-Dimensionator, he imagined giving the necklace to Jenny; he imagined each of her possible responses in exquisite or excruciating detail, depending on the nature of the response. His reveries were so complete, in fact, that when three strange men came into Building Three around lunchtime, he was one of the last apprentices to notice.

When he finally did look up, he saw that all the other young men were frozen in watchfulness; pens hovering over papers, places in books held with still fingers.

Building Three did not get many visitors, for Grig liked to keep the projects they were working on a matter of strict secrecy even from the other groups on the Compound. But while visitors were not unheard of, none had ever provoked such a response.

The men were all very large and strong-looking, and they all bore the same official Tesla Industries insignia that the apprentices did—except these men's badges read "Security."

The visitors strode across the large workfloor, coming to a stop before Roher's desk. Roher looked up at them. The squeak of his chair fell silent. Every apprentice in the room seemed to hold his breath.

"Mr. Max Roher?" one of the men asked crisply.

Roher nodded assent, but did not speak.

"We are here to escort you from the premises. It has been determined that you have violated the terms of the apprenticeship contract you signed."

Will watched with dark satisfaction as all the color drained from Roher's face.

"We have received a report that you have been maintaining unauthorized contact with one Miss"—here he consulted his notes—"Greta Zuffenhausen. Having verified the accuracy of this report, it has been determined that the only recourse is your immediate expulsion. Please come with us. You are to take nothing with you. Your personal belongings will be collected and sent."

Roher stood slowly. He looked around the room, his fat face stricken.

Will smiled to himself. He did not think of himself as a mean-spirited person, so he wasn't quite sure what compelled him to call after Roher's back, as he was being escorted out by the three men:

"Goodbye, Blockhead!"

After they left, the room was deathly silent. All the other apprentices turned their eyes to Will. Will was surprised to find that their gazes were uniformly hostile. He glared back at them before returning to his work. None of them had liked Roher any better than he had! What were they all so angry about? Court came over to his desk and roughly gestured for Will to follow. Once they were outside, Court thrust his face close to Will's, his eyes bright with fury.

"*You* did that?"

"Hell yes I did!" Will snapped back. "You know how he was always digging me! And you yourself were the one who told me about his little flirtation with Greta whatever-her-name-was!"

"I didn't mean for you to use it to get him kicked out!" Court yelled, shoving Will backward. Will stumbled, but caught himself.

"Court!" he blurted, shocked.

"You were supposed to tell *Roher* that you knew," Court said. "It would have gotten him off your back. But for God's sake, you weren't supposed to rat him out to *Tesla*."

Will swallowed hard. Shame contended with anger, and anger won. "Well, he broke the apprenticeship contract!" he barked. "He deserved what he got."

"We've *all* broken the apprenticeship contract, Will!" Court yelled, then quickly clapped his hand over his mouth, anxious at having yelled it so loudly. When he continued, it was in a quiet intense hiss: "Have you *read* that contract? It's impossible *not* to break that contract! One bite of meat and you've broken the contract! One night in the sack with your wife and you've broken the contract!"

"They took that part out of mine," Will muttered.

Court's eyes narrowed. "Oh, that's right. Because you're so *special*. Because being held to a contract is for other people, for people you don't like."

"Look, I'm sorry you feel that way," Will said finally. The words sounded petulant even to him.

Court shook his head and stared at him.

"You have no idea what you've done, do you? Roher will never work again, Will. Tesla will ruin him. There won't be a university or a high school or even a goddamn *kindergarten* that will consider him now. All because you couldn't take a few tacks on your chair."

Then, turning on his heel, Court was gone, disappearing back into Building Three. And Will realized that he had lost his only friend at Tesla Industries.

None of the other apprentices spoke to him after that. Not at all, not even when he addressed them directly. And it was clear that none of them intended to do so again.

Fine, Will thought acidly. *To hell with all of them.*

Later that day, when Grig finally returned to Building Three, he looked worn down. He did not return to work on his

Tri-Dimensionator, as he was accustomed to do, but rather called all the apprentices together.

"We've all had a very upsetting day," he said, his voice quavering. "I would be guilty of great disloyalty to Mr. Tesla if I were to defend Mr. Roher's actions. But I must say, I will miss him. He was a young man of exceptional intelligence and insight, and I am very sad that he has thrown away, with one foolish indiscretion, what promised to be a brilliant career."

Walking back to his desk, Will stumbled over an outstretched foot. It was Court's.

"Blockhead," Court hissed at him, before returning to his work.

Later, walking home with Grig, Will wasn't sure what he should say. Grig would certainly know that he'd been the one who'd written the letter to Tesla, telling him of Roher and his blonde-braided girlfriend. Will had signed his own name to it, sent it through the interoffice mail, unsure if a letter from a lowly apprentice would reach the notice of the great man. But clearly it had. And clearly the great man had taken it seriously.

They walked very slowly through the slanting evening light. Grig kept clearing his throat, as if he wanted to speak about the events of the day but was having a difficult time doing so.

"Mr. Edwards," he began formally, then softened. "Will. I want you to know that I blame myself."

Will had been expecting anything but that. "What?"

"I allowed Mr. Roher to bully and abuse you, and for that I apologize. I know how he treated you when I was out of the office. In some ways, I thought it would help you. It gained you the sympathy of the other apprentices. Mr. Courtenay, in particular, would never have taken you under his wing had he not felt you needed a friend."

Grig was apologizing to *him*? It made Will feel unutterably low.

"I care very deeply for all my young men," Grig continued. "For all his flaws, there was much to admire in Mr. Roher. And no small amount of genius."

There was a long silence between them as they came to the front steps of the Winslow Street Apartments.

"In the end, however, you behaved just as Mr. Tesla would have. Strictly, and with respect for the rules. Mr. Tesla is a great admirer of the rules." Grig paused. "But just between you and me, Will, while Mr. Tesla has most of the qualities it takes to make a great man—I do not believe he has all of them."

Will blinked. Tipping his hat to Will, Grig said before vanishing inside:

"Good night. I will see you in the morning. As usual."

Will stood there for a long time, staring at the closed door. Then, quietly, he went inside and climbed the stairs to his own apartment. Letting himself in, the first thing he saw was Jenny, sitting on the couch facing the door, her face pale.

"Oh William, you're home, thank goodness!" She rose swiftly. "You didn't come home at all last night! Where were you? I was worried sick!"

"I was just out," Will said softly. "Walking." Breaking the contract, just as Roher had, but in an infinitely more flagrant way. And in a way infinitely more disloyal to the woman standing before him. He couldn't tell her about following her, about seeing her with Atherton Hart. He felt terrible about it now. Dirty and sneaking and unkind. With his thumb, he stroked the velvet box in his pocket, as if to reassure himself that it was still there. "I'm sorry if I worried you."

"You did," Jenny said. Her lip trembled as she said it.

He took a step closer to her. "Why would you worry about me? We've both got our own plans. Just business, right?"

"Sure," she said uncertainly. "But we're friends too, right?"

"I don't know," Will said. "Friends usually tell each other things and trust each other. You don't seem to trust me at all."

Hurt softened Jenny's features. "I trust you, William. But you have to trust me. I promise you, I have it under control."

"Sure you do," Will said. "You always have everything under control."

Will realized that they were now very close to each other. He could feel Jenny trembling. He could smell her skin. Without thought, he touched her flushed cheek, cradling it in his palm. Her soft brown curls brushed his fingertips.

"I don't always have *everything* under control," she murmured. She leaned her cheek into his hand and closed her eyes.

Drawing her toward him, he kissed her. Her lips were warm and soft. He kissed her and he didn't want to stop.

But being so close to her made him dizzy, and not in a pleasant way. The voice in his head was suddenly back, and it was ... laughing. Laughing, cackling and cruel. His heart raced and he pushed her away, alarmed.

"Oh, shucks," she said, stumbling back. Her face was suddenly beet red. "I ... I guess I'm not a very good kisser. I'm sorry."

"You're a fine kisser," Will said curtly, not trusting himself to look at her, not wanting to risk the return of the laughter. "I'm just not feeling like myself right now, Jenny."

She cast her eyes down. "You're tired," she said. "I worked you too hard. But it's all over now."

"Yes, Jenny," Will said. "It's all over now."

Chapter Fifteen

Seven Stones Unturned

And even though it was all over, and the only thing Jenny had to do was finish preparing the filing papers so they could be sent to the patent office in Washington D.C., and Will could sleep as much as he liked, catching up on the rest he so desperately craved and knew that he so desperately needed, he found that sleep was even more a stranger than it had been before. All the rest of that week, Will suffered from terrible dreams, each night's horrors more terrible than the last. He would wake gasping, the light of the waxing moon casting terrible shadows across his sweat-tangled bedclothes.

His dreams always had blood in them.

One night he dreamed of killing a man, stabbing him in the chest with a kitchen knife. There was a lot of blood that came out when you stabbed a man in the chest. There was also a child in that dream, a little girl. And for some reason he hated her. The violet-eyed little brat was hiding from him. He kept calling to her, trying to find her, telling her that he would kill her, but of course he would not. He needed her. He could not live if she did not grow up someday, have little violet-eyed brats of her own. But he liked making her afraid. And she knew something. She knew something that he wanted to know, and she wouldn't tell him what it was.

He had many other dreams like this, but in each dream, he was always a different person. In each dream, people looked at him with fear in their eyes. For some reason, they never knew who he was. They always expected him to be someone else. Someone they trusted. And he did not know why, in those dreams, he found it so deliciously sweet to disappoint them, to betray them, to hurt them.

He didn't tell Jenny about these dreams. He didn't talk to her at all, just went to work every morning and closed himself in his room when he got home at night. Sometimes he heard her outside his door, lingering as if she wanted to knock. But he did not want to talk to her. *Couldn't* talk to her. He couldn't get the thought of kissing her out of his mind. Or rather, he couldn't get the thought of what he'd wanted to do *after* kissing her out of his mind. Those thoughts were as bad as the nightmares. Worse. Sometimes he thought it was better to sleep and have nightmares than think about Jenny.

Ben still wrote to him every night, his letters short and friendly. There were no more terrible revelations—it was as if his brother knew that Will could not stand any more of them. And Ben was coming to Detroit. He was coming to Detroit on December 16th, and Will was to meet him at the Michigan Central Depot. It would all come out all right.

Will wrapped that thought around himself. It was insufficient armor, but it was something.

Ben was coming.

It would all come out all right.

On Thursday night, he woke from the worst nightmare he'd yet had. In it, he had been screaming a word, just one word—*maledictus*. His hands were covered in the blood of a woman he loved, and a man was putting a sword to his throat.

Will felt that he was still screaming when he woke, but as he sat in his bed, panting and trembling, he realized that the apartment was still and silent and he hadn't made a sound. It was very bright outside, the light of the almost-full moon multiplied by the harsh light of the moonlight towers.

I'm sick. It was the only explanation. He thought about the way the Exunge had slithered and burrowed under Selvaggi's skin. What was wrong with him? Why was he hearing voices in his head? He would ask Ben. Ben would know.

Climbing out of bed, he moved quietly across the room and into the hall. Ben would know why he was hearing voices. Ben would know what was wrong with him. As he walked past the door to Jenny's bedroom, he saw that it was half open.

He slowly pushed it open, careful not to make a sound.

She was very beautiful when she slept.

BEAUTIFUL AND HELPLESS AND AT YOUR MERCY.

He cradled his head. The voice again, the goddamn voice. He forced himself to look away and in doing so, saw something else. Jenny's calfskin grip. Seizing it, he fled from the room as if in a fever.

He carried the grip to the breakfast nook and sat down. It was secured with a small lock, but he didn't care about that. Using the sharp point of a kitchen knife, he jimmied it open, ruining it.

He pulled out the papers and spread them on the table. There were sheaves and sheaves of notes on his patent, drafts of the filing marked up with comments and corrections in a fine law-yerly script. Will frowned. It had to be Atherton Hart's writing. At least there was nothing incriminating there, no little love notes, no hearts or flowers or rhyming couplets. Even so, it didn't make Will feel much better.

Setting these aside, he got down to some more interesting documents. Investment records. When Jenny had said she had deposited the gold certificates, he'd thought she'd meant in a bank. But instead, the receipts were from Hart Financial, and they indicated that all of the money had been invested in a bewildering tangle of short-term options on the Detroit Stock Exchange. Will had no idea what any of it meant, but most of the investment orders were accompanied by more notes, this time in Jenny's fine strong hand—intricate calculations and equations, with notations about hedge parameters, velocity and put-call parities. Will remembered how Jenny had corrected the equation on the board when they'd come to Detroit. Her little hand sliding across the slate, rubbing out the chalk. Will was good at mathematics, but these equations defied his understanding; he set these aside as well.

He recognized the paper that sat on top of the next bundle. It was the telegram the landlady had given him, removed from its envelope and folded smooth.

Received your message. Hart has been informed of your arrival. Waste no time. Hetty.

The letters bundled with this telegram were from a Brooklyn address, scribbled on cheap pieces of scrap paper. They were all signed Hetty Green.

Will sat back in his seat, stunned. Even he knew who Hetty Green was. She was the richest woman in America, a cutthroat financier in New York City and a famous miser. Will scanned the letters. They were all notes of friendly encouragement from an old, wise woman to a young, ambitious one. He didn't have Jenny's letters, but he could tell from Mrs. Green's replies that she must have written about investing. One sentence caught Will's eye:

If you are looking to parlay a hundred thousand dollars into a million in the space of a few weeks, I am afraid I cannot offer you any words of advice. I have always been content with six percent interest, steady over time. That is all a Christian woman should expect.

Will stared at the paper. A million dollars? What could Jenny be trying to do that required a million dollars? Briar's words came back to him.

Money makes people do terrible things.

He sorted through the papers more quickly now, anxiety rising. He was looking particularly for anything about the Consortium that Jenny had spoken of, the organization that she had used to scare Dr. Smyth. But there was nothing in any of the papers, nothing at all.

What he did find, at the very bottom of the pile, was their marriage license. And with it, the envelope that he had glimpsed in her purse when they were in San Francisco. It had the logo of the Hansen Timber Company in the top left-hand corner. He unfolded it and read the contents:

Dear Mr. Sawtelle:

I am pleased to inform you that my daughter, Jennifer Elaine Hansen, has married Mr. William Edwards. I have known Mrs. Emily Edwards since childhood, and I consider her my oldest and dearest friend. I am overjoyed that my daughter has chosen to marry her youngest son, and I wish to give the newlyweds every comfort and luxury as they begin their new life together. To this end, I direct you to immediately disburse to her $100,000, the entire balance of the emergency fund of cash you hold on my account.

My apologies for not being able to arrange this with you personally, but matters of immediate concern require my presence away from San Francisco over the Thanksgiving holiday.

I remain respectfully yours,

Mr. Dagmar Hansen, President
Hansen Timber Company

Will stared at the signature on the letter. It was a reasonable facsimile of Mr. Hansen's signature. But he knew it had to be just that. A facsimile.

A fake.

That's why Jenny had been so panicked in San Francisco.

She hadn't gotten the money from an inheritance or a trust. She'd *stolen* it. She'd embezzled it from her father. The marriage license had been a pretense, but not of the kind she'd said.

"What are you doing?" Jenny's voice came from behind him. She was dressed in a long white nightgown trimmed with soft lace. Her hair streamed around her shoulders. She stared at him.

He did not speak, only held up the letter. It took her a moment to realize what he was holding, but then she saw the calfskin grip at Will's feet. First she reddened, then she went deadly pale. Flying across the room, she snatched it out of his hand furiously.

"How dare you go through my papers!"

"How dare *you* mix me up in this swindle!" Will jumped to his feet, fury flaring in response.

"You were happy enough to be mixed up in it when it meant you could get to Detroit!" Jenny snapped. "And it's *not* a swindle. I do have an inheritance waiting for me, and that $100,000 is only a patch on it. But not even the crookedest lawyer on earth could have gotten that for us—it's sewn up tighter than a drum. So I had to ... borrow it another way."

"Borrow it! Jenny, you *stole* it!"

"I *borrowed* it!" Jenny stomped her foot. "I am going to pay him back every penny, with handsome interest!"

"Is that what all this is?" Will gestured to the financial papers on the table. "All of these investments?"

"I am going to make a million dollars," Jenny hissed. "I *have* to, and this is the only way I can do it."

"For what, Jenny?" Will advanced on her, cold rage rising in him. The voice was screaming, just as it had in his dream, joyous and cruel. "What is the Consortium? Goddamn it, *tell me!*"

"I *can't!*" Jenny cried. "William, I *can't!* If I do—"

"Tell me!" he yelled, seizing her by the arms and shaking her. Jenny wrenched away from him.

"Don't you touch me, William Edwards!" She staggered across the room. Falling against the bookshelf, she seized a heavy bookend and pressed herself back into a corner, brandishing it.

"What about Atherton Hart, Jenny?" Will spoke in a low voice as he crossed the room toward her. "I know about you sneaking off to see him every day."

Jenny looked at him, her knuckles white around the bookend. "What are you talking about?"

"I followed you," Will said softly. She was afraid of him, he saw. Why did that give him so much pleasure? "I saw things."

"You didn't see anything because there wasn't anything to see!" she screeched. "He's my financial agent. Recommended to me— "

"By Hetty Green," Will completed the sentence. "An old miser you've been writing schoolgirl mash notes to. Even *she* thinks you're a fool trying to make a million dollars out of a hundred thousand. And for what, Jenny?" He was close to her now, towering over her. "What is the Consortium?"

"Stop asking me that," she said, voice trembling. "You have no right."

"I have every right," Will sneered, seizing the bookend out of her hand and throwing it to the ground. It landed with a heavy thud, denting the beautifully polished hardwood floor. "I'm your *husband*, remember?"

"You're a stupid bumpkin I used to get what I wanted!" Jenny darted past him, quick as a fish. She ran across the living room and down the hall, seizing the knob of her bedroom door. "You're not even a business partner! You're a sneaking, two-faced son-of-a-bitch! I got you what you wanted. I paid your way here. Now leave me alone!"

She slammed her bedroom door and Will heard it lock. Behind the door, he could hear her sink to the floor, sobbing. He went to the door and laid his forehead against it. He felt spent and remorseful.

"Jenny," he began.

"Leave me alone!" she screamed through the wood.

"Jenny, I'm sorry. I'm ... I'm worried about you."

"Don't worry about me." Jenny's voice trembled. "I can take care of myself."

Will stood there listening to her cry for a long time. Then he went back and gathered up her papers and put them back into the calfskin grip. As he did, a tiny slip of paper fluttered to the floor. Picking it up, Will saw that it was the paper from the fortune cookie that she'd gotten at the chop suey restaurant.

Loss is the crucible of the spirit.

Tucking it inside with the other papers, Will closed the grip and left it outside Jenny's bedroom door.

Chapter Sixteen

Nikola Tesla

Dear Will:

I will arrive in Detroit at 6:15 p.m. on December 16th. Please meet me at the Michigan Central Depot, under the clock tower, without fail.

It'll all come out all right.

Your brother always,

Ben

When Will woke the next morning, Jenny was gone, the calfskin grip gone with her.

GONE, GONE, GONE. The voice—now familiar and pervasive, hardly separable from his own thoughts anymore—echoed mockingly. AND YOU LET HER GET AWAY.

"Mr. Tesla has taken a sudden interest in you," said Grig as they were walking to work. He spoke with stiff formality, as if Will was a stranger, but there was concern in his eyes. Will didn't know why Grig was concerned about him, except perhaps it was that he hadn't shaved, even though he did have the straight razor in his pocket. He had started to shave that morning, but then he had been more fascinated by the gleam of the metal. It was a beautiful blade. Jenny had bought it for him.

WHERE DID SHE GO? SHE PROBABLY WENT TO MEET THAT HAND-
SOME MAN.

"No she didn't," Will muttered to the voice. "She said it was just
business."

THAT'S WHAT SHE SAID ABOUT YOU TOO. AND THEN SHE KISSED
YOU. SHE WAS LYING TO YOU, MOONCALF. DON'T YOU KNOW THAT?

"No, I kissed *her*," Will said, confused. Then he realized that Grig
was looking at him and the voice in his head laughed, and Will was
silent.

Grig did not speak again until they were in Building Three, and
Will had slumped into his chair, staring down at the papers on his
desk. "Mr. Tesla is now very interested in having you reconstruct
your Otherwhere Flume for his review. What did you say it would
take you, two weeks?"

WHAT DO YOU THINK THEY ARE DOING RIGHT NOW? CAN'T YOU
JUST IMAGINE? WHAT KINDS OF SOUNDS IS SHE MAKING?

"I don't need two weeks," Will said dully. He felt for the straight
razor in his pocket, as if to reassure himself that it was still there.

If Tesla wanted the Flume, he'd build it for him. To hell with
Jenny. To hell with that deceitful, sneaking, lying ...

Jumping to his feet, Will began gathering parts from the storage
bins around Building Three. Throwing these together on a table he
began working furiously. The ferocity of his efforts didn't silence
the voice—nothing did—but at least it gave him something to think
about other than what it was saying.

CAN'T YOU JUST IMAGINE, MOONCALF? THE TWO OF THEM
NAKED, HIS HAND MOVING UP HER THIGH—

"Shut up!" Will shrieked. The other apprentices looked up at
Will's outburst. But it was Court who finally came over.

"Hey, Will," he said softly. "Are you all right?"

"It's all *your* fault," Will growled at Court, low this time. "*You*
did this. *You* made me sick, with all your stories about witches and
cabals. Why did you tell me about those things? Terrible things that
can't be undone!"

Then he turned furiously back to his work. He felt, rather than saw, Court back away. He felt, rather than saw, Court cross the floor of Building Three to go talk to Grig.

"Will," Grig's voice interrupted Will's work a few minutes later. "Court says you're sick. Perhaps you should rest a bit."

Taking a deep breath, Will lifted his head. He made his face smooth and pleasant. When he spoke, it was in a completely normal voice.

"Gee, Grig, I don't know what Court means by that," he said. "I don't feel sick at all." He gestured to the work in front of him. "And look, I'm making swell progress."

Grig looked down at the work spread on the table before Will. His brow knit with uncertainty. "Are you sure? You've been behaving very strangely—"

"I'm just swell, Grig," Will interrupted, smiling so hard it made his cheeks ache. "It'll all come out all right."

By late afternoon, Will had completed the new Otherwhere Flume. It was a day of unbroken and intense effort, his fingers flying with greater dexterity than he'd ever imagined them capable of, their accuracy and swiftness seeming almost unnatural. When he was done he went to Grig's desk and set the Flume down before him with a thump.

"Done," he barked. Grig looked up at him slowly, then at the Flume. It had been built to Will's new specifications, and was far more elegant and impressive than his cigar-box prototype.

"I will call Mr. Tesla and let him know," said Grig softly.

Will said nothing in reply, just turned on his heel and returned to his desk. He threw himself down on his chair. But something was missing. Rising, he went to Roher's empty desk. He wheeled Roher's chair to his desk, shoving his own chair aside. Then he said down and started rocking back and forth.

Squeaking.

Yes. That was better.

Mr. Tesla arrived about an hour later.

When he arrived in Building Three, everyone leapt to their feet. All the other apprentices stood stock-straight, some hastily slicking back their hair, others straightening their ties or tucking in their shirts. But Will just continued rocking back and forth in his chair.

Will and Jenny Edwards, sitting in a tree ...

Nikola Tesla was in his early fifties. He was very tall and trim, and every article of his clothing was as crisp and precise as a wiring diagram. His hair was templed with gray and he wore a small, neatly groomed moustache. He did not even glance at the other apprentices, but walked straight to Will's desk, Grig at his elbow.

"I am very pleased to meet you, Mr. Edwards." His voice was soft and melodic, spiced with the sounds of the Black Sea. "I am glad that you wrote to me about Mr. Roher. There is no greater tragedy than a brilliant young mind wasted in debauchery. You clearly understand the vital importance of discipline and focus." He paused, scrutinizing Will with clear, blue-gray eyes. "You will go far here at Tesla Industries."

"I doubt it." Will smiled up at him. Tesla's brows lifted with surprise. Grig hurriedly placed Will's newly-built Otherwhere Flume on the desk before him.

"Here it is, Mr. Tesla," he said.

Tesla did not reach for the device, nor did he do anything but look at it.

"Grig says that you have somehow overcome the Connection Drop Problem," he said. "I am eager to understand how."

Will pushed the Otherwhere Flume closer to him, and said with supreme indifference:

"Figure it out for yourself. It's all right there."

"Mr. Edwards!" Grig gasped, but Tesla lifted a fine-boned hand to silence him. Then he reached into his pocket and withdrew a pristine white handkerchief. Unfolding it, he used it to pick up the device. He turned it over and over, slowly. He stared at it for a long time, his eyes luminescent.

"Yes," he murmured finally. "Yes, I see. Of course. It makes perfect sense."

"Does it?" Will said. "That's good. I'm glad something does."

Then Will stood up and walked out of the door of Building Three, not even looking back to meet the astonished gazes that followed him.

He walked past the gatehouse toward Grand River Avenue, pulling his coat tight around him. Winter twilight was gathering cold and purple. He put his head down against the frigid wind. He walked faster.

He was supposed to meet Ben at the Michigan Central Depot. The Michigan Central Depot was right across the street from the Hotel Acheron. The hotel where people didn't care if you screamed.

Will walked downtown. He *needed* to walk. It was the only thing keeping him from flying into a million pieces. But when his feet stopped, he saw that they had carried him someplace unexpected. They had carried him, as unswerving as metal filings to a magnet, down Griswold Street, to the tall white building in the financial district where Atherton Hart's offices were.

He pushed open the brass and glass door. Steam heat enveloped him. He got in the elevator, and let the elevator man take him all the way to the top, to the 23rd floor.

The offices of Hart Financial occupied the entire penthouse. The silken carpets were brilliantly colored, the wood paneling dark and polished to a high gloss. Will approached the massive reception desk, behind which sat a neatly dressed receptionist. She looked up with a pleasant smile as he approached, but when she saw his face, her smile vanished abruptly.

"Hello," Will said to her. "I'm looking for my wife."

The receptionist blinked at him. "Excuse me," she said. "I'm sorry, but who are you looking for?"

"My wife," Will repeated. "Her name is Mrs. William Edwards."

"I ... I'm sorry, sir," she said. "But I don't know anyone by that name."

"Her name is Jenny," Will thundered, pounding the reception desk with his fist. The girl jumped, her face going ashen.

"You mean Miss Hansen?" she squeaked. "I'm sorry, but she's not here!"

"I don't believe you," Will snarled, striding past her to open the door to the offices beyond. The girl was on her feet in a moment, wringing her hands.

"Oh no, please! You can't go in there, I'm sorry—"

But Will had already stormed into the private office of Atherton Hart.

As Will entered, Atherton Hart rose from behind his huge mahogany desk. Seeing him up close made Will hate him even more. He hated his neatly slicked hair, his mirror-polished shoes, his dark horn-rimmed glasses that only seemed to make him more handsome.

"Excuse me, who are you?" Even Hart's voice sounded pressed and starched and expensive.

"My name is William Edwards," said Will, taking two slow steps toward him. "And I'm looking for my wife. Your secretary says you call her Miss Hansen. But her name is Mrs. Edwards. She's my *wife.*"

Atherton Hart blinked and said nothing for a moment. Then he looked past Will at the receptionist standing behind him. She must have looked terrified, for Hart spoke very gently to her.

"It's all right, Miss Leydeker," he said. "Please hold my calls. I will speak with Mr. Edwards."

Will heard the door being closed behind him. Then he was alone with Hart. He felt in his pocket. The straight razor was still there.

"Your wife *is* a client of mine, Mr. Edwards," Hart said. "But I'm afraid I don't know where she is."

"I think you do," Will took another step forward. "You and she have been going around together. *Sneaking* around."

"We have hardly been sneaking!" Hart lifted an eyebrow, smiled slightly. "I have taken your wife to lunch once or twice. But it's only business."

"Only business," Will whispered. "That's what she said to me. Only business."

"Mr. Edwards, are you all right?"

"No!" Will barked. "I'm not all right. I don't know where my wife is. It's not only business. I'm not all right."

Then, turning, Will slammed the door behind himself hard enough to make the wall rattle.

Will stalked up Grand River Avenue, arms clenched around himself, muttering low. It had grown much colder, and the streets glistened with moonlight, pallid and deceiving. Maybe she was home. Maybe she'd gone home. Maybe that's where she was.

He didn't even notice Harley Briar was beside him, matching his hurried stride, calling his name, until Briar grabbed him by the shoulders and shook him.

"Will! I've been looking everywhere for you!"

"Why are you looking for me?" Will snarled. "Are you one of them? Are you one of the Consortium, or the cabal? Were you the one who turned the Earth against us? It's trying to kill us all."

Deep concern passed over Briar's face. "What are you *talking* about? You're not making any sense."

"There's Exunge inside my head," Will whispered. "Big fat worms of it."

"Then you need help." Briar spoke carefully, using the same infuriatingly reasonable tone he'd used with Selvaggi at the Mayflower factory. He tried to take Will's arm. "Come on. I'll take you to Dr. Gore's."

"No!" Will shrieked, shaking off his hand. "They're sangrimancers! Who ever heard of sangrimancer *doctors*?"

"It's going to be all right, Will," Briar said. Instead of trying to take Will's arm again, he just rested a steadying hand on his shoulder. "Just come with me, okay?"

"I have to go *home*." Will stared down. The pavement beneath his feet wheeled and spun. He felt dizzy. The moonlight was too bright, too bright. It hurt his eyes. He covered them with a shaking hand.

"You can't go home like this," Briar murmured. "You'll scare your wife. You'll scare *Jenny*—"

"Don't talk to me about Jenny!" Will roared, shoving Briar square in the chest. "Do you think you can just talk about her? However you like?"

"No! I never said—"

"Do you want her, just like Atherton Hart does? Do you want to take her away from me?" Will kept shoving Briar, and Briar staggered back.

"Will, stop it!" Briar finally shouted in a commanding voice. It was so loud that it made Will cringe. He lifted his hands to his head, pressing the heels against his temples.

"My head has been screaming," Will said.

Briar took that opportunity, when Will's hands were pressed to his head and his eyes covered, to launch himself at him. He tried to pin Will's arms to his sides just as he had with the screaming man. But something wild and bitter rose in Will, gave him strength and quickness he never knew he had. Lashing out at Briar, he struck him in the face once, twice. Briar went down like a stone, and Will fell on top of him, beating him.

When Briar was finally still, Will stood slowly. He looked at the blood on his knuckles, Briar's blood mixed with his own. He lifted it to his tongue, tasted its salty richness.

LET'S GO HOME, MOONCALF, the voice said.

Chapter Seventeen

The End of the Beginning

When he came inside the apartment he knew that Jenny was there before he even saw her. He could smell her.

She sat on the couch facing the door, waiting for him. She was wearing her dark soft fur coat and all of her things were packed and ready for travel. He stood looking at her for a long moment. She blinked when she saw blood on his shirt, but said nothing.

"Where have you been?" he said finally. "And where are you going?"

"I took the overnight train to Washington. I filed the papers for your patent." She paused. "And ... and I'm not going to tell you where I'm going. Remember?"

"I gave Tesla the Flume, Jenny," Will said.

"What?" Jenny whispered.

"Gave it to him *personally*!" He sneered the words with savage glee. "Built a new prototype in one day. One day! It's his now. I *gave* it to him."

"But ... but all that work ..."

"I. Don't. Care." Will advanced on her. "I'd rather give it to the richest man in the country than see you get one dime of it, you greedy whore. If it's money you want, go fuck Atherton Hart. I'm sure it won't be the first time."

Jenny stared at him for a long moment, fury draining her face of all color.

"You ... bastard!" Jenny launched herself at him in a storm of fists. But she was small, and she didn't have the power to hurt him. Her soft, warm violence was little more than a pleasurable provocation. The smell of her brown curls, the tangy pungent perfume of her rage fired him. He seized her, pulled her close. Pushing the fur from her shoulder, he buried his face in the bare place where her shoulder met her neck. He pressed his mouth to her skin, tasting its rich sweetness.

Jenny screeched, and her fingernails found the side of his face. Burning pain seared through him. And with the intense pain came clarity. He saw Jenny through unclouded eyes—her brown curls falling out of their pins, her blue eyes full of hurt and rage.

What was *wrong* with him?

He staggered back. The clarity brought something else to his mind.

Ben.

He was supposed to meet Ben.

He was supposed to meet Ben but now it was too late and Ben would be gone.

"Oh God, Jenny," he said. "Oh God."

Fleeing the apartment, he staggered out into the street. It had begun to snow heavily, and everything was blindingly white, illuminated by the full white moon that appeared and disappeared behind scudding clouds. He looked up at it, and it filled his vision, and he could not take his eyes off its screaming, insane brightness.

—Part II: Waning —

Chapter Eighteen

The Beginning of the End

When Will opened his eyes again, he felt horribly sick. Hunger and thirst were the first things he noticed; then, crashing in behind them—pain. His whole body ached, bruised and scratched, as if he'd just been thrown down a hill of brambles.

He ... was inside. Inside a room. He blinked away confusion. The room was familiar. There was peeling wallpaper that looked like demon faces, and a grimy orange bulb and a window that looked only onto a brick wall. He thought about it, and realized that it was the hotel he'd stayed in with Jenny when they'd first come to Detroit.

The Hotel Acheron.

He was sitting ... no, not sitting, *crouching* ... by the door. He rose, unsteady on his feet, stiff muscles screaming. There was a chair nearby, and he had to hold onto the back of it to keep from falling over. Then he noticed that there was something in his hand. Lifting it, he looked at it. It was his straight razor.

There was a small whimper from the corner. Will looked in the direction of the sound.

It was Jenny.

He narrowed his eyes, nausea rising afresh. Jenny was huddled in a ball, knees drawn up to her chest. She was wearing her fur coat, clutching it tightly around her throat. She was just looking at him. Staring at him, her eyes wide and glowing with fear.

"Jenny," he began, his voice cracking. Speaking to her made the fear in her eyes grow even more intense. He saw that she was looking at the razor in his hand. He looked at it again. Why was it open? Why was he holding onto it at all? He closed it and slid it into his pocket. Then he steadied himself against the chair again, feeling disoriented and miserable. "Hey, Scuff. What are we doing here?"

He saw Jenny's face soften slightly. But she did not relax.

"William?" she whispered. "William, is it you?"

"Sure it's me," he said irritably. "Who else would it be?" He sat heavily in the chair. The act of sitting made him realize how completely exhausted he was. He felt like he could sleep for a month.

"Jenny, something's gone wrong with me," he said. "I don't feel well. I think I've been sick."

"Yes, William." Her voice trembled. "You've been sick."

"I remember ... I went to look for Ben," Will said. "I needed to find Ben."

"You didn't find him," Jenny said.

"Why are we here?" Will said. "Why did we come back here? It's not clean."

The kind of place where people don't care if you scream ...

"I followed you. I was worried about you. You said we should come here." She paused. "You locked the door."

"Why would I do that?" Then he said, "I'm so hungry, Jenny."

"So am I," she said. "We haven't eaten for five days. I drank water out of the tap."

"I don't understand what's going on," Will said.

"You locked the door," Jenny said again, in a queer tremulous monotone. "But it wasn't you, William. It wasn't you. You were sick."

Will didn't answer. He went to the basin in the corner of the room and turned the spigot. He gulped the cold water greedily, then put his head under the stream.

"You haven't eaten either?" he asked. The cold water on his head wasn't helping him think any more clearly. "Why didn't you go get food?"

"You locked the door," Jenny said again. "You have the key in your pocket."

"Why didn't you just fish it out?" Will reached into his pocket, and his fingers found the key with the bakelite fob on it. As he crossed the room to give it to her, he saw that one side of her face was swollen and purple-yellow.

"Jenny," he whispered. "You're hurt."

And then he saw that the bruises weren't her only injuries. Her arms were covered with dozens of shallow cuts. Razor cuts. His breathing quickened, and he reached for her, and she screamed. Her eyes went blank with panic and she scrambled away from him. As she did, the fur coat she'd been holding closed around herself fell open. She was stark naked beneath it. And her body was covered with ... signs. Sigils, magical charms, drawn in blood.

Will staggered back from her, heart racing. He steadied himself against the wall farthest from her. Jenny had pressed herself into a corner with her back to him. She had curled her body into a tight ball, head covered by her arms. Will stared at her back, rising and falling with quick shallow breaths, for a long time.

"Jenny," he said softly. "What happened?"

"You were sick," Jenny said, her voice muffled and dull, and he realized that she was just saying the same things over and over. "You were sick. But you're better now, William. It's going to be all right."

Will didn't move. He suddenly remembered the key in his hand. He threw it to her. It skittered on the floor, coming to rest beside her leg. She made no move to take it for a long time. Finally she uncurled slightly, looking down to see if it was really there. When she saw that it was, she snaked out a hand and snatched it, clasping it close to her chest, curling over it as if it were a small animal in need of protection.

"Are you all right, Jenny?"

Her shoulders twitched—with bitter laughter or a desperate sob, he didn't know which. In one swift movement she jumped to her feet and ran to the door. As she slid past him, it aroused a tingling echo in his memory, something dark and cruelly sweet, whispering to him in the back of his mind, the light of the full moon illuminating falling snow ...

Will braced himself against the wall against a sudden rush of dizziness. He was sure he was going to vomit or pass out, but he did not, he just stood there, holding himself up.

Jenny paused by the door, watching him fearfully. She was clutching the key so hard her knuckles were white. It was as if she was waiting for him. Waiting for him to do something.

"Should I go with you?" His voice sounded plaintive even to his own ears; he was so confused and he didn't want to be in this place. He knew it was a bad place. Bad things had happened here and he did not want to stay here with them.

"No," Jenny said softly. "No, William. You have to rest. You have to stay here and rest. I will go and get food. I'll get lots of food. I'll get lots of food and come back."

"All right, Jenny," he whispered. "You go."

It was as if she had required his permission to actually move. Even then, her hand touched the doorknob hesitantly. She brought the key to the lock, but did not put it in. He could see that she was turning a question over in her mind, some deep uncertainty playing itself out on her face. Then, instead of putting the key in the door, she seized the doorknob. She turned it with a jerking movement. The door opened, creaking.

Jenny's face drained of color, and he almost thought she would collapse.

"You never really locked it." Her voice was a strangled whisper. "It was never locked."

And then she was gone, slamming the door behind her. He heard her footsteps moving swiftly down the hall, then breaking into a panicked run.

Will barely made it to the bed. There was blood on the sheets. There was a lot of blood on the sheets. But there was nothing he could do about that. He fell onto the bed. And despite his hunger, despite everything, his body crumpled into sleep.

Will was woken by rough hands pulling off the thin blanket that covered him. A destroyed face, half of it swallowed by swollen slimy black flesh, thrust itself close to his.

"Rent's due," the night-man said, feeling through Will's pockets, turning all of them inside out. Finding the straight razor, he withdrew it—but when he saw the blood crusted on the blade, he shoved it quickly back into Will's pocket. He straightened, the heavy brace on his leg making him stand at a queer angle. "You got the money?"

"I don't think so," Will said softly.

"That girl you had up here ... she threw money at me when you two came in here, so I didn't bother you about it. But it's been more than a week now, and what she gave me don't cover it." He paused. "What happened to that girl, anyway?" His tone was both harsh and insinuating. "The two of you were making a hell of a racket."

"What happened?" Will staggered to his feet, seizing the man by his worn lapels. "What did you hear?"

But the night-man was quick, and much stronger than he looked. Breaking Will's grip, he threw him to the floor.

"People do what they like at the Hotel Acheron," the man sneered down at him. "I don't make it a point of listening too close."

Then, seizing Will by the back of his coat, the night-man lifted him and threw him out the door. Will tumbled, and the man followed, grabbing him again, throwing him down the stairs this time.

Will landed in an aching heap.

One last lift, and the night-man threw Will down the cement front stairs and into the street. Will rolled against the cold pavement, landing on his back, looking up at the waning moon. It was a bright cold night, snow swirling.

"Merry Christmas, you bum!" the night-man yelled, kicking the door shut behind him.

Will did not move for a while, the chill of melting snow seeping up through his coat. He squinted against the brightness.

It can't be Christmas already, he thought. That would mean eight days had gone.

Why hadn't Jenny come back for him?

Rolling onto his knees, he climbed to his feet slowly and unsteadily. The cold seemed to reach all the way down into his gut. He wrapped his arms around himself and walked. Probably Jenny was back at the apartment.

He stumbled through the cold streets, feet slipping on ice. He didn't even have the nickel he needed to get on a streetcar. He was starving, weak as a newborn lamb. All the restaurants along Woodward Avenue were closed, but he could smell festive dinners being laid on tables in faroff homes, and just the smell made him feel weaker.

He could not walk, he kept stumbling and falling. Finally, he didn't want to try anymore. The next time he fell, instead of trying to get up he just sat there, head down over his knees.

He had been sitting like this for a while when a concerned voice broke into his thoughts. "Is something the matter, son?"

A kindly-looking old man with a luxurious white beard looked down at him. He wore a warm overcoat and his arms were full of presents wrapped in gold and silver paper. For no reason that he could understand, Will burst into tears. Helpless, childish tears.

"My goodness, that's no way to spend Christmas Eve!" The man clucked his tongue. "What's wrong?"

"I'm trying to get home," Will sniffed, wiping his nose on the back of his sleeve, "And I don't have any money."

The man quickly dug in his pocket and retrieved a handful of small change. He pressed the coins into Will's hand; they were still warm from his body.

"You go on home, I'm sure people are waiting for you." The old man put down his packages and helped Will to his feet. "It'll all come out all right. You'll see."

"Ben?" Will whispered. But the old man had picked up his presents and was walking away.

Will got off at the streetcar stop nearest Winslow and walked to the apartment building. Seeing lights blazing from the sitting room in the front, he snuck quietly along the side alley and up the back stairs. When he got to the apartment, he saw that the door was standing half open. He stumbled through it.

"Jenny?" he called, softly.

But Jenny did not answer. And when he saw the apartment, he prayed she wasn't there.

The apartment had not just been ransacked, it had been destroyed. Furniture was broken and the pieces scattered. The suitcases Jenny had packed had been slashed open, their contents strewn carelessly. Cold air streamed in through broken windows.

Will moved through the wreckage carefully, glass and shattered wood crunching under his feet as he moved. Weariness and hunger vanished; his whole body was suddenly awake and alert and anxious.

There were three men waiting for him in his bedroom. Three men—and a woman. But it wasn't Jenny. It was Mrs. Kosanovic, the landlady, probably drawn upstairs by the sounds of destruction. She lay on the floor, hog-tied and gagged and blindfolded. Will's heart thudded.

The men reminded Will of the men who had come to take Roher. But these men wore black suits, and instead of a badge, each man had a red orchid in his lapel.

One of the men—diminutive, with large dark eyes and a small moustache—had Jenny's calfskin grip at his feet. He was reading her papers.

"Merry Christmas, Mr. Edwards," the man said without looking up.

"Who are you?" Will said, taking a step toward him. "What are you doing—"

Quick as thinking, the other two men, who had been standing at the first man's flank, rushed forward and seized Will, pushing him back against the wall. One of them got a thick arm against Will's throat and held him there.

"Get him a chair," the first man said. "If there are any left."

A chair was fetched, and Will was put into it, each of the two men standing beside and behind him, resting a heavy hand on his shoulder, holding him down.

The man who had spoken laid the papers aside. He rose and came to stand before Will.

"My name is Bernays," he said. "And my boss is not happy with you. Not happy at *all.*"

Will stared at him, waiting for him to explain, but Bernays seemed in no hurry. Rather, he looked down at Will contemplatively.

"You're so *young,*" he observed. "Your body should not be able to withstand that much magic, not without an allergic reaction severe enough to kill you immediately. You should be dead. Why aren't you?"

"I don't know what you're talking about," Will said again. "I didn't ... do any magic." But then he remembered the charms he'd seen on Jenny's body, the charms sketched in blood, and his head spun. "I don't think I did."

"We know you did magic," Bernays said. "That is not in dispute. It is our job to know when huge amounts of magic are released. And it is our job to track down the warlocks who release them."

Will blinked, remembering what Court had told him.

"The Settlement," he said. "Killing Old Users. The Agency. You're ... you're from the *Agency.*"

"Very good, Mr. Edwards." Bernays' eyes flared. "You've been doing your reading. But you might want to choose your material with more care. *The Goês' Confession* is a piece of seditious trash, and we work very hard to keep such falsehoods from propagating."

He took a step toward Will.

"The information in that book is neither accurate nor fair. We are a kinder, gentler Agency now. Now, we offer the warlocks who have had the misfortune to come to the attention of our boss a choice."

He made a strange ornate gesture, the flourish of a stage magician producing a dove from a silk hat. But instead of a dove or a silk hat, Bernays suddenly held a small phial—and a silver knife.

"You will see that I hold two objects, Mr. Edwards," he said. "In my left hand—well, I hardly need tell you what this is." He turned over the sharp silver blade, and it gleamed in the low light. "In my right hand ... that requires only slightly more explanation. Do you know what's in this phial?"

Will shook his head.

"This is the Panchrest," Bernays said. "Drink it now, and you will no longer be able to channel magic. And you will no longer be of any interest to us."

"But I've already had the Panchrest," Will hissed. "I had it when I was a child."

Bernays looked at him with astonishment.

"What an *incredibly* stupid thing to say." He grinned. "And here I'd heard you were supposed to be a genius or something. Haven't you the slightest capacity for self-preservation? In any case, I know that you have *not* had the Panchrest. My boss has it on absolute authority that you have not."

"Who is this boss you keep talking about?" Will snapped. "And how the hell would he know?"

"Oh for pete's sake, will you just choose?" The man holding him down hit him hard across the face. Will felt blood blossom from his nose, trickling warm down his chin.

"Stop it, Trotter," Bernays spoke with annoyance. "You know that never works. Mr. Edwards has decided to be stubborn. As we were told he might be."

He went over to where Mrs. Kosanovic lay on the floor and lifted her to her feet. The old woman's eyes snapped with fierceness and fear.

"In the bad old days, Mr. Edwards, in the early days of our nation's history, when a warlock was accused of the crime of practicing magic, he was also required to make a choice. He was required to choose his plea—guilty or innocent. It wasn't much of a choice, for pleading guilty meant death and pleading innocence meant a slower and more painful death. So some tried to get out of the choice all together, and they refused to plead anything at all. Do you know what happened to the warlocks who refused to choose?"

Bernays did not handle Mrs. Kosanovic violently at all. Instead, he just put his lips next to her ear and began to whisper. The whispered words, Will could hear, were in Latin. Mrs. Kosanovic began to tremble. Then she began to ... collapse. It was as if she were being sucked inward upon herself. Her flesh compressed as if she were being crushed by heavy stones.

"Stop it!" screamed Will, blank with terror. "Please!"

But Bernays just kept whispering, and Mrs. Kosanovic began making horrible squeaking sounds through her gag. The sound of bones fracturing into a million tiny pieces was like the pop and sputter of dry, burning wood. Blood welled from her skin in fat droplets like water being wrung from a sponge. She became smaller and smaller, crushed by the weight of Bernay's words.

After a long, long time, Bernays stopped whispering. Mrs. Kosanovic was no longer there. All that was left of her was a dense lump of meat in a pile of bloody clothing.

Will must have passed out, because the next thing he knew, Trotter was slapping him hard across the face to wake him.

"You are *going* to choose," Bernays promised him. "We can't choose for you. It's against the rules. But to *make* you choose—well, we can do anything we like to you." He felt in his pocket and pulled out the little purple velvet box that Will had left on his bedside table. Bernays opened the box, looked at the silver dollar within, turning it to glint in the waning moonlight. "Or to your lovely wife, when she comes home."

The bedroom door crashed open.

All of the warlocks turned, and Will saw Harley Briar standing in the doorway. His face was yellow and purple with days-old bruises, and his nose—badly broken—was still swollen to twice its size.

"Let him go!"

He had something raised in his hand—a two chambered pendant, filled with a dark liquid. The same kind that Irene wore.

A sangrimancer's alembic. Briar muttered a command that made it glow faintly, warm and red.

Bernays did not smile, but rather regarded Briar with a low dark gaze. "Oh wonderful. A hobo sangrimancer."

"Who are you?" Briar barked.

"I think you know who we are," Bernays said. "I'm sure you've heard of us." He touched the red orchid on his lapel.

Seeing it for the first time, Briar paled, his battered face going corpse-white beneath the bruises. The alembic in his hand trembled.

"I'm used to long odds," Briar said. And then he barked a command in some kind of strange language. Jenny's papers exploded into ash-fine dust, filling the room with a blinding, choking cloud.

Briar was at Will's side in an instant, grabbing his arm, pulling him toward the door.

But Bernays simply muttered something in Latin, and a cold fresh wind blew through the room, dispelling the cloud. With the precision of three who'd always worked as one, the assassins attacked Briar in perfect unison, lifting their hands to sketch the same charms; chanting the same flawlessly matched Latin. Briar held the alembic high, screaming his bitter acrid spell words, both defending and attacking, summoning tendrils of light from the floor that lashed wildly at them. One of these searing whips caught Bernays across the throat, slashing it open. It staggered the trio for a moment, but only a brief one; Bernays choked an imprecation, placed his hand on the gushing wound and closed it with one curt command: "*Sanare.*"

Then, with a snarl, Bernays and his men intensified their efforts, their voices rising to unearthly volume. The same whips of magical light that had been lashing out at them now turned, wrapped themselves around Briar, held him fast. He struggled desperately as he dropped to his knees.

Will fumbled in his pocket for the razor. He knew that he could help Briar. Save him. The voice didn't come back to his head, but whatever had been speaking to him then was how he knew it now.

Not quite sure what he was doing, Will used the razor to gash his arm. He rubbed the blood between his hands, and strange power tingled on his fingertips. Then he reached down into himself, to a place dangerous and only vaguely remembered. The memory of the charms on Jenny's body filled his vision. Lifting his hands, he spoke unfamiliar words, words that tumbled out of him, words that he knew had never really existed until the very moment he spoke them.

He saw the look of shock in Bernays' eyes as the warlock assassins were wreathed in cold blue flame. They all screamed—in perfect unison—and vanished, leaving behind nothing but the smell of sulphur and silence. Dead silence.

Will collapsed against the wall. He felt exhausted and unclean. Looking at the place where Bernays had been standing, he saw that the warlock had dropped something. The purple velvet box. With an angry cry, Will bent to snatch it from the floor.

Then he went to where Harley Briar lay, writhing and moaning in agony. Briar had used so much magic. And beneath his skin, black rivers of Exunge were beginning to blossom and swell.

Chapter Nineteen

The Tender Sangrimancers

Will didn't know how he was able to get Briar to the Gores—he hadn't eaten in days, and hadn't an ounce of strength left—but somehow, he did it. And when they arrived at Dr. Gore's front door, Will didn't bother knocking; he just threw it open and dragged Briar inside.

Briar had stopped screaming somewhere along Gratiot Street, and now just hung limply off Will's shoulder, his feet dragging. As they collapsed together onto the tiled floor of the entryway, Irene fell to the floor beside them.

"Harley!" she exclaimed with anguish, bending over him. Her fingers traveled swiftly over his face, over the insane pattern of black writhing beneath his bruised skin. "He knows never to use so much magic! *What happened?*"

"We were attacked," Will rasped, laying on the floor beside him, unable to move. "By warlocks wearing red orchids."

Irene's eyes went wide, and she looked up at her father, who had hurried in from the back room.

"There is no time to waste," Dr. Gore said. "Irene, help me."

"He's *dying*," Irene keened. "Harley—"

"If they've been followed, we're *all* dead!" Dr. Gore bellowed, pulling a knife from his belt and kneeling at Will's side. "Now. Quickly."

Seizing Will's arm, he used the knife to make another deep incision, drawing a fresh hot gush of blood, and both Irene and Dr.

Gore coated their hands in it. Irene's had her alembic at the ready. Clasping hands with her father, she held the alembic high as Dr. Gore spoke words in the bitter, pungent language that Will knew as the language of sangrimancy—the language Briar had spoken to banish the Agency warlocks. He suddenly realized that it was very familiar to him. It was the language the voice in his head had always spoken in.

Her father's words made Irene's alembic glow, and with it she began tracing patterns in the air. She sketched swift hexes over Will's body, then over the doors and windowsills.

"What are you doing?" Will murmured.

"We're sheltering you," Dr. Gore said. "Hiding you. Quiet now. Rest."

They proceeded around the whole house in this fashion, Dr. Gore chanting and Irene sketching, until finally they returned to where Will and Briar rested. Irene looked exhausted from the effort, but she did not stop for even a moment; she bent and lifted Briar up, carrying him into the receiving room and laying him tenderly on the table. Dr. Gore followed her.

Will lay on the cold floor, his own blood smeared on the tiles around him. He curled up into a ball and closed his eyes. And even much later, when a soft knock came at the door, he could not bring himself to open them.

The hem of Irene's skirt brushed his cheek. She paused, and he heard her slide open the little viewing window. After a moment in which Will could feel her weighing her decision, she opened the door. Will felt cold air stream in over the threshold. He opened his eyes a crack, just enough to see a pair of leather shoes on the doormat.

"I'm looking for Will Edwards," the shoes said. They were scuffed, Will noticed. Not polished. "Please let me in, I know he's here—"

"You shall not enter here," she replied in a calm, ceremonial voice. "Begone, *kallikantzari*. This home is fortified against you."

"I'm not one of them." A pause. "I swear it upon my blood."

Irene weighed the shoes' formal response for a long time. "Who are you?"

"I'm Will's brother," the shoes said. "Ben."

Chapter Twenty

Kala Christouyenna

Hunger woke him the next morning, gnawing at his gut with a ferocity even more powerful than his lingering weariness. The smell of food suffused the house—the scent of garlic and rosemary and roasting pork heavy in the air.

He had been put into a bed in an upstairs room. Climbing out of it, he stood for a moment on shaky legs, steadying himself. Winter sunlight illuminated the shade covering the window. He pushed the shade aside, looking out over the roofs and back alleys of Greektown, narrowing his eyes against the intense glare.

Then, slowly, he made his way downstairs. In the kitchen, Dr. Gore, wearing a long ruffled apron, was bent before the gas oven poking at a roast. An unfamiliar man was sitting at the kitchen table. Will stopped in the doorway, looking at him.

"Ben," he said.

Ben was tall and slender, with walnut-colored hair and green eyes. He wore a rumpled suit—it matched his scuffed shoes—and the impression he gave was of a bank clerk in a very small bank with very few clients.

Ben rose quickly, and came over to where Will was standing. Without a word, he hugged Will. Will held on to him for a moment, steadying himself against his brother.

"It's all right," Ben murmured. "It'll all come out all right."

Will shook his head and pushed himself away from his brother's embrace. But he didn't say anything. Instead, he shakily crossed the kitchen to the table, steadying himself against the back of one of the chairs.

"I'm hungry," he said.

"I can imagine," Dr. Gore said. "But I'm afraid dinner is not yet ready." He gestured to a plate that had been put out on the table to accompany two half-drained cups of coffee. "Have some *kourambiedes*. The sugar will help you."

The plate was piled with cookies, round and white and thickly coated with powdered sugar. They looked like tiny full moons. Will devoured them, one after the other, licking his fingers between bites. Dr. Gore did not seem surprised at how quickly Will ate the cookies, he just went to the icebox and retrieved a glass bottle of milk. He poured a large cupful and set it before Will.

"Drink that," he said. "Then help your brother set the table. Irene will be home from church soon, and then we will eat. We will be glad to have you, and you will need your strength to decide what is to be done."

Will drank his milk as he was told, then followed Ben into the dining room, where a colorful cloth, plates and silver were collected on a heavy walnut sideboard. The eastern wall of the room was dominated by a holy shrine. An olive-oil lamp flickered low before gold-leafed icons of Jesus and the Virgin Mary, as well as a saint Will did not recognize, a beardless young man with dark curly hair.

Silently, Ben and Will began working side by side, laying the table for Christmas dinner.

"How did you find me?" Will finally asked. When Ben did not answer immediately, Will instead asked what he'd wanted to in the first place: "Why couldn't you have found me sooner?"

"You were supposed to meet me at the train station," Ben said. "You never showed up. I spent days looking for you. Some people had said they'd seen you with a man named Harley Briar, and they told me that he often came here." He paused. "Look at the letter."

Will remembered Ben's letter, still crumpled in his jacket pocket. He took it out and smoothed it, and saw that it did bear a message, written in a desperate hand.

Where are you, Will? Why can't I reach you? Why didn't you meet me at the station?

There was more written on the letter than just that—instructions for where he should go, pleas to come as quickly as possible, comforting reassurances—but they were all useless to him now. Exhaling, Will carefully folded the letter and put it back in his pocket.

"I blacked out, Ben," Will said softly. "I woke up five days later, in a hotel. And Jenny was there. In the room with me. She thought I'd locked the door, but I hadn't. She had blood on her. And ... cuts. Something happened, Ben. Something bad."

Ben drew a deep breath, but said nothing.

"I don't understand what happened to me," Will said. "Do you, Ben? Do you know?"

Ben stopped for a moment, plate in hand. He laid it down, straightened it.

"I think I do," he said softly. He looked at Will, and Will suddenly noticed that his brother's eyes were very green.

"You remember, in one of the letters I sent you? I said that to explain things, I kept having to go back farther? Well, to explain this, I have to go very far back." He paused. "I have to go back to 1690, to one of our ancestors. A man named Anson Kendall. He was a witch hunter, and one of the warlocks he hunted was named Aebedel Cowdray."

The very name sent shivers up Will's spine. He knew that name, he'd heard it spoken in his nightmares a million times. But never in plain English, only in the language the voice spoke to him in.

"Anson Kendall crushed a warlock named Aebedel Cowdray to death beneath seven stones. And with his dying breath, Aebedel Cowdray cursed Anson Kendall and his descendants for all eternity. It's a moon-curse. It reveals itself only after the victim's eighteenth birthday. The curse becomes more powerful as the moon waxes, gaining its full strength when the moon is full. And as the moon wanes, so does the power of the curse."

Will remembered another moon-curse ... the one that had afflicted the farmboy in the story Jenny had read to him. He blinked, thinking through it ... in fact, it was all the same! Moon-curse, vengeful warlock ...

"Ben ... that's a goddamn *story*," Will hissed. "*The Warlock's Curse*."

"There certainly are similarities," Ben allowed, but said nothing more.

"That was the book you told me to use to unlock the letter." Will narrowed his eyes, taking a step toward his brother. "Why did you choose that book, Ben? Did you know? Did you know this would happen to me?"

"No," Ben said firmly. "I knew about the curse, yes. And I knew that all of us—all of the brothers—could have potentially inherited it ... except that Father gave us all the Panchrest. And the Panchrest should have made it impossible." He paused. "You shouldn't have inherited the curse, Will. It wasn't supposed to happen. But somehow it did."

"The Agency warlock ... Bernays ... he said that I hadn't had the Panchrest. That his boss had told him I hadn't."

This comment gave Ben pause—but then he shook his head dismissively. "Well, his *boss* wasn't there. I was. I saw Father give it to you."

"Did *he* know?" Will said. "Father? About the curse?"

"Of course Father knew," Ben said, trying—and failing—to keep bitterness from his voice. "Father knows everything."

"So Father didn't give us boys the Panchrest to protect us from the Black Flu at all," Will spat. "He gave it to us to prevent us from getting the curse. Which is a far better reason than you gave me. Why did you leave that part out of your letter?"

"Because I didn't know the truth until later," Ben said. "And even when I did know, I still couldn't forgive him."

"So you decided to let me believe the worst as well?"

"I wanted to tell you in person." Ben raked a hand through his hair. "I couldn't ... Will, I couldn't tell you everything. Even on the Sophos' stationery, it was too dangerous."

Ben fell abruptly silent as Dr. Gore entered the dining room, carrying two small glass dishes filled with glossy black olives. Will began eating them in greedy handfuls as soon as Dr. Gore placed them on the table, swallowing them pits and all. Dr. Gore slapped his hand away.

"Irene will be home soon," he said. Then he murmured to Ben, "Is everything all right? Have you told him?"

Ben nodded. "I've told him. He understands now."

But Will didn't understand anything. He looked between his brother and Dr. Gore, and in the long moment of silence, he heard singing.

The sound came from the street outside. Women's voices, sweet and solemn, singing a holy song in Greek. The front door opened and closed, and the sound of song faded as the women continued on down the street.

Irene came into the dining room, dressed head to toe in sober black, head covered by a scarf.

"*Kala Christouyenna*, daughter." Dr. Gore pressed a kiss to her forehead. "Did you ask a blessing of the Reverend Father for me?"

Irene nodded, glancing at Ben and Will but then looking quickly away.

"Has Harley woken up?" Her voice was soft and anxious as she laid aside her scarf and smoothed her shining black hair.

"Briefly," Dr. Gore said, and Irene said nothing more as she hurried off to check on him.

"Here's what I *do* understand," said Will, picking up the thread of their conversation once more. "I've inherited a family curse. And there are warlocks after me. Agency assassins, wearing red orchids. They were waiting for me in my apartment."

"You've mentioned the Agency twice now, which means you've read *The Goês' Confession*," Ben murmured. He looked at Dr. Gore, then at Will. "I would advise you not to go around telling people that."

"I didn't read it. My friend told me about it. He said that the warlocks who wear red orchids are from the Agency. And that they kill Old Users to abide by the terms of the Settlement. So why would they be interested in me?"

"The powerful possession you suffered would have created an intense magical beacon," Ben said. "They are trained to watch for such high levels of magical activity."

"They will be even more interested in you now," Dr. Gore added grimly. "Harley said you were able to banish an entire Trine of Agency warlocks. That would have taken a hundred times more magical force than Harley himself expended. You should be in much worse shape than him—in fact, you should be dead. But, besides being hungry enough to eat all of our *kourambiedes*, you aren't showing the slightest sign of damage."

Will absorbed all this information silently. That's what Bernays had said. That he should be dead.

"But Bernays wasn't old." Will knit his brow. "His men weren't any older. They were all of my generation—Malmantic. But all of them did as much magic as Harley." Nausea rose in him as he recalled what Bernays had done to Mrs. Kosanovic. "More, even."

"They're credomancers," Dr. Gore said, with a dismissive shrug. Ben shot him a warning glance, and the old man fell abruptly silent.

Will narrowed his eyes. "If they're credomancers, then you must know who they are. The Sophos of the Stanton Institute must know, at least—"

"There are many kinds of credomancers, Will, just as there are many kinds of churches," Ben interjected. "They all have their own unique power structures. The Stanton Institute trains credomancers, but we don't own them, any more than Tesla Industries owns you." He paused. "No, the Agency is something different. It recruits credomancers because they are the least restricted in their use of magical power."

"Why would that be?"

"Credomancy uses the least amount of free magic of all the great traditions," Dr. Gore said, straightening a knife alongside a plate. "In fact, the credomancer himself channels very little magic. He draws his power through the bodies of those who believe in him."

"So every time Dreadnought Stanton uses magic, he doesn't suffer for it ... rather, the people who believe in him do?"

"Something like that," Ben said.

Will's head spun. Trying to make sense of it, he thought through the events of the night before, forcing himself remembering every terrible detail. When he came to the part where Bernays had shown him the little purple velvet box, alarm seized him.

"What if they're looking for Jenny?" He suddenly realized he didn't know where she was ... Where could she have gone?

YOU KNOW WHERE SHE WENT.

Will winced visibly, hands going to his head. Dr. Gore laid a steadying hand on his shoulder.

"Natural after-effects," he murmured. "Your body is accustoming itself to the new presence that has invaded it. Aebedel Cowdray does not control your body at the moment, as the moon is on the wane. But he may still bleed through when you are tired, or weak, or under great stress."

Will sank heavily into a chair.

"They have no reason to look for her," Ben said. "She's not who they want. And as for where she's gone—"

"No," Will said. "I know where she went. At least I think I do." He felt spent and tired and hopeless.

Dr. Gore looked at Ben. "Would you please go find Irene and tell her that it is time for supper?"

Ben hesitated for a moment, but then nodded and left the dining room. Pulling out a chair, Dr. Gore sat next to Will, looking into his face.

"It is a very terrible thing that has happened to you, Will," he said. "And I understand, more than you know. The Agency found me too, many years ago. I am an Old User—or at least, I was."

Will stared at him.

"They found me in the winter of 1894," Dr. Gore continued in a soft contemplative voice. "My dear wife had been very sick, and finally she died—but not until after I had used too much magic trying to save her life. The Agency assassins tracked me down." He paused, remembering. "They gave me a choice. I could either take the Panchrest—stripping me of my ability to work magic at all—or they would kill me. The leader of the Trine who found me held out the Panchrest in one hand, and a silver knife in the other. I chose the Panchrest and was glad of it."

"Glad of it?" Will echoed.

"Yes, *glad* of it," Dr. Gore said. "It was not a choice they offered Old Users before the Panchrest was developed. If they had found me just a few years earlier, they would have killed me in secrecy and silence, a knife in the dark, a silver bullet through the heart." He paused. "My daughter was very young and her mother had just died. There was no one else to care for her. So yes, I was glad that they gave me the chance to live, even if it meant I could no longer work magic."

Will shook his head slowly, trying to understand.

"But if you took the Panchrest, how are you still able to work magic?" He looked at Dr. Gore. "You healed that man from the factory. You sheltered me when I came here. How?"

Dr. Gore clenched his jaw and did not answer. Will suddenly noticed that Ben had returned from speaking to Irene, and was standing in the doorway of the dining room.

"He needs to know everything," Ben said. "He can be trusted."

"Perhaps *he* can," Dr. Gore said. "But what about Cowdray?"

Ben dismissed the older man's reluctance with an impatient gesture. "There is a way around the restriction, Will. It's a technique known as 'vamping.'"

"The flow of magic through the human body can never be entirely blocked. Some magical conductivity must be retained to sustain life," Dr. Gore continued resignedly. "This small amount of residual conductivity can be used to make a low-level magical connection with another person. In this way, someone who has taken the Panchrest can 'vamp' upon the body of another—direct the flow of power through the magical channels of that person's body."

"You use Irene's body," Will said, suddenly remembering how Dr. Gore always held hands with his daughter while he did magic, how it was always she who held the alembic.

"It is a very dangerous practice," Dr. Gore said gravely. "Irene and I have worked together for many years, and I know her limits as well as is possible. But even so, the slightest miscalculation could result in Exunge building up in her body to levels from which she could not recover." He paused. "And of course, if such a miscalculation were ever to occur, I would be powerless to bring her back."

"That's why the warlocks from the Agency don't care too much about it," Ben added. "Because the one vamped-upon so frequently dies. The practice is self-limiting."

"But it explains how Cowdray can control my body the way he does," Will whispered, looking at Ben. "He's ... *vamping* on me."

Ben inclined his head. "The magical mechanism of a curse is fundamentally similar to vamping," he said. "But if the Panchrest was given to you—as I saw Father do—then it should not be possible for Cowdray to work so much magic through your body, as most of the magical channels of your body would have been fused in infancy." Ben paused. "On the other hand, if you were somehow *not* given the Panchrest, as the Agency warlocks have said, then you should be dead from the amount of magic you worked." He sighed. "Neither explanation fits, little brother."

Will's eyes searched the worn carpet. Ben was right. But then he realized that he didn't care about explanations—explanations weren't solutions. He sat back in the chair, rubbing his face vigorously before letting his hands drop with a sound of anguish.

"So what am I supposed to do?" he finally said. "How do I get *rid* of him?"

Dr. Gore said nothing. And Ben could not meet his eyes.

"I don't know, Will," Ben said. "I'm sorry."

Will stared at his brother for a long time.

"What about Dreadnought Stanton? Your Sophos?" Will remembered Jenny's dramatic reading of *The Warlock's Curse*. "The Dreadnought Stanton books are supposed to be true life tales. He saved that farmboy, the one who was cursed. He banished the spirit that possessed him. Could he save me?"

"Nothing is impossible," Ben said. But there was no encouragement in the words.

"There is one thing I do know," Dr. Gore said regretfully, "and that is we cannot shield you here forever, Will. You must leave here very soon. And you must go far away."

Will looked from Ben to Dr. Gore.

"Whatever the reason—however it has happened—you are nothing less than an Old User in a young man's body. And the Agency has targeted you as such." He paused. "There are avenues open for those who have attracted the Agency's attention in this way. I can put you in contact with people who can help you escape the country. They will send you up through Canada, and then across the Atlantic. There are places in Europe where Old Users can live in safety. Belgium, I hear, is very pleasant."

Will looked at him incredulously. "*Belgium?*"

"There are places even the Agency cannot reach," Ben mused.

"I'm not going to Belgium," Will snapped. "I'm not leaving America. I have to find Jenny. I have to tell her—"

"She won't want to see you." Ben cut him off. "And even if you do think you know where she is, you'll only put her in more danger. Stop thinking like a kid. You can't afford it anymore."

Will curled back in his chair, stung. A deep feeling of bitterness rose in him. Goddamn Cowdray. Goddamn the filthy cruel *thing* that now lived inside him.

At that moment, Irene came into the dining room, and Briar was with her. He limped at her side, leaning heavily on her, and between his broken nose and the puffy bruises on his face—*I gave him those*, Will thought miserably—and the deep inky smudges on his skin he didn't look like he should be able to walk at all. But he was, and he was even dressed nicely in the secondhand suit Will had seen him in before. When he saw Will he smiled crookedly.

"Hey Will," he said, his voice soft and weak, as if he had been screaming. "*Kala Christouyenna.* That's 'Merry Christmas' in Greek, in case they ain't told you."

Will stood quickly, letting Irene guide Briar to the chair he'd been slumped in. Irene hovered over him for a moment before Briar gently pushed her away.

"C'mon, stop fussing," he said. "That food smells good enough to kick the guts out of a badger. Let's eat, huh?"

Irene hurried into the kitchen, followed by her father, and as steaming platters were being carried in and laid on the table, Will crouched beside Briar and spoke quietly.

"How are you?"

Briar chuckled grimly. "That thing in you has got some fight in it," he said. "I ain't had the stuffing knocked out of me like that since the McKees Rocks Strike in Philadelphia. And even then it took six Cossacks on horseback with billy clubs." He shifted in the chair, groaning. "But I'll be all right. I told you, I'm tougher than I look."

"Thank you for helping me," Will said. He was silent for a moment before adding, "I didn't know you were a sangrimancer."

"I kind of guess I wasn't much help at all, really," Briar said. "And sure I'm a sangrimancer. I ain't ashamed of it. Why do you think I took to organizing the magical factories as my specialty?" He paused. "They're my people, Will. Your people too now, I reckon. Seeing as this makes you kind of a warlock, just like the rest of us."

Will clenched his teeth. "No offense, but I'm not a warlock and I'm not going to be. I'm going to get rid of this thing somehow."

"My gran'dad once told me a story about a cursed man," Briar shrugged. "The curse was like yours; some kind of family feud, someone did someone else wrong. Gran'dad said the only way to break a curse like that is if both sides forgive each other. Truly and completely."

"*Forgive* each other?" Will said. "Forgive *Cowdray?*"

"Truly and completely forgive," Briar reiterated. "And he's got to truly and completely forgive you."

"Well then," Will muttered, "I guess I'd better learn to speak Belgian."

The table was soon piled with food: chicken and rice soup, stuffed cabbage, beet salad and fried potatoes, and roasted pork, rich savory mounds of it. Before eating, the Gores stood together before the little shrine on the eastern wall—Irene dipping her finger into the olive oil in the lamp and crossing her forehead with it—speaking a low, reverent prayer:

The poor shall eat and be filled, and they that seek the Lord shall praise Him; their hearts shall live forever and ever.

And as Will stuffed himself, feeling strength return to him, the last words of the prayer continued to echo in his mind.

Lord, have mercy. Lord, have mercy. Lord, have mercy.

After dinner, there was strong Greek coffee and a sweet bread decorated with walnuts that Dr. Gore called *christopsomo*. But stuffed with food and uncomfortable new knowledge, Will did not feel like further celebration. He pushed himself away from the table without a word. No one tried to stop him.

He climbed the narrow stairs to return to the bedroom he'd woken up in. But as he came into the room, he realized that something had changed. The room was now very cold. Air was blowing in through the window. The window that had been closed when he'd woken up.

Something caught Will's eye. On the pillow of his bed was a handwritten note, stabbed through with a knife. The note bore just one, terrible line:

Come immediately, and come alone, or Jenny will die. AH.

Atherton Hart.

Will trembled with sudden fury. It was just as he had suspected—just as he had *known*. Jenny had gone to Hart. But how had Hart found him here? How had he gotten in through the Gores' wardings?

If Atherton Hart could get in here, anyone could. And even though Will knew leaving the house meant risking another encounter with the warlock assassins, he knew that hiding from them was just forestalling the inevitable. They were going to come after him anyway, eventually. Unless he fled the country. Learned to speak *Belgian*.

And he wasn't going to do that.

The Gores didn't deserve to be put in danger by him. Nor Harley, nor Ben. Will couldn't ask any of them for help—none of them could help him anyway. Whatever lay in his future, he had to face it alone. *Worse* than alone.

Ripping the note from the pillow, he left the knife. He had a better blade. It had been given to him by the woman he loved, the woman he'd hurt. He had to help her.

And if Atherton Hart had done anything to her, Will swore, he would use that blade to slash the man's throat.

Will climbed out the window, and was gone.

Chapter Twenty-One

Rush to Justice

The creamy white terra-cotta of the office building on Griswold glowed in the cold purple light of late afternoon. And even though it was Christmas day, and the streets were still and deserted, Will knew that the front door would be open.

He crossed the silent lobby, footsteps echoing. The elevators were not running, so he had to take the stairs. But the meal at the Gores' had strengthened him; Will's muscles warmed as he took the steps two at a time.

The stairs did not bring him to the reception area, but rather to a small hall just off it. The offices had a hushed, deserted feel. The door of Hart's office stood open, revealing the large silent space beyond.

The lights were not on; the only illumination came from the afternoon sunlight streaming through the tall windows.

Atherton Hart sat behind the large mahogany desk. A half-open bottle of whiskey and a revolver sat before him. He stared steadily at Will, not speaking as Will stopped to stand in the doorway. Instead, he poured himself another glass of whiskey, and downed it in a swallow.

"I should kill you, you son of a bitch," Hart said.

"Funny," Will answered. "I was just thinking the same thing."

Hart slammed down the glass. "I'm not the one who hurt her," he barked. "I'm not the one who—"

"Where is she?"

"Do you really think I'd let you see her?" Hart's lip curled in disgust. "She said it wasn't you. She swore it wasn't you. But I don't believe it."

"Then why am I here?"

"Because I need you," Hart said. He did not hurry to take the revolver, rather laid his hand on it as casually as if he were picking up a pen. Pulling back the hammer with his thumb, he leveled it at Will. "You're the only one who can save her."

Fists clenched, Will did not move as Hart held the gun on him. And Hart's aim did not waver as he lifted the receiver on the sleek black enameled desk telephone. He asked the operator for a number in Chicago.

"Yes, he showed up," were the first words he spoke. "I've got him." Then, a long pause as Hart listened to the voice on the other end of the line. Grunting acknowledgement, Hart replaced the receiver on the hook and stood.

"Come on," he said, gesturing with the gun. "We've got a train to catch."

Hart kept the gun in the pocket of his cashmere overcoat and pressed it into the small of Will's back as they walked down Fort Street to Third, where the old Union Depot stood.

"Are you going to tell me where we're going?" Will made no move to resist Hart, and he did not intend to. Hart knew where Jenny was. For that reason, if for no other, Will needed him. And Hart had not taken the time to search him, so Will still had the razor in his pocket. He had options.

The heavy sandstone walls of the Union Depot glowed cold and blood-red. They boarded a train bound for Chicago. Hart had purchased a private compartment, and after he had shoved Will into one of the seats, he closed the door and locked it. Then, taking the seat across from Will, he withdrew the gun from his pocket and rested it on his knee, pointed toward him, his finger on the trigger.

"I'm not going to fight you," said Will, looking not at the gun but into Hart's amber eyes. "I will do anything you say if it will help Jenny."

Hart snorted. "You lying son-of-a-bitch," he muttered. "If you wanted to help Jenny, you would have stayed away from her. Kept that thing inside you away from her."

"You know?" Will narrowed his eyes. "About Cowdray?"

"Of course I know," Hart snapped. "Jenny showed up on my doorstep a week ago, half dead. I know everything you did to her."

Will's heart lurched painfully in his chest. He swallowed hard. He did not want to hear it from this man. He didn't want to know.

"Where are you taking me?" he asked finally.

"I'm taking you to the Consortium," Hart said. "They want you. If they don't get you, they'll hurt her even worse."

"Why do they want to hurt her?"

"They don't *want* to hurt her," Hart spat. "But unless they have you, they'll have to. They'll have no choice."

"What do you mean they'll *have* to? Why will they have to?"

Hart stared at him in silence, the only sound the rattle of the train swaying over bright steel tracks. Outside, the sun was setting, and long slanting rays made the air golden.

"You hang around with warlocks," Hart finally said. "How much do you know about magic?"

"I don't want to know anything," Will said bitterly. Hart hmphed.

"Well, I'd advise that you learn. And quickly. Because that's why the Consortium wants you. For your cursed blood. For Aebedel Cowdray."

"What would they want with Aebedel Cowdray?"

Hart just stared at him, hatred in his eyes. He said nothing more.

"Why are they going to hurt Jenny?" Will asked, after a very long silence.

He did not think Hart was going to answer, but finally he did.

"They were supposed to capture you before the full moon," he said. "The Consortium had men waiting for you. But you weren't where they thought you'd be."

Will looked away, frowning. The sun had finally set, sliding down behind dark hills. The waning moon glowed like a half-smile. "But how could they have known?" he said. "How could they have known to wait for me? No one knew I had inherited the curse. I didn't even know."

"The Consortium has ways of knowing things," Hart said.

"Who *are* they?" Will barked, annoyed by the cryptic statement. "What do they want?"

"The Consortium wants to make the world a better place," Hart said flatly, as if quoting a marketing pamphlet. "That's all you need to know."

"That's not even the tiniest bit of what I need to know!" Will hissed. "Jenny was mixed up with them, and so are you. What do they want with her?"

"The Consortium needed to raise money, and Jenny was helping them," Hart said. "And I was helping her." He paused, his voice softening. "Not that she needed my help. She's brilliant. I've never encountered a mind like hers."

Will must have made a sound of anguish at the tenderness in Hart's voice, for the man looked up, his eyes suddenly becoming hard. "Yes, she's brilliant. And in the time I have worked with her, I have come to care for her very much. Which is more than you can say."

"You don't know anything," Will said.

"I know that you broke her." Hart's voice was flat. "*Almost* broke her. Even you couldn't break her all the way, thank God. She's stronger than you, stronger than Cowdray. But you both gave it your best try, didn't you?"

Will stared at him, his jaw held so tightly that it ached.

"When she came to my office after she escaped the hotel, I called a doctor to take care of her physical wounds. And then I called someone else. The Consortium's magical advisor, a man named Professor Coeus. I wanted to understand what else it was you'd done. You drew charms all over her body, in her own blood. Do you know what they were?"

"No," Will said. "I don't know."

"Some were to hold her down, bind her." Hart spoke the words in a clipped, businesslike tone. "I'm sure those were necessary, because she probably put up a good fight." His voice grew harsher with every word. "Some of them were to cause her pain. Because causing her pain was apparently very amusing to you." Now Hart's breathing began to quicken with fury. "But the rest ... oh, the rest! They were to make her *want* you. After everything else you did. You worked magic on her to make her believe she wanted it."

Will closed his eyes. Anguish screamed between his ears, keening and sharp as the sound of the train's steel wheels. He couldn't have. He couldn't have done that ... to *Jenny*.

Hart was silent. When Will opened his eyes again, he saw that Hart's hand was gripping the gun so tightly that his knuckles were white.

"I would give this gun to you right now if I thought you'd do the right thing with it," Hart said softly. "Nothing would give me greater satisfaction than to see your brains splattered on that upholstery behind you. But if you weren't strong enough to keep Cowdray from doing what he did, then I'm sure you're not strong enough to do that, either."

"Why don't you do it for me?" Will murmured. In that terrible moment, it was a request, not a question.

"Because if they can't use your cursed blood, they'll use the next best thing." Hart paused, finger twitching on the trigger. "The blood of your unborn child. Conceived while Cowdray was in your body."

Chapter Twenty-Two
The New Faith Seat of Praise

They did not speak again, but Will could not have even if he wanted to. He sat with a trembling hand over his mouth, holding in the urge to scream. The world reeled around him, blank and unreal.

Your unborn child. Conceived while Cowdray was in your body.

And when they arrived at the Union Depot in Chicago near midnight, Will could barely walk, only shuffle like a drunkard, his whole body leaden and heavy. Hart held his arm with painful firmness, almost having to hold him up as they walked.

Outside the station, piles of dirty snow were frozen hard in the gutters. At the curb, a black truck painted with the words "Dept. of Police, Oak Lawn" idled. The driver and a passenger sat in the open cab, heavily bundled and muffled against the cold. As Will and Hart approached, one of them got out and opened the back of the truck. Hart shook his hand firmly.

"Mr. Trahern," he said.

"So this is him?" Trahern looked at Will's face for a long moment. He had pale eyes that made Will feel as if the man was looking past him, through him. "He doesn't look like much."

"He isn't." Hart bit the words. "Let's go."

Trahern held the doors as Will and Hart climbed inside. There were two rows of hard wooden seats and a place where shackles could be locked. Trahern climbed in after them, pulled the back doors shut, and knocked three times on the truck's steel roof. The truck pulled away from the curb.

Trahern looked at Will. "You didn't tie his wrists?"

Hart lifted an eyebrow. "I don't keep rope in the office." Then he showed Trahern his revolver. "He didn't put up a fight."

"Where we're going I don't like to take chances." Trahern took a pair of cuffs from his belt. As he leaned in close to snap the icy metal around Will's wrists, Will smelled raw onions and cheap aftershave.

"Where are we going?" Will asked, shoulders slumped as he let his bound wrists hang between his knees.

"Little town," Trahern said, glancing at Hart. "Outside Chicago."

"It's called Justice," Hart added softly.

Justice.

It sounded familiar, Will thought dully. But perhaps it was only his guilty conscience that made it seem so.

The drive to Justice took another hour, and the ride was bitterly cold. Staring out the tiny back window, Will could see snow blowing in small hard pellets. Hart held his cashmere overcoat tightly around himself and breathed out clouds of white. When the truck finally stopped, Will's fingers were stiff and his whole body was numb. When Trahern opened the back doors, they stepped out into deep snow.

Wherever this place was, it was very far away from any kind of civilization. The truck had parked in the middle of a large area bulldozed flat by heavy gasoline machines that still hulked in the distance, blanketed with snow. Tall black trees ringed the perimeter, cast in sharp relief by the waning moon, hanging low above dark distant hills.

The men crunched across the snow in the direction of something looming and dark: an enormous hulking building. Clearly, construction on it had only recently been completed—moonlight shone on piles of leftover lumber covered with snow-dusted canvas. But electric light blazed from the building's windows, powered by lines strung to slender poles that receded into the dark distance. It was strange that there would be electricity all the way out here, in the middle of nowhere. But shifting his eyes, Will saw something even stranger.

A Tesla Tower—and a broadcasting one, he could tell, judging by the small building that squatted at its base.

Looking away from the tower, Will brought his eyes back to the main building. The skeleton of a steeple was outlined against the night sky. Atop it was an enormous cross.

They entered through one of a dozen doors that stretched across the building's front—clearly designed to allow hundreds of people to pass at once—and came through a long wide room that reminded Will of a theater lobby. At the lobby's far end, a pair of doors twenty feet tall stood open just slightly, but that was enough to allow the men to pass abreast.

Beyond the doors was a cavernous space—a sanctuary. So this *was* a church, as the cross had suggested. But Will had never imagined a church could be so enormous. Thick support columns carved of fine white marble soared into an inky void. The place smelled of sweet new wood and varnish, candle wax and sacred oil. The main lights were not switched on, and the only illumination came from a handful of electric bulbs set in decorative gold sconces.

Will and Trahern remained near the large doors while Hart and the man who had been driving the truck crossed the vast space. Will could barely see the group of men they went to speak to, who stood clustered around the distant altar.

As they waited, something pale and small flitted at the corner of Will's vision. He looked harder, trying to see what it was. And there it was again, a tiny white form in ruffles and lace, darting between two dim marble columns. Will watched as a small girl, no older than six or seven, leaned slowly out from behind the column where she was hiding. Her skin was fish-belly white, as white as the platinum ringlets that curled wildly around her face. When she saw Will looking at her, she darted back behind the column and did not come out again.

"What is this place?" Will asked.

"This is the New Faith Seat of Praise," Trahern said. "The biggest house of worship ever built in the whole United States. There's seating for ten thousand in here."

Will knit his brow. Who would build a church like this in the middle of nowhere? But then, in a flash, Will remembered where he'd heard of the little town called Justice. It had been in Claire's room, back in Stockton. On the Teslaphone broadcast.

Coming to you live, from Justice, Illinois...

That explained why there was a broadcasting Tesla Tower outside. But while it answered one question, it raised so many more. Why would Hart bring him here? And why was Brother Phleger— the charismatic Scharfian preacher whose blot-marked face Will had seen on a hundred handbills on a hundred walls around Detroit, on a thousand tiny missionary pamphlets—now walking toward him?

Brother Phleger was square and heavily built, like a well-tailored wrestler. He wore a warm, heavy coat with a collar of thick fur. As Phleger came near, Trahern seized Will's arm, drew him close, and held him firm.

Brother Phleger was strong and good looking, despite the famous sickle-shaped mark that slashed his face from eye to chin. He looked like the kind of man who ate potatoes without salt. He thrust his hand forward.

"Welcome to Justice, Mr. Edwards," Phleger said. "I'm glad you have come."

"I didn't have much choice," Will growled, ignoring Phleger's outstretched hand and lifting his wrists to show the cuffs. "Where's Jenny?"

"Miss Hansen is here, and she is safe and comfortable," Phleger said. He looked at Trahern. "You can remove the handcuffs, Mr. Trahern. They're not necessary."

"But, Brother—"

"Just take 'em off," Phleger said a bit more roughly, and Trahern hurried to comply.

"I never do business with a man until I've shaked his hand," Phleger said pointedly, extending his hand again after Trahern had removed the cuffs.

Will rubbed his wrists, which were cold and raw, but he made no move to extend his hand. "I don't know that I have any business with you," he said.

With a grunt, Phleger reached out and seized Will's hand, crushing it. He pumped it powerfully as he took a step closer to Will, bringing them face to face.

"Dolphus Phleger," he said in a low voice. "And we *do* have business, Mr. Edwards. Very important business. I would like to explain it to you, if you will give me the chance."

Will took a deep breath. He nodded.

A bright smile lightened Phleger's face, making the slash across his cheek seem even darker. "Wonderful," he said. "Come with me to my office. We'll be more comfortable there." Then, nodding to Trahern, he turned and began strolling back in the direction from which he'd come. Trahern pushed Will forward, compelling him to walk at Phleger's side. As they walked, Phleger gestured around himself expansively.

"Isn't it glorious, Mr. Edwards? We completed work just before Christmas. I had planned to consecrate it on New Year's Day, to give good Christian people a higher-minded spectacle than that sensationalist moving-picture garbage Edison Studios is premiering." He paused, then lowered his voice with reverence. "But I have had a Vision. The Lord has commanded me that it must be consecrated more quickly. The ceremony must take place just two days from now. His will be done."

Will looked sidelong at him. "Seems like short notice to get ten thousand people to change their plans," he said.

Phleger gave him a warm smile. "Obedience to God's command is not always convenient." He pointed upward, toward a vague multicolored smear that seemed to make up most of the far wall. "It's a shame you cannot see our stained glass. It was all done by Mr. Tiffany's studio. When the sun shines through that window, it is like bathing in the light of Jesus' own redemption."

"All paid for by Jenny's money, I suppose?" Will said. "The money she stole from her father? The money Atherton Hart was helping her make into a million?"

Phleger shook his head, sighed.

"You don't understand anything," he said. "But you will."

Phleger's office was finished to an even finer degree than the rest of the building, but perhaps it just seemed that way because all the lights were on and Will could actually see the room's rich details. The wood flooring was so new that carpets had not yet been laid upon it, and it smelled of linseed oil and lacquer. A large framed painting of the man Will recognized as Brother Scharfe, founder of the Scharfian sect, hung in a place of honor above a vast desk of carved mahogany.

Seated behind the desk, engulfed in the enormous leather chair, was the little white-haired girl Will had seen in the sanctuary. Glaring down at the desk, she was tearing papers in half with intense concentration. Trahern shoved Will into one of the large chairs that were arranged before the desk, but the little girl didn't even look up, just kept tearing the papers slowly, as if liking the sound.

"Why you little heathen!" Brother Phleger roared, but it was the mock roar of a cartoon lion. He seized her, lifted her, rumpling her white ruffled skirts as he spun her around with rough playfulness. She screamed and tried to bite him, but Phleger just giggled like a naughty boy and began kissing her face all over, with big dramatic smacks. "You little scamp! Those are my notes for the broadcast! I should give you such a tickling!"

The girl writhed desperately in his clutches, and when she finally broke free she ran across the room. From the safety of that distance, she stuck her tongue out at him, pink eyes filled with hatred.

"Get out of here," Trahern growled at her. The girl—whom Will now realized must be "God's Special Snowflake," the famous Little Sanctity Snow—kicked him hard in the shin before running out the office door.

"I bought the little savage off some sharecroppers in Arkansas," Phleger commented, watching her go. "Haven't got her quite tamed yet. Damn good on the organ, though."

Trahern made a soft noise of inscrutable implication, then went to take a watchful position by the door. Phleger continued to stand for a moment, looking down at Will.

"Are you hungry, Mr. Edwards?" Phleger asked, voice dripping with concern. "Would you like some hot coffee, perhaps?"

"No."

Phleger nodded approval. "A young man of action. No time for niceties. Good. That's the kind I like to do business with."

Then he went to a very large safe that seemed to take up almost an entire wall. It was as heavy as any bank vault, gleaming black and scrolled with gold. The massive door bore the emblem of a red cross. Laying his hand on the safe, Brother Phleger bowed his head and murmured something—a prayer, Will thought, for he heard the word *amen*—and then he carefully turned the dial of the safe, shielding the action from Will's eyes with his large body.

He reached into the safe and took something out. Sitting at his desk, he placed the object before himself, holding it with two thick fingers on either side, as if he were afraid it might wriggle away. When Will leaned forward to look at it, Phleger made a warning noise and pulled back slightly. Will felt Trahern tense behind him.

"Do not attempt to touch it, Mr. Edwards," Phleger warned. "Not yet."

"What is it?"

"This is a snuffbox," Phleger said. "Do you know what snuff is? Powdered tobacco. Our forefathers used to take it in pinches. Nasty stuff. But the snuff is not what interests us. Rather, it is the box itself."

He drew in a long breath, stroking the box's top with his thumb.

"It really is a beautiful little thing," he said. "Crafted in the seventeenth century, chased silver. Very nice, as snuffboxes go. But it is more than an object of antique fascination, Mr. Edwards. Much more."

"You sure use a lot of words for someone who wants to get down to business," Will growled.

Phleger's eyes widened, but he seemed to take pleasure in Will's curtness. He smiled. "Then I will speak more plain." His voice dropped by one dark shade. "This box has hell inside it, Mr. Edwards. An eternal hell of tormented souls. And I want you to help me unlock it."

Will stared at him.

"It is, of course, a *synthetic* hell," Phleger commented. "Though I don't suppose that matters to the poor souls who have been trapped inside it for the past two hundred and twenty years—more than that, really, because within this unholy realm, each year seems ten thousand. It was created by Aebedel Cowdray, the warlock whose spirit now curses your body. He stole the souls of living men and consigned them to this hell so that their unimaginable suffering could fuel his damned practice of sangrimancy. It is Cowdray's dark masterwork, a monstrous magical artifact of incredible power. And its power has been building, untapped, since Cowdray's death.

"The box has been secretly guarded since the late seventeenth century by a parish in Massachusetts, an admirably observant sect. They always prayed that they might find a way to free the tortured souls within, but the dark magic Cowdray used to create it was an impenetrable mystery." Phleger paused. "We recently absorbed this church into our own Scharfian Fellowship, and the box came into our possession. We redoubled the efforts to discover how the artifact could be cleansed of its evil. And, praise the Lord, he sent us help."

Here, he made a gesture to Trahern.

"I find that I really would like some coffee," he said. "And bring some for Mr. Edwards as well. He looks pale."

As Trahern was opening the door, Phleger added, "Oh, and you might bring the other thing we discussed. I believe this is a good time for it."

When Trahern was gone, Brother Phleger leaned further over the desk, his large body hulking over the snuffbox. Clasping his hands together, he rested his forehead on them in an attitude of prayer.

"Yes, the Lord sent us help. Help in the form of a man—a creature of sin who has spent his entire scholarly career studying the magical history of Aebedel Cowdray. But good works may be the path to Grace! He is the only one who knows the secret of how the box may be unlocked. How the eternal suffering of the poor souls within might be ended." Phleger lifted his eyes, peering at Will over his clasped hands. "He is called Professor Coeus. He told us that we must find you—a Kendall descendent who labored under Cowdray's curse. He said we must take your blood while the curse was active, during the five days surrounding the full moon, for your blood could be used to force Cowdray's spirit to unlock the snuffbox."

"But you *didn't* find me," said Will softly. "And now it's almost a whole month until the moon is full again." His stomach turned at the thought of Cowdray returning, seizing control of his body.

Phleger shook his head regretfully. "No, we did not find you. You did rather ruin our plans, running off the way you did—" He stopped abruptly, his face becoming grave as he seemed to remember how much more Will had ruined. "But the Lord works in mysterious ways. For He has blessed you with an extraordinary—a *miraculous*—ability. You can channel Cowdray's power even when the moon is not full. You used it to banish an entire Trine of Agency warlocks, I am told."

"I don't know how I did that," Will said in a dull voice.

"It doesn't matter if you know it or not," Phleger said. "Professor Coeus knows. He knows everything. He will tell us what we must do. He will be here in the morning."

There was a long silence, during which Trahern returned with a tray bearing two cups of steaming coffee. He was not alone. Two people followed him. Hart—and Jenny.

As Trahern set down the coffee, Will had to clutch the sides of the chair to keep from leaping to his feet.

Jenny clung to Hart's arm, pressing herself against him. She looked tiny, snuggled deeply into her fur coat. Her face was set with strange bitterness.

"Jenny," he breathed, her name catching in his throat. But she did not look at him.

"I thought you might like to say hello," Phleger said. "As I have promised you, she is safe and well. And she agrees with our plan. Don't you, Jenny?"

"They can help Claire, William," she said, her voice hard and distant. "That's all I ever wanted to do."

"How can unlocking the snuffbox possibly help Claire?" Will turned his eyes back to Phleger, not able to bear the pain of looking at Jenny any longer. "And what about the million dollars Jenny was raising, why did you—"

"By sacrificing the unholy works of this fiend upon the altar of our faith, the Lord will reward us with more righteous power than all Satan's forces combined!" Phleger interjected loudly, rapturously. He turned moist eyes onto Jenny. "Imagine it, dear child. All the poor suffering victims of the Black Flu—healed in an instant. Your sister Claire made healthy and whole. We can do it, if this young man will help us. Don't you think he should?"

Jenny did not answer, rather she just made a sound. A strange sound, a throaty growl. Hart laid a comforting hand over hers.

"She's still very tired," Phleger said, deep compassion making his voice sound oily. "Take her out, Mr. Hart. She needs to rest."

When they were gone, Will did leap out of his chair, a cry of rage on his lips. Trahern crossed the room in two steps, grabbing Will's arm and twisting it behind his back. Phleger watched Will calmly.

"Hart said that if I didn't help you'd hurt Jenny," Will breathed, gasping as Trahern pushed his arm higher. "How does that fit in with this plan of Christian charity you've outlined?"

Phleger's face became thoughtful, and sad. "Even you must be able to see, Mr. Edwards, that one little life cannot be privileged over the lives of so many who now suffer. Yes, we could use the child in Jenny's body. But hurting her—forcing her—would be monstrous. That doesn't mean, however, that we would refuse if she ... *offered* herself. She loves her sister. And just as our Lord Jesus Christ, the lamb of God, offered himself as an all-sufficient sacrifice for the redemption of mankind's sins—"

Will cut off the words with a horrible noise, a strangled cry of pain and anguish.

"Do not ask her to make that choice," Phleger concluded. "Do not give her that cross to bear. Bear it for her. You owe her that much."

Will released a long breath, his body slumping in defeat. As he did, Trahern loosened the grip on his arm.

Phleger leaned back, drawing the box closer to him as he did. He closed his eyes in an attitude of reverie. "Sometimes I can feel the souls inside it, screaming. This box is an unholy evil that must be purged. It is a crime of unimaginable vastness that must be avenged." He opened his eyes quickly, and fixed Will with a piercing gaze. "Help us, Mr. Edwards. Help us in this great holy crusade. Help Jenny's sister, and all of those like her. Help the tormented souls in that box obtain their release from the anguish they've labored under for so many countless aeons."

When Will said nothing, Phleger stood and put the box back in the safe. He closed the heavy steel door, turned the dial. Then he picked up his cup of coffee and sipped at it delicately.

"Take some time to pray on it, Mr. Edwards," he said, warming his hands with the cup. "Professor Coeus will be here in the morning. We will talk more then."

After this interview, Trahern escorted Will to a "cell"—a word he clearly used in its penitentiary rather than religious sense—and locked him in. The cell reminded Will of Claire's room at the asylum—bare, sparse and clinical. Just as in Claire's room, there was a Teslaphone, playing soft organ music, but it was installed behind a wooden grate in the wall, and could not be turned off.

The room contained few furnishings—little more than a narrow bed and a simple pine desk and chair. Sitting on the edge of the bed, Will rested his face in his hands. His face felt very hot, and he rubbed it slowly.

Phleger told a good story. A good story, told in the smooth persuasive language of a preacher. But applying his rigorous scientific mind to what Phleger had said, Will began to see all the holes, and all the questions he wished he'd asked piled on top of each other. Hart had said that the Consortium had intended to capture him on the night of the full moon ... but that would mean they'd *known* he would inherit the curse. And how could they have possibly known that? Were they just going to kidnap him on the off chance that he had? That didn't seem like much of a goddamn plan.

And furthermore, if their intentions were so Christian and just, why not just ask him? Why hadn't they come to him *before* the full moon and presented their case? Why had they waited? And what about the million dollars Jenny was trying to raise for them? Phleger had never answered his question about that.

Hissing frustration through his teeth, Will rolled back onto the narrow bed, flinging his arm over his eyes. As he did, something pressed against his leg. Feeling the pockets of his trousers, he remembered that no one had thought to search him. They had not taken his razor. That was good, Will thought. But what could he do with it? While the thought of slashing Trahern's face—or better, Hart's—gave him a kind of savage pleasure, he realized that even if he managed to escape it would do him no good. They had Jenny, and if he was gone, they'd use her, just as Phleger had said. Ask her to sacrifice herself for her sister, and for the greatest good. Having just experienced Phleger's overpowering rhetorical skills, Will had little doubt the preacher could persuade her. Make her think it was her idea. He wouldn't force her, no. But he would make her agree.

There was something else in his pocket as well, he realized. The little purple velvet box. Clicking it open, he stared at the shining silver dollar. Jenny had looked so small, clinging to Hart's arm.

A key scraped in the lock. Will sat up, closing his hand quickly, hiding the box as the door jerked open. Trahern looked at Will up and down, frowning.

"Yes, he's awake," said Trahern, to someone behind him. "But I don't think Brother Phleger would like it."

"I don't care what Brother Phleger likes." Jenny's voice was harsher than Will had ever heard it—harsher even than when she'd threatened Dr. Smyth at the asylum. "He may be your boss, Trahern, but I'm the one paying your salary. Don't forget it."

The steel edge to her voice was sufficient to make Trahern redden and step back. And then Jenny came briskly into the room, coming to stand just near the door, which Trahern left half open. She stood with her hands clasped sternly beneath her breastbone, and Will hardly recognized her.

She was beautiful, of course, beautiful as she'd always been—but it was as if the soft, sweet girl he'd known had been replaced with a woman carved of stone. She had cut off all her loose edges. Anything untucked, unsmoothed, had been restrained with perfect severity. Even the loose curl that had always fascinated him was firmly pinned back, as tightly as if it were being punished.

She looked around the room angrily, as if she too were reminded of Claire's prison. She frowned at the Teslaphone, at the weak strains of silky organ music.

"I have to tell you what happened," she said crisply, as if delivering a report. "There's a lot you should know. Maybe it can help you. Cowdray asked me things. He asked me about you, first. He asked me about your family, and I told him. I told him everything he wanted to know."

"Jenny—" Will began softly.

"He seemed to know your mother." She continued as if he hadn't spoken, hitting every word with precision. "I don't know how. He said she must be the Russian's brat. I don't know what that means. He asked about something called the Anodyne. I told him I didn't know what that was." She paused, a tenseness in her jaw indicating the terrible force of whatever it was she was holding under restraint. "It made him angry that I didn't know."

Will didn't speak. Court had read in *The Goês' Confession* that scientific alteration to the magical structure of the Earth had been wrought with something called Lyakhov's Anodyne. But how could Cowdray know about that?

Jenny drew a deep quavering breath. "He hates you, William," she continued very quietly. "I've never known someone with so much hate in him. He kept asking me which would hurt you more, if he killed me or left me alive. He decided leaving me alive would be worse. He took steps to ensure that it would be."

Will could only stare at the floor, numb and distant. He clutched the little velvet box in his hand, holding on to it for dear life. Organ music hummed softly in his ears.

"But I am glad that I'm alive," she finally concluded. It sounded as if she were trying to convince herself of it. "He likes to hurt people's bodies. But he likes to hurt their minds more. That's something else you should know about him."

"I don't want to know anything about him," Will murmured. "I want to kill him."

He felt Jenny staring at him. When he looked up to meet her gaze, he saw that there was a queer kind of disgust in her eyes.

"Well, you can't. You're stuck with him." Her hand slid to her belly unconsciously. "Just like I am."

She paused.

"It's strange how I feel like I used to know so many things," Jenny said. The words were wistful, but the tone was not. "I was sure of everything. But now I'm not sure of anything at all. It feels dangerous to be sure of anything."

She paused again.

"But I am sure of one thing. I know it wasn't you. You're my friend. You'll always be my friend."

Will looked at her. Moving very slowly and carefully, he stood. He saw her tense, saw fear enter her eyes. But then she lifted her chin and glared at him defiantly—she would not be cowed by him, or her memory of him. He lifted a hand.

"It's all right," he said softly. "Please."

He did not try to move near to her, but rather stretched his arm out as far as it would go. He was careful not to touch her as he laid the velvet box in her palm. For some reason, he remembered how Brother Phleger had told him not to touch the snuffbox. As if doing so would be very dangerous.

Then he stepped back from her, returning to the narrow bed and sitting down, back straight, hands clasped between his knees. He watched as she opened the little box. When she saw what was inside it, she drew a tiny breath. And then she smiled, her face softening. Will exhaled, his whole body suddenly warm. *That* was Jenny, he thought, feeling as though he might weep. *There* she was.

"I remember this," she murmured, touching the silver with her fingertip.

"We won't see each other anymore, Jenny," Will said. "I know we won't. It's better that way." He paused, then added, "But if you ever do think about me, will you please try to think about me like that? Like the way things were then?"

She closed the box quietly. She didn't say anything else. She turned, and was gone.

When she had left, Trahern came to the door and looked at Will. His eyes, so very pale, were filled with something ugly and insinuating. Shaking his head, he barked a laugh as he closed the door and locked it once more.

Slowly, Will lay back on the bed, staring at the ceiling, listening to the organ music. He did not feel better or worse. He just felt heavy and tired, as if he'd walked a hundred miles.

And then he remembered something that made his heart race. He remembered that there was one more thing in his pocket.

Ben's letter.

He took it out and unfolded it. There was new writing on it.

Will:

I know where you are.

Whatever happens, say nothing. There is more to this than you know. Trust me.

Your brother always,

Ben

Chapter Twenty-Three

Professor Coeus

Many hours later, Will woke to the sound of Brother Phleger's voice.

This is a message to all the faithful. It is perhaps the most urgent call you will ever receive.

The words were charged with such intensity that Will sat bolt upright. After a disoriented moment, he realized that the sound was coming from the Teslaphone.

Brothers and Sisters, beloved sons and daughters redeemed by the all-sufficient grace of Jesus Christ our Savior—I have received a Vision. A Vision from most Holy God Almighty, with whom we walk in faith.

Will was aware of his own breathing, shallow and quick. Golden afternoon sunlight streamed down through a high barred window, making a perfect square on the floor. He stared at it as he listened.

The Lord has directed me that the Consecration of our Great Temple in Justice, Illinois must happen not on New Year's Day, as I originally decreed it should be. Rather, it must happen tomorrow night ... tomorrow night, brothers and sisters, on the 28th day of December, at the very hour of midnight!

Here, Brother Phleger's voice began to rise.

This is a call, my beloved ones! A call that each servant of Christ should be proud to answer! It is a once-in-a-lifetime chance to demonstrate your obedience to His Holy Will! Will you show your faith? Will you prove your ever-submissive obedience to his Holy command?

Phleger's voice was becoming louder and louder, rising to an impassioned crescendo. Will pressed his hands to his ears against it.

Will you lay aside your worldly concerns? Will you come today, this very hour, this very moment?

Then Phleger's voice dropped almost to a whisper, and even across the crackly speaker of the Teslaphone, Will could hear the preacher breathing hard.

Come now, my brothers and sisters. Come immediately. Bring friends, your families, loved ones. Climb on board trains, automobiles, horse-drawn carts if you must! Come now, that your name might be written in the book of Glory alongside all the true servants of the Lord Jesus Christ.

There was a long moment of silence. It sounded as if Brother Phleger might have collapsed in a fit of religious ecstasy.

And then, the broadcast repeated.

This is a message to all the faithful. It is perhaps the most urgent call you will ever receive.

The broadcast kept repeating, and Will had to listen through it twelve times before Trahern came for him.

"Professor Coeus made it on the afternoon train." Trahern glanced at the Teslaphone. "He could hardly get a ticket; everything to Chicago is sold out, thanks to the brother's impassioned appeal— Praise the Lord."

Will you lay aside your worldly concerns? Will you come today, this very hour, this very moment?

"He and the good brother are waiting for you in the office," Trahern said. "Come on."

As they walked to the office, they passed through the vast sanctuary that Will remembered from the night before. Then, it had been a cavernous realm of shadows and ghosts, but by day it glowed with brilliantly colored light that streamed through acres of stained glass. An enormous electrical organ with no fewer than four tiers of keys hulked against one wall. The space was even bigger than Will could have imagined.

And already, it was filling with people.

A thousand, at least, had arrived already. How could they have gotten there so quickly? They sat in the new polished pews, having brought their traveling bags with them, women and men murmuring prayerfully among themselves. A few knelt in the aisles, bathed in soft, colored light, oblivious to all earthly concerns.

When Will entered Phleger's office, he saw that two men were already waiting for him. Phleger was seated at his desk, bent over a mountain of papers, clearly in a frenzy of preparation for the moved-up Consecration ceremony. Another man—Will guessed this was Professor Coeus—stood behind him, his back to the door. He had his hands clasped behind him, and was looking up at the picture of Brother Scharfe. He was tall and slender, with walnut-brown hair. He wore a suit of no distinction. He did not even have to turn for Will to realize who he really was.

Ben.

Will clenched his jaw so tightly he thought his teeth might crack.

Trust me, Ben had written. But if Ben was the man Phleger knew as "Professor Coeus," that meant he'd been working with the Scharfians since they found the box. It meant he was the one who'd told them about the curse, about Aebedel Cowdray—about everything. But Ben hadn't told him any of it.

Ben turned then, his face held with smooth indifference. There was nothing on it that showed he recognized Will at all. He remained standing with his hands behind his back, his bearing stiff and formal. He looked different—older, heavier, weightier. He commanded respect. Before, his rumpled suit had made him look like a bank clerk. Now, its very shoddiness seemed to assert a kind of arrogant superiority—the mark of a man with far more important things on his mind than well pressed trousers.

"Good morning, Mr. Edwards," Phleger said, standing to welcome him. "Allow me to introduce you to Professor Coeus."

Ben made no gesture of greeting, just continued to peer at Will with supercilious contempt.

"He must be prepared," Ben said in a loud clipped tone. He didn't even sound like himself. He spoke—like Father or Uncle Royce—with a note of command that assumed compliance. "I will speak with him privately."

Phleger nodded, gathering up a stack of papers and squaring them neatly. "The office is at your disposal, Professor. I've got members of the international press waiting to speak with me. They, too, have been arriving in droves, clamoring for information about our holy work. His will be done!"

Will managed to hold his tongue for a few seconds after Phleger had gone—trailing Trahern behind him like a shadow—and the door was closed behind them. Finally, though, he could remain silent no longer.

"You bastard," he whispered.

"Will, stop and listen to me."

"You lying bastard," Will continued, as if his brother had not spoken. He crossed the room in a furious rush and seized Ben by his lapels, forcing him back against the wall. Putting his face close, he hissed, "How much of what you made me believe was a lie? Were they all lies? All of them?"

"I didn't lie to you," Ben said. His green eyes regarded Will steadily as he spoke. "I just didn't tell you everything. I *am* a researcher. *And* a Jefferson Chair. *And* a secret agent for the Stanton Institute."

He let the words hang. Slowly, Will released him and stepped back, breathing hard, heart pounding.

"Now listen to me, and listen carefully. Use your fine mind, not your hot head. There's a lot I have to tell you if we're going to survive this."

Will growled, turning away abruptly.

"I know what Phleger has told you about me. And much of it is true," Ben began. "My name actually *is* Coeus—Benedictus Coeus. It's the professional name I took when I was hired by the Institute. And I *am* an expert on Aebedel Cowdray. I have studied him for years—that's why the Institute gave me this assignment." He paused.

"But as I'm sure you've already guessed, if Phleger finds out who I really am, or what my real relationship is to you, we're all dead. You, me ... and Jenny."

"Phleger wouldn't have even known about Jenny if it hadn't been for you," Will spat. "Hart told me that you saw her. *Examined* her. Was it you who told Phleger that the blood of her child—*my child*—could be used to unlock the box?"

"Phleger didn't need *me* to tell him!" Ben spat back. "A child conceived when a curse is active bears the cursed blood, that's fundamental magical theory—and Phleger knows enough about magic to know that!" He paused, his expression pained. "It's Atherton Hart who doesn't. He bought a goddamn dime-store pregnancy charm and worked it on her to find out. By the time they called me in, Phleger already knew. Hart had already told him."

Fury rose in Will's chest. That fool. That damn fool.

"Now *listen*," Ben said again, more sharply. "I was assigned by the Institute to infiltrate the Scharfian Fellowship and get the snuff-box away from Phleger. We cannot allow him to unlock it. I'm sure he told you that he wanted to free the tortured souls—just like he told Jenny that he wanted her money to save her sister. And when he said those things, they were the truth—at that moment." Ben paused. "But the *real* truth, the bigger truth, is that every action he's taken has been toward a more ambitious and infinitely more dangerous goal."

"What do you mean, the *real* truth?" Will interjected. "How can he be telling the truth and lying at the same time?"

"That question is the very foundation of credomancy," said Ben.

Will raked a hand through his hair. "Then you're saying Phleger is—a *credomancer*?"

Stepping behind the desk, Ben sank heavily into the leather chair. He rubbed his face with his hands.

"No, Will. He's not a credomancer—but he's the most sophisticated practitioner of credomancy I've ever encountered. He's nothing less than a magical savant."

Will made an exasperated gesture. "How can he practice credomancy, but not be a credomancer?"

"Because a credomancer must have *some* degree of self-consciousness. Phleger is no more self-conscious than an amoeba. There isn't an ounce of hypocrisy in him, not the slightest bit of calculation or guile. He believes every word he says at the moment he says it, and that's what makes him so powerful—and so dangerous." Ben paused, leaning back in the chair and looking up at Will. "You've heard him speak of his Visions, haven't you? They are how he rationalizes his conscious actions—by attributing them entirely to his God. He does not want what he wants—he makes God want it for him."

"And what does he want God to want for him?" said Will, resting both hands on the desk so he could look more closely into his brother's face.

"What Phleger wants—*really* wants, though God has not yet told him this—is to use the power inside the box to change the entire structure of American society," Ben said.

Will narrowed his eyes. "What?"

"His Vision—his Great Vision—is of a sanctified America where the human ability to channel magic has been wiped out for good, through the implementation of mandatory Panchrest immunization. I can't even begin to explain what kind of havoc that would unleash ... but he intends to make this Vision into a reality. And that's why, tomorrow night, at the conclusion of the Consecration ceremony, he will announce his bid to become President of the United States."

Will straightened, bringing a hand up over his mouth. He turned, took a step away from the desk.

"The money Jenny raised is manna from Heaven for his campaign war-chest," his brother's voice came at his back. "But while a million dollars is a lot of manna, it's not just money Phleger needs. It's power. Enough power to destroy the one individual who stands between him and the achievement of his Great Vision." Ben paused. "Dreadnought Stanton."

Will turned back and stared at his brother blankly. Ben took a deep breath.

"As a credomancer, Dreadnought Stanton gains power when people believe in him, when they are inspired by his grandiose achievements. Over the past thirty years, as he has continued to find new ways to capture the public imagination, he has steadily gained in strength."

Ben rested his chin on his steepled fingertips.

"But the popular imagination is a finite resource—and the very large share that Dreadnought Stanton commands is a share that Brother Phleger can never fully access. Without it, he can never achieve his Great Vision. So he's got to capture it. Capture it, sanctify it, and place it in the service of the Lord Almighty." Ben paused. "Dreadnought Stanton is a *distraction*. While that distraction exists, Phleger has no chance of turning those minds to Christ. So the distraction must be ... eradicated."

"Are you saying he intends to—kill Dreadnought Stanton?" Will forced the words through clenched teeth.

"Well, facilitate his demise, at any rate," Ben said. "Phleger's faith would never allow him to commit cold-blooded murder. But holy vengeance is just as bloody." Ben lifted an eyebrow. "I have no doubt that Phleger would rationalize the act beautifully. It would not be *murder*, rather it would be *chastisement in the name of all Holy God—*"

"I get it," Will cut him off sharply. "Enough."

"If Dreadnought Stanton were dead, all of the Institute's power would come up for grabs—and no one would be in a better position to seize it than Brother Phleger." Ben gazed down thoughtfully at the work-strewn desk before him. "Really, it would be simplicity itself—all he'd have to do is preach a sermon of condolence to a grieving nation. Adding, at the end, a twist of the knife about how, despite his well-publicized heroism, Dreadnought Stanton had clearly been judged by the Lord Almighty as nothing better than a sinful *warlock*."

Will absorbed this silently. He could just hear Phleger speaking those very words, the sermon crackling across Teslaphone speakers from coast to coast. He looked up at Ben. "But how does he intend to kill Dreadnought Stanton?"

"That's another bit of untutored brilliance." Lifting his eyes, Ben smiled grimly. "Dreadnought Stanton's whole mythology is built on his quests to retrieve powerful and malign magical artifacts, right? That's the central plot of just about every one of his books. As a magical artifact, the snuffbox is as powerful and malign as they come. Phleger believes that my Sophos will try to reclaim it—*must* try to reclaim it. And when he does, Phleger will use the power in it to kill him."

"Well, if you already know that, just tell your Sophos not to come!" Will threw up his hands. "He doesn't have to come for the snuffbox!"

"Of course he's not going to come," Ben snapped, annoyed with Will's slowness. "I just told you Brother Phleger's *plan*—as much as he *has* a plan within that welter of half-formed subconscious impulses that he attributes to divine guidance. What's going to *happen*, however, is that we're going to get this box out of here—get it away from Brother Phleger, and back to the Institute, where it can be kept safe."

"And how exactly are we going to do that?"

"The only way we can. We must unlock it and use its power before Phleger can."

"We have to unlock the box—to keep Phleger from unlocking the box?" Will shook his head. "That doesn't make any sense!"

Ben drew a deep breath. "Will, we are inside a credomantic organization that is as strong as the Institute. And tomorrow at midnight, when they perform the Consecration, it will become infinitely stronger. We are trapped within walls of impenetrable faith. Our only possible means of escape is brute force—the kind of force contained within the snuffbox."

Will thought through all this.

"But if Dreadnought Stanton is in no real danger ... and the box is no threat to anyone if it's not unlocked .... and Phleger says you're the only one who knows how to unlock it ..." Will made a gesture that suggested the conclusion was obvious. "Why should we unlock it at all? Why not just leave it as it is, locked and useless? Then no one could use it—not the Scharfians, not anyone."

"Oh yes, that's a *wonderful* idea," Ben sneered. "Just exactly what do you think Brother Phleger will do when I tell him no? When I tell him that I've decided not to assist him in accomplishing his highest holy crusade?"

"God will probably tell him to kill you." Will regarded his brother coldly. "But I don't see why he'd hold it against Jenny or me."

Ben blinked at him in astonishment. Then he exhaled slowly.

"You've got more Cowdray in you than I imagined," he said harshly. "No, Will. He wouldn't kill me. He would tear my mind to shreds with righteous indignation, looking for the information. And very quickly, he would discover the truth."

"And which kind of 'truth' is that?" said Will, with faint irony. He was beginning to be very wary of that particular word.

"That he doesn't really need me at all." Ben said, his glossy green eyes reflecting Will's silent astonishment. "There's no secret to opening the snuffbox. It is true, it does require a magical connection to Cowdray's spirit, a connection that could be established using you or—" Ben stopped abruptly, looking away. "But beyond that, it only requires overcoming Cowdray's resistance with sufficient magical force. Of course I know how to do it—but so would even the most casual student of magic."

"Well, why doesn't God tell him this?" Will snapped.

"Because at the moment, Phleger perceives me as a necessary evil. The good brother protects his holy self-image by believing that I am the only one who knows how to open the box," Ben snapped back. "He doesn't keep me around for my magical knowledge. He keeps me around to be his sin-eater."

Ben leaned forward, his voice becoming both softer and more intense. "But if I cross him, or thwart him in any way, I will become an *unnecessary* evil. Phleger's subconscious defenses would swarm against me. And I have no doubt that God *would* tell him—in the form of a well-timed Vision—that anything I can do, he can do a million times more powerfully. When he decides he wants God to want that for him ... we really are all dead."

Ben paused to let these words sink in. Then he continued.

"Unlocking the box is a risk, yes. An enormous risk. But given the amount of power Phleger has, it's going to get unlocked one way or another. Using you—or the blood of your child." This time Ben did not pull the punch, but rather hit the last few words with painful emphasis. "The only way any of us are going to get out of here alive is if we control how it happens, and control what happens to the power afterwards."

Will thought about this for a long time. The sound of organ music, soft and muffled, filtered in through the walls. *That must be Little Sanctity Snow playing*, Will thought. He thought of how she'd sat at Phleger's desk, intensely ripping his papers to shreds. He looked up at his brother.

"Just tell me one thing, Ben. And tell me the truth. Did you know that I would inherit the curse?"

"No!" Ben said, a note of anguish in his voice. "I *didn't* know. I've told you that already, and it *was* the truth. I saw Father give you the Panchrest. How could you possibly inherit the curse? But to infiltrate the Consortium, I had to be of value to them. I had to give them information, and there had to be truth in it. I had to make them *believe*." He paused. "It *had* to be you. You were a Kendall descendant, just turned eighteen. The Consortium knew that none of the other Edwards brothers had inherited the curse. You were the only plausible candidate. I gave them a *story*, Will. That's all I have the power to do, tell people stories and make them believe them. I had no way of knowing it would turn out to be the truth."

"But if you believed I *wouldn't* inherit the curse, how did you intend to get the snuffbox?" Will said, following the logic through. "What did you think would happen when they found out I didn't have the cursed blood they needed?" He gestured around himself broadly. "How did you expect to get the snuffbox out of this great center of power then?"

"If things had gone as they were supposed to, the snuffbox wouldn't be *in* this great center of power," Ben said bitterly. "Brother Phleger was in Detroit on the night of the full moon—December 16th. He was holding an old fashioned revival at the Detroit Scharfian Fellowship. I had convinced him to bring the snuffbox with him to Detroit. It was almost impossible to get him to take the chance—you've seen how careful he is with it. But I did. I convinced him. I told him a very good story."

Ben paused, his face dark and intense. He stared down at the desk for a moment, fists clenched. Then he took a deep breath, and released it slowly.

"And if things had gone according to plan ... if you'd met me at the station as you were supposed to ... then Trahern would have taken us both to him. To wherever he was keeping the snuffbox. And the Institute warlocks shadowing me would have followed, and they would have seized the box in a place *away* from Phleger's center of power. It would have been a difficult battle, but they would have prevailed."

He paused again. "But you didn't meet me. And Trahern did not take me to Phleger. And so, here we are."

Will bowed his head. The organ music had become heavy and slow.

"I didn't know where you were," Ben continued. "I didn't know what had happened to you. But I never imagined it was actually the curse, until Hart contacted Phleger and told him about Jenny." He paused. "When I saw the charms on her body, I knew. I knew it had to be Cowdray."

He looked at Will.

"I also knew that the most sensible course of action was for me to return to the Institute. Extract myself from the situation; put myself out of Phleger's reach. He believes I hold the secret to unlocking the box—so the best move would have been to keep myself, and the secret he believes I possess, away from him. It would not have been a permanent solution, but it would have slowed him down. It would have made him waste valuable time. And the Institute needed that time. It needed it very badly."

Ben stretched his hand out flat, staring hard at his own fingers, as if there was some kind of secret within them.

"But I knew what he would do with that time. The only thing he *could* do—figure out some way to use Jenny. And no matter what God told him to do to her, it surely would have hurt her more than she's already been hurt. If I let that happen, you'd never forgive me. That's why I put that note on your pillow."

Will was shocked. "You?"

Ben nodded.

"The Gores warded their whole house against Agency warlocks ... do you really think a fool like Atherton Hart could get past them and stab a knife into your pillow?" Ben scoffed. "No, Will. I sent you to him, so that he would bring you to me. Because I knew that you and I together could have a chance of making this work. As long as I keep Phleger fooled about how important I am to him, and you do everything exactly as I say, we can save Jenny, get the box, escape to safety, everything. I know we can do this, little brother. Trust me." He grinned crookedly. "It'll all come out all right."

Will absorbed all this. Finally, he sighed. "You could have told me all this at the Gores', and spared me the trouble of climbing out the window."

"Phleger would have known." Ben lifted an ironic eyebrow. "You're not a very good liar, Will. Besides—I couldn't have told you earlier; that's not how credomancers operate."

"You're not a credomancer," Will said.

"But I *am* a storyteller," Ben said. "And we happen to work in much the same way."

Chapter Twenty-Four
The Sanctum Sanctorum

The jangling ring of the desk telephone shattered the silence, making them both jump. Ben lifted the receiver quickly, and listened.

"Yes, the preparations are complete," he replied sharply. "You must return immediately. I have discovered something very important." Ben replaced the receiver in its cradle and turned to Will.

"Phleger is coming." Ben leapt out of the chair. "Things will happen fast now. Try to keep up."

A suitcase, damp from melted snow, sat near the office door. Retrieving it, Ben unlocked it with a key he drew from his pocket.

"It is of utmost importance that we escape with the box *before* the Consecration ceremony," he said, opening the suitcase. It was filled not with clothes, but rather with books and papers. "The ceremony will cement this place as Brother Phleger's center of power. After it is complete, these walls will be magically impregnable. That's why Phleger moved up the ceremony. He knows that you can access Cowdray's power, and he knows that the Institute knows it."

Will knit his brow, puzzled. "How does the *Institute* know it?"

"I told them, of course—"

"But how could *Phleger* know that?"

Ben's eyes flashed alarm, but the look quickly coagulated into annoyance. He shook his head sharply.

"I don't have time to explain everything, Will. All you need to know is that Phleger expects that Dreadnought Stanton will try and get the box before the Consecration puts it out of his reach. He's fortifying his center of power to keep my Sophos from getting in …

and if we don't get out before the ceremony is complete, we might not get out at all."

Ben swept all of Phleger's paperwork to one side and began pulling his own papers from within the suitcase. He spread these out over the desk as if he'd been working on them during Phleger's absence. He set a pen and pot of ink nearby to complete the illusion. Will peered down at the sheets—they were all covered with hastily scribbled astrological charts and horary calculations.

"I have to convince Phleger to attempt to open the box before he's completed his defenses—and I have to do so without making him question his faith in me." Ben paused, his face going slightly pale, as if realizing the enormity of the task before him. Visibly steeling himself, he pulled several leather-bound astrological reference tomes—tables of houses, ephemeredes, sidereal atlases—out of the suitcase and thumped them down in dusty piles. "So I've cooked up a damn good story. My best yet."

Having arranged the papers and books to his satisfaction, Ben then reached into his pocket and produced a silver tin that rattled. He opened it and thrust it at Will. "Quick, take one of these—no, take two."

Will looked into the tin. "Candy?"

Ben rattled the tin at him insistently. "They're a magical potion, just in a different form. Come on!"

Will took two of the candies and popped them into his mouth. They were sweet and bitter at the same time, tasting of ginger and honey and sulphur.

Ben tucked away the tin, put both his hands on Will's arms, and looked him full in the face, his green eyes searching Will's violet ones. "Listen carefully. Before I came here, I alerted the Institute. There are warlocks waiting to come to our rescue. But they cannot enter here unless Phleger invites them in."

Will almost choked on the candy. "*Invites them in?* How are we supposed to—"

At that moment, the door to the office jerked open. Trahern entered first, glaring at Ben and Will as he stood aside to let Brother

Phleger pass. The press conference must have gone very well, for the beaming preacher strutted through the door chest-first, in mid-command: "Of course they must print it! I have it here somewhere ..."

Going quickly to his desk, he sank into his chair, clearly meaning to retrieve some important document. When he saw the heaps of astrological papers and books, he frowned deeply, and his nostrils flared as if smelling brimstone. Lifting his eyes to Ben, he hissed, "What kind of demonic sorcery is—"

But then he caught sight of Ben's face, and the words stopped in his mouth.

Will himself was shocked by his brother's transformation. He had become "Professor Coeus" again in an instant, his chin raised high, his back strong and straight, his whole body as taut as a predatory cat's. But that wasn't what caught Phleger's attention—rather, it was the fervent, intense gleam in Ben's eyes.

"What's the matter?" said Phleger, concerned. He glanced at Will. "Is there something wrong with the boy?"

"Wrong!" Ben exhaled, his voice trembling with excitement. He gave a wondrous little laugh. "Wrong? No, Brother Phleger. Nothing is wrong. As a matter of fact, things couldn't be more right. I have discovered something incredible—astonishing!"

Phleger's brow furrowed even more deeply. "What have you discovered?"

"I almost cannot believe it," Ben mused, looking not at Phleger, but rather past him. "It cannot be, and yet it is—"

"What?" Phleger barked. "What is it?"

Ben's eyes focused, and he turned his keen gaze on Phleger. "This young man has just provided me with his birth information," he said. "I used it to quickly calculate his astrological chart, thinking it might be of some use in our efforts. And I discovered that Mr. Edwards was born under ... a *Grand Cross*."

Ben paused to let the import of the statement sink in. But it was lost on Brother Phleger, for he merely made an impatient gesture.

"Yes? And? So?"

"Aebedel Cowdray was also born under that particular astrological configuration. And while I have never told you, for I know you do not countenance such practices, when I cast your own chart, I discovered that you too were born under a Grand Cross."

Phleger's eyes widened. It was clear that the symbology of a Grand Cross shining on his birth was of intense and immediate interest to him—and so pleasing, in fact, that he seemed willing to overlook the fact that he shared the holy-seeming birthright with the wicked Cowdray himself.

"But that is not the incredible thing," Ben seized a sheaf of papers from the desk, and thrust them close to Phleger's face, jabbing at specific notes as he spoke. "At this very moment, in the heavens above us, yet *another* Grand Cross is forming. This exceedingly rare and powerful configuration, which occurs when each of four planets stands at a square to the others, creates massive tension— the eternal tension between good and evil, taken to its furthest extreme. The stage is set, Brother Phleger, for a magical event of such unimaginable power ... of such exceptional intensity ... that it literally takes my breath away." As if to demonstrate this, Ben drew in a deep gulp of air.

"All right," Phleger said, slight wariness creeping into his voice. He pushed the papers aside with disgust, as if Ben were waving a soiled handkerchief at him. "What does it all mean?"

"It means the box must be opened at the moment the Grand Cross reaches its most precise alignment," Ben said. He quickly consulted a battered pocketwatch. "In exactly one hour."

The words hung in the air for a moment—but it only took a moment for Phleger's face to go from consideration to conclusion.

"No," he said.

Ben looked stricken. "But Brother—"

"It is impossible," Phleger interjected coolly. "The Consecration must happen first. We must fortify this Temple, dedicate it and all of its power to the Lord Almighty. If we conduct the ritual without that holy sanction, then it is nothing more than *witchcraft*. And God will not tolerate it."

"You *are* the Temple!' Ben cried. "You are sanctified, a man of God—"

"Precisely so!" Phleger flared. "I am just that—a *man*. If we fail, our enemies would gain great comfort—enough, possibly, to empower them to move against us." He drew a deep breath, closed his eyes. "God tells me very strongly that I must wait. I must wait until the time is truly right, when the ritual can be conducted with all the power of the faithful behind it."

Ben made a sound of extreme annoyance and threw the papers down onto the desk. He seemed ready to storm out of the office in disgust—but instead, he made a great show of collecting himself. When he did speak again, Professor Coeus' haughtiest sneer tinged his voice. He spoke very slowly.

"Clearly, Brother Phleger, you do not understand the gravity of this discovery. This combination of astrological omens is so powerful—and so utterly unprecedented—that not to take advantage of it would be the very apex of foolishness."

Phleger met Ben's infuriating condescension with an even more infuriating grin. "I understand that faith can sometimes seem like foolishness to a man who does not know God, Professor."

Phleger's grin made Ben bristle—but then, all at once, he relaxed. He took a deep breath, and then he, too, smiled—the knowing, weary smile of a man recognizing his defeat.

"No, you are right," he said. "I am not a man of faith. I am a man of the world, and as such, the ways of the world seem very urgent and important to me." He began gathering his charts and books from Phleger's desk and carefully replacing them in the suitcase. "I was thinking more of your secular aspirations than your holy obligations, and I apologize. It's just that you have no idea how much additional power this could lend to the announcement you're planning to make after the Consecration."

Brother Phleger said nothing, just stroked the black blot on his cheek, absently fingering the discoloration's slightly-raised edge.

"Of course, most of that power will still be available even after the astrological alignment shifts," Ben said, as if trying to find comfort in the fact. "Not all of it—nowhere *near* all of it—but I'm sure it will be enough." He sighed as he buckled the suitcase shut. "It's just that they say it's going to be a four-man race next year, and ..." He trailed off. "Well, never mind. His will be done, as you so often say."

"It is—not *safe*," Brother Phleger said, in a quiet voice. He let his hand drop, and when he looked at Ben his eyes were pleading. "Don't you understand, Professor? A great responsibility has been placed upon me. I must not fail."

"You are burdened," Ben said, and there was real sympathy in his voice. He laid a hand on Brother Phleger's shoulder, and the preacher made no move to shrug it off. "I *do* understand. I know there are great forces that oppose you, and you very wisely wish to protect yourself and your followers from them." He gripped Phleger's shoulder more firmly. "I just want to make one thing very, very clear. This set of astrological circumstances is so unlikely as to be outside the realm of possibility. It is, in a word, impossible."

Ben paused, as perfectly still as a wax saint.

"As I said, I am not a man of faith." His voice was low and rhythmic and thrilling. "But if I were to believe in miracles, I could not help but believe this to be one. If I were a man of faith, there is only one word I could use to describe the opportunity we are presented with." He paused before hitting the last word with an intensity that made it seem almost physical: "*Foreordained.*"

Phleger was not looking at Ben now, he was just listening, his eyes narrowed with careful thought—or rather, with prayer, Will saw, for his lips were moving and his hands were clasped.

"When the Lord sends a man of faith such a message, Brother Phleger, should he question it? I don't know the answer, you must tell me. And should he question the power of the Lord to shield him?"

Phleger slumped over his desk, resting his forehead on his clasped hands. He muttered to himself for a long time. Ben did not move a muscle. No one in the room did. When Phleger finally raised his head, his eyes were distant and unfocused, glistening with tears.

"*Many are the afflictions of the righteous, but the Lord delivers him out of them all,*" he whispered, his voice choked with emotion. "Just as the Lord protected Shadrach, Meshach, and Abednego when they were cast into the furnace's fiery depths, so will He protect us."

He wiped his eyes quickly with the back of his cuff. In an instant, his gaze was as keen and sharp as it had ever been. "We will show our faith by proceeding as you suggest, Professor. We will take the risk, secure in the ever-loving protection of the Lord. His will be done!"

"We cannot conduct the ritual in the sanctuary," Phleger muttered as he went quickly to the large safe. "It is already filling with the faithful. If the ritual were to be presented as a part of the Consecration, that would sanctify it in their eyes. But as a piece of deviltry on its own, it would merely befuddle and worry them. That would not do at all."

"A wise choice," Ben murmured, clearly admiring Phleger's perceptivity, untutored as it was.

"We will use my *sanctum sanctorum*, the private chapel where I retreat for personal prayer and reflection." Laying a hand on the safe, Phleger whispered a prayer, then unlocked it. Withdrawing the snuffbox, he tucked it inside his coat pocket.

Phleger and Ben strode from the office, and Trahern took Will's arm, pulling him to follow. As they walked, Will rolled the candies around in his mouth. The taste was beginning to change; now the candies had the flavor of grass and memory and blood—and Will's body was beginning to feel strange. He was powerfully aware of each of Trahern's fingertips digging into the flesh of his arm. They burned.

Brother Phleger's *sanctum sanctorum* was situated directly behind the vestry. It was an intimate space, without the sanctuary's grandeur—but in some ways, it was even more impressive. The walls were stark, pure white—so white it hurt Will's eyes. There were no windows and no trace of ornamentation. Just white walls that stretched up to high white ceilings, lit by stark white bulbs.

The floor was of glittering white marble, polished mirror smooth. The room was as cold as an icebox.

There was only one spot of color in the room, and that was on the far wall—an enormous red cross of stained wood, at least twelve feet tall.

There was no altar before the cross; instead, there was a single piece of furniture, low and wide and armless, covered in smooth white leather.

"I think only the three of us need to be present for this," Ben said, looking meaningfully at Trahern.

"Think again," Trahern growled.

"No, the Professor is right," Phleger said. "Having four doesn't seem right. Three is a more hallowed number." When Trahern made no move to leave, Phleger waved him away with an impatient gesture. "Guard the door. I will call if I need you."

Ben helped Will lie down on the low ottoman. Will was feeling very strange now. The brilliant whiteness of the room seemed to press against his skin, and his very bones ached.

"I will conduct the ritual," Ben said to Phleger. "You must assume an attitude of prayer. Beseech God to cover us in his holy Grace."

Phleger grabbed both of Ben's hands, and held them for a moment.

"Even though you are not a man of faith," he said, "may the Lord be with you."

Then he went to kneel before the cross. When Phleger could not see, Ben shuddered and shook his hands as if he'd been shocked by electricity.

"What is in this candy?" Will murmured to Ben. The words slurred as he spoke them, and his voice sounded strange within his own ears. His muscles burned as if he'd just run for miles. Ben looked into Will's eyes, assessing something in them, then nodded with silent satisfaction.

"The Gores compounded this potion to help us keep Cowdray at bay while we conduct the ritual."

"Help *us* control Cowdray?"

Ben nodded. "You're not trained in magic, but I am. We're going to do exactly what Dr. Gore and Irene do. I am going to vamp on you."

"It hurts," Will whispered, his voice hoarse. "It hurts a lot."

"I know, Will," Ben whispered. "I'm sorry. But Cowdray will resist us with every means at his disposal. And we have only one advantage over him. Your body. Your physicality. The pain is the only way you'll be able to keep from being overwhelmed by him. You must use the pain—be intensely aware of it. You need to use the pain, just like you used it to break Mother's Send."

Will nodded, his head wobbling loose on his neck. The movement sent agony screeching down his spine. He remembered pressing his arm against the steam radiator, the pain tearing away the tendrils of magic that had tried to insinuate themselves through his mind. But that had only hurt for a little while. This pain was already so much greater than that. And it was getting worse.

"Ben, it's too strong," Will whispered. At the sound of his real name, Ben quickly looked behind him to see where Phleger was. But Phleger had not heard; he was kneeling on the cold hard floor before the cross, shoulders hunched in prayer.

"It's too strong," Will gasped again, as a fresh wave of pain surged through his body. Involuntary tears sprung into his eyes as all his muscles clenched against it.

"I just hope it's strong enough," Ben said as he unbuttoned Will's shirt, laying his chest bare.

"I don't know what I'm supposed to do," Will rasped, feeling as if his words might catch fire for speaking them. He felt himself panting heavily. "Ben, I don't know what I'm supposed to do!"

"Stop calling me 'Ben' for one thing," his brother growled low. Then, in a louder voice, he called over his shoulder to where Brother Phleger was kneeling. "Brother Phleger! I will need the box now."

Will did not see Phleger rise; he did not see him until the preacher was standing over him, looking down at him, the snuffbox in his hand. In Will's pain-swimming vision, Phleger seemed to be— *glowing*. Wisps of brilliantly colored light entwined his entire body, shimmering threads of red and purple and gold and yellow. The black mark that slashed from his eye to his chin seemed to throb. Will could not stop staring at him.

Ben made an urgent gesture. Slowly, reluctantly, Phleger reached into his pocket and withdrew the silver box. Ben had to take it from his hand. Ben placed the box gently on Will's bare chest—over his panic-thrashing heart—then laid both his warm hands over it.

Focus on my voice. Ben's thoughts rang abruptly through his head, and Will closed his eyes in concentration. Ben's response was abrupt: *No, keep your eyes open. <u>Open</u>.* He seized Will's chin, gave his head a little shake. It felt like broken glass was rattling inside his skull. Will whimpered.

I told you the warlocks cannot come unless Phleger invites them in. So make him. Tell him to invite them in. Tell him to invite his enemies into this temple.

Will's mind swam with confusion. How could he! Phleger would never—

Ben pressed down on the box. It was the worst agony Will had ever known, as if his very heart was being burned in the fires of hell. Will screamed.

Say it! Tell him to invite them in! Command him!

"Invite them in," Will gasped, but it was a mere whisper against a maelstrom of suffering.

Louder! Ben pressed down on the box again, and Will thought he would die. *Use Cowdray's voice! The command in Latin is <u>Invado</u>— scream it!*

"Invado!" Will shrieked, and his voice was Cowdray's, ringing and cruel. It made the walls shudder around them. "Invite them in! Invite in your enemies!"

Phleger leaped to his feet, alarmed. Will's magically-enhanced vision allowed him to see the panicked colors glowing around the preacher. Will could see how deeply Phleger's power suffused the very structure around them, how the gleaming threads of magic that surrounded him ran like blood-veins through the walls. The light that pulsed from Phleger pulsed all around them.

"What is he saying?" Phleger bellowed.

"It's not the boy—it's Cowdray!" Ben bellowed in response. "He's attempting to invade your mind, to take control of you!" Ben pressed the box down again, making Will babble and thrash uncontrollably. "You must not let him! Defend your temple!"

With a cry, Phleger whirled and fell to his knees once again, lifting his hands to the cross and pleading loudly for salvation, for shelter, for deliverance. Ben slackened his pressure on the box, and Will's agony relaxed slightly. He felt himself sobbing.

I'm sorry, Will. Stay with me just a little longer. Will was faintly aware of his brother stroking his hair. *All of Phleger's energy will be directed outward now, flowing out of the temple. We can ride it out. You just have to break the walls, Will. Break the walls. Believe that we are outside them. Me, you, Jenny, and your child. All of us. Outside and free.*

FREE? WHY SHOULD YOU BE FREE? I AM NOT, AND NEVER WILL BE.

Ben clenched his teeth at the new presence. *Cowdray.*

ANOTHER KENDALL! Cowdray seemed to recognize the very flavor of Ben's thoughts. AND A EUNUCH AT THAT. SEEKING TO STEAL A BIT OF YOUR BROTHER'S POWER FOR YOUR OWN?

Cowdray will try to bully you, Will—don't let him! Keep your eyes open. Stay here. Stay with the pain—

OH, BUT THERE ARE SO MANY KINDS OF PAIN, Cowdray said. AND YOU DON'T KNOW HALF OF MANY OF THEM AS I DO.

Will was suddenly seized with the uncontrollable urge to close his eyes. They slammed shut, clenched tightly as fists. But instead of darkness, Will found that he was seeing through different eyes.

Different eyes—but the memories were his.

His, and Aebedel Cowdray's.

Walls.

Walls of buildings. Buildings made of stone. And lights—so bright. And the moon—and not the moon.

It is cold here.

Having just taken a new body, Aebedel Cowdray tries to remember the last life he lived. The last body he owned.

Where am I?

Cowdray pauses in the street, paved with some hard, smooth substance. Everything around him is smooth, strong, tall. There is so much light.

He pauses and runs his hands along his arms, his torso. He is a man this time. That is good, very good. It is good to be a man again. A young man. Strong. He looks at his hands, places them on his firm abdomen, feels himself breathe. He smells the air, cold and fresh, tinged with the smell of steel. He is in some very large city, and he is outside, and it is snowing very hard.

"Will!" Ben's voice, distant, another time and place. A place where a huge red cross burned. Will could feel Ben slapping him hard across the face, but compared with the rest of the pain, the sensation was barely noticeable. "Will, open your eyes! For God's sake, don't let Cowdray pull you into memory! Use the pain, Will. Stay here! Open your eyes!"

Will tried. He tried desperately. He struggled against Cowdray, struggled to crack his eyes open. He summoned all the pain in his body and all the hatred. He focused on his brother's words.

"Use the pain!" Ben was roaring. "Use the pain! Think of *Jenny*—"

AH, YES! Cowdray's exclamation was bright with cruel inspiration. LET'S THINK OF JENNY! TENDER, SUPPLE, MOIST LITTLE JENNY—

"No!" Will screamed, and he realized that he was screaming it aloud, the extended shriek scorching his throat. He felt Ben's fist slam down on his chest, cold silver driving through his heart like a stake. This time, though, he arched his back to meet the pain, desperately seeking to intensify it.

The night is bitterly cold, and the snow is falling heavily. And the moon is full, beautifully full.

Cowdray moves unsteadily along the pavement, remembering how to walk, savoring the cold. As he walks, he sheds the memories of his last body, discarding them like rags of old clothing. He had a woman's body before. It was weak. He killed that woman's husband with a large knife. That woman's husband had been a scientist. A Russian. Cowdray had stabbed him with the woman's hand, as she had screamed for him to stop. He decides that he will keep that memory. He will keep it with the others he carries with him from life to life—bloody, brutal, beautiful memories.

That woman had a child, Cowdray remembers. A tiny girl with disturbing violet eyes. Cowdray wonders idly what became of her. Squealing little get of a Kendall. He wishes he could remember what he did to her. That might be a fine memory, well worthy of keeping. But he doesn't remember killing her. Perhaps he let her live so that she could get other squealing little Kendalls. Squealing little Kendalls like the boy whose body he now possesses.

Thinking of the boy, Cowdray feels for his mind. It is pinned like an insect, wiggling. Panicked, terrified, completely devoid of understanding. Cowdray regards this squirming little creature.

"What are you called?" he inquires aloud, breath congealing white then falling with the hard-driving snow. The boy does not want to answer, but Cowdray's power is sufficient to compel an immediate response:

WILL EDWARDS.

Cowdray grunts. It is good to know the body's name. The body's name will be useful. Especially since there is someone following him, someone just as young and clumsy as the new body he possesses. He turns, startling her.

She is exquisite.

The body he possesses thinks so too, for just seeing her releases a rush of desire in his blood. The boy feels shame at this, but Cowdray is older. Much older. He knows what to do with such feelings.

"William!" the exquisite creature says, breath white. She is breathing hard, her pretty face flushed pink with cold and the exertion of

following him. She is wearing a coat of lustrous animal fur, downy with white flakes. "What's wrong with you?"

It is better, for the moment, to pretend.

"I feel strange," he says, putting weakness in his voice. He rests a hand on her shoulder to steady himself. Her shoulder is warm and firm and soft, and he leans heavily against her, hungry to let his hand wander. But not here.

She draws closer to him, helps him stand. So she trusts him, then. There is concern in her eyes. Concern, and something else.

Love.

Oh, Cowdray thinks bitterly. This will be sweet. Very, very sweet.

"What's your name, my pet?" he asks, nuzzling her as he whispers it in her ear, smelling the fragrance of her hair.

"Jenny," she says, drawing back to look at him with surprise. "What's wrong with you?"

"I'm sick, Jenny," Cowdray whimpers pathetically. "I'm so cold. We have to get out of the cold."

He searches the boy's memories for a place he can take her. This time the boy senses his intentions and struggles against him. But it only takes a moment for the perfect place to reveal itself.

No, Will screams.

"I have to hide," Cowdray says to her. "You shouldn't stay with me. I am in danger. Terrible danger."

"I'll stay with you," she says, wrapping her arm around him to hold him up. Oh, how loyal she is! How sweet! "I will help you. We'll go back to the apartment—"

"No," Cowdray says curtly. "We cannot go there. It is too dangerous. We must go someplace else. You have to trust me. You have to trust me ... Jenny."

Smiling, he leans against Jenny, and she helps him stagger to the Hotel Acheron.

"Will!" Ben is yelling. "Will, fight him. Fight him!"

In the real world, Will is screaming.

Will is screaming, and he cannot stop.

The place is so perfect that Cowdray wonders if the boy is less reluctant than his constant screaming would suggest. He does desire the girl, after all. Cowdray is just helping nature along. He closes the door behind them. He puts the key in a pocket inside his vest.

Jenny is standing with her arms wrapped tightly around herself. Snow is melting into the soft folds of her coat. Her eyes are worried.

"Why have we come back here, William? This is a terrible place—"

He seizes her. The worry in her eyes becomes something different as he kisses her hard, roughly.

"Stop it!" She tries to pull away, but Cowdray holds her fast. His body is strong, strong and young. Her struggle fires it.

"Your hair smells like snow," he says, "Like cold air and ice on the water. I want to know what your skin smells like."

With a cry, Jenny pulls away, whirling to the other side of the room, pressing her back against the wall. Cowdray lets her go. This is just the first salvo, the first foray. He is assured of victory. There is no need to achieve it too soon.

"I want to leave," she says. She is breathing hard. She is trembling.

LET HER GO, *the boy moans.* PLEASE.

Cowdray removes his coat. He does this very slowly. Once his coat is off, he removes the key from his vest pocket. He shows it to her.

"The door is there," he says. But as Jenny is moving toward him to take the key, the boy remembers something else. The boy is so very obliging. Cowdray pulls the something else out of his pocket, something that shines. A straight razor with a smooth tortoiseshell handle. The girl is forgotten for a moment as Cowdray unfolds the shining silver blade. It is a beautiful piece of steel. When he finally does look up at Jenny, he sees that she has frozen like a startled fawn.

"You bought this for him," he says wonderingly. Glee bubbles up within him. He is young, he is armed, and there is a beautiful girl at his mercy.

"I bought it for you," Jenny says, voice breaking. "Please. I want to go now."

Cowdray holds up both hands. In one hand is the key to the door, in the other hand, the open razor.

"You can go," he says. "If you can get the key before I can open your throat. But I don't think you can."

Jenny withers like a dying plant. She collapses in on herself. Cowdray has seen this moment many times. It is the moment when someone realizes that they are going to die, and there is nothing they can do. Fire courses through his blood again, filling him with desire.

Jenny creeps backward, away from the door, away from him. Cowdray steps forward exactly as many steps as she steps back, a lover's dance.

He shows her the key again, but she makes no move to take it. He puts it away with an indifferent shrug. But the razor he does not put away. He holds it in his hand, turning it over and over.

"Who are you?" Her voice is miniscule. She understands now. She understands that something is very wrong. She understands that he is not the boy she knows, the boy she trusted.

"My name is Aebedel Cowdray," he says. "I have taken this body, and I will do with it as I wish."

"How?" The word is a soft moan. "How did you ... take it? Who are you? What did you do to William?"

"I am an old warlock with an old grudge against his family," Cowdray says. He takes another step toward her, watches her cringe. "The moon is full. His body is mine for the next five days. As is yours."

STOP IT! LEAVE HER ALONE! *The boy's incessant screams have become loud enough to give Cowdray pain. He touches his fingertips to his temples with annoyance.*

"You want this as much as I do," Cowdray snarls, putting all the force of his power into the words, and the boy's cries are silenced. But Jenny thinks he is speaking to her. She says, in a surprisingly clear voice:

"I don't want this." She is trying to catch the boy's eyes, trying to find him within Cowdray's cold approach. "William, please. Please."

The words fill Cowdray with sudden fury. As if the boy, the pinned insect, another weak squalling Kendall in a lineage of weak squalling Kendalls, could do anything to help her. The very idea is a monstrous insult. With an ugly epithet, he lunges at her, catching the neck of her dress with the razor. It slashes with a very satisfying sound, the slither of steel on silk.

And then she is the one doing the screaming.

Will felt Brother Phleger and Ben holding him down, holding him hard. He was aware of his own body, consumed with anguish, thrashing insanely.

"Trahern!" Phleger screamed. And in an instant Trahern was there too, his entire weight thrown across Will's legs.

"Cowdray's too strong for him." Ben's voice.

Will felt tears streaming down his face. The pain was unbearable. But it wasn't the physical pain. It was the pain of memory, of Cowdray's body against Jenny's, his lips against her skin, his hands on her throat ...

Will fought now as he could not fight Cowdray then. Trahern, Ben, Phleger ... he fought them all.

"We have to stop this," Ben said. His voice was edged with panic.

"But the snuffbox! It must be unlocked! He must—"

"It will never be unlocked if he dies, or is driven mad!" Ben barked.

Something was placed at Will's lips. Glass, warmed by someone's body. A phial. Liquid filled his mouth, bitter as death. He swallowed, and it filled his body with emptiness and chill. He felt himself subsiding and dying. He stopped screaming, and let himself fall gratefully into oblivion.

Chapter Twenty-Five
Will of God

Will woke to the sound of someone being beaten.

"Devil! Devil, demon, filthy, foul, accursed!" A grunt, and the sound of flesh slamming against the wall. "Deceiver! Tempter!"

Will opened his eyes slowly, cringing against the brilliant searing whiteness. Moonlight? No, a white room—a hideous room of snowstorm white, dominated by a blazing blood-red cross. The *sanctum sanctorum*, Will remembered. His head ached, but his throat ached more. His whole body ached. He wanted desperately to fall back into blackness. But someone was being beaten.

"Can the Ethiopian change his skin or the leopard its spots? Neither can he do good who is accustomed to doing evil! A bad tree cannot produce good fruit! And whatsoever does not proceed from faith is sin!" It was the voice of a preacher, quoting indiscriminately from the Bible, and it made Will's flesh crawl. He felt as though he might vomit.

He turned his head just enough to glimpse Ben, and Brother Phleger. The back of Ben's coat hung in shredded, bloody tatters—it looked as though he'd been lashed. The preacher's face was purple with rage. Phleger clenched his fingers and lifted his hand, and Ben rose into the air. When Phleger struck the air with his fist, Ben slammed hard against one of the ice-white walls.

"But now I see you, Satan! Old Scratch, monstrosity of evil! I know your works!" Spittle flew from Phleger's lips as he stood with one hand raised like a claw, fingers pointed skyward.

Ben hung suspended against the smooth wall. With a furious gesture, Phleger thrust his hand down, and Ben slid to the floor, his torn flesh leaving bloody smears. He slumped, dazed and half-conscious. Fat drops of blood fell from his bruised face, splashing the cold marble floor.

Will stared at the blood. He remembered blood. He remembered so much blood. Everything he'd done to Jenny was in his mind, bright and sharp as the blade of the razor he'd held. He now remembered every moment of it.

"You fooled me! You befuddled me with your magic, with your unholy prophecies. You have made me untrue to myself! You have made me betray my all-sacrificing Savior!" Brother Phleger stood over Ben, and as Ben tried to pull himself up to his hands and knees, Phleger kicked him viciously in the ribs. Ben collapsed again, curling over on himself.

"Cowdray was too powerful," Ben rasped, wiping blood from his lips.

"I knew I should wait," Phleger hissed down at him. "God told me I should wait, but you deceived me! You seduced me with your black sorceries like the snake in Eden! And now you account your work complete, do you not, son of Lucifer? You will see this great work fail, the works of the righteous trampled in sin and ignorance—"

"There is still the girl," Trahern interjected in a low voice. The bodyguard was rubbing his chafed knuckles, clearly having started physically what Phleger had finished magically. "Shall I go and fetch her here?"

"No." Ben staggered to his feet, and the effort made blood stream from his nose. He spat it away weakly. "I understand Cowdray's strength now! You must let me try again—"

Phleger roared, a wordless scream of rage so forceful it made the walls shudder.

"*Get back, Devil!*" The words rang with all the force of a holy judgment, and Ben was thrown backward against the wall again. And then Phleger seemed to go insane. He opened his eyes so wide the whites gleamed. He pulled at his hair until it stood on end, tore at his clothes. He reeled like a drunkard, coming to stand in the middle of the room, hands raised in wild supplication. "I am beset on all sides! How the devils surround me! Who knows how God will punish me now! Forgive me, Lord, for I have had fellowship with the unfruitful works of darkness! Forgive your unworthy servant! I have been weak! Forgive me!"

His livid face drained of color, but the black slash across his cheek seemed to darken. He began to jerk and twitch, and his eyes rolled back in his head. He collapsed to the floor, writhing. Babbling, nonsense words poured from his mouth.

"Brother Phleger!" Trahern cried, falling to the preacher's side. He held the man's head tenderly as he spasmed and shuddered. "He's having a Vision, a divine inspiration from all-holy God!"

Trahern held Phleger until his body stopped twitching and flailing. There was a long moment of silence as the holy man lay on the floor, panting. Finally, he reached up and clutched Trahern's hand with the gratitude of a man just pulled from a sinking ship.

"God has shown me," he whispered. "God has shown me what to do."

He climbed slowly to his feet, his balance unsteady. He looked over at Ben, shaking his head sadly.

"You poor lost soul," he said softly. "I never needed you. I never needed your research nor your damned astrology. My weak human mind made me believe the answer was very complicated when really, I needed only what I already had. The all-sufficient grace of Jesus Christ our Savior."

Ben released a long breath then—a long, shuddering, defeated breath. He lowered his head, as if he could not bear to look at the preacher any more.

Phleger turned toward Will. He extended a hand to him, helping him to sit up, then knelt before him. Will was surprised at how gentle and compassionate his gaze was.

"I can chastise the demon that is inside you, my poor child," he said softly, raising a hand to stroke Will's cheek. "You have suffered so much under his cruelty. You, and Jenny."

The words were so tender that Will had to choke back a sob.

"Tonight, at midnight, we will proceed as I originally planned. We will conduct the Consecration ceremony and fortify this Holy temple. And we will sacrifice the power of that miserable creature to the greater glory of the Lord. His will be done."

Then, slowly, Brother Phleger staggered to the far end of the room. He looked up at the giant red cross for a moment before falling, once more, to his knees. But this time he did not lift his hands. He made no extravagant gesture. Instead, he merely bowed his head and pressed his forehead to his clenched fists.

"I am humbled by Your forgiveness, Lord," he whispered, his voice soft and tremulous. "And I thank You. From the bottom of my sinning soul, I thank You."

Will knew that the prayer was more sincere than any the preacher had ever made. He knew it from the streams of light that were emanating from Phleger's body, red and purple and gold and yellow, haloing his form with the brilliance of a hundred stained-glass windows. Phleger knelt like that, hands clenched, his body perfectly rigid, for a long time. And then he fell forward, sobbing.

Trahern helped him to his feet. Phleger leaned on him heavily. Trahern helped the preacher walk slowly from the room, holding him up when he stumbled.

Ben crawled slowly across the room to the low couch where Will was sitting, leaving a trail of blood droplets behind him. When he finally made it, he collapsed against the ottoman's side, the wounds on his back smearing the white leather.

"We're in trouble, Will," he rasped.

The words made Will laugh. And not just laugh, but laugh hysterically. He collapsed backward onto the ottoman, shaking with humorless convulsions that made tears flow from the corners of his eyes.

Memories burned in his mind like acid. The razor slicing Jenny's skin. How it had made the smooth pink flesh blossom red, and how he had drawn his finger through it. How he had used her own blood to draw charms on her body, how he'd made her beg for mercy beneath them.

You want this as much as I do, Cowdray had said.

Yes, he had wanted her. He had wanted Jenny. But not that way. Not the way Cowdray had taken her. Will wanted to die. It made him laugh even harder.

"William!" Ben barked. Fresh blood trickled down his chin, and he wiped it away. "Get ahold of yourself. You're the only one who can save us now. Phleger is going to use you himself. He'll vamp on you somehow. You have to stop Cowdray from—"

"I *can't!*" Will screamed at him. "I couldn't make him stop hurting Jenny. I did everything I could to make him stop hurting her. I wanted it more than anything." He stared up at the red cross. "I wanted it more than living. If I couldn't make him stop then, how can I stop him now?"

"There's still a chance. There's *always* a chance," said Ben, though he clearly had to struggle to put any hope into the words. "Cowdray has the most power over you when the moon is full. But when the moon is dark, you have as much power over him. It's only a few days until the new moon, Will. Maybe you'll be able to use that extra bit of control to your advantage."

Will shook his head in despair. It didn't matter if the moon was full or dark. He would never be able to match Cowdray's cruelty. Never.

"Why did you tell me to think of Jenny?" he finally said, bleakly.

"Because I hoped your love would be stronger than your guilt," said Ben.

At that moment Trahern came back into the room, striding toward them, his face dark with purpose. He dug his fingers into Ben's jacket coat, pulled him to standing.

"Praise Jesus, the Brother has finally seen the light about you, you smug charlatan." Trahern gave Ben a hard shake. "I would kill you now, but he doesn't want the Temple sullied by your unredeemed blood before the Consecration." He smirked back over his shoulder at the gory trail Ben had left on the floor. "Any *more* of it, anyway."

Spinning Ben around, Trahern shoved him hard toward the door, following as he stumbled forward. "But just you wait until after the Consecration, Professor. Just you wait and see what kind of fun we're going to have *then*."

Trahern did not return for Will until just before midnight. And when he did, he had changed into the long, pristine white robes of an usher. He did not speak, just set to work with gruff efficiency, lashing Will's hands together before him with a piece of stout white cord. He bound Will's ankles and gagged him with a piece of red cloth.

Will did not resist any of this. He felt incapable of resisting. He felt incapable of caring. He just lay on the low couch, limp, staring up at the red cross.

He had said nothing as Trahern drew the cords painfully tight. And he said nothing even when Trahern was finished and hissed in Will's ear:

"You're going to make this work, understand? Or I will slice her belly open myself. I'll hurt her as much as you've hurt the good Brother. That's a promise. *An oath*."

Will let his eyes slide closed. The image of the red cross burned behind his lids. He felt Trahern lifting him, throwing him over his shoulder like a feed sack. And then Trahern carried him to the sanctuary.

The sanctuary was already buzzing with energy and anticipation. While there was no sunlight to illuminate the stained glass, all the electric lights blazed. A team of Teslaphone technicians had set up their equipment in a corner near the front of the great room. They had hung a broadcasting microphone near the enormous electrical organ—where Little Sanctity Snow, in a frothy white dress of silken ruffles and lace, sat poking at the keys ill-temperedly as she waited for the power to be switched on.

Another technician was laying a carpeted runner over the cord of a second microphone, on a slender stand of black iron that had been placed a few feet in front of the altar. Muttering a curt "Beat it!" to the man, Trahern placed Will in a kneeling position behind the microphone stand, facing the crowd.

Bound hands clenched before him, Will stared out into the crowd. Phleger had not just filled the sanctuary, he had packed it. Every pew was crammed to capacity, and the faithful who could not find seats clustered at the edges of the broad aisles. And all of them were eyeing Will with a mixture of fascination and dread, whispering between themselves.

They don't know what Brother Phleger intends to do to me. And they're dying to find out.

As Will's eyes roamed the vastness of the crowd, he saw that Ben had been put into a special seat in the roped-off front row. Ben's battered face was puffed and purpling, and one eye was swollen shut. He was not bound—but what did it matter? There was nothing he could do to help. Not with Trahern and a hundred of his ushers, all dressed in white robes, having taken up positions along the sanctuary's walls.

Looking away from Ben, Will caught sight of Atherton Hart—and Jenny.

Just like the petulant child at the organ, Jenny was dressed all in ruffled white. But her dress had a very high neck and very long sleeves, and Jenny sat so rigidly in it that the ruffles seemed chiseled, not draped. Hart sat next to her. He did not sit close, and he did not touch her, but there was something about his presence that encompassed her, enveloped her in his protection.

Hart was not a bad man, Will realized, his heart breaking. He was a fool ... but he was not a bad man.

As if sensing his gaze, Jenny looked at Will. Her blue eyes held his, and he saw the worry in them. But he looked away quickly, lowering his gaze to the deep red carpet. He stared at the carpet for a long time.

Then, suddenly, the organ boomed—one crashing chord, flooding the sanctuary with sound.

Someone had switched on the organ, and Little Sanctity Snow became like one reborn. She fell upon the keys with the eagerness of the starved, tiny fingers flying. There was no sheet music propped up before her; she seemed to play purely from spirit.

The organ music began with a powerful melody, but before long, it settled into a strange looping rhythm. A pulsating cascade of sound that set every member of the congregation swaying. Will couldn't quite tell when they began singing along with the organ's boom and storm, raising their voices to ride upon its swelling waves, but soon the song was as loud as the organ itself. But the faithful did not seem to be singing words. Rather they sang a kind of pure unified chaos, the sound both perfectly coherent and perfectly meaningless.

Little Sanctity Snow—"God's Special Snowflake"—was whipping them into a frenzy.

And when Brother Phleger finally emerged from the vestry, dressed only in a simple black Sunday suit—nothing flashy, no worldly adornments, only a simple red cross worn around his neck— all of the thousands of worshippers rushed as one to meet him. But not a single person actually *moved*. It was their energy that flowed toward him, streams of color and light stronger than any Will had seen around him before. Closing his eyes, Phleger lifted his hands and received the adulation, absorbed it with the calm assurance of the righteous.

He did not speak, did not gesture to Little Sanctity Snow to stop her playing. He probably could not have stopped her playing if he tried. The girl was in a state of holy seizure, standing now to reach the keyboard's topmost tiers. Her white-blonde ringlets flew around her small screwed-up face. Her eyes were closed tight. It was as if she was playing the organ with her whole body, not just her hands.

Arms still raised, Phleger began a slow processional circuit around the sanctuary. First he walked west, and when he came to the westernmost wall he fell to his knees, flinging himself against the glittering stone, embracing it, kissing it.

The worshippers moaned in unison. Some of them had leapt to their feet, swaying, arms held high; some had clustered around Brother Phleger, and were trying to help him stand. These zealots were hustled roughly back by Trahern's white-robed ushers. When Phleger finally did stand, he wheeled like a drunk, crossing the sanctuary's broad expanse along the wide aisle that bisected it. Trahern followed him protectively, fists clenched, menacing any supplicant who came too close.

Phleger seemed barely able to make it to the east wall. He collapsed against it, resting his forehead on the marble, breathing hard. Throwing his head back, he bellowed, beating his fists against the wall with intense, furious passion. Brilliant coruscations of power crackled over the white stone, like lightning seeking ground. Several women fainted. The organ screamed.

Phleger had to crawl along the aisle to reach the huge double doors at the sanctuary's southern end. Trahern tried to reach down and help him along, but Phleger batted him back. And though the preacher seemed weak as a kitten, his rebuff made Trahern stagger, tumbling backward into the pews. The faithful set him back on his feet, dozens upon dozens of hands caressing him as they did.

When Phleger finally did make it to the huge double doors, he climbed to his feet. It seemed to require a mighty effort. He stood before the doors on trembling legs, lifting his hands.

Thus is this mighty tabernacle Consecrated, in the name of God most holy, justified by our Savior's all-sufficient Grace, in Jesus Christ alone, for His glory alone, according to Scripture alone.

Phleger did not speak the words. Instead they saturated the air. They were a part of the driving beat of the organ, they formed themselves in the throats of his congregation. He was not speaking *to* them, he was speaking *through* them.

Then Phleger whirled, all his weariness erased in an instant. He was revitalized, resurrected. He seemed ten feet tall. His body was heavy with beneficence and compassion. He proceeded up the broad center aisle toward the altar slowly, bathed in colored light brighter than any that could have streamed through the stained glass on the brightest day, and his feet did not touch the ground. He reached his hands out as he walked, touching and stroking the followers who fell before him. He tenderly cupped a sick man's cheek and the man collapsed, writhing like one possessed. Phleger lifted a supplicating old woman and pressed a kiss to her forehead, and when he released her she dropped like a stone and did not move again.

When finally he came to where Will was kneeling, Will could feel the heat pouring from his body. His dark suit was soaked with sweat. He came to stand behind Will, and as he lifted his arms to compel him to rise, acrid stink poured from his damp armpits. When Will was standing, Phleger stepped even closer to him, pressing his hot chest against Will's back. Taking the snuffbox from his pocket, he wrapped his arms around Will's sides, holding him tight, and holding the snuffbox out before them both. Gently, he nuzzled his chin into Will's shoulder.

"Witness the power of the Lord Almighty," he whispered in Will's ear. "He is our shield and our sword, our ever-ready protector. He will annihilate the devil that possesses you. He will set things to right. You have only to *believe*, dear child. Believe."

Will shuddered and stiffened as Phleger's power seized him. As before, his eyes clenched shut, and he was unable to open them—and as before, it was not darkness that greeted him. This time, however, he was in the cold room of snowstorm white with its looming, blazing red cross. The *sanctum sanctorum*. It was not the *real* room, Will knew—rather, it was Phleger himself who was the room, and the sound of the organ was his walls, and the singing of the faithful was his voice.

And Cowdray was there.

In the room that was Phleger, the old warlock appeared as he must have in life—elegant and slim and cruel, decked in jewels and embroidery. Standing with his back to the cross, Cowdray regarded Will curiously, eyes gleaming like a malicious bird's.

You have returned. Are you very brave, Mooncalf? Or just very stupid?

But Will could not answer, only move his lips in unison with Phleger's voice:

In the name of most holy God, I compel you to my will, demon!

Cowdray cringed, hissing, as if he'd been sprinkled with acid. Wisps of acrid smoke, smelling of burnt flesh, curled up from the folds of his coat. Will's heart leapt with vengeful joy. Phleger's power flowed through him—Holy power, the power of the faithful. It was good power, clean and strong.

The Word compels you, spawn of misery! Phleger spoke again, and the Word became Truth. **You are subject to God's command now.**

Never! Cowdray shrieked, falling to his knees. Flames flickered around him, blue and orange. Behind him, the red cross pulsed like a beating heart.

Will suddenly saw that the silver box was in his hands. He did not hold it; rather, his hands bracketed it, and it hovered between them. The brilliant light of the snowstorm room bent and wavered around the box, as if it were submerged in very dark, clear water.

You will open the box so that the power can be sanctified.

The flames engulfing Cowdray flared up, and Cowdray shrieked, a sound of agony wrenched from the deepest part of his lost soul. His shrieks filled Will with pure, perfect pleasure—and alongside it, a desperate hunger that was just as visceral. He wanted to hurt Cowdray *more*. He wanted to take everything from him, everything—every iota of his power, every scrap of his self-control.

Once the power in the box was sanctified, Will knew, it would be at his disposal. He could use it to shatter Cowdray's spirit into a million screaming, smoldering bits.

Open it. Will's lips moved with Phleger's voice, but the words were his own. **Show me how to unlock it.**

It is unlocked, Cowdray whimpered, curled on a ball on the floor. It always has been. Open it yourself.

Will looked at the box more closely. And through eyes opened by the power of the Word, he perceived the reality of it.

It was not a box at all.

It was a door—a door Will recognized.

The door from the Hotel Acheron.

With the urgency of desire, Will reached for the doorknob.

When he touched it, a rush of suffering more intense than any he had ever known burned through him. Despair, black and hopeless, made the white brilliance of the room around him vanish into oblivion. His ears burned with the agonized cries of the souls trapped within that void. Will felt, in a horrible eternal instant, all of the hell that lay behind the door.

Gasping, Will opened his eyes.

The reality of the world rushed back in on him—the sanctuary, the mass of chanting faithful, the thundering crash of the organ, the smell of Phleger's body behind him, the tight press of the preacher's hot trembling arms against his sides.

Then Will's eyes met Jenny's.

And in Jenny's eyes, he saw the truth. The *real* truth. She had opened the door of the Hotel Acheron, and she had run away from the horrors within—but she had not escaped. And, Will realized, neither had he. They were both still locked inside, trapped together in misery, and they always would be.

He couldn't do it.

He couldn't open the door.

Opening the box would not sanctify the power, or alleviate the suffering of the souls, Will understood suddenly. The power would poison the world. The suffering inside would not be let out. No. Rather, all the joy in the world—all the hope, all the love—would be sucked *in*.

Open the door! Phleger commanded, the organ commanded, the voice of the faithful commanded in unison. **Make the demon suffer in the hell he created!**

And oh, how Will wanted to. How he wanted to make Cowdray suffer within that hell. But Jenny's eyes told him that he could not. That he must not. That he had to find another way.

Returning to the snowstorm room that lay behind his tightly shut eyelids, Will withdrew his hand from the doorknob, retreated from the door. Cowdray, curled up on the floor, breathed like an injured animal—quick and shallow, yet still ready to strike.

Phleger was the room. But Will was Phleger's ability to act upon Cowdray within the room. Phleger could command—but only Will could *act*.

Will reached down to Cowdray, his hand trembling.

I cannot allow him to open the box, Will said, and gave Cowdray his hand. Cowdray took it, and as he helped the warlock to his feet, Will hated himself. Despised every molecule of his being.

DO YOU THINK THIS ACT WILL EARN YOU MERCY? Cowdray growled, thrusting his face close to Will's. Will barked a bitter laugh.

Just tell me how to stop the preacher, Will said, the words soaked in bile. *Stop him so that he cannot attempt to open the box again, ever.*

GET ME INSIDE HIS MIND, Cowdray whispered insinuatingly. I WILL HANDLE THE REST.

With a cry of disgust, Will opened his eyes again, returned to the sanctuary. Phleger was clutching him more tightly now—it was clear that he realized something was going wrong. He was furiously muttering prayers into Will's ear, his breath hot and moist.

Will's bound hands hung before him. He inched them to one side. Struggling against Phleger's tight embrace, Will was able to get one hand into the pocket of his trousers. He carefully withdrew the straight razor. Opening it, he first used it to cut the cord that bound his wrists.

And when his wrists were free, he reached up and placed a hand on Phleger's arm, feeling for the place where the preacher's flesh emerged from his starched white cuff. With his other hand, Will brought up the razor. He drew it along Phleger's skin, slowly, making it hurt as much as he knew how.

The pain opened Phleger's mind, just a tiny crack. But that crack was enough for Cowdray. With a joyous, brutal cry, the warlock's spirit slithered into it like a black snake. Tendrils of his spirit probed the crack and stretched it wide.

NOW YOU ARE SUBJECT TO *MY* COMMAND, he hissed gleefully.

Phleger screamed.

Will felt Cowdray sending fat, filthy tentacles of control into Phleger's mind, invading him. Within an instant, Phleger began spewing a vile stream of blasphemous foulness into the microphone before him. He swore, he spat, he raved. He roared every unclean word and sacrilegious profanity that Cowdray had collected in every life he had ever lived.

The shock of recoil from Phleger's followers was like an icy wave. Where there had been song, now there was silence—the shocked silence of betrayal. Will felt Phleger's power waver, then crack, then crumble.

Then, clenching his fists around Phleger's arm, stroking his fingers through the preacher's warm blood, Will used Phleger's mind to blast a message out on a wave of magical power:

Invado!

The sanctuary's huge double doors burst open in a blaze of light.

Warlocks, hundreds of them in black suits, swarmed inside. The faithful, already bewildered and terrified, began to scream and run. They became a stampede, a panicked whirlpool.

The warlocks, operating in Trines, made their way through the frenzy with calm purpose. They separated off small groups of the horrified worshippers, raising their hands to speak words in Latin. Where they did, the worshippers dropped, collapsing upon each other in unconscious, quiescent heaps.

Some of these warlocks began pushing their way toward the altar, where Will and Phleger were still standing, Phleger still holding Will tight within an unbreakable embrace, still mindlessly spewing profanities into the microphone before them.

As the warlocks drew closer, Will saw something.

He saw that they all wore red orchids on their lapels.

Panic iced him. He struggled within Phleger's arms.

They weren't *Institute* warlocks. They were *Agency* warlocks.

But it was not the Agency warlocks who reached Will and Phleger first.

It was Ben.

Ben darted up to the altar. Seizing the broadcasting microphone that stood before them, he swung the iron down, knocking the snuffbox out of the preacher's hands. The magical connection was severed abruptly, in an explosion of ice-white brilliance. Brother Phleger fell backward, unconscious; Will fell forward, into Ben's arms. But Ben didn't hold him long. Casting a swift glance over his shoulder, he let Will slide to the floor.

And then, reaching down and grabbing the snuffbox, Ben ran.

Will screamed after him, a wordless shriek of betrayal. He tried to leap to his feet, forgetting that his ankles were bound. He fumbled for the razor, slashed the cord.

And then, he heard Jenny screaming.

People were closing in around her, falling around her—and she was panicking. Her eyes were stark-wide with terror. Atherton Hart had gotten an arm around her, and was sheltering her with his body, trying to muscle a path through the chaos.

And then Will saw Trahern. And Trahern, his face purple with rage, saw Will. He saw where Will had been looking—and a fierce, frenzied smile curled his lips. Pulling a silver knife from his boot, he began pushing his way through the crowd, toward the struggling Hart and Jenny.

"Jenny!" Will cried.

But neither Jenny nor Hart could hear him over the cacophony. And they didn't see the bodyguard coming.

Clutching the razor, Will ran with unearthly quickness, Cowdray's magic still surging through his body.

Trahern did not stab Hart—just hooked a foot around his ankle and shoved him to one side. Hart stumbled and fell into the stampeding swarm around them, and did not rise again. Then Trahern seized Jenny's hair and pulled her head back. She struggled against him for just an instant before the knife flashed down, sinking into her chest.

Will fell upon Trahern with a brutal cry, pulling him away and slashing his throat in one movement. Blood sprayed, and Trahern's fingers fumbled helplessly at the gaping wound. But he fumbled only for a moment; then he dropped, gurgling.

Will fell at Jenny's side. Blood was spreading across the white lace of her dress, spreading very quickly. He pressed his hand to the wound, raised her gently, tried to make the blood stop. But it would not stop.

"Oh William," she sighed softly. "Everything came out all wrong, didn't it?"

Fresh hot blood welled up through his fingers with every beat of her heart. He prayed for any kind of guidance, any kind of grace.

I love you, Jenny.

He did not speak the words, but he saw them reflected in her eyes. She placed a bloody hand over his, clasped it tightly for a moment.

Then something very heavy came down on his head, and everything went black.

Chapter Twenty-Six

Alcestis

Will was dimly aware of the sound of his own voice, moaning Jenny's name. Someone was trying to comfort him, trying to calm and soothe him.

"Where is she?" he murmured. "Is she all right?"

"She is alive," the voice said. A soft, female voice, one that he did not recognize. "She is alive, Will. She is alive."

Relief surged through him, and it was enough simply to feel himself breathe.

Feeling his own breathing made him conclude that he, too, must be alive. He tried to open his eyes, but the light sent pain knifing through his skull. He retreated back into darkness.

Jenny was alive, he thought.

Praise the Lord.

He did not wake again for some time. When he did, he found that the room was dark, and he could open his eyes—but only very slowly. He swallowed, his throat dry and scorched. His body ached, but he was used to the aching by now. He now couldn't even remember a time when his body didn't ache.

He didn't know where he was. He was in a room, surely, but he knew he was no longer in the New Faith Seat of Praise. He didn't know how he knew it, he just felt the difference. There was energy here, power—but a much different kind of power. It ... *tasted* different. Smelled different.

He looked around himself, his eyes slowly coming into focus. The room was luxurious, with high ceilings and carved cornices. It was lit by old-fashioned gas jets, turned down low. He lay under a duvet of fine light silk.

When he tried to sit up, he discovered that he could not move. He was bound even more tightly than when Phleger had held him. He could turn his head though, just slightly, enough to see that there was an old woman sitting at the side of his bed, watching him.

She sat in a high-backed wicker wheelchair, slender and erect, her hands clasped in her lap. She wore all black, in sharp contrast to her paper-white hair. She regarded him through tortoiseshell glasses.

"How are you feeling?" she asked, and Will recognized the soft, kindly voice that had comforted him.

"Not very well," he managed hoarsely.

"I imagine not," she said.

"Is Jenny all right?" he asked again. He was afraid the words he remembered her speaking might only have been a dream. But the old woman smiled gently.

"She is alive," she said. "She was wearing a necklace beneath her dress. A silver coin. It deflected the blade just enough to save her life."

Will released a long breath. The relief he felt was no less intense for feeling it a second time. He met the woman's gaze. "Where am I? And who are you?"

"You are in the Stanton Institute in New York City," she said. "I am Mrs. Zeno, the Institute's Executive Director." She paused. "Where is your brother?"

"Which one?" Will did not mean to sound insolent, for at the moment he could not be if he tried. His mind was a muddle and a haze. But Mrs. Zeno frowned slightly.

"Benedictus Coeus," she growled. "Ben."

Will stared at her, eyes fixed and blurry as he tried to make sense of his shattered fragments of memory. He remembered the New Faith Seat of Praise ... the Consecration. He remembered the blood spreading across Jenny's breast. He remembered slashing Trahern's throat.

And he remembered the last time he had seen Ben. His brother had taken the snuffbox and he had run away.

He was opening his mouth to tell all this to the old woman, but something made him stop. Because suddenly, he remembered something else.

Warlocks wearing red orchids.

Agency warlocks. Ben had said the Institute would help them—but it had been Agency warlocks who had stormed the New Faith Seat of Praise. The woman said that he was in the Stanton Institute. But if it had been Agency warlocks at the New Faith Seat of Praise, then how the hell had he ended up here?

"Where is Jenny?" he finally said.

"I swear to you that she is safe," Mrs. Zeno said, with the careful formality Will recognized as having the magical weight of a guarantee. "And I swear to you that she will remain so. But if I were to tell you where she is, I could not swear that either of those statements would be true anymore."

Will absorbed this, and then nodded. He believed her. He did not know for sure who this woman was, he did not know if she was telling the truth about anything else, but he felt that she would not lie about this. There was something about it that was too close to her.

Will tried to stretch against whatever force bound him, but it was futile. It was as if he'd been wrapped in an invisible cocoon of unbreakable silk.

"Why am I bound?" Will asked. "Will you at least let me sit up to talk to you?"

"You have been very combative in your delirium, and it was not known how much of a threat you might pose." She paused. "I can unbind you, but I'm not sure I should. Do you have Cowdray under control?"

"It's almost the new moon," Will said, but did not elaborate.

The old woman considered this, then drew a deep breath and lifted her hand. She murmured a soft command under her breath.

Will felt the cocooning restraints dissolve away. He sat up slowly, stiff muscles screaming.

"Thank you," he said.

There was a brisk knock on the door—more of an announcement of entry than a request for it—and another woman bustled briskly into the room. She was not as old as Mrs. Zeno. Rather, she looked about the age of Will's own mother. Her hair was pulled back in a tidy ashen bun, and her brown eyes were piercing and hawk-like. She wore many layers of ruffles, as if they were sentries of fabric she had set to guard her.

"This is Professor Coeus' brother?" Her gaze flickered over Will. "Doesn't look much like him."

"Will, this is Miss Hibble," Mrs. Zeno said. "Miss Hibble is Sophos Stanton's personal secretary."

"They have all arrived," Miss Hibble said to Mrs. Zeno, not sparing Will another glance.

"I will come and speak to them, but Will must answer my question first." Mrs. Zeno turned her eyes back to Will, and behind her glasses they were clear and strong. "Where is Ben?"

There was strange force behind the question. It made him want to answer more than anything. But he recognized that force. It was the same kind Phleger had used—a credomancer's force of will. He was not a warlock—and he swore to himself he never would be—but he had learned many lessons in the past few horrible days. He held himself firm.

"Why do you want to know?" he countered mildly.

Mrs. Zeno raised an eyebrow. "I should think the answer to that is patently obvious."

"Is it?"

"Answering questions with other questions is a very annoying habit, young man," Mrs. Zeno snapped.

"Ben taught it to me."

Mrs. Zeno's gaze was appraising. "It seems Ben taught you many things."

Will stretched his aching muscles, tested his strength. Looking down at himself, he saw that they had left him in the same clothes he'd been wearing at the Consecration, and they were stiff with crusted blood. Phleger's blood, Trahern's blood, Jenny's blood. He fought down a wave of nausea.

"I'm sorry we could not change you out of those clothes." Mrs. Zeno saw the direction of his gaze, and the regret in her voice indicated that she found the clothes as offensive as Will did. "But I could not release the restraints until I had spoken to you."

Will said nothing. He forced himself to be strong, to think. He did not know where he was. He did not know if this woman was who she claimed to be, or why she wanted Ben—why she *really* wanted Ben. He did not know where Ben was. He did not know why Ben had run away. He had nothing but questions. This woman might not have all the answers, but she certainly had some of them. So there was only one course open to him.

"You must want Ben because he has the snuffbox," Will said softly. "You have me. And you know he can't use it without me. He can't use it at all, really, because he can't work magic. But I can. I can work a lot of magic, more than anyone my age should be able to. And before I tell you anything, I want to know why."

Mrs. Zeno said nothing. Then, with a gesture of her hand, she magically bade the wheelchair turn. Miss Hibble opened the door for her and they were gone.

After a while, Will felt able to climb out of bed. He found that a pitcher of water had been left for him; he drank it all, not realizing how thirsty he was until the water touched his lips. Then he went to look out of the window. The room was on a high floor, much too high to climb out of. The window looked out over a white landscape of smooth snow. In the distance, he saw the buildings of a large city, glowing with electric lights. New York City. Well, at least the old woman hadn't been lying about that.

The door, of course, was locked. That was to be expected. And it was also to be expected that his refusal to answer for Ben's whereabouts would not stand unchallenged. About a half hour later, Miss Hibble returned.

"You're wanted in the Sophos' office."

"Who wants to see me?" Will asked warily. "Dreadnought Stanton?" As soon as he spoke the name he prayed that the answer would be yes. He'd asked Ben if the great Sophos of the Stanton Institute could banish Cowdray from his body just as he had in the pulp novel—and now he wanted to ask the man himself.

But Miss Hibble just laughed, fluty and deprecating.

"Certainly not!" she said. "The Sophos is far too busy to trouble himself over a trivial matter such as this. It's your parents. They've come for you."

She gestured for him to follow, but he made no move to do so. The thought of seeing his parents sent his heart into his shoes. God, what was he going to tell them? He couldn't stand in front of them in these blood-crusted clothes. He was dirty and spoiled and broken. He'd cut a man's throat. And did they already know? Did they know about Cowdray? Did they know what he'd done to Jenny?

"Come on!" Miss Hibble chirped impatiently. Then, seeing Will's apprehension, she added more kindly, "It's all right. They're your parents, not monsters!" She extended her hand, as if cajoling a small child. "Besides, your mother is very worried about you. Come and let her see that you're all right."

Lowering his head, Will did not take her hand. He was not all right. But he did want to see his Ma'am. So he followed Miss Hibble from the room, and followed her as she led the way through the halls of the Institute. It was a very old building, only recently rewired for electricity; the electric bulbs were bright and harsh. The floors were smooth marble, veined with gold. The place had a hushed, sober feeling, and as they walked, dozens of young men peered out from behind half-opened classroom doors to watch the pair of them pass.

But Will hardly noticed this scrutiny, for he was transfixed by the fact that everywhere—massed in vases, twining up the walls—were fragrant red orchids. The exact same kind the Agency warlocks wore in their lapels.

"Those are very pretty flowers," he murmured to Miss Hibble.

Miss Hibble smiled brightly. "Yes, aren't they divine? They're the Institute's signature flower. Emeritus Zeno used to grow them."

They finally came to an office with a very grand door. Just inside the door was an antechamber lined with books, and beyond this antechamber, an even grander office. The stained-glass window behind the massive desk reminded Will of the bright glass behind the altar in the New Faith Seat of Praise.

Enthroned behind that massive desk, Mrs. Zeno seemed younger and stronger and healthier. She lifted her chin, and Will saw that she had once been quite beautiful.

And in front of her sat his parents, and Uncle Royce.

No one spoke or moved as he entered, but everyone watched him. It was clear that they'd all been discussing him. Discussing what was to be *done* with him. But Will had been through too much to allow others to decide his fate. He had learned too much. And he was going to use what he'd learned.

"I suppose you've called me here to ask where Ben is," he said before anyone else could speak. "But I've decided I'm not going to tell you."

Uncle Royce narrowed his eyes. "What?"

"Before the Consecration, Ben and I made an arrangement." Will was surprised at how smoothly the lie rolled off his tongue. "We agreed on a meeting place. But I'm not going to tell you where that is. Unless you answer my questions."

"We don't have any answers for you," Uncle Royce said, looking between Father and Ma'am. "We've just come to bring you home."

"That's a lie," said Will, turning a calm gaze onto him. "I don't know where we really are, the Institute or the Agency, but these people are not about to let me go back to California, not with Cowdray's power inside me and that snuffbox just waiting for me to find it."

Mrs. Zeno tensed. "I have already told you. You are in the Stanton Institute."

"Am I?" Will said. "But why would *Agency* warlocks bring me here? And why do Agency warlocks wear the Institute's signature flower in their lapels?"

"The Institute has an amicable enough association with the Agency," Mrs. Zeno lifted an eyebrow. "We are an institution of credomantic learning. Of course we train—"

"And why is it the *Agency* who destroys those books? *The Goês' Confession?*" Will continued, as if she had not spoken.

Mrs. Zeno eyed him warily. "They destroy them because they are seditious trash, designed to undercut our noble Sophos," she said.

Will smiled to himself, nodded. "Seditious trash. That's exactly what Bernays called them too." He narrowed his eyes at her. "But why should the Agency care about your noble Sophos' reputation? He's *your* leader. Unless—" Will fell suddenly silent as understanding overtook him. "Unless he's *their* leader, too."

Will suddenly perceived that his father was looking at him strangely, in a way Will didn't recognize. What was that in his eyes? Admiration?

But it was Ma'am who rose and rushed over to where Will was standing, and hugged him desperately close.

"Will, *stop*," she whispered. "Please. Please stop ... *thinking.* Just tell us where Ben is."

And Will hugged his Ma'am back, but he did not stop thinking. Instead he thought harder.

"So if the Institute and the Agency are the same thing, then does that mean that Dreadnought Stanton is the head of the Agency too? Is he the one who receives the messages from Alcestis? Is he the one who receives the names of Old Users that the spirit of the Earth wants killed and sends assassins after them?"

"God, no!" Father and Uncle Royce both blurted, at almost exactly the same time. They looked at each other, and Will looked between them.

"Then who is?"

Silence.

"One of you knows," Will said. He looked down at his Ma'am, who was still holding onto him fiercely. "I'm guessing all of you know."

Ma'am released him from her embrace and went back to sit by Father, sinking heavily on the couch. Father placed a steadying hand on her shoulder.

"It seems we're going to have to tell him after all," Mrs. Zeno said. "Apparently he already knows much more than we expected."

Apprehension paled Ma'am's face. "No, don't." She looked anxiously at Father. "I don't want him to know."

"He has to, Emily," said Father softly.

"*I'm* the head of the Agency," Uncle Royce spat, as if disgusted by the sudden upwell of emotion in the room. For a moment Will thought Uncle Royce was simply making a stupid joke, but then he realized that his uncle was dead serious.

"You? How could *you* be the head of the Agency?" Will gestured around himself. "The Institute is in New York, and you live in San Francisco!"

"My house has a private Haälbeck door. I can come through to New York any time I like." Royce leveled his gaze on Will. "But I don't need to. My primary duties are in California. With your mother."

Ma'am had pressed her face into Father's shoulder. She wasn't crying, only hiding her face. Father remained still, his hand resting on her back.

"The head of the Agency ... works with the witch called Alcestis," Will was unable to believe the words even as he spoke them. "The witch who made a psychic connection with the spirit of the Earth. The witch who tells the Agency ... who to kill." He paused, anguished. "*Ma'am?*"

Ma'am said nothing, just rocked her face back and forth against the fabric of Father's coat in silent refusal—not of the fact, but of Will's knowledge of it.

"But ... you're my *mother*," Will said. "You bake pies and feed chickens and grow flowers. How could you be ... *that?*"

"Leave her alone, Will," Father growled in warning.

"Is that why you went mad after Catherine died? Because it was you who told the scientists to implement the Anodyne? Because you knew it was your—"

"Leave her *alone*," Father roared, surging to his feet. He had to catch himself for balance when his game leg failed him.

"What really happened to your leg?" Will whispered, looking at his father. "Ben said it wasn't a riding accident."

"It wasn't a *riding* accident," Father hissed. "But it was an *accident* nonetheless." He sat back down slowly, putting his body close to Ma'am's trembling one.

"So I'm not the only one in this family who's been cursed," Will said. "Who's been forced to live with something—terrible."

He went over to his Ma'am and touched her shoulder. "I'm sorry," he said. "I'm so sorry." She reached up and clutched his hand, but did not look at him.

"Now we've told you everything you wanted to know," Royce snapped. "So tell us where Ben is."

"You haven't told me anything I *wanted* to know," said Will, releasing his mother's hand. "And you certainly haven't told me what I *need* to know. And that's why Bernays—your employee, a murdering son-of-a-bitch—said what he said to me in Detroit. He said that his *boss* told him that I hadn't had the Panchrest. But you were there, Uncle Royce. You helped Father give it to us. So why did Bernays say that?"

Uncle Royce narrowed his eyes, frowning at Will. But it was Father who finally spoke.

"Because I never did give you the Panchrest, Will."

"*What?*"

"It's why I didn't want you to take the apprenticeship at Tesla Industries. It's why I tried so hard to find you in Detroit, to make you come home. Because I knew there was a chance you might inherit the curse."

"Why didn't you *tell* me!" Will's whole body felt suddenly numb. "Do you know, Father? Do you know what I did? What Cowdray made me do?"

Father's eyes slid closed for a moment, his face anguished. "Yes, I know."

"Why *didn't* you give me the Panchrest?" Will's voice was so thin it was hardly a voice at all, rather a thread of pain. "Why protect all my brothers but not me? Did you hate me even back then?"

"I never hated you," Father said very softly. "And I'm sorry. But I had no choice. I swear it to you. I had no choice."

Will stood looking down at his father for a long time. He didn't recognize him at all. His face was familiar, he knew that it was his father ... but he didn't know who the man *was.* The tension of the moment was broken when Uncle Royce stood, stretching with an exaggerated groan. There was a broad smile on his face—strangely enough, he seemed to have found the whole exchange darkly humorous. He clapped Will on the shoulder.

"You see, William," he began, "your father—oh, and by the way, he and I are not really brothers, thank God, so you needn't call me Uncle anymore—your father has always been, and always will be, a traitor and a cheat. And a liar, of course. But as the old saying goes, all credomancers are liars."

"Father's not a credomancer," said Will.

"He used to be," Royce said, leaning forward to put his head close to Will's. "A very notorious one. So notorious he was forced to sell his name to the Institute simply to live in peace. And we have done so much with it ever since."

"What name?" Will whispered.

"Dreadnought Stanton," Royce said.

Will whirled on him, eyes blazing. "My mother's Alcestis and my father is *Dreadnought Stanton*?"

"No!" Father barked. "I am *not.* I am nothing and no one. I've been a father and a husband for over thirty years—and that's *all.* What the Institute has done with the name has nothing to do with me."

"With one very notable exception," Royce looked at Father hard, and there was challenge in his eyes. "The little matter of the Defalcation. Would you care to explain that to your son? Explain to him how you're not only a liar and a traitor and a cheat, but a *welcher* as well?"

Father looked down at the floor, his gaze hard and resigned.

"You see, when your father sold us his name, all those many years ago, part of the deal was that he would never attempt to reclaim his power," Royce said. "Of course, we knew better than just to take him on faith—we required him to seal the magical channels in his body so that reclaiming it would be a physical impossibility. In effect, he took the Panchrest himself, though in a much different form. This was our assurance that it would be safe to use his name to build our power."

"Use *his* name—to build *your* power?"

"Dreadnought Stanton's heroic exploits fuel the power of the Stanton Institute," Royce said. "It doesn't matter that they're not the exploits of a real man. It doesn't even matter that they're not real exploits, just thrilling fictional accounts with the sketchiest foundation in magical truth. What matters is that people *believe* he is real, *believe* he is our Sophos, and *believe* that he is the most powerful warlock in the United States."

"Then there really is no Dreadnought Stanton," Will said softly. "So what is this—Defalcation?"

"It happened in 1892, just after you were born," Royce said. "Your father decided that he wanted to be Dreadnought Stanton again."

Ma'am was sitting up straight now, listening. Her violet eyes were intense and bright, and Will realized that they'd never told her any of this either. He felt a strange comradeship with his mother at that moment. You didn't tell things to the magically afflicted— whether they were cursed by an ancient vengeful warlock or by the spirit of the Earth itself. You didn't let them make their own choices. You made the choices for them.

"You developed Black Flu almost immediately after you were born," Royce continued. "And if nature had taken its course, you would have died even more quickly than Catherine had, eight years earlier."

"I ... had the Black Flu?" Will struggled against shock.

"Yes. And you would have died, and Emily never would have survived it." Father's eyes held Royce's with the heat of an old fight rekindled. "I took just enough power to save him—to save my *son*."

"You *vamped* on me," Will murmured.

"No," Father said. "I vamped on *Ben*." He turned his green gaze onto Will. "I couldn't have vamped on you, Will—you were already dying from Exunge allergy. Ben was there. He wanted to help."

"He helped you—he saved my life—and then you betrayed him," Will said. "You gave him the Panchrest. No wonder he hates you."

"You've read *The Goês' Confession*, Will," Father said. "You know there are only two choices. It was either the Panchrest—or the knife."

"Personally, I would have preferred to drown the whole litter of you—" Royce began, but Mrs. Zeno silenced him with a curt gesture. She turned her intense gaze onto Will.

"The Institute demanded that you and your brothers be given the Panchrest. Your father had violated his contract with us, and it was necessary to eradicate the possibility that he might attempt to do so again." Mrs. Zeno drew a deep, weary breath. "But more importantly, Will, it was necessary to give the Panchrest to *you*. Because your father stole something far more precious than just a small amount of Dreadnought Stanton's power."

Father groaned softly, but did not speak. Will looked from him back to Mrs. Zeno.

"What did he steal?"

"A piece of Dreadnought Stanton's soul," Mrs. Zeno said. "He grafted it onto your own to give it strength. To save your life. But it did far more than that. It gave you a magical claim upon *all* of Dreadnought Stanton's power. It is why you can use so much magic without physical harm. And it is why, I'm sorry to say, you're so dangerous to us."

"That means ... he's like an Old User in a boy's body," Ma'am mused, almost too quietly to be heard.

"That's *exactly* what he is," Royce snapped at her. "A *boy*. A boy who has been handed power that he doesn't deserve, hasn't earned, and hasn't the slightest idea how to use."

Royce walked around behind Father. Resting his hands on the back of the chair Father sat in, he leaned over him to whisper accusingly, "But you just couldn't stand the thought of really giving up all that power, could you? If all the boys had the Panchrest—why, that would be too *permanent*. Too final. You had to make sure there was still a loophole—one just big enough for a *rat* to scurry through someday." Royce pushed himself up and stood straight. He looked at Will. "And so your father palmed the real Panchrest and gave you a dummy." He shot an acid glance at Mrs. Zeno. "I *told* you I should have been the one to give them the Panchrest. You should have insisted. *Forced* him to comply—"

"He is their *father*," Mrs. Zeno interjected softly. "And he was once my Sophos. I owed him that, at least."

"An Old User ... in a boy's body." The words came from Ma'am. She had risen, and was clutching her gut. Her face was ghastly pale, and she looked stricken.

"Ma'am?" Will said.

"No," she whispered, bringing her hands up to her head. "Oh God, no. No ..."

Father reached up to her, concerned, but she pushed his hand away, folding over herself in sudden pain.

"Why did you let me hear?" she screamed at them—at Father and Royce particularly. "Why didn't you tell me to *leave*?"

She collapsed to her knees.

"Not Will," she murmured, and her voice sounded strange—hollow and vibrating. "Not Will."

But then she lifted her face.

And her eyes were entirely black, from lid to lid.

He must be destroyed, Ma'am roared, her voice shaking the walls, shaking the floor beneath them with the force of an earthquake. It was not Ma'am speaking, Will realized. It was Alcestis, the voice of the spirit of the Earth, delivering a terrible judgment. Delivering it to the head of the Agency—

This is my command.

"Emily, no!" Father screamed, falling beside Ma'am. "Royce, help me!"

But Royce could do nothing as Ma'am threw Father violently aside. His body slammed against the wall with bone-shattering force.

You will comply with the terms of the Settlement.

Her voice was low and resonant and old, and it did not come from her body, but from all around her, from the very earth and air. She rose slowly, pulled up like a puppet on threads of magical brilliance. Her hand came up. She leveled a damning finger at Will.

Kill him.

"That. Is. *Enough!*" Mrs. Zeno, rising behind the desk, brought both fists down on the wood with a thunderous slam. The resounding power of the sound buffeted Ma'am, and she staggered. Anger crackled across her face like a snapped whip. She barked a command.

The panes of the stained glass window behind Mrs. Zeno wobbled, then bowed, then shattered inward. Will threw up his arm reflexively, but none of the sharp shards made it that far. Instead, with unerring accuracy, they pierced the body of Mrs. Zeno. She stood standing for a moment, her face sad and surprisingly lovely, and then she slumped forward slowly, blood spreading across the papers on which she had fallen.

Comply! Ma'am roared. Cold air streamed in through the ruined window, and Ma'am's skirt whipped around her ankles. Her hair, unbound, caught flakes of snow as they blew in. Her black eyes gleamed. She turned to Royce.

Kill him. She howled. **Kill the Old User.**

Royce's face was grim but resigned. Lifting his hands, he began to chant in Latin.

RIDICULOUS, Cowdray's voice echoed in Will's head.

And strangely, Will found that he agreed.

Seizing a piece of glass from the floor, he slashed himself with it, rubbed blood between his hands. Power surged within him, as if his whole being had been charged with electricity. He lifted his hand, and brilliant force gushed in a crackling torrent from the very center of his palm. Royce staggered back, unable to withstand the enormity of the onslaught.

Ma'am shrieked ferociously, and made a gesture of terrible violence.

Her attack made Will feel as though he were shattering into a million pieces. Ma'am's magic was infinitely more powerful than anything Royce had been able to muster, or Phleger even. It was an insane kind of power, wild and primal and heedless, like thundersnow and earthquakes and towering waves. Will could not perceive any end to it.

The world tumbled around him. He could not tell if he was standing or falling. That power would break him, like being crushed beneath huge ancient stones. Cowdray screamed, WHORE OF A KENDALL! and tried to lash out, but Ma'am's power constrained the vile old spirit easily. It tightened around Will like vines, like roots, choking him. He felt himself being smothered—so quickly and easily overpowered. Panic gripped him.

"Ma'am," Will gasped. "No!"

Ma'am blinked.

Her eyes remained black, but she had heard him. *Ma'am* had heard him. She put her hands over her mouth.

"Will—" she whispered.

In that moment of opportunity, Will struck. He did not know why he did it—was it Cowdray? But power surged within him, pure reflexive power, unbidden, uncontrolled. Every ounce of force within his body surged against his mother. And all around her, everything caught fire. Every book, every scrap of paper, every broken splintered shard of wood, every tumbled bit of debris, burst into brimstone-blue flame, all consuming, flaring up with unearthly intensity.

His mother fell.

It took Will several moments to come back to himself, and in those moments the fire spread with devastating speed, billowing up the walls, licking the tin ceiling. Thick black smoke choked the air. Glowing embers fell like rain.

"Will!" Father's voice, coming from somewhere within the black smoke and chaos.

Covering his mouth and nose with the fabric of his sleeve, Will staggered across the room toward the sound of his father's cry, stumbling over ruined furniture and shattered glass. With a horrible cracking sound, a large beam of the roof collapsed in a fountain of sparks, and the blue flames rose to consume it with fresh intensity. The heat drove Will back, and he reached into himself for magic, for anything he could use to help—but the magic was no longer at his command. There was nothing left inside him. He was empty, bled dry.

The heat drove him back, step by agonizing step, toward the open window, toward the cold clear night air and the wildly whipping snow, toward the perfect darkness in which no moon showed.

Epilogue

On New Year's Day, an enormous crowd began gathering for the premiere of *The Warlock's Curse* well before sunrise. After the ball dropped in Times Square, the throngs pushed their way down 44th, jamming the narrow street in front of the Belasco Theater. They came even though it was snowing heavily—in freakish, unaccountable amounts. They came, drawn by the stark, enormous headlines that had dominated the front pages of all the newspapers for the past two days:

Fire razes the Stanton Institute. Hundreds Killed.
Sophos Dreadnought Stanton—Dead.

The headlines were of sufficient enormity that they had pushed even the most titillating reports of Brother Phleger's horrifying mental collapse (which had been broadcast to tens of thousands of homes live on the Teslaphone) below the fold.

Everyone, all the hundreds and hundreds of people waiting outside the theater in the driving snow, wore black.

Everyone except one young man, who did not have any black clothes to put on. He had only burned and dirty ones, stiff with so many kinds of blood he'd lost count. As he pushed his way through the crowd to the door of the theater, press-camera flashbulbs—aimed at some more important personage—exploded around him. The young man cringed like a repulsive crawling thing from which a rock had been lifted away.

It should have been difficult to sneak into the theater with so many people clamoring for entrance and so many Edison Studios representatives guarding the doors. But the young man merely rubbed a few drops of blood between his fingers, muttered bile-bitter words under his breath, and the theater ushers and public-ity representatives turned their heads the other way as he passed. He hated the blood, hated the charms—but he was discovering that they could be useful.

The young man knew only what he had read in the newspapers. Dreadnought Stanton was dead. *That must mean Father is dead*, he thought. Because there was no real Dreadnought Stanton, only a name on a page, soon to be a picture on a screen. He did not know if Ma'am was dead, because the papers didn't say anything about her. But he knew that Mrs. Zeno was dead. And Royce ... well, the young man found that he didn't care what had become of Royce.

The newspapers reported that the Institute had burned with an unearthly flame that all the city's firefighters, working in shifts, had not been able to extinguish. The blue flames had raged for days until everything, everything had been consumed—leaving nothing but baked earth.

But the young man did not need the newspapers to tell him that. He had watched the Institute burn with his own eyes, blue and purple flares shooting from the roof like fireworks.

WELL DONE, Cowdray had said admiringly.

The moon was dark, and the young man had more control over Cowdray than at any time during the month. So when Cowdray had spoken, the young man had sunk his teeth into his own arm, hard enough to draw blood. He had given Cowdray the pain. And Cowdray had winced, and stored another grudge to be paid back when the moon was full again. But the young man wasn't ready to think about the moon being full again. He wasn't sure he wanted to live that long.

The young man didn't know where Jenny was, but he felt certain that Mrs. Zeno had been right. It was better that he didn't know.

And he didn't know where Ben was, either. The young man reached into his pocket and withdrew a crumpled piece of stationery. *Ex Fide Fortis,* read the scroll clutched in the eagle's dirty claw. *From Faith, Strength.* Midnight had passed. The world had rung in a new year. Perhaps there would be new writing on it.

But it was still completely blank, front and back.

"Do you want some candy?" It was a girl asking him this, a girl standing behind the refreshment counter. She was dressed in a tidy white apron, and she had a round, soft face framed by shining brown curls. The young man stared at her for a moment. She was looking at his scorched and ragged clothes—but her eyes were filled with sympathy, not contempt. She smiled at him, leaned in a little closer. Her hair smelled like flowers.

"I've got plenty," she whispered. "I'll give you some."

She bent down behind the counter, and as she did the young man felt suddenly angry. Why should she be able to smile like that? Quickly, he snaked a hand into her till and grabbed all the paper money he could. By the time she had risen, a box of chocolates in her hand, he had vanished into the crowd.

He stuffed the money into his pocket and climbed the stairs to the balcony, climbing all the way to the back row, high enough almost to touch the coffered ceiling set with octagons of stained glass. He did not take a seat, but rather pressed his back against the wall. While the theater's deep stage had been fitted with a special projection screen of Edison's own design, it was not a very good place to see the picture. But he didn't need to see it. He knew the story.

Still, he watched as it all unfolded on the screen. The story of a farmboy, possessed by a devil, his face bisected into halves. Good and evil. The celluloid images flickered, silver shadows on a silver screen. He watched the farmboy destroy the girl he loved— ah, but no, in the movie she was saved. They were both saved. They were saved, and redeemed, and blessed, and they lived happily ever after.

In the audience, people were crying.

But in the balcony, the young man was crying the hardest of them all.

Acknowledgements

The publication of *The Warlock's Curse* was funded by 249 Kickstarter backers from all over the world. Each and every one has my heartfelt thanks. Their support and encouragement has made me feel a whole lot better about this strange, sprawling multi-generational saga that I've got rattling around inside my head. The idea that people other than myself might find the Stanton/Edwards clan of interest makes it slightly less annoying when I wake up in the middle of the night having to scribble down some obscure detail of the family's magical intrigues that I've just "remembered."

As always, I owe a huge debt of gratitude to my family and friends. Writing, funding, producing, and publishing this book ended up being a demanding full-time job. Considering that I already *have* a full-time job, it left precious little of me to go around. Without the patience and good humor of my husband Dan and my daughter Nora, *The Warlock's Curse* would never have seen the light of day. They have always supported me, sometimes in ways I didn't recognize or appreciate at the time. They have my eternal devotion and adoration.

Finally, I want to thank my mom. Because I don't think I've thanked her in a book yet, and I think it's about goddamn time.

Thanks, Mom.

Kickstarter Sponsors

— SOPHOS LEVEL SPONSORS —
Stefanie "Finny" Deveaux
Kelly Robson

— MAGISTER LEVEL SPONSORS —
Karen G. Berry • Cie McCullough Buschle • Vivian Caethe
Nicolas Cagnard alias Neogandalf • Robin Catesby
Simone Cooper • Christian Decomain • Kate DeWitt
Sandi Gray • Helenmarie Hobson • John Idlor • Sally Qwill Janin
Marguerite Kenner and Alasdair Stuart • Rachel Koroloff
B.A. Lawhead • Deb Layne • William Long • T. L. Morganfield
Sara A. Mueller • Sandra M. Odell • Mary Christine Reese
Rhel ná DecVandé • Gene Scott • Carrie Seidman
Michael Shumate • Dave Thompson
Kevin Ward • Erica Warren • Bruce Williams

— PRAEDICTATOR LEVEL SPONSORS —
Shannon Moss • MeiLin Miranda • Katherine Nyborg

— CULTOR LEVEL SPONSORS —
Amanda A. Allen • Emma Bartholomew • Emma Bengtsson
Heidi Berthiaume • Jamaila Brinkley • Serge Broom
Lexie C. • Erin Cashier and Paul Goodman • Venetia Charles
Connie Chinn • Patrick Clare • Brenda Cooper
Barb Florence • Wilson Fowlie • Curtis Frye • Anne Lesley Groell
Gwennah • Hammer and Nails • Elizabeth Hillmann
Ann Leckie • David D. Levine • Shira Lipkin • Elise Matthesen
Mahesh Raj Mohan • Eugene Myers • Derek Reynolds • SAMK
Rebecca Stefoff • Rachel and Michael Swirsky
Melinda A. Smith • Dawn Vogel
Tinatsu Wallace • Carmen Williams

Creative Team

Cover Artist: Lee Moyer
Development Editor: Juliet Ulman
Copyeditor: Amy Garvey
Literary Agent: Ginger Clark
Digital Publishing Strategist: Steve Kasdin
Publicist: Jaym Gates

Special Thanks To

Mary C. Reece and Igor Spectre for letting me use their beautiful music in my Kickstarter video • MeiLin Miranda, Tim Pratt and Douglas Lain for letting me pick their brains about Kickstarters and indie publishing • Kelly Robson & A.M. Dellamonica for their chronic awesomeness • A.S. Kline, Sonya Taafe & Liz Bourke for their help with Euripedes • Peter Honigstock at Powell's Books for his ongoing support and commitment to the F&SF genre • And last but not least, for being as forgiving as it is fascinating—American history.

About the Author

M.K. Hobson's debut novel, *The Native Star*, was nominated for a Nebula Award in 2010. She lives in the first city in the United States incorporated west of the Rockies. Her favorite authors are Theodore Dreiser, Sinclair Lewis, Booth Tarkington, Gore Vidal, and William S. Burroughs. *The Warlock's Curse* is her third novel.

www.demimonde.com

A Note on the Type

The text of this book is set in Linux Libertine (a proportional serif typeface inspired by 19th century book type) and Linux Biolinum (an organo-grotesque non-linear sans-serif type-face.) Created by the Libertine Open Fonts Project, these are free and open alternatives to proprietary typefaces. For more information, please visit www.linuxlibertine.org

The display face used is Birch, an Adobe Originals typeface designed in 1990 by Kim Buker Chansler. Based on a Latin Condensed wood type found in a 1879 William Page specimen book, Birch is a particularly legible condensed display typeface notable for its angled serifs.